UNCIVIL LIBERTIES

A Pug Connor Novel

Book Two

BY

GORDON RYAN

Nov, 2010

Jim:

all the very best,

Gordon Ryan

© 2010 Gordon Ryan

Library of Congress Cataloging-in-Publication Data

Ryan, Gordon, 1943–

Uncivil Liberties - A Pug Connor novel, Book Two

ISBN 978-1-4538773-3-3 (softcover)

Printed in the United States of America

All rights reserved. Without limiting the rights under copyright, no part of this publication may be reproduced, stored in or introduced into a retrieval system, or transmitted, in any form, or by any means (electronic, mechanical, photocopying, recording, or otherwise) without the prior written permission of both the copyright owner and the above publisher of this book.

This is a work of fiction. Names, characters, places, brands, media, and incidents are either the product of the author's imagination or are used fictitiously. The author acknowledges the trademarked status and trademark owners of various products referenced in this work of fiction, which have been used without permission. The publication/use of these trademarks is not authorized, associated with, or sponsored by the trademark owners.

Author's Note:

If you have first obtained a copy of Book Two, *Uncivil Liberties*, I strongly recommend that you acquire *State of Rebellion*, Book One in the series, where I introduced a new character, Pádraig "Pug" Connor, who initially is a career Marine Corps officer. In Book Two, *Uncivil Liberties*, Pug's role increases dramatically and he becomes central to the plot. As I explained in the Author's note to *State of Rebellion*, Pug is not the traditional, thrust-and-parry, seek-and-destroy protagonist of many thriller action heroes. His sidekick, retired Command Sergeant Major Carlos Castro is more that type of hero. Together, they form a unique team, directed by the President of the United States to defeat a growing domestic terrorism that threatens to destroy individual liberty on our home shores. As you read the Pug Connor novels, I hope that Pug and Carlos become part of your reading enjoyment.

"It is the liberals who fear liberty . . ."

— George Orwell

"We need a constitutional convention in the State of California. We need to change the framework of governance."

— Gavin Newsom, Mayor, San Francisco,
1 Feb. 2010, Fox News

Prologue

**WHITE HOUSE
WASHINGTON, D.C.
PRESIDENTIAL INAUGURATION DAY
JANUARY, 2013**

Clay Cumberland had been president of the United States for less than two hours when his understanding of the magnitude of the office changed dramatically. Following the inauguration ceremony at noon, the first order of business for the new president—a fulfillment of his major campaign promise—was conducted in the Oval Office amidst great fanfare, in the company of a clutch of key political supporters and the full leadership of the Senate and the House of Representatives. All of them projected their best campaign smiles for network television.

Inscribing his signature using one of two dozen gold engraved pens—each of which he then distributed to senior officials in the room—Cumberland signed the Aspers-Kendall Health Act, extending expanded health care benefits and a greatly broadened pharmaceutical package to senior citizens throughout the United States.

The second order of business, accomplished some fifteen minutes later in a much more secluded setting, was not of his choosing and marked an undesired, but immediate, departure from his other campaign promise—to seek peaceful solutions to America's escalating terrorist problems. Acting as commander in chief, President Clay Cumberland verbally authorized a horrific, unprecedented military action, a decision that would, ultimately, end his presidency.

Instinctively, President Cumberland knew he would not be in attendance at any of the nine gala inaugural balls planned throughout Washington that evening.

ONE

BIRD DOG NINE ONE
EAST OF WASHINGTON, D.C.
JANUARY, 2013

A three-hour combat air patrol over Washington, D.C., wasn't bad duty, especially if the shift started at midday. Cruising at 16,000 feet in a loose, forty-mile, counter-clockwise racetrack pattern certainly didn't tax a pilot's ability to navigate, least of all Major Harrison 'Dutch' Witherspoon's, leader of Bird Dog Nine One, a flight of four F/A-22 Raptors.

Deputy Commander of the Air National Guard component assigned as part of the 27th Fighter Squadron, 1st Fighter Wing, Langley AFB, Virginia, Witherspoon had pulled rank to get on the day's flight schedule so he could observe the crowd gathered for the swearing in of the new commander in chief from three miles above. Security was extremely tight for the inauguration, including combat air patrols overhead, but beyond the hype surrounding a new presidential change of command ceremony, this crisp, blue-sky afternoon in January was destined to be unlike any other day. Or any other mission, for that matter, including the forty-seven combat sorties Witherspoon had flown over Iraq.

At the age of thirty-six, Witherspoon had traveled internationally, especially while he was on his brief active duty tour with the Air Force, but he was still regarded by his peers as an upper-class home boy—a landed-gentry Virginian who had never left his roots.

He had a solid Dutch heritage, a result of his New Amsterdam/New York ancestors, the first of whom arrived in America in 1685. Since then, fourteen generations of Witherspoons had prospered in what became a solidly English Tory colony, taking their place among the leading families of the upper and middle-eastern seaboard, eventually moving to the coastal tidewater area, and by the end of the War of 1812, into central Virginia.

A graduate of VMI with a bachelor of arts in economics and business, followed by a law degree from Georgetown University, Witherspoon had followed his father, a former mayor of Richmond, into politics, and three years earlier had been elected to the Virginia General Assembly. His recently announced plans to run for Virginia's 1st Congressional District seat had surprised no one, least of all his father. As a partner in Witherspoon, Witherspoon, and Templeton, one of Richmond's oldest law firms, 'Dutch' Witherspoon's future was, by general consensus, blue chip.

Appointment to the Air National Guard through Virginia's "good old boy" network offered, even in hard economic times, two or three sorties a month in a high performance Air Force fighter. Air Guard membership provided the thrills, male bonding, and locker room camaraderie fighter jocks find essential to their well-being. More importantly, membership in the Air Guard had offered the ultimate political resume, at least in Virginia—combat experience in a war zone during the liberation of Iraq, and the requisite air medals.

He'd even earned a Purple Heart during a temporary assignment following the Iraqi defeat. While he was serving as a ground observer for close air support, and traveling by convoy with a battalion of combat Marines, an improvised explosive device (IED) had detonated, delaying the movement temporarily while minor wounds were attended. The small shrapnel wound Witherspoon received to the left side of his neck required only three stitches, but the Marines, in a jocular ceremony, had declared the Air Force "Weenie" a certified leatherneck.

All in all, Harrison Witherspoon was the product of the perfect political family in the traditional mold of Virginia aristocracy. Every aspect of his life and his family's colonial genealogy smacked of military, a genealogy that had almost been wiped out during the Civil War as the family line was threatened when two of the three male Witherspoons were killed. Only Captain Colton Witherspoon, riding with the 43rd Battalion of Virginia Calvary, better known as Mosby's Rangers, had survived the Yankee onslaught, surviving to become Dutch's third great-grandfather.

Dutch's wife, the former Melinda Phillips, added her own component to his military credentials. She was the eldest daughter of Admiral Tarkin Phillips, recently retired as the Superintendent of the United States Naval Academy at Annapolis. According to the party hacks, Harrison Witherspoon's political "tally points" pointed to nothing less than a sweeping victory in the next congressional elections.

As his four-ship flight of Raptors assumed patrol over the nation's capital, Dutch could clearly see the assembled crowds on the streets of Washington dispersing after the inaugural speech, followed by the parade with the ever-present knot of cars and trucks on every major artery of the city.

The first squadron in the Air Force to convert from F-15s to the hot rod F/A-22 Raptor, the 27th Fighter Squadron had been flying the Air Force's newest stealth aircraft for four years. Dutch's wingman on this momentous day, First Lieutenant Teal "Rocky" Simmons, was only five weeks out of Raptor qualification training at Tyndall AFB, Florida, and on only his second Combat Air Patrol, or CAP mission, since being assigned to the 27th. Short, solid, and confident, Rocky's flat nose betrayed his collegiate boxing career. Class of '10 at the U.S. Air Force Academy, Lieutenant Simmons was the cadet wing boxing champion and national runner up in the 167-pound class. He was archetypical of the combative, do-or-die warriors that filled the ranks of the 27th Fighter Squadron. The envy of every other pilot, the Raptor had put the 27th in the forefront of America's first line of defense, and the Fighting Eagles, as they proudly called themselves, were determined to stay there.

Over a decade into the 21st century, the Raptor was America's latest entry in the air supremacy race. Despite the absence of any credible enemy air force, the Pentagon's senior Air Force brass had, nonetheless, applied a full-court press on Congress for at least fifteen years, lobbying the military's need for the latest "must have" weapon, pressing hard for the full-scale development, testing, and production of a new airship that would boast super-cruise, super-maneuverability, and super-stealth capabilities. Once approved, even the subsequent decision by the Pentagon that the fighter was no longer needed did not stop congressional representatives, in whose district the production occurred, from continuing to press for further orders.

Every pilot who was given the chance to take the stick and get airborne in a Raptor emphatically praised the latest generation air weapon. A single-seat stealth aircraft, the Raptor flew effortlessly, and, with its engines' unique thrust-vectoring nozzles, was capable of nearly unbelievable acrobatic maneuvers. The acceleration of its overpowered engines was astonishing, even to a seasoned fighter pilot. The first production fighter capable of maintaining over Mach 1 without the need for afterburners, and with an operational ceiling of over 60,000 feet, the Raptor could get *anywhere* in a hurry, limited only by fuel capacity. It was armed with a variety of air-to-air missiles, a 20mm Gatling gun that could fire 6,000 rounds a minute, a state-of-the-art electronically scanned array radar, and a helmet-mounted display to aim its sensors and weapons with a mere turn of the pilot's head. The Raptor was, by any measure, formidable.

The weapons package for this day's domestic CAP mission was the medium range AIM-120C missile with its own internal radar to lock onto targets, the incredibly agile AIM-9X short-range, heat-seeking missile, and over 500 rounds of 20mm ammunition.

Ninety minutes into Dutch's patrol, the Northeast Air Defense Sector air traffic controller, his primary source of information, unexpectedly contacted him, redirecting his communication to the airborne controller, call sign Chalice.

"Bird Dog Nine One, this is Whetstone."

"Whetstone, Bird Dog Nine One, go ahead."

"Bird Dog Nine One, vector east. Bogie bearing 065, range two hundred twenty-five miles. Contact Chalice on three one eight point six."

"Bird Dog Nine One vectoring east, switch three one eight point six."

"Two!" acknowledged Rocky, his wingman.

With a dip of his wingtip, Dutch silently signaled Rocky to turn with him toward the northeast, then punched in the new frequency on his digital keypad, switching his radio to the airborne AWACS controller, a military version of the Boeing 767, coordinating all aircraft on patrol that day.

"Chalice, this is Bird Dog Nine One."

"Two!" said Rocky quickly, confirming he was on frequency as well.

"Bird Dog Nine One, Chalice, go secure."

"Bird Dog Nine One," acknowledged Dutch as he and Rocky switched their radios to a secure, encrypted mode. This could only mean that AWACs had some classified information to transmit. Dutch was hoping for some news of interest to make the monotonous sortie pass a little quicker, but a secure communication was not likely to be a replay of the president's inaugural address. His pulse quickened.

"Bird Dog Nine One, Chalice, radio check."

"Chalice, Bird Dog Nine One loud and clear," answered Dutch, despite the fact that the secure radio mode was akin to talking to a deep sea diver through a face mask 300 feet down in the Caribbean.

"Two, loud and clear," lied Rocky.

"Bird Dog, I've got you loud and clear. Snap to heading 067. Your bogey is a 747, range two hundred five. We've had no radio or transponder response since initial communications."

"Chalice, Bird Dog Nine One copies. Bird Dog Nine Three flight will remain on station. Bird Dog Nine One snapping 067 to intercept the bogey." With that, the third and fourth Raptors in the flight remained on station while Dutch and Rocky swung northeast.

The Delaware coastline passed beneath them as they headed over the Atlantic. With a few moments' reflection, it seemed a strange coincidence to Dutch that precisely when the presidential inauguration was taking place, an airliner would approach Washington with its radios and transponder off. He hadn't seen an airliner with these malfunctions during any of his previous CAP missions. His pulse climbed yet another notch as an adrenalin rush engulfed his body.

"Bird Dog Nine One flight, push it up!" Dutch ordered as he slammed his throttles forward. Within seconds, he was supersonic, chopping the throttles back to maintain Mach 1.5.

Ninety seconds later, Chalice called.

"Bird Dog Nine One, Chalice. Bogey aircraft is KL6051, a commercial 767. Aircraft is renegade. Repeat—aircraft is renegade."

Renegade! A hijacking on his watch. Dutch felt instant nausea. The bile rose in his throat, threatening to fill his oxygen mask. He glanced across the narrow space between the two fighter aircraft at his wingman, Rocky, who was monitoring the communication. "Chalice, Bird Dog Nine One copies. KL6051 confirmed renegade. Say mission."

"Bird Dog Nine One, mission is to shadow and stand by for further words. Suspect is 067 for one ninety, Angels thirty-three. Report contact."

"Bird Dog Nine One copies shadow and stand by for words. Bird Dog Nine One is in radar contact with bogie."

WHITE HOUSE
WASHINGTON D.C.
JANUARY

As the cluster of well-wishers began to filter out of the Oval Office following the signing of the new Aspers-Kendall Health Act, Marilyn Cosgrove, the president's White House chief of staff and the architect of his brilliant, two-point election victory, gave him the look he knew so well: *I need to see you.*

Shaking hands with the Senate majority leader as he departed, Cumberland nodded slightly to Marilyn. She then stepped into a small anteroom, accompanied by two men, one in naval uniform. In a moment, the president moved to join them, pausing momentarily as he heard, and then observed, the Marine helicopter landing on the broad lawn.

Cumberland acknowledged Admiral Thornton Barrington, chairman of the Joint Chiefs of Staff, and Hank Tiarks, the president's secretary-designee—as yet unconfirmed by the Senate—for the Homeland Security Department.

"Good afternoon, Admiral. I didn't expect to see you this quickly.

This isn't another world situation briefing, is it?" he said, extending a handshake and a warm smile.

"No, sir, Mr. President. I apologize for the interruption to your schedule, but we have an urgent matter at hand. You will have noticed Marine One landing. We need to talk for a moment, then I have to ask you to board the helicopter as quickly as possible."

President Cumberland looked toward Secretary-designee Tiarks, who gave a slight shrug of his shoulders and a brief shake of his head.

"Please explain, Admiral. I have appointments throughout the afternoon and was not advised I would need to leave. I presume you're the only one in the room who knows what this is all about."

"Mr. President, there is a hijacked commercial airliner inbound to Washington. At 1315 hours, air traffic control at Washington Center received a communication from KLM Flight 6051, a civilian 767 en route from Amsterdam to Dulles. At that point they were just over an hour from their projected ETA. Sir, the radio transmission stated that KL6051 was now under 'Allah's control.' The aircraft hasn't responded since."

Cumberland looked toward Marilyn, his eyes displaying his incredulity at such news his first day in office. In fact, his first two *hours* in office. "You're telling me this airliner has been hijacked and is headed toward Washington?"

"That's what it looks like, Mr. President."

"Can you divert it?"

"Only if the pilot, or whoever is in control, is willing to change direction."

"Can't you direct your fighters to *force* it to change course?"

"Sir," Admiral Barrington said, "No aircraft, military or civilian, can force a very large aircraft to change directions if the pilot doesn't want to change directions. It's not as simple as nudging a vehicle off the road."

"What do they want?" the president asked.

"They've made no demands. At this point, we've only been advised that the aircraft is under hostile control. I'm sorry to be so abrupt with this news, but we have less than . . ." he glanced at his watch, ". . . eleven minutes until the aircraft goes feet dry."

"Feet dry?" Cumberland asked.

"He means that's when it crosses the coastline, Mr. President," Secretary-designee Tiarks, a former Air Force officer, offered. "What are the president's options, Admiral?"

"Mr. Tiarks, given the brief time remaining, we have only two options: escort it while they continue to wherever they decide to take it . . . or shoot it down."

"*Shoot* down a civilian airliner?" the president said, his face suddenly flushed.

"Mr. President—" Barrington started.

"That's *not* an option, Admiral," the president said, his voice now tense, the veins in his neck prominent, his breathing beginning to accelerate.

"Sir, with all due respect, it's your *only* option unless you're willing to allow him to choose his target."

"What in blazes are you talking about? What do you mean, his *target?*" the president continued, anger welling up in his voice and coloring his face. "What are his objectives?" Cumberland took a deep breath and tried to calm himself.

"Mr. President, he's already met his objectives. He's leaving the final choice up to you."

Cumberland's eyes opened wider. "To *me?*"

"Yes, sir. Consider this, Mr. President. A suicide bomber boards a bus in Tel Aviv, detonates an explosive, killing himself. . . or herself, and five or six people, perhaps wounds another ten. Their mission has been accomplished. When this terrorist, or terrorists—we don't know how many are on board—gained control of this aircraft, their objective was met. There are only two outcomes: they choose a target, perhaps the White House or the Capitol building or even the Pentagon again, and crash the aircraft into the building. They kill everyone on board the aircraft, plus hundreds or even thousands on the ground. We have no time remaining for evacuation. They know that. They also know that the alternative is for *you* to order the plane to be shot down before it reaches its target. They know these are your only choices, Mr. President. They're forcing you to decide, and timing it to coincide with the inauguration is no accident. They know you have to let them crash the plane where they choose, or that you have to order the death of the people onboard the airliner. They're prepared to die in either case."

"Fanatics! They're *insane!*"

"My thoughts exactly. We have eight minutes, Mr. President."

Silence filled the room for several long moments, broken by a softly worded question from the president, his anxiety growing more apparent, despite his attempts to control his emotions. "How many people are on board?"

"Amsterdam has advised us of 316 passengers and crew, Mr. President."

"Are your aircraft in position?"

"Yes, sir. We have two fighters escorting the airliner."

"We're absolutely *positive* it's been hijacked? Are you sure it's not a communication problem?"

"The aircraft's transponder signal indicates that the crew is no longer in control, and the voice on the radio was definitely from someone other than the pilot. The message was not garbled, Mr. President. He clearly stated, 'Allah is in control of this aircraft.' "

Cumberland lowered his head for a moment, then looked up at the United States' senior military officer, a man he had only met once in his preparatory intelligence briefing several weeks earlier.

"Your advice, Admiral?"

Barrington took a deep breath and exhaled slowly. "We have to assume the passengers are as good as dead already, Mr. President. This is a suicide bombing on a scale we've dreaded and hoped would never happen again. But, sir, we *must* bring this plane down before it reaches our soil."

"Hank?" the president said, looking to his old friend.

"I agree with Admiral Barrington, Mr. President. It's abhorrent but the alternative is unthinkable."

"Mr. President," Marilyn said, her political antennae fully extended, "the public will *not* understand this choice."

Cumberland nodded his agreement, stood silent for a brief moment, then retrieved his handkerchief and wiped the perspiration on his brow. "Neither do I, Marilyn," he said, stepping backward and reaching to support himself as he sought the refuge of a nearby chair. "But it appears that Harry Truman was correct: the buck stops here. And it wasn't very long before Truman also had a tough decision to make, but he got more time than I have." Cumberland hesitated for what seemed to those in the room like minutes, his eyes closed and his breathing now raspy and shallow. Finally he looked up, locking eyes with Barrington. His voice was weak, his breathing ragged. He was nearly gasping as he softly spoke. "Admiral, order your pilot to attempt, uh, communication directly with this aircraft. If . . . they fail to respond to your pilot . . . to turn around . . . then you have my authorization to ... to ... to prevent this aircraft from crossing our coastline." His eyes closed, and the president leaned his head back against the chair.

Marilyn moved closer to his side, kneeling down next to the chair. She took his hand, wrapping her fingers around his wrist, then turned to Secretary Designee Tiarks. "Call for his doctor, quickly." Tiarks stepped out of the room.

Admiral Barrington immediately picked up the telephone, spoke a few terse words, and hung up, turning back to Cumberland. "You've made the right decision, Mr. President."

The ashen-faced man who, only moments before, had been the center of attention as he began his presidency by signing a wide-ranging health initiative, opened his eyes briefly and again looked at Barrington, his voice barely a whisper. "Perhaps you're right, Admiral," Cumberland said, his right hand clutching at his chest, "but I believe, uh . . . uh . . . I'm about to find out if God sees it that way."

Two

**BIRD DOG NINE ONE
OFF THE DELAWARE COASTLINE
JANUARY**

"Bird Dog Nine One, Chalice."

"Go ahead, Chalice."

"Bird Dog Nine One, the NORAD Commander is on frequency and needs to pass you words."

Witherspoon paused, his heart performing an internal stress test. "Roger that, Chalice. This is Major Witherspoon. Go ahead, sir."

"Major, this is General Wilson. I authenticate zebra foxtrot at 1940 Zulu."

"Bird Dog Nine One copies zebra foxtrot. Good authentication, sir."

"Major, are you in contact with KL6051?"

"Off my left wing, sir. They refuse to acknowledge me, but I can see two people in the cockpit. They do not, repeat, do *not* appear to be in flight crew uniform."

"I understand. Now listen carefully. Are you prepared to carry out the orders of the commander in chief?"

"I am, sir."

"Major, I want you to try again to contact whoever is in control, tell him of your orders to destroy the aircraft, and, if you fail to receive a response, you are to shoot them down before they go feet dry. *You have launch authority.* Do you understand that order?"

"Attempt contact, then splash the airliner. Yes, sir, I understand, sir."

"Both of you. I want you *and* your wingman to fire."

Witherspoon didn't respond for a moment, deciding in that instant not to include his young wingman in this distasteful task, then he responded. "Copy all, sir."

"Major . . . do it quickly. The airliner must *not* be allowed to go feet dry!"

"Affirmative, sir.

"Good luck. Wilson out."

Dutch squeezed the transmit button on his inter-flight radio. "Bird Dog Nine Two, stay in cover position and remain armament safe. I repeat, armament safe, nose cold."

Rocky remained two miles dead astern of KL6051 with a radar lock-on, and Witherspoon changed frequency on his #2 radio. He continued to fly parallel with the huge airliner, clearly visible to those in the cockpit.

"KL6051, this is Air Force 1005," he called, using his tail number. "Do you read?"

No response.

"KL6051, this is Air Force 1005. Please acknowledge. I have been instructed to prevent your entry into American airspace. Please acknowledge this transmission."

For ten seconds there was no response. Dutch reached with his left hand to flip the master armament switch to ARM and squeezed the trigger, letting a few hundred rounds of 20mm fly in front of KL6051's nose. The noise of the gun was almost as deafening as the silence that followed.

"KL6051, this is Air Force 1005. *Acknowledge!*"

Witherspoon's headset crackled with Rocky's voice. "Dutch, he's under four minutes to feet dry. Do you want me to arm hot?"

Witherspoon quickly shifted frequency back to Washington Central. "Whetstone, Bird Dog Nine One arming hot. Is there any change of order?"

"Negative, Bird Dog. Proceed as ordered."

Major Harrison Witherspoon extended the speed brake and quickly drifted to a position roughly a mile aft of KL6051, his thoughts turning to his wife and her effort that morning to change his mind about flying today. She'd wanted to attend the inauguration celebrations in downtown D.C., but he'd been adamant that he needed to fly. She'd taken the kids on her own and left him to his intention, her silence sufficient evidence of her displeasure.

"Bird Dog Nine One, Whetstone. *Engage* the target!"

"Roger, Whetstone, locked on target." The warbling tone in his headset confirmed an AIM-9X lock on target, and the AIM-120Cs were set to launch as well. The growling of the missile's infrared seeker grew louder as it shifted lock directly to an engine.

How often had the Fighting Eagles debated this precise moment in the pilot's ready room at the squadron? How many variables and no-win scenarios had entered the minds of those pilots assigned to Operation Noble Eagle, commenced after the attack on the World Trade Center? And what *were* the overall objectives of Noble Eagle? To protect innocent civilians on the ground? By killing innocent civilians in the *air?* Even his wife, Melinda, had cast her vote. As they lay in bed late one night several years earlier, discussing his new assignment, her head nestled in the crook of his arm, her tears trickling down his chest, she had softly voiced her innermost thoughts. "I don't understand how they can ask you to do this. I couldn't *stand* it, Harry. I can't comprehend the thought of all those people crashing to their deaths from an airliner that *Americans* . . . that *you* shot down. There's got to be another way. There's just got to be." She lifted her head slightly, shifting her gaze to meet his eyes. "Harry, if you were ordered to . . . to . . ."

Witherspoon had pulled his wife closer, kissing her forehead, brushing back her soft, auburn hair, and comforting her in this moment of despair. "It'll never happen again, Millie." But his words brought little solace as they drifted toward sleep. It *could* happen again, and they all knew it.

And now it had.

The moment they had all dreaded had arrived. Dutch had drawn the short straw in this lottery of life and death. He knew he could refuse the order, simply fly away, and someone else would have to make the kill once the airliner had crossed the coast, or Whetstone would shift the burden to Rocky, and he would have to carry out the order. In that split second of vacillation, an indecisive moment born of months of mental gymnastics and personal angst, Dutch realized that he had subconsciously determined the end result long ago. If he ran, he would betray his commitment. His career would also be over. His professional life would be destroyed. And if he obeyed his orders, he was equally dead, politically and professionally speaking. He would forever be the man who killed hundreds of civilians with his Air Force jet, and his missiles would not present a good image on the campaign trail.

In the end, it came down to duty. That's what the Fighting Eagles had determined in their cavalier approach to tough choices. It was fate. They were as good as dead if they were called upon to accomplish such a publicly abhorrent mission. It would haunt them for the rest of their lives, much as it had Colonel Paul Tibbets, the pilot who had dropped the first atomic bomb on Japan. The Fighting Eagles had come to the conclusion, mostly unspoken, that the only way to view it was to accept that it was combat—kill the enemy and die. There was no other honorable way.

KL6051 thundered on, the vacuum behind the giant aircraft attempting to pull the Raptor closer. Dutch could hear his pulse deep inside his inner ears, his heart heaving and thumping deep in his chest. His years of training took over, and in a practiced reflex action, not taken in reality since his sorties over Iraq, he climbed a few hundred feet to position himself above the airliner and loosed three of his six missiles at the behemoth dead ahead.

"Bird Dog Nine One, fox one! Fox two! Fox three!"

Moments later, the inboard engine on KL6051's right wing exploded with a direct hit, followed by a slow disintegration of the wing. Hunks of jagged metal streaked below Dutch's Raptor. The fatally wounded airliner lurched to the left as two larger missiles impacted the tail and fuselage, severing the aft third of the huge aircraft. In the stream of suitcases and clothing that followed, Dutch thought he saw two passengers, still strapped to their seats, tumble past.

KL6051 began a steep dive toward the ocean, trailing thick black smoke from its stub of a wing. Bird Dog Nine One with Nine Two in tow followed the shattered Boeing 767 as it gathered momentum in its downward spiral, continuously spewing litter from the gaping hole where there once was a tail. The impact was tremendous, with the water splashing hundreds of feet into the air. It was as if a pod of dozens of whales had jumped high out of the water and flopped as one. Flaming debris could be seen scattered along the surface as they flew past the gruesome impact site.

"Bird Dog Nine One, Whetstone. Report?"

Dutch hesitated for several long seconds. "Splash one . . ." he responded, his voice weak and distant.

He made three slow circles over the impact site, observing debris now scattered over a two-mile-wide area as Rocky resumed formation with his flight lead. "Whetstone, debris location is north 3861, west 7479 . . . No survivors seen . . . Bird Dog Nine One returning to CAP."

As the flight of two Raptors began to climb away from the scene of the carnage, Lieutenant Simmons watched as Dutch suddenly rolled his aircraft inverted and pulled back down toward the water. Rocky pursued, trying to maintain formation with his flight lead.

"Bird Dog Nine One, this is Bird Dog Nine Two. Dutch, are you okay?"

Silence filled the air for several long seconds before Bird Dog Nine One, Major Harrison "Dutch" Witherspoon, heir apparent to Virginia's 1st congressional seat, made his final radio call.

"Rocky, tell my family I love them . . . and I'm sorry."

Lieutenant Simmons stopped his pursuit and leveled off, watching in horror as Bird Dog Nine One knifed into the cold grayish water, a half-mile short of the deserted Delaware beach.

WHITE HOUSE
WASHINGTON D.C.
JANUARY

At the moment Bird Dog Nine One entered the ocean, Roger Turnbill, the president's personal physician for nearly a dozen years and the man who had repeatedly warned him—privately, of course—that his heart would not stand the stress of the presidency, rose from beside the chair which held the remains of the former president of the United States. Four Secret Service agents were now also in the room.

"There is nothing further to be done," Dr. Turnbill said, placing his stethoscope back in his bag. "This time it was just too massive."

"Resuscitate him. Put him on life support," Marilyn Cosgrove demanded.

Dr. Turnbill shook his head. "It's no use, Marilyn."

Several staff members had gathered in the room. Secretary Designee Tiarks motioned to one of them, a young woman. "Find the vice president." Rendered speechless by this moment of history, she just nodded and left the room.

Admiral Barrington, thinking along the same lines as Secretary Tiarks but not confident the young staffer would hold herself together long enough to perform her task, nodded toward one of the Secret Service agents. "Clear the room except for Ms. Cosgrove, Secretary Tiarks, Dr. Turnbill, your security detail, and myself. Then see that the vice president is informed. Also, see if you can locate the chief justice and escort him here."

Under Secret Service control, three paramedics entered, pushing a gurney. They began to work with the president, unwrapping a blood pressure cuff and feeling his neck for a pulse. "That won't be necessary," Dr. Turnbill said. "Please place the president on the gurney." The three medics hesitated for a moment, uncertain of their next action. Again, Admiral Barrington spoke.

"Gentlemen, please follow Dr. Turnbill's instructions. The president has been pronounced dead. Let's all follow procedure here and do this with the proper degree of respect."

The three men gently lifted President Clay Cumberland's limp body from the chair, placing him on the gurney and covering him with a green sheet. Tears were now streaming down Marilyn Cosgrove's face as she leaned against the wall, her well-known, unflappable, take-charge demeanor suddenly subdued.

Secretary designee Tiarks stepped close to Admiral Barrington and the senior Secret Service agent. "When the body is removed, I think we should gather in the Oval Office and meet the VP there."

"Agreed," Barrington said. "Shall we try to reassemble the congressional leadership? They can't be far."

"Yes," Tiarks said, nodding his head, "but first we should speak with Vice President Snow. He may have a preference or some concerns that will need to be addressed before we take the next step."

"What about the media?" Barrington asked.

"Let's speak with Vice . . . uh, President Snow first," Tiarks said, shaking his head. "I wouldn't want to be in his shoes over the next forty-eight hours. He's about to reap the whirlwind and he had no part in the decision. What a state of affairs. Two dead presidents in four months. For better or worse, we've got yet another president. God help us!"

"And God help *him*," Barrington added.

Three

DUBLIN, IRELAND
JANUARY

Carlos Hernandez Castro was dressed in slacks, pull-over golf shirt, and a dark blazer. At five feet, ten inches tall, with a muscular upper body, he looked more like a halfback than a wide receiver. His dark hair was closely cropped, a twenty-year affectation instilled by the military. He had deep-set, dark brown eyes and a swarthy complexion, compliments of years in the field and multiple generations of Spanish, Central American Indian, and the occasional European ancestor. His smile was rare, but when delivered, had been known to win a few bucks from his colleagues when put to the test against some unsuspecting female.

He descended the front steps of the American Embassy in Dublin at a hurried pace, turned west, and strode briskly down Pembroke Street toward St. Stephen's Green and a pre-arranged meeting. Once there, he stood on the northeast corner for about five minutes, during which his mind wandered over the events of the past sixty days. Major changes had recently occurred in his life. The death of President Cumberland two days ago only compounded the confusion. Carlos had already departed on this assignment, having no ability to speak with General Connor about the new development. That would have to wait for his return.

Strictly speaking, Carlos was still a Sergeant Major in the United States Marine Corps, but he was on terminal leave, pending his retirement on February 28, 2013. Officially, he was in Ireland in the capacity of his new position as Deputy Director, Office of Public Relations and Information, Department of Homeland Security. In fact, Carlos was second in charge of the president's new terrorism task force, code name Trojan. Juggling his multiple official and unofficial roles was something he found amusing, and about as convoluted as his life story.

Entering the United States illegally over thirty years earlier with his mother and two siblings, after walking the length of Mexico from their rural village in Guatemala, Carlos had matured well beyond his age. He used this new found confidence to immediately take command of his Los Angeles barrio—at least, command of the 'under twelve" age bracket, the training ground for prospective gang members. He stayed in charge for several years until the police began to wonder about several recently absent gang leaders and the unknown teenager who had apparently assumed control. In less than four years, everyone living in the barrio of East Los Angeles knew of the boy who had come to be called CC.

After one of his increasingly frequent incarcerations in juvenile hall, a benevolent youth gang detective saw something others had not. Seeking to kill two birds with one stone, he gave CC the hard news—he was headed for one of three places: jail, the cemetery, or the military. When the detective explained that CC could join the biggest, baddest gang in the world, the United States Marine Corps, seventeen-year-old Carlos Castro signed up.

Within two years, his peers in the Corps had joined forces to beat the crap out of him and, in the process, a different Castro had surfaced. Still tough, still seeking leadership, and still the best one-on-one street fighter he knew, Carlos was learning to work within the confines of a team. And now he had a new family, had earned his stripes as a Recon Marine, and had been recognized by his command structure—for all the right reasons—as a leader. As a Recon Marine, he was with his peers, the best of the best, despite the Navy SEALS claim to the title.

Twenty-five years later, Carlos had become an American citizen, risen to the highest attainable enlisted rank in the Corps, and earned two bronze and one silver star and a host of lesser decorations. He had also acquired an Associate's degree in Middle Eastern Languages from the Defense Language Institute, a Bachelor's in History and a Master's in Economics from the University of Phoenix at various locations during his career, and most recently, a law degree from Loyola University's evening law school. The man who had started as a young, illegal Hispanic immigrant had completed his transformation. Becoming a senior executive in the Department of Homeland Security was merely a bonus.

The most unique aspect of this transformation, Carlos thought as he waited for his Irish rendezvous, was that he was still doing the same thing: seeking out and intimidating or killing his, or his country's, enemies. A law degree hadn't changed that hard-won talent, but it had provided one other professional characteristic that set him apart from most of his peers: he could write a grammatically correct after-action report.

Three days earlier, in a meeting with his boss, General Pádraig 'Pug' Connor, in their new offices in the Eisenhower Executive Office Building across the street from the White House, Pug had briefed him on the man he was to meet.

"His name is Kevin Donahue. He's in his mid-sixties now, but don't underestimate the man. I've met with him before, several years ago. He was a brigade commander in the IRA, essentially a terrorist similar to what we're fighting now, but with a different purpose. Paradise wasn't his goal, but a united Ireland was, and in those days, he had no qualms about placing a bomb in the public square. Those lads hadn't agreed to *be* the bomb, but they certainly wreaked havoc."

"From what I understand, they've been at peace for a decade, notwithstanding the claimed assassination of the vice president and prime minister last year. What does he have to offer us now?" Carlos asked.

"The main tool of intelligence: information. He just might know where to locate the elusive Jean Wolff. There's no need for you to go armed. And you're not a credentialed diplomat in Ireland. If they wanted to kill you, they would, but those days are, for the most part, gone. I won't say you should trust him, but he'll most likely tell you the truth. He'll tell you nothing if he doesn't want to, or doesn't know, but he has no reason to lie. Just give him my regards and see what he brings to the table. In my message to him through our resident CIA agent at the embassy, he knows what we need. Shouldn't take more than a couple of days for him to make contact. In the meantime, if this is your first visit to Ireland, enjoy yourself. Some great old Irish pubs throughout Dublin."

Carlos nodded. "It's not the type of insertion I'm used to, General, but I guess I'm in a new world."

"Get used to it, Carlos. Your days of 'dropping in' through a HALO insertion are likely over." The 'high altitude, low opening' parachute drop had been Carlos's favorite part of being a Recon Marine.

"You've just earned a desk, like I did a few years back," General Connor continued, "and you've crossed the big forty. It's not easy to accept. You and I have to put Trojan together piece by piece and we can't expect much help from anyone outside. The Pentagon certainly won't like our *carte blanche* mandate to call on their special ops assets without even telling them how we intend to use them."

"That's putting it mildly," Carlos replied. "That was the primary reason I decided to retire. A sergeant major wouldn't get much cooperation from the puzzle palace. Maybe as Deputy Director Castro from Homeland Security I'll fare better."

"Don't count on it," Pug said, "but if you start to miss the Corps, check your bank account. Your current salary should help ease the pain." He laughed. "Anyway, keep in touch while you're in Ireland. You have full authority to go where, and do what, you need. But you're not 007. No license to kill, at least not in Ireland on this trip. If you need additional backup, just contact me. I want Wolff dead. That would be the exception to my earlier statement. If he's in Ireland, which I strongly doubt, then kill him. President Cumberland takes office day after tomorrow. If you can locate Wolff, let's try to get this done before the change occurs."

"Aye, aye, sir." Carlos stood and headed for the door, pausing to look back and grin. "Or rather, 'yes, sir,'" he said. "Got to change the language too, I suppose."

"Carry on, Sergeant Major," Pug had replied with a loose salute.

Carlos had flown out the next day and waited two days for contact from Donahue. In the interim, President Cumberland had died.

As the Irish evening began to descend, a black Mercedes approached St. Stephen's Green, pulled up sharply, and the back door opened. A burly, red-faced man quickly got out. Even though Castro was expecting the vehicle, the manner of approach had all the earmarks of an abduction, and his pulse began to quicken.

"Welcome to Ireland, Mr. Castro, is it?" he said, a slight sneer on his face and his tone anything but welcoming.

As Castro slipped into the backseat, another man slid over to the far side and Red-face quickly climbed in, sandwiching him in the middle. As the car sped away, he flinched when the man to his right pulled out a blindfold.

"Not to worry," the second man said, "we'll treat you better than your lads did the Dutch tourists." After several seconds of silence, Red-face spoke again. "How'd you like Ryan's Pub? I noticed you didn't try the Guinness." Carlos had assumed from the moment he stepped off the plane that he might be under observation. He'd confirmed it the night before in the pub.

"No, I didn't," Castro responded, "but *you* did. And your companion left a bit early, didn't he?"

The male pissing ritual completed, they rode in silence for about twenty-five minutes, the sounds of the city varying as they traversed multiple suburban communities. Castro tried to estimate, by sound and timing, the direction and possible location of their destination. Eventually, the vehicle seemed to enter an enclosure and the ambient noise grew quiet.

"Right, here we are now," Red-face announced. Helped out of the car, Castro was led blindfolded several feet where he was guided into the back seat of another vehicle. Immediately, the second vehicle exited the building, and the sounds of city traffic once again were audible. In about three minutes, the blindfold was removed. Even though it was full dark outside and the vehicle windows were heavily tinted, Castro blinked to clear his eyes.

Only one man was in the back seat with him and the vehicle was much larger inside, a limousine, by all appearances. He glanced to his right and immediately recognized the other man. Two men were in the front seat behind the sound proof glass enclosure that separated the two compartments.

"So, my old friend Colonel Connor gave you my file, did he?" the man next to him said.

Castro didn't respond.

"Come now, Mr. Castro, let's not play games. You haven't much time before your flight. You recognized me. Surely you've read my file and seen my picture. And Pug Connor sent you to discuss a mutual friend."

Castro nodded, and then stared directly into Donahue's eyes, neither man blinking. "I know who you are, Mr. Donahue."

According to American intelligence documents which the general had provided to Castro, most of which were received from British Special Branch and the SAS surveillance unit, Kevin Donahue was, or at least had been, a brigade commander in the Provisional Wing of the Irish Republican Army, better known as the PIRA or Provos. In the seventies in Northern Ireland, he'd been suspected of at least a dozen killings and knee-cappings, plus several bombings. More recently, there was American and British intelligence community speculation, but no proof, that he had been behind the assassination of the American vice president and the British prime minister about six months earlier.

For the past decade, there had been an uneasy truce in Ireland and the IRA had refrained from their traditional course of open rebellion, which they had followed through much of the previous century. Still, the former IRA leaders remained in the shadows, fearing retribution from the British intelligence community.

"Colonel Connor asked me to present his compliments and to ask how you were. He specifically asked about your progress with the current peace accords." General Connor had told Castro not to mention the recent promotion to general.

"I keep my nose in the wind," the older man answered. "You know how it was in the American west. The gunslingers often became the town marshal, didn't they? Corporate security is a big business, no matter what side of the fence one chooses. I've made a few contacts. Even in America. Big bucks riding on security in America these days."

"Indeed, security operations are springing up everywhere. Perhaps that brings us to the subject of our meeting, an international weapons operative who goes by the name of Jean Wolff," Castro replied.

"What makes the *'office of public relations'* interested in Wolff?" Donahue asked.

Carlos kept his surprise at Donahue's knowledge of their new designation hidden beneath a stoic mask. "Let's just say he's been active in our neck of the woods. My boss said you might have some knowledge of his activities."

Donahue was silent for several seconds, then nodded. "Right then, let's get down to business," the older man said, turning his body slightly to face toward Castro. "What's in it for us if I can provide a lead to Wolff?"

"My bosses' undying appreciation," Castro replied. "Maybe the more appropriate question is, 'why would you be willing to give him up'?"

"There's no love lost between Wolff and the Irish. The bastard has double-crossed us in the past and I thought it might be an opportunity to pay him back. If you're interested, I'm willing to help. If not, then we can just drop you at the airport. As to what's in it for us, just tell Connor that I'll chalk it up and call in the chit some day."

"I'm listening," Castro said. Glancing out the window, he confirmed that they were heading in the direction of the airport on the north side of Dublin.

Donahue anticipated his concern. "Not to worry, Mr. Castro. We've retrieved your suitcase from the hotel and are happy to escort you to your flight. We also made certain you were booked on Aer Lingus, and not on a KLM flight. Although you'll undoubtedly check, there are no surprise packages in your suitcase, either. Dutch airline flights are rather dangerous these days, so I hear. Far safer on Aer Lingus."

Castro nodded.

"Now, what was I saying? The identity of an arms merchant, was it? Would that fall within Colonel Connor's new area of concern?" "He's of interest to several organizations, Mr. Donahue. My boss heads one of those. Let's stop dancing. Do you know where Wolff is located?"

Donahue looked at his watch before responding, then he leaned forward and tapped on the window, alerting the driver with a pre-arranged signal. "Diplomacy's not your long suit, is it, Mr. Castro? You could learn something from your boss. But of course, Connor is already Irish, so it comes naturally. As for Wolff, I *might* be of some assistance. I'll get back to you."

The vehicle left the side street they were on and quickly entered the M1, a dual carriageway, the Irish equivalent of a freeway, and increased speed toward the airport.

They drove in silence for about ten minutes, pulling up in front of the Dublin International Airport terminal. Donahue turned toward Castro and smiled. "Here we are, Mr. Castro."

The driver was already at the boot of the car, placing Castro's suitcase on the footpath in front of the international terminal.

"You're a hard man, Mr. Donahue," Carlos said, looking directly at the former IRA operative. "Any message for my boss?"

"Tell the *general* congratulations on his promotion and new assignment. I look forward to meeting him in person again one day. In a *peaceful* context, of course," he said, chuckling.

Castro broke into a smile, his first friendly gesture of the meeting. "General Connor said you might surprise me."

"Satellites can't see *everything*. With all your American high-tech capability, you lads seem to have forgotten the good to be had from a bit of fossicking around by a man with a good nose. Of course, you knew that in east LA, didn't you? All good intelligence still comes from a man, or a woman, on the ground. Fortunately, '*Paddy*' has been emigrating throughout the world for two centuries, but they all remember where they or their parents were born. Best intelligence network in the world, bar none. Maybe the Jews are as good, but they don't frequent the pubs."

He paused, offering Castro a handshake. "Perhaps we'll meet again, Mr. Castro. Now that we're friends, perhaps you'll allow me to call you CC. I'll get in touch with you about our mutual friend. I should hear something soon—probably sooner than you think. Have a safe trip home, lad. The world's become a dangerous place, even for innocent bystanders. By the way, since you and your boss are into, what did you call it, *public relations,* do you think your new president, Bill Snow, will survive his own public relations storm? From the sound of it, Cumberland took the easy way out and Snow has to carry the can for the decision to shoot down the terrorists. From my perspective, it was the only decision to make, you know."

"Gracious of you to concur," Castro replied. "But one can never tell about the public, or the politicians. One thing's for certain—the next lot of fanatics will think twice."

Donahue shook his head. "Don't be naïve, lad. The terrorists won that round. And you lost an eighty-million-dollar fighter and a fifteen-million-dollar pilot. You're still a bit young, lad, but if you've read that the old Irish groups were terrorists, it would seem that these jihadists have put a whole new light on political action. In my father's day, they *brought* the bomb in a suitcase. These new fanatics *are* the bomb. Someone bent on a trip to paradise is hard to deter. Not much defense against that, lad. Safe journey, Carlos."

Castro exited the vehicle, then stood by his suitcase and watched as Donahue departed the terminal drive. He then picked up the bag and turned to enter the building.

At the Aer Lingus flight center, Carlos worked his way to the front of the check-in counter. The young woman appeared barely twenty, her dark red hair cascading down her back as her fingers flew over the keyboard, her intense concentration masked by the bright smile on her face.

"That will do it, Mr. Castro. You're all checked in, and, as I've already explained, upgraded to first class. You're welcome to use our VIP lounge just inside the security area. Please have a wonderful flight."

Apparently Donahue had made the final parting gesture, upgrading his flight accommodations. Carlos Castro smiled at the thought. He picked up his boarding pass and his leather laptop case, stepped away from the counter, and moved behind the line of passengers seeking to discard their luggage in care of the airlines, thereby freeing themselves to hit the duty-free shop.

Passing the roped-in area, Castro felt his Blackberry vibrate. He stepped out of the traffic aisle as best he could and clicked the icon, slowly reading the e-mail as people flowed around him, jostling for position.

> *Dear Irish Tourist:*
>
> *Asshole convention will be held in East Timor first week in March. Attendees include a lone wolf, traveling as Juan Hernandez on a Portuguese passport. Remember, always wash your hands after attending an asshole convention . . . or bring your local wiper!*
>
> *A friend of the Old Sod*

Carlos smiled, clicked to store the message into the Save folder, and returned the Blackberry to its holder on his belt. He then cleared security, entered the VIP lounge, and took a seat near the overhead television. A room attendant dressed in the Aer Lingus uniform brought him a small plate of cheese and crackers and took his order for a Heineken. On the television, a discussion was in progress on Fox News's "The Factor," with Bill O'Reilly voicing his normal opinionated commentary. Carlos placed his laptop case on the small table beside his chair and watched the proceedings. He quickly recognized O'Reilly's guest as Donald Read, a well-known liberal columnist syndicated across the nation.

" . . . in all respects, Bill, he should do the honorable thing and resign."

"Why, for heaven's sake? He was the legally elected vice president. That's how our system works, whether the president has been in office for three years or, in this case, three hours. Why should he resign?"

"He campaigned for the presidency in the primary, Bill, and Cumberland beat him. Two others beat him also, so they should be given the opportunity to compete in a special election. Snow never appealed to mainstream America. They didn't like him as governor of Arizona and they don't like him now."

"*You* don't like him, Read. Sorry to break it to you, but you're not America. And that's not how our system works. Snow was elected to the vice presidency."

"Not really. *Cumberland* was elected, and Snow came along for the ride to pull in the western states."

"Your version of American politics is a bit distorted, Read. Snow might have brought geographical balance to the ticket, but there was more to it than that. There always is."

Read shook his head in disagreement. "It doesn't matter. He has no right to be our president. He's opposed to abortion, and Cumberland was, at least, open-minded. As governor of Arizona, Snow opposed increased funding to the needy. Plus, those rumors of an affair are probably spot-on."

"What are you talking about, Read?" O'Reilly said, his voice rising and his body language aggressive, leaning forward. "Bill Snow said he would follow the law of the land on women's rights. The funding he opposed was to the labor unions, who demanded exorbitant multi-year contracts, and he's the only Republican primary candidate who's been married once. Absolutely no corroboration of those rumors has surfaced, and that's with an army of corrupt media clamoring to find incidents of infidelity, reporting rumor as fact when they failed. Tell me *that's* fair and balanced. You're spewing garbage, Read."

"What about his racially biased stance on immigration? His granddaddy and great-granddaddy were Arizona Rangers, killing Mexicans even before Texas or Arizona became a state. He's a racist, from racist origins, pure and simple."

Becoming exasperated by his guest, O'Reilly just shook his head. "I'm sick of all this racist crap. It's gutter politics, Read, and beneath you. Look, you're from old New England stock. Are you prepared to have someone poke into *your* patrician family history four generations back? You got any family members who killed off the original inhabitants of Massachusetts? Any rum runners who profited off the poor? Any railroad barons who stole Indian land in the west for right-of-way?" O'Reilly taunted. "What you claim is hypocritical. Every family has skeletons in the closet. The fact is, William Snow is now president of the United States, for better or worse. And I, for one, can think of a lot worse. That's how I see it, but I'll give you the final word."

"Just wait and see, Bill. The American people will not stand for it. Now he's in charge of the federal government and immigration. The Hispanic people deserve better. His true colors will surface, and then the

American people will see who he really is."

"Give the man a chance, Read." O'Reilly turned to face the camera, shaking his head again. "We'll be right back with the voice recording and transcripts of the Dutch airliner cockpit voice recorder. They clearly show that both pilots were killed—their throats were cut—by the terrorists at least thirty minutes before the Air Force brought fighter jets on scene. Those who are second-guessing President Cumberland's decision to shoot down the airliner should listen carefully to these tapes and drop their ridiculous assertions that the downing of the airliner was not needed and that it was only a communication problem. Stay with us."

Carlos turned away from the television screen and pulled out his Blackberry again. He sent a quick email to the general's secretary to advise her of his arrival time at Dulles International Airport. Then he began to make notes for his briefing to General Connor the following morning. Pausing for a moment as he tapped the keyboard, he reflected on the first time he'd met Captain Connor, his newly assigned company commander, back in the early nineties. Several battalion sergeants made bets that the new, soft-spoken guy couldn't handle a tough situation. Two weeks later, returning from a covert Pakistan insertion, Carlos had new respect for his captain. When they had been ambushed by a local guerilla band, Captain Snow had killed four terrorists—two with a knife, hand-to-hand. Carlos never doubted Pug Connor again.

But whether the new president was tough enough to meet the challenge facing America was another story. The media had made a big deal of his supposed anti-Hispanic stance during the campaign, making so many false assertions. Even the rumored infidelity issue did not bring Snow to anger. As a candidate, Snow had never lost his temper in situations where Carlos would have knocked the media hack on his ass. Carlos himself had been an illegal immigrant, but he supported control of the borders.

Since his conversion to Islam over a decade ago, Carlos Castro, of Catholic heritage and the former leader of El Toro, the new name he had given his east Los Angeles gang, had become a gentle person in almost every circumstance. But like Pug Connor, when called upon to fight, Carlos Castro was a natural warrior, instantly and usually fatally violent to his opponent, as he had proved on many occasions.

The new president was an unknown quantity, certainly pertaining to Trojan. As General Connor had explained it to Carlos when he reported for duty, former President Clarene Prescott had formed Trojan within thirty days of her ascension to the presidency after President Eastman had been assassinated during his congressional address the previous September.

According to the general, President Elect Cumberland had been briefed in December, before taking office, and had agreed to continue the formation of the unpublicized domestic terrorism task force. But what about President Snow? How would he handle it? Resigning from the Corps to take this new position had been Carlos's choice, and Connor had offered him a way to decline, but now the die had been cast. How long would the job last? Would Snow kill Trojan? That question was yet to be answered.

Four

LAS VEGAS, NEVADA
JANUARY, 2013

As the year 2012 ended, the state of California had entered into a twenty-four month countdown toward secession from the United States of America. Despite considerable opposition from state and national political leaders over the past eighteen months, a U.S. Supreme Court ruling that it was unconstitutional, and a brief, but violent military confrontation in Sacramento that the press had dubbed The Battle of Capitol Mall, the people had spoken—three times, actually—at the polls. Preparation for the formation of the Republic of California began in earnest. The date for implementation was January 1, 2015.

California Governor Walter Dewhirst, initially a staunch opponent of the secession, had responded to his constituents' demands and called for international recognition of his new nation. Mexico, along with half a dozen other sovereign Pacific Rim nations, had responded affirmatively.

The previous August, when secession seemed imminent, Daniel Rawlings, a young, newly elected state legislator from Davis, California, had found himself immersed in both a secret presidential task force investigating the origins of the secession movement and a gubernatorial assignment to draft the new California constitution. For several months, he had wrestled with the dichotomy of the two assignments: one to stop the secession, and one to prepare for its eventuality.

Even the discovery by the presidential task force that the elections had been rigged, electronically, by a group of corporate financiers for whom the secession was a means to an end, did nothing to stop the steamroller effect. Convinced by the false vote tally that their fellow citizens were in favor of secession, the people demanded freedom. Freedom from Washington D.C. and burdensome taxation; freedom from confiscatory redistribution of wealth; freedom from myriad government regulations that invaded areas that most people knew were historically private: religious affiliation, sexual preference and even medical records. And freedom, when the judicial system was stacked against them, meant separation. Even in a state known for its liberal, 'anything goes' philosophy, enough was enough. The conservative voters, along with the vast array of independent middle-of-the-roaders, had overwhelmed the activist liberals and made history at the polls.

Rawlings and the task force had discovered one of life's truths: no matter the fallacy of the origin or the deception perpetrated in the process, the end result was the determining factor in public acceptance of change. The decision of President Clarene Prescott, following the assassination of her predecessor, Bill Eastman, not to reveal the source or even the presence of a fraudulent election, put the final confirmation to the issue. Legally achieved or not, California was on the road to secession, and so far, no one in national power had agreed to use military force to stop it.

A month before the November 2012 presidential election, in an effort to broaden his understanding of America's founding principles, Rawlings had contacted The Montclair Advocacy, a prestigious political think tank in California with a known conservative persuasion. Dan also solicited the assistance of other outside sources, including Horatio Julius, his former law professor at Stanford and a renowned constitutional scholar.

Several meetings with Professor Julius and principal officers and analysts at Montclair gave Rawlings an entirely new perspective. In fairly quick order, these learned scholars opened Dan's eyes to various philosophical components of the existing national Constitution that were intended by America's Founding Fathers, but which had been abandoned. More importantly, their presentation of how these various components of governance had become corrupted over the ensuing two centuries by the political adoption of progressive philosophy that was antithetical to the 'natural, God-given rights' theory had broadened Dan's concept of central versus local governance. Constant bombardment by Glenn Beck and other conservative talk show hosts sealed the lesson.

The upshot was that after several months of study and analysis, Dan Rawlings, to his own surprise, had shifted his thinking, slowly becoming more open to the idea of secession as possibly the only way to truly start anew and restore the original principles. His approach was not directed at open, confrontational revolution, but instead, a reestablishment of the original founding concepts, thereby bringing America back to a nation based upon an equality of rights, rather than a nation striving for equality of condition, acquired at the expense of the more successful members of society.

After the presidential election, Dan had been contacted by several legislators from neighboring states, specifically Nevada, Arizona, and Oregon, who asked to meet with him to discuss California's impending secession. He had agreed to their request, considerably encouraged by the fact that states he, and other political pundits, had assumed were solidly liberal in their thinking, including his own California, had suddenly developed a strong, vocal, moderate, if not conservative, voice.

When discussing the issue with his new wife, the former Nicole Bentley, a medically retired FBI agent Dan had met as a result of the presidential task force, he had expressed his feelings more openly.

"Nicole, I had no idea there were so many conservative thinkers in California. Even in other West Coast states."

She'd laughed at his naiveté. "Did you think that West Coast people were all airheads, part of the 'anything goes' crowd?"

Rebuffed, Dan joined in her laughter. "Maybe I did, despite my family's long-standing conservative leanings. The media has duped me, I guess. They present their ideology as the ruling—and prevalent—philosophy."

"My father told me something once, Dan," Nicole continued. "Most conservative people are just that: conservative. They don't advocate, press for change, rebel, or march in demonstrations. Not until they're provoked. They are, in fact, what has been called the silent majority. But since they *are* silent, the liberals believe that because they're *not* present, they don't care, and the media promotes that perception. Then, when they *do* speak up, they're called stupid because they can't see the logic and intellectual superiority of the liberal position. Who do you think makes up the bulk of today's Tea Party movement? No," she said, shaking her head, "the conservatives are there. Just give them a reason to rear their head. Inform them, inspire them, and you'll see the result. I think they've finally had enough of the 'some work, all benefit' attitude, the stereotypical one-sided liberal view of *equality for all*."

On the flight to Las Vegas to meet with the other legislators, Dan recounted Nicole's remarks while she cat-napped. The growth of the meeting, eight states now being represented, was ample evidence of her reasoning. Or was it? Notwithstanding a public display of a more openly conservative philosophy, both in rhetoric and action in their respective state legislative matters, these other elected state legislators had requested their meeting be held in confidentiality and had suggested they meet in late January, after the presidential inauguration. Were they ashamed of their involvement? That would become apparent soon enough, Dan thought as the plane began its descent into McCarran Airport.

By the time of the meeting, five additional western states—Alaska, Idaho, Montana, New Mexico, and Utah—had joined the convocation, and what later became known as the First Vegas Gathering was convened. To date, they had successfully kept their planned assembly low-key, confidential, and, at last count, limited to approximately thirty individuals, all current or former elected state officials, including one former governor. Most important to the group, they appeared to have succeeded in being undiscovered by the media.

Dan had not briefed California Governor Walter Dewhirst of the gathering. The governor had made it clear that Dan was to continue with his assignment to draft the new constitution, but Dewhirst had also made it clear that he was not going to run for public office again and was going to limit his involvement in the transition. He remained privately opposed to secession, and it was almost as if the governor was abdicating his responsibility to serve as the chief executive. Dan accepted this limitation and had proceeded almost unilaterally in his efforts to create a document that would contain the governing principles for the new Republic of California.

Nicole had come with Dan to Las Vegas, but was not going to attend the meeting of legislators. Although it was still January, southern Nevada was enjoying a warm spell, and the temperature was in the low seventies. The morning of the meeting, Nicole drew Dan to the window of their hotel suite.

"See that patch of sparkling blue water down there, with the scantily clad people all around the edges?" she said.

"Yeeessss," he responded easily, dragging out his answer.

"That's where *I'll* be, Mr. Assemblyman. Don't call me unless your group declares an insurrection."

"Fair enough," he replied. "I'll join you when I can."

"I won't hold my breath," she said, kissing his cheek and patting his behind as he left the room.

At nine A.M. on the last Tuesday in January, 2013, thirty-seven people convened in the Cascade Room at the Bellagio. Morning coffee, juice, and pastries were on the side table, and several people were speaking in small groups as Dan entered the room. Inasmuch as Dan had not initiated the gathering, he was not coordinating the meeting or the agenda. He had come by invitation prepared to discuss his current work on a new California constitution, but to date had received no request to speak or instruct. The meeting was, to Dan's understanding, ad hoc.

Dan poured a cup of coffee and placed a sweet roll on a plate, taking a seat at one of the small tables placed around the room. Although the people in the room were state and local officials, rather than federal officers, several faces in the room were immediately recognizable as a result of their national prominence. Two other people, one male and one female, were already seated at his table. He introduced himself and they reciprocated. Both were from Oregon. Then three people seated near the front, two men and one woman, stood and moved to the rectangular table placed at the head of the room. The woman, one of those whom Dan recognized, remained standing as the two men took seats on either side of the table-top lectern.

"Good morning, everyone. My name is Joyce Jefferson," she began. Everyone in the room knew her as the former governor of Arizona, presently dean of the James E. Rogers College of Law at the University of Arizona, and currently on the Board of Directors of the Black American Conservative Caucus. She had also served as lieutenant governor to President William Snow during his term as Arizona governor.

Ms. Jefferson was acknowledged as the great-great grandchild of Georgia slaves who had moved west shortly after the Civil War. Her published novel, *A Colored Cowboy*, had become a New York Times bestseller and recounted the life of her great-grandfather as he established his ranch in the Arizona territory in the early 1870's.

"Let me introduce my associates this morning. On my left is Doctor Erasmus Hennington, Speaker of the House in the New Mexico state legislature. To my right is Donald Tompkins, attorney general for the state of Utah. Both gentlemen have agreed to moderate with me this morning as we commence our meeting.

"I must first acknowledge that I am not the originator of this gathering, nor was I involved with the smaller group who proposed the initial contact with Mr. Rawlings of California. Those three men are sitting to the front left of our gathering. Please, gentlemen, raise your hand to identify yourselves. Harry Philips, mayor of Eugene, Oregon; John Tustin, minority leader in the Oregon state legislature; and finally, Tim Pollock, lieutenant governor of the state of Nevada. When Mayor Philips contacted me, he asked that I moderate and choose two associates. I was pleased to be asked and honored to be here this morning. But before we proceed, I would like to acknowledge and express sympathy to those of you who were personally associated with President Cumberland. A most tragic circumstance." She paused for a moment as the room remained silent.

"As I have said, I'm a latecomer to your assembly, as over half of us are today, but make no mistake, I come willingly. And, Mr. Rawlings," Jefferson said, turning her head to look at the near table where Dan sat,

"I come with admiration for what you and your California colleagues have been able to accomplish in so short a time. The political world was astonished at the boldness of California's secession movement, but, like most politicians, we wrote it off as election hyperbole, a campaign ploy by Senator Malcolm Turner. How wrong we were.

"As recently as two months ago, I dare say that most of us in this room would not have even considered being part of a secession movement. Look around the room. We don't all know each other, but a quick read of our sign-in list shows our diversity. There are thirty-seven people registered on this morning's roll. We have twenty-two men and fifteen women. Nineteen are Republicans, fourteen are Democrats, and four are independents. I think it would be fair to say that over our careers, we have each been cast as either conservative or moderate . . . and some as just plain ornery," she said to open laughter from the participants. "Even in our fledgling status, having barely gotten out the word regarding our intent, our eight states collectively represent about sixty million people, roughly twenty percent of the population of the United States. If Texas and Colorado join us—and I have reason to believe Texas would be with us in a heartbeat—that will increase to over ninety million people and about thirty percent of the nation's population. I don't doubt that by mid-year, long before we process our intentions regarding the formation of a new nation, nearly every state west of the Mississippi will join our movement." She waited for a moment to allow her words to settle with the audience.

"Yes, I *did* say the formation of a new nation. Why else are we all here? As I said, all of us in this room are either conservative or moderate thinkers. What I like to call *reasonable* people, absent extreme rhetoric and ideology. I don't think any of us would be accepted into the society of liberals. But from the moment we leave this room, our confidentiality, and perhaps even our credibility, will no longer be assured. We'll be Tea Party lunatics. The concept we have met to discuss is too controversial. The ideas we'll discuss are too volatile. And the purpose for which we are gathered is too important. When we complete this assembly, we'll be committed to the track we've entered. So let's be certain of our intent. Once we voice our agenda this morning and announce our intentions, we must each decide to remain or to withdraw. I don't mean to suggest that it's all or nothing—far from it. There will be ample room for debate, disagreement, compromise . . . after all, we're *politicians*, right?" Again, more laughter.

"But perhaps I should start with what we are *not* about this morning. We are *not* about revolution. We do *not* seek the overthrow or disestablishment of the United States of America, nor the present government of our nation. Those are treasonous acts. But what I think we *can* agree upon is that we are *for* the reformation of a national government according to the original principles enacted by our nation's Founding Fathers. We are *for* the establishment of equal *opportunity* for all people regardless of race, color, creed, and religious affiliation. Be clear about my meaning: I said *opportunity*, not *entitlement*. We are for the fulfillment of that historical promise of life, liberty, and the pursuit of happiness, without the need for class-based prejudice, minority assured preference, or affirmative action programs to elevate one class of people over another in a misguided attempt to redress real or perceived historical assault on the rights of those particular groups. Ladies and gentlemen, we must not give lip service to those ideals. We must enact those principles without fear or favor. These are the core values we are gathered in this room to discuss. If you do not share these ideals, then this morning is the time to express your reservations and to speak your mind. This first gathering will cast us for or against these principles, at least in the minds of those media representatives and liberals dedicated to the elimination of any obstacle to their incremental socialist agenda. Those are the people who will swarm to the attack when they become aware of our objectives.

"Within this room, we have the cadre of leadership from the elected legislatures of eight states. I submit that within ninety days of the public announcement of our intentions, that number will swell . . . and our enemies will mobilize. They will fight tooth and nail to deter our success. But be assured, ladies and gentleman, we do *not* seek revolution—we seek to resurrect the basic principles, eternal principles . . . *God-given principles*, that our forefathers enacted when this great nation was founded. I would be the first to acknowledge that it took America over one hundred years to extend that equality to everyone who lived here, my family included, but extend it they did. Then, over the past fifty years, these rights were rescinded, piece by piece, in a misguided attempt to 'protect' us from ourselves. Papa government and his liberal cousins wanted to make sure we had milk and bread, but they didn't want us to learn how to raise the cow or grow the wheat. Our overly protective government stepped in to assure that the big bad wolf wouldn't eat the babies. Absolute rubbish if you ask me," she said, shaking her head. "In words taken from my great-grandmother's journal, when the *real* wolves came near their cabin, '*ain't nobody gunna' eat* this *baby.*'" The room began to applaud amidst laughter.

"If we restore the rights that the founders promised to all Americans, and we do so correctly, *and,* if we do so with increasing public support, this nation will once again be united in purpose and practice. What has been called for over a century the "Eastern Establishment" will probably not join with us. And again, make no mistake: they are formidable opponents. But I firmly believe that we can reverse the geographical formation of this nation we all love, moving from the west to the east this time. The only mountains we will have to cross in re-tracing our ancestors steps are the mounds of ignorance and deception that have grown over the last century.

"If all states do not choose to join us—and I doubt that they will— we will honor their right of self-determination. But I believe this fact with all my heart: within three years, the newly established Republic of Western America will be the majority government on the North American continent, stronger and more confident than ever before, both morally and economically.

"The task before us will not be easy. I believe it can be done and it can be done economically rather than militarily. I believe it *must* be done without force of arms, but with economic measures designed to withdraw financial support from the existing national structure and with the intent to return that financial control, to a large extent, to the individual states, to the lowest political level feasible with good oversight, thereby limiting the new national authority to a very small, defined set of responsibilities. We are going to enact a completely new redistribution of wealth, ladies and gentleman, not from the rich to the poor, but from the government to the people. And what will be the end result if we restore government to the people? The District of Columbia will no longer control the price of corn. Nor will they dictate that your seven-year-old child must learn the benefit of alternative lifestyles—at least, not before they are emotionally ready to make those choices. A one hundred-million-dollar appropriation for a new water treatment plant will no longer contain fifteen million dollars of unrelated earmarks for the favored few. And, no longer will Washington determine the extent to which God—anyone's view of God—may be displayed in the public square." Another round of applause greeted Jefferson's comments.

"If we design this correctly, for the most part, government will be conducted at the lowest level to which adequate resource can be assembled to perform the function. Our new nation will immediately have vast tax resources, at greatly reduced levels, redirected from the USA to the RWA. A flat tax on income, or if we work it right, *no* personal income tax. A national sales tax, evenly applied, and many user-pays options to consider.

"So, let's move forward, begin our discourse, and see what the future holds for our effort. I suggest that we ask Mr. Rawlings to take a few moments and describe what he has discovered in his current attempt to develop a constitutional document suitable for the governance of California. I submit that what we discuss here this morning is larger than California. Larger than any of us. Larger, in fact, than any single or collective group of people. Perhaps from Mr. Rawlings we can discover some ideas that can be applied to the new constitution for the Republic of Western America. After that, we can hold an open discussion and take it from there." Jefferson paused a moment and scanned the room, her smile bright, her head nodding gently. "I admire your courage in convening this convocation. Once publicly acknowledged, many of us will be branded as foolish, rabble-rousers, and even stupid. Of course, *stupid* will only apply to the conservatives in the room," Jefferson said, laughing at her own remark. "Thank you all for listening to me ramble this morning. I am encouraged. I am excited. And I am proud to be among you. Now, Mr. Rawlings, are you prepared to speak to us for a few moments? The floor is yours and we're grateful for your attendance."

"Tell me, Dan, what do you think of our results this morning?"

Joyce Jefferson asked as they sat around a shaded table in the pool area outside the Bellagio. Nicole had joined the group, which included Nevada's lieutenant governor and Utah's attorney general.

Dan kept a straight face and reached for a bread roll, pausing to open a small, tinfoil butter packet. "I had thought that the California movement proceeded at lightning speed . . . until today. In four hours, we've just formed the basis for an entirely new nation and decided among ourselves to divorce the United States. Quite a morning's work for thirty-seven people," he concluded.

"And what do you think, Mrs. Rawlings?" Jefferson probed.

Nicole looked briefly at Dan and then back at Jefferson. "Governor, it's a good thing I'm no longer an FBI agent. I'd have to report the possibility of a treasonous action being perpetrated within the confines of the famed Bellagio Casino in Las Vegas. As it is . . ."

Joyce Jefferson nodded. "Quite surprising, isn't it? I've seen a lot in my lifetime, and I, too, find it hard to fathom what we're proposing. Yet, what are the options? For several decades—at least, during my political career—we've incrementally moved down the road of liberalism, some even go so far as to call it socialism. Bit by bit, we haven't even acknowledged the distance we've traveled from the original concept of American freedom—a people free to pursue their personal interest, to own property, to rise above their station. When Mayor Philips called me a few weeks ago and asked me to attend this gathering, I politely declined. I've not been known as a rebel, despite my years of advocacy for one cause or another. Compromise, negotiation, conciliation. Those were the tools of my success these many years. But the mayor asked me to take the long view . . . backwards. He asked me to consider where I was when the Civil Rights Act was passed in 1964. By the way," she said, a sheepish grin forming on her face, "I tried to tell him I wasn't born then, but he wouldn't bite. He then asked me to consider how far minorities have come over the subsequent years. And he asked me to look beyond the success of those minority people, not just my own race, but Hispanics, Native Americans, even women. Then he dropped the bomb on my head. He said, 'Joyce, how many of these success stories are celebrated if they are *not* in line with liberal thinking? How many black, Hispanic, or female leaders are celebrated by liberals or even female advocacy groups if they espouse conservative views? What is freedom of choice if not the right to oppose a view with which you don't agree? And why is that opposition—that open debate—not acceptable today as it was originally?'" She paused, taking a drink of her iced tea, and looked away toward the people milling around the pool.

"I thought of Clarence Thomas and wondered why the first black conservative on the Supreme Court was not lauded by his people. And Condolezza Rice as National Security Advisor and then Secretary of State. Why did they not receive their accolade for achievement? Were they not deserving of their honor? Did they not rise above their birth station by their own merit? And is that *not* the reason we believe in the equality of humanity? No," she said, shaking her head again, "liberals give lip service to minority rights. Minority *success* is lauded only if it conforms to the liberal slant of human rights. They believe in human *entitlement*, not human rights. And that's why I'm here today. That's why it's my intention to pursue this agenda to fruition. It may cost me tenure at the university. It may end my political career. It may end *all* our political careers. But it's the right thing to do, in my opinion.

"Mr. Rawlings," Jefferson said, looking straight at Dan, "I would like to ask you to go with me to see President Snow. We've worked together before and I owe him a great deal. I want to address this with him before we go public, and, as our group decided this morning, we're going to go public in early March so we can place the issue on each states' ballot for primaries this summer and the general election in November. But before we do that, I owe the president the courtesy of advance notice."

"I'm flattered, Governor, but what can I add to your presentation?" Dan asked.

"Dan, much of America, for better or worse, recognizes you as representing California in their secession process. But I'd like the four of us to go, gentlemen. Utah, Arizona, Nevada, and California. Then I will feel that we have fulfilled our obligation to the president. I also want to assure him, and perhaps hear from him, that we—and he—will do everything in our power to prevent this from becoming a military affair. We do *not* want insurrection or bloodshed. Can I count on you three gentlemen?"

The small group was silent as they sat around the table for several seconds. Finally, Dan smiled. "I guess I'm sort of pregnant again," he said. Nicole started to laugh, and Joyce Jefferson and the two men remained silent.

"Mr. Rawlings?" Jefferson asked, confused.

"I'll explain it later, Governor Jefferson, but for the present, you can count on me to stand by your side in this venture. However, before you proceed down this road, I think you need to hear how California *actually* came to her conclusions about secession. The back story might not be as you've been led to believe." Dan reached for Nicole's hand and smiled at her, essentially seeking her confirmation that what he was proposing was correct. Seeing her slight nod, he turned again to Jefferson.

"Governor, gentlemen . . . Californians were duped."

Five

OFFICE OF JOHN HARFORD, PRESIDENT
STRATEGIC INITIATIVES, LLC
ARLINGTON, VIRGINIA
FEBRUARY

"I don't pay your firm two million dollars a month so I can leave a message on your *voice* mail. That's more than I pay my bloodsucking lawyers. For that kind of money, I damn well expect you to be available 24/7."

John Harford stood behind his massive desk, his eyes boring into the visitor who had just entered his office, the door closing behind him. Harford's company, Strategic Initiatives, was known in the military world as SI, a multi-national security firm specializing in government contract work around the globe, legal and not so legal. Harford was used to employees, or sub-contractors, which was how he saw Ted Rowley's PR firm, placing him at the top of their priority list. And from Harford's perspective, since he paid the biggest fees, *everyone* would put him at the top of their priority list or he'd find someone else.

Forty-two, a West Point graduate, and a self-professed hard-ass, Harford had served as an Army Ranger and a Delta Force operative. He left the Army after eight years when a fellow ring-knocker recruited him to work with the CIA. Within three weeks of his recruitment, two Latin

American citizens had died of apparently self-inflicted gunshot wounds. When Harford discovered that his partner on that job, a freelance, contracted "security expert," had made over three times the money the CIA had paid him, Harford quickly left their service. Thirty-one, ten years out of West Point, he had resigned from both the Army and the CIA.

Recruiting a few of his former associates, Harford branched out, starting his own security firm with primarily bodyguard work initially, then progressing to contract killing, mostly on foreign soil.

A decade later, Harford remained in top physical shape, although his current position did not require "wet" work or even strenuous activity. He now had "people" for black ops. The only killing he did personally was character assassination of politicians who stood in his way.

Within those ten years, Strategic Initiatives had signed contracts with multiple U.S. government agencies and about a dozen foreign governments, ranging from personal protection to outright destabilization of smaller governments with shadow leaders who thought it was time for a change at the top. The bread-and-butter work came from domestic security in malls, sporting arenas, and federal buildings.

SI employed over 10,000 people, with several hundred more black ops staff who were paid off the books. Gross revenues in the previous fiscal year had topped fourteen billion dollars. Security work had been good to him. The prospects since 9/11, with the increased concern for domestic terrorism, had only enhanced his reputation and his revenue.

Noting the tone of rebuke in Harford's voice, Rowley responded cautiously. "I apologize, John. I called you within twenty minutes of receiving your message, but I was in the South African bush with a client. In your business, I know you can appreciate the need for occasionally being out of touch."

Harford just looked at the man standing before his desk for several long seconds, grunted his acknowledgement, then waved his hand toward a chair.

"Clay Cumberland's dead, as the whole world knows. I put five million into his presidential campaign, and I got three hours from him. Worst investment I ever made. Where will Snow stand on issues of importance to SI?" Harford asked.

"In all candor, I don't know," Rowley said, "but it doesn't matter. We have the votes we need in Congress, and our inside Pentagon source is moving, even as we speak, to close the loop. Snow won't even find his private toilet before we have this locked up."

Theodore Justin Rowley, T.J. to his associates, was the president of his own company, a public relations firm that worked exclusively for politicians, governments, and the military, both domestic and foreign. Not in any respect as large as SI, T.J. Rowley & Associates was, nonetheless, a force to be reckoned with when image was needed. From political campaigns to outright deception and manipulation of public interest, Rowley knew exactly how, and just as important, when, to present the "truth" through his vast media resources. No longer referred to as public relations, the high concept term had become "perception management." T.J. Rowley and Associates was the best in the world at creating it. His boiler room Internet chat sites spewed forth his personal brand of truth twenty-four hours a day, ridiculing anyone who thought differently. If you wanted your idea to be "true" and popular with the public, Rowley could make it so. On Facebook, Twitter, YouTube, and a hundred other blogs his operatives, mostly stay-in-their-room teenage nerds, had specific orders to combat any ideas contrary to T.J. Rowley & Associates' opinion *de jour*.

Harford picked up where he left off. "And what about our progress for passage of the Domestic Tranquility bill? Is everything in place in the House and the Senate?"

Rowley nodded. "All done. Your choice of a project name was masterful. Even the liberals are onboard with the concept. Every congressman who addresses the issue invokes the Constitution when he's speaking about it. I love it. It's made my sales job that much easier."

"That's fine," Harford commented. "On the operational side, I've arranged for an Irish associate to drop information into the European underground network. If all goes well, they'll troll the bait. Then either the CIA or Homeland Security intelligence operatives will pick up on a warning, and if they act quickly, they'll be fully aware of the coming domestic threat. Internal intelligence briefings to the congressional committee should do the rest, as far as passage of the bill is concerned."

"Excellent," Rowley said. "Are your operational people ready to react?"

Harford remained quiet for several long seconds before responding. He had long ago learned his basic premise: don't share any information with subordinates. "You create the public perception, T.J. I'll handle the rest."

"Consider it done. Our congressional supporters have planted the seed, and General Wainscott has already created the position paper to reflect the insufficiency of an Army National Guard response to domestic terrorism. John, the upcoming California secession, whether it happens or not, only adds to our cause. America is in turmoil. SI will be the resource they turn to when domestic violence commences. Wainscott's on it."

Harford raised an eyebrow and cocked his head. "Don't let him get too far ahead, T.J. Being prescient is one thing—being clairvoyant is another. Do you believe California will follow through? Will the president let them go without military action or declaring martial law?"

"We've had four presidents in as many months. What this newest one will do is uncertain, but after the Battle of Capitol Mall in Sacramento—well named, I might add—who knows? I doubt he wants military bloodshed any more than Eastman did. A civil war over freeing the slaves was a moral cause which much of the world understood. Sending troops to keep California in the Union is another matter. In my opinion, it would not justify open combat—body bags—in American cities."

Harford nodded. "And Senator Culpepper? Is he convinced of the need for more domestic security resources—that the Domestic Tranquility bill is the answer?"

Rowley chuckled. "Culpepper used the term 'promote the domestic tranquility' himself the other day in committee. Ironic, isn't it?"

"You better hope it's only irony. We need Culpepper to support our White Paper on the need for increased domestic surveillance measures and arrest powers for the private security guard force. We need the Patriot Act expanded, more law enforcement authority. We also need to be able to offer a private security alternative to an unpopular activation of the National Guard."

"I'll stay on it. Culpepper is not quite as susceptible as some of the others. He's in his last senatorial term and looking for his legacy, not more campaign funds. But he's always been in support of security measures, and from the tone of his last public announcement, he understands that Americans are going to have to make some tough choices between personal liberty and security."

"If he's not going to be with us, T.J, then it's time he retired, voluntarily or otherwise. I've got over fifty million tied up in the latest generation metal detectors, bomb sniffing apparatus, unmanned aerial vehicles, camera equipment, and public building security measures, not to mention getting ready for over 150,000 security guards in public facilities around the country. This operation will dwarf the TSA build-up to secure airports. I need this policy accepted and the Patriot Act enhanced to permit its implementation. Domestic Tranquility hinges on Culpepper's committee and the Pentagon's recommendation."

"The Pentagon is a lock, John, and Culpepper is only one man. With or without him, we'll see it through Congress."

"See that you do. Are you convinced that our new president can't stand in the way?"

"What can he do? He doesn't even have a cabinet lined up yet, and from what we hear, he's considered turning his nose up at Cumberland's promised appointments. That alone will set him against his own party. He'll be impotent to get his initiatives through Congress, much less stand in the way of all these 'patriotic' congressman who are only thinking of their country and the security of the people. Perception management. That's my business, remember?"

"Save your damned perception management spiel for those more gullible, T.J. As for cabinet officers, what can we do to override Snow's reluctance to appoint Pat Collins as Secretary of Defense? That was part of my deal with Cumberland."

"Actually, I hear that still might go through. Nothing firm yet, but my Pentagon source says Snow has requested that the background check continue."

"If you can massage that appointment, by all means get it done. Collins is 'in the loop,' if you understand my meaning. Did you arrange my interview with General Wainscott?"

"Friday. He's champing at the bit to join SI."

"Well, we need him to remain as Deputy Chief of Staff for the Army for the immediate future, but that doesn't prevent him from going on salary—surreptitiously, of course. Sweeten the pot. Tell him we'll put him on salary now and hold it until he signs with us, then we'll call it a signing bonus."

"Of course. I better go, John. I've got a few more legislators to convince that America is in need of *domestic tranquility*."

"Keep me informed," Harford said.

Six

EISENHOWER EXECUTIVE OFFICE BUILDING
OFFICE OF INFORMATION & PUBLIC RELATIONS
DEPARTMENT OF HOMELAND SECURITY
WASHINGTON, D.C.
FEBRUARY

President Cumberland's immediate death from a heart attack and William Snow's elevation to the presidency, as traumatic as it seemed, had provided much grist for the mill of late night comedians. Hank Carter on *Late Night Today* quipped: "Did you hear that the president ordered his new business cards the other day? They came back with 'President of the United States,' followed by a signature line that says 'fill in the blank.'" In two hundred twenty-five years, America had never experienced such turmoil in government.

With the creation of the Homeland Security Department over a decade ago under President Steadman, many of the traditional intelligence-gathering agencies had consolidated under the new banner. President Prescott, in her brief tenure, had been a bit more creative in forming a small group of military intelligence and special operations people reporting directly to the Secretary of Homeland Security, Anthony Weyland.

To head the new operation, a combat-experienced Marine Colonel,

Pádraig 'Pug' Connor, with whom Prescott had worked on the California secession task force, was promoted to Brigadier General and placed in charge. The new team, still in its formative stages and recruiting staff, had been in place less than ninety days when President Cumberland took office.

The cover name given to the team was the Office of Information and Public Relations. It was designed to be a part of the president's immediate advisory and quick reaction staff, without the need to consult the Joint Chiefs. In truth, it circumvented the established approval process for application of military force and was strongly opposed by the Pentagon.

They worked out of the Eisenhower Executive Office Building, known as the EEOB, after its name was changed in 1999 from the Old Executive Office Building. The ornate structure, decried by some and praised by others, was located directly across the street from the White House.

General Connor, Sergeant Major—now Mr.—Castro, three Special Ops officers, and two enlisted NCO's, plus a new secretary, composed the entire staff. With room for two more on the permanent staff, Connor had quietly solicited certain individuals from the special operations network to become a part of the team. The initial TO, or Table of Organization, numbered only seven people, plus two administrative support staff. But as General Connor had explained to Castro, Trojan was much more extensive.

For any mission that had been designated as security level "Troy" by the president, they had unrestricted access to military assets, including small, covert special ops units around the world, Army Delta, Recon Marines, or Navy Seals. They had authority to coordinate action with British, Australian, or New Zealand SAS troops, but only on a voluntary basis. Trojan's tasking of military units did not require Pentagon approval, which was the primary source of military opposition. However, General Connor had decided to attempt coordination, if not cooperation, by giving notification as a matter of protocol mainly to assure that the field teams requested were not already involved in other missions.

President Prescott had given Pug free reign to develop the team, but since the change of administration, they had received no briefing on how the Office of Information and Public Relations, OIPR, would operate under the new president, either Cumberland or Snow. The turmoil of transition from Prescott to Cumberland to Snow, all within a matter of hours, had only exacerbated the situation.

Unfamiliar with such high-level political maneuvering, Pug had consulted his old boss at the CIA, Lieutenant General Bill Austin. Under Austin's guidance, and in established military tradition, the Trojan team continued to 'operate until relieved,' pressing forward to establish a further foothold against intrusions, foreign or domestic. In this case, "domestic" was defined as any political or Pentagon-based assault on their domain. It was common knowledge that the Joint Chiefs of Staff, the JCS, would love—and had tried—to assume control over the group, resenting their ability to call upon military assets without standard approval procedure.

The widespread uncertainty among Cumberland's designated cabinet officers, none of whom had received Senate confirmation, and all of whom were concerned about retaining their own anticipated power base, aided in Trojan's ability to remain operationally independent. Everyone at an authority level, or presumed to be heading in that direction, was more concerned about their own survival than an assault on a small, non-descript military outfit.

The morning after his return from Ireland, Carlos Castro arrived at the EEOB and contacted Alice Hall, General Connor's secretary, who now stood in the general's doorway. "General, Mr. Castro is asking if you have a few moments to see him."

"Thank you, Alice. Have him come in."

Carlos was wearing civilian clothes, as was General Connor, a routine procedure for the Homeland Security military personnel working in the central Washington complex. Military officers working at DHS frequently dealt with other civilian government departments and had come to realize that uniforms sometimes put them at a disadvantage. The use of civilian attire had also reduced the military post atmosphere and the rank-induced protocol that existed at the Pentagon. The civilian atmosphere only carried so far, however, and even when a general officer wore a Brooks Brothers or Armani suit and referred to his military staff officers with a degree of informality, it was not intended to be reciprocal.

Carlos stopped in front of the general's desk. "Good morning, General."

Pug looked up. "Welcome back, Carlos. How did it go in Ireland?"

"Quite well, actually. I've been invited to an asshole convention," Carlos said.

Pug smiled and shuffled a stack of papers into a pile, shoving them toward the corner of his desk. "Some might say you qualify."

"Touché," Carlos acknowledged. "I didn't see anyone until I received a cryptic note at the embassy, instructing me to be on St. Stephen's Green at a designated time. Then, after being driven blindfolded out to a secluded location, we switched vehicles. I then had a twenty-minute personal meeting with Kevin Donahue while he drove me to the airport. He knew about our new public relations function and your promotion. He said to give the *general* his regards."

Pug nodded. "I told you he was well informed."

"After I checked in and was waiting for my flight, I got this email at the Dublin airport," Carlos said, placing a printed version on General Connor's desk.

Pug scanned the paper quickly. "East Timor's far too small to hold all the assholes I've met," the general continued, a sharp grin crossing his face as he handed the note back. "Do you believe this information?"

Carlos nodded. "Yes, sir, I do. As you told me, Donahue had no reason to provide *any* information. He was not the least bit evasive. Why would he lay a false trail? I called Brigadier Colin McIntyre, military attaché at the British Embassy here in Washington, early this morning. He's heard Wolff's name through his channels. He felt certain this would get instant response from MI6 and suggested we'd be hearing from the Brits within a couple of days, if not immediately."

"You think they'll want to crash the convention?" Pug asked.

"Wouldn't surprise me, General. Sounds like something right up their alley."

"What about the Indonesians or the Timor government?"

"I doubt the Brits would share this information. They'll probably just send some SAS guys in as tourists and snatch him."

"Something a recon marine might like to get involved in while working with a FAST team, I suppose?" Pug said, referring to one of the main components of their available assets, a Fleet Anti-Terrorist Security Team, mostly Force Recon Marines, located aboard each CBG, or Carrier Battle Group, throughout the world. Pug himself had commanded such a team several years before coming to the NSA and then the CIA.

"We *could* get some worthwhile information, sir. We've both been down that path before."

Pug nodded. "I do miss that part of the game, Sergeant Major, but I'm on the bench now, and in short order, you'll most likely become indispensible to this office. When that happens, I'll bench you too. We might have to rely on our new assets to handle the field work. Don't turn in your web gear just yet, but understand what I'm saying. Operational planning is just as important, maybe more so, than field ops. Speaking of that, we have three SEALS and two ranger candidates to interview tomorrow for our last two slots. I want you to go over their service records today. All good men, by first accounts. I know two of them. You probably do too. Besides, if we're both benched, Trojan has to learn to rely on these guys. I think that after last week's KLM drama, we'll get more authority to go operational. The climate is feverish in the west wing."

"General, have you met the new president yet?" Carlos asked.

"Not since he's become president," Pug replied.

Carlos remained silent, but tilted his head slightly, questioning the meaning.

"I'll fill you in later, Carlos, but I knew President Snow over twenty years ago. He and my father and two other men were partners in a law firm in Phoenix. He taught me to play golf and my older brother is married to his daughter."

Carlos whistled softly. "So you're *family*."

Pug bristled at the inference. "I don't see it that way, Sergeant Major, and that information goes no further than this room until I decide how to address the issue."

"Yes, sir. About the SAS and the extraction of Wolff?" Carlos said, a quick subject change seeming appropriate. "I'd like to be involved. He's my first Trojan assignment, and if I'm likely headed for the bench, I'd like a bit more field time."

"True, you're not on the bench *yet*, and I agree that it's probably necessary for you to accompany whoever is sent to get him. We might decide that it will be *just* you, with a small team to back you up. And . . . we might decide that it's *not* an extraction."

"I understand," Carlos replied.

"But remember this, Carlos: there's more than one way to fight a war. Especially the type of war we currently face. We both better get used to it. While we're on the subject of East Timor, what do you make of this Intel?" he asked, handing Carlos a sheet of paper.

More than once, Pug had come to the same conclusion he was suggesting to Carlos—the necessity of stepping out of field operations—but for far different reasons. He had counted it up once when he was reviewing his life and his poor choices along the way. Pug had married Cheryl the week after he graduated from Annapolis in 1992. Within four months, he had gone to sea with a Marine Expeditionary Unit as a platoon commander. Out of eight years of marriage, over four and half of them he had either been at sea, commanding a platoon or company of Marines, or on a special covert assignment where he couldn't even tell her where he was going, when he would be back, or where he had been. Finally, she'd had enough and told him, essentially, that she needed a husband who worked nine to five, cut the grass, went to bed with her, woke up next to her, and was going to be around to help raise the kids, if he was ever home long enough to participate in *making* any children. They'd parted ways in 2001, shortly before 9/11, and he'd remained single every since, notwithstanding the opportunities that had come his way. Fortunately they'd made the decision to divorce before children had complicated the process.

Scanning the document the general had handed him, Carlos assumed the role of analyst.

"It's from Security Intelligence Service, Canberra," Carlos said, basically to himself. "This confirms what we got last week from the DHS Intel Day Sheet, General. Increased indication that Al Qaida leadership is expanding operations in the Indonesian theatre and the South Pacific. They've got a lot of Muslim support there, just as many fanatics, but not much in the way of sophisticated weaponry. And the island Muslims are not happy about Australia's support of the coalition forces in the war zone. They proved that a few years ago with the bombing in Bali, which targeted mostly Australian tourists, and more recently in Fremantle during the yachting regatta."

"No sophisticated weapons, you say? Carlos, you know as well as I do that a reliable weapons delivery system in the Middle East, Indonesia, or anywhere else for that matter, can be nothing more than one single religious fanatic, a bulky overcoat, and a dozen sticks of dynamite plus several hundred ball bearings and nails strapped to his—or her—body. I want you to give this top priority. It coincides with your search for Wolff, at least geographically, and it may help to clarify why he's going to East Timor in the first place. Put together an analysis of capability, timing, anything you can conceive of that terrorists could mount in the south and west Pacific theatre. You might need to have a chat with the Aussies."

"I understand, sir. I'll get right on it."

"And let me know what the Brits decide. I think Brigadier McIntyre is right that they'll be a bit anxious to get the SAS involved in this . . . what is it the Brits would call it, an *arsehole* convention?"

"Yes, sir."

"One further thing, Carlos," Pug said, stepping behind his desk. "Your retirement is not until February 28th, but let's drop the Sergeant Major and commence immediately with Mr. Castro, Deputy Director, especially for the interviews tomorrow. Some of these guys may know you, and those that don't will check us out with the SOG network. Since most of them are officers, we have to ascertain that they can work under the direction of a former enlisted man. Leave that part of the interview to me."

"Yes, sir. No problem."

"And Carlos, I'm going to remain on active duty as a general officer. In private, feel free to call me Pug, but in a public or staff setting, we will retain protocol."

Carlos smiled again. "No problem . . . Pug."

Carlos walked down the corridor toward his office, his thoughts mixed with regard to the possibility of going after Wolff, and the new, certainly more dangerous possibility of Al Qaida developing a new geographical base of operations in Indonesia. As he entered his office, he saw a Post-it note on his telephone, signed by his secretary.

Carlos, Brigadier McIntyre has called twice in the past hour.

Carlos looked at the note briefly, closed the door, sat behind his desk, picked up the phone, and dialed.
"British Embassy, Military Attaché's office. May I be of assistance?"
"Brigadier McIntyre, please. Carlos Castro returning his call."
"Certainly, sir, one moment please."
A slight pause ensued, and then McIntyre came on the line. Brigadier Sir Colin McIntyre had served Her Majesty through three decades and part of a fourth, as a young officer with the Coldstream Guards, eventually rising to command the regiment, and then as a member of MI6, Britain's Secret Intelligence Service, posted abroad the past decade.
"Carlos, thank you for returning my call. Your Irish information has stirred up the proverbial hornet's nest, dear boy. Are your swimming skills still in good form?"
"Sir?"
"About now, or certainly within the hour, I suspect General Connor will be getting a call from the Pentagon. The thrust of the message, lad, will be that Her Majesty's government shall be requesting the use of your personal skills."
"In what capacity, Brigadier?" Carlos asked.
"*Who dares, wins*, I should think, Carlos. You know those Stirling Lines SAS boys, of course. The CRW, our counter-revolutionary warfare wing, will probably be assigned this mission, although given the proximity of the target, they might farm it out to the colonials. That would be the Aussies to you." He laughed.
Carlos smiled briefly, recognition of a previous assignment in the Middle East drawing distant memories. "It seems I'm destined to spend a portion of my career seconded to Her Majesty's Special Air Service. And we're going swimming, you say?"
"Indubitably, my dear boy, but not to worry. It's quite warm in the South Pacific this time of year, so I'm led to believe, and with six to eight inches of snow due here in Washington later this week—well, I

envy you. Were I twenty . . . no, make that *thirty* years younger, I'd see about a set of togs and flippers for myself. Let me know when you hear something."

"Certainly, Brigadier. Thanks for the heads-up."

SEVEN

WHITE HOUSE OVAL OFFICE
WASHINGTON D.C.
FEBRUARY

President William Snow, 5' 11", trim and healthy at age 59, with a thick shock of salt-and-pepper hair and a piercing set of steely gray eyes, sat comfortably on a soft, terra cotta-colored lounge chair, its new smell faint in the Oval Office.

Former President Joshua Steadman, 71, was a native of South Carolina and had retired to a secluded, Hilton Head Island estate. His hair was now thinner and a slight paunch had begun to appear in what had remained, well into his 60's, a stocky, athletic build. He sat across from Snow on an equally new, burgundy-toned settee.

Steadman had served two terms as president, departing just over eight years ago after transferring power to President Eastman. He had returned to Washington to participate in President Clay Cumberland's inauguration, and had stayed for the funeral ceremony. Six weeks later, he had graciously accepted an invitation to meet with President Snow.

Despite his advancing age, Steadman was visibly animated in his actions and speech, his mind clear, decisive, and his verbal presentation authoritative, yet not directive. Both men had spent the previous thirty minutes in discussion, alternating between casual chatter and more serious, penetrating, conversation. From opposite political parties, they had only met once previously. However, on this second occasion, arranged at the personal invitation of President William Snow, each had taken an immediate liking to the other, notwithstanding their philosophical differences.

"I could beat around the bush, Bill, but to get to the heart of the matter, there's only one real question you need to answer," Steadman said. "Do you want a chance at a second term?"

Bill Snow smiled and nodded his head, agreeing with the other man. "That *would* be the bottom line, wouldn't it?"

"Indeed," the older man replied. "The answer to that question will form all your other decisions in these first few weeks. If you act forcefully, relying on your own counsel and those you *know* you can trust, and if you make your own decisions and are determined in what you seek, you'll undoubtedly set some of your own party against you. Unfortunately, there's no way around that. I came here today, at your invitation, to discuss this with you as candidly as possible. You've got an unprecedented opportunity, Bill. You can do what few of us who have sat behind that desk have truly been able to do."

"How so?" Snow queried.

Steadman smiled broadly, reaching to retrieve his coffee cup from the side table. "Despite what your party hacks are going to claim to the contrary, you have absolutely no obligation to honor *any* political deals Cumberland made. All bets are off. They died with that poor unfortunate soul at the end of his three-hour presidency. You owe 'nothing to nobody,' as the saying goes. You can make your own cabinet nominations without fear or favor to those who supported Cumberland, and you can set the agenda for your first, and perhaps your *only*, term." He chuckled. "In short, Bill, you've come to this office without baggage—without owing an arm and a leg to everyone who claims he brought you his county, his state, or a bag of electoral votes. That in itself is rare, practically unheard of in this day and age. But," the former president said, "if you have any thoughts of a second term, they'll hold you over the barrel and demand you support their favorite nominees, programs, or hare-brained ideas."

Snow leaned back into the soft, yet firm cushions of his chair, crossing his legs and pursing his lips. "I'd certainly anger all those in my own party who made the promises, those who paid the bill for Cumberland's—and my—election."

"True. But at what price? Four years with a management team someone else chose, some of whom will be inclined to repeatedly remind you that whatever you want to do, it was *not* what President Cumberland would have done. Or would you prefer freedom to do what you think is right? What—in your own opinion—the country needs? With a top-level team of your own choosing? To be perhaps the first president to ever come in here with a clean slate and no human debt? It's not only the economy, security and general national issues—you've got this dammed secession issue to consider. What will you do about California? Cumberland voiced his determination to take any and all measures necessary to put a halt to it. Personally, Bill, I think military intervention would be the worst thing you could do."

Snow remained silent, a slight smile played across his lips as he listened to the highly popular former president, a man who had left office after eight years still possessed of a sixty-three percent favorable poll rating. Steadman sipped on his coffee and watched the younger man.

"You've thought all this through, haven't you, you desert fox?" Steadman asked, using the term the Arizona press had coined when Bill Snow had—against all odds—run for governor and won.

"Choosing my own team has certainly crossed my mind, Josh, but I haven't made any firm decisions yet. I'm also not certain how to handle California. In some respects, we'd lose a lot of problems if we just let them go. Let them fend for themselves. At last look, they were bankrupt. We either need to let them go it their own way, or bail them out."

"That's true, but don't underestimate the precedent. We might end up with two nations between the Atlantic and the Pacific. I've heard rumblings from some western colleagues."

Snow nodded. "So have I, but let's get back to cabinet appointments and my immediate problems. California can wait until next week." He laughed. "I'm not anxious to get crossways with my own party, but the thought of a clean slate, choosing my own cabinet, is enticing. Other vice presidents who took over from their president did so well into their terms of office and had to show at least a semblance of completing the guys' work. I don't see it that way in this case. Cumberland made campaign promises, but had no initiatives started yet. There truly is an opportunity to put the right people in the right places—*my* people—regardless of the clamor it would raise among your party or mine. Of course, there are the Senate confirmation hearings to consider, and the Republicans are still in the minority where I need the votes. And the first consideration is a vice president."

Steadman nodded in agreement. "In light of the events that have transpired, if you move quickly, decisively, the American people will support you and the Senate won't have the ability to deny confirmation of your nominees. Even the press will take up your cause, loving that 'in-your-face' attitude it will throw at Congress."

"You *really* believe that, Josh?" Snow asked, his interest suddenly heightened.

"I'd work with you to see that it happened. You have my word on it."

"A truly bi-partisan effort, you mean?"

"Oh, no," he said, placing his coffee cup back on the saucer. "I'd have to be completely covert. Totally behind the scenes to try to convince some of my party that it would be a good time to get political hacks and lobbyists out of the executive recruitment business, putting their lackeys in office, then coming to them for favors. And I could support you in the media, with the obligatory cautionary statements to distance myself, of course," he said, a small laugh following. "Remember, I *am* a South Carolina Baptist." He laughed even louder. "I can't be openly seen to be supporting an Arizona Catholic. Goodness gracious, how would all those fire and brimstone televangelists raise money if Christian religions starting *agreeing* with each other, admitting they weren't the *only* ones who spoke for God?"

"You mean Jesus *isn't* a Republican?" Snow said, joining Steadman in laughter. Turning serious, the new president leaned forward. "Josh, I'll probably be in touch with you again on California, but for today, you came prepared to offer sage advice, right? Who you would recommend for the half-dozen key jobs? Vice president, for instance?"

"I have a few thoughts," Steadman replied, "but I'd rather hear yours. I was sincere when I said this is *your* opportunity, not mine, for another go around. I served my time in that chair." He nodded toward the chocolate-brown leather executive chair positioned behind the mahogany desk that once sustained Andrew Jackson's presidency.

Snow rose from his seat and stepped over to the desk, retrieving a leather folder and walking back. He stood behind his chair for a moment, leafing through several papers in the folder. "Most of Cumberland's selectees," he said, waving the documents, "have already been through this office or on the phone, subtly and not so subtly trying to remind me of the promises made and of their willingness and capability to serve."

"I'm sure they have," Steadman replied, shaking his head. "It doesn't matter."

"Some of them are good men and good women, Josh. Good choices."

"Well, then *nominate* them. But make sure they're *your* choice as well as Cumberland's. Even then, remember that they will be inclined to remind you that when Cumberland offered them the job, he '. . . *gave them to understand, this and that . . .*'"

President Snow nodded his agreement. "And as for the vice president, I really haven't had a good thought about it. No name has jumped to the surface." He paused, looking at his folder. "Hank Tiarks is a really good man, Josh," he commented, again leafing through the papers. "But I think due to their friendship and level of trust, Cumberland wanted him in Homeland Security because he felt domestic security was going to be a real problem as these terrorist threats continue. I actually think that Cumberland wanted Tiarks as his vice president, but our party forced him to select me."

"That could be, Bill, but don't let it deter you from choosing someone you want. Are you thinking of Tiarks for VP?"

"Maybe. He's well respected. Cumberland mentioned to me that he thought Tiarks would stand up to the heads of the various intelligence agencies. But I think his talents lie elsewhere. Law enforcement or direct action planning are not his strengths, at least as I see it."

"What *is* his strength," Steadman asked, "in your opinion?"

"Possibly VP, or Secretary of State. Perhaps even the United Nations. He's well thought of abroad."

"I agree. He could fill either of those slots. See, you're on the right track already. And Homeland Security? Cumberland was right, you know. You'll need someone you can trust who has exceptional judgment and the courage to implement his decisions. Someone who's not beholden to the political world and not afraid of ruffling feathers in the intelligence community. It will take a tough individual, one who's not constantly looking for his next higher office. Also, someone who isn't inclined to push for military intervention in California. Someone familiar with the problem out there."

"I don't know about Homeland Security yet," Snow said, flipping through a few more pages, "but I do know it will be at the forefront of a lot of action and public reaction, good *and* bad. I'm inclined to stick with Collins for SecDef. He's come out publicly against military intervention in California, and he served well as Secretary of the Army under Eastman during his first term. Besides California, we anticipate much more domestic terrorism this decade. This is a long war, Josh. If history serves, it may even outlast the European Thirty Years' War, or, heaven forbid, the Hundred Years' War. It started during your term, Josh, but most attacks were abroad in those years. It's a lot different now, even in the short time you've been out of office."

"Well," Steadman replied, rising from his seat and placing his coffee cup back on the table, "since you asked for my advice, let me tell you a bit about someone who is currently hidden away. Someone I came to trust explicitly. Someone who doesn't give a hoot about higher political office."

A quizzical look appeared on President Snow's face. "Someone from Washington whom you *trusted*?"

Steadman laughed. "He's not from Washington. Far from it, but he's served his country in peace and in war, including the Washington wars, for nearly forty years."

"You've got my attention," Snow said, beginning to rise to the game.

The former president walked toward the small table in the corner of the room, a silver coffee service in place on its polished surface. "Let me refill my coffee cup and I'll give you a couple of thoughts. Would you like a refill?"

EIGHT

WHITE HOUSE OVAL OFFICE
WASHINGTON D.C.
FEBRUARY

Lieutenant General William Austin, USAF, Ret., and Brigadier General Pádraig Connor, USMC, were escorted into the Oval Office by Dixie, the president's temporary secretary. President William Snow came out from behind his desk and greeted both men, smiling broadly.

"It's been a long time, Pug," the president said. "When I heard you were part of the president's extended staff, I was surprised and quite pleased. How are your parents?"

"Very well, Mr. President."

"General Austin," the president said, turning his attention to Austin. "It's a pleasure to meet you." He offered his hand. "Please, gentlemen, take a seat. General Austin, can I assume that General Connor has explained our distant family relationship?"

"Yes, Mr. President. When Pug... uh, General Connor called to advise me that you had requested my attendance this morning, he discussed your former relationship. I also understand his older brother is your son-in-law."

"That's correct. And has he explained our other former connection?"

"Sir, General Connor has also advised that you were partners in a law firm with his father. He casually mentioned that you taught him to play golf as well."

The president laughed. "Too well, I'm afraid. I wouldn't stand a chance against him, should we tee it up again. So, now that the familiarities are completed, I'm the one who needs to be brought up to speed. Pug, as my secretary mentioned yesterday, the purpose for this impromptu meeting was to brief me on your current position and the confidential task force you head. Can you succinctly describe the function of your office—what's it called? The Office of Information and Public Relations? What does that office do for Homeland Security?"

Pug hesitated momentarily, a pensive look crossing his face. "Well, Mr. President, we *don't* do public relations."

President Snow smiled back at his former law partner's son. "I surmised as much, General Connor. And I confess to a short briefing—yesterday morning, actually—from President Steadman. He said President Prescott had called him to discuss her intention to create your task force and wanted his opinion. He supported her intentions. I have no knowledge of where President Cumberland stood on the issue."

"I see, sir. Then you understand that President Prescott organized our office under the Homeland Security Department specifically to give her direct control over a quick reaction, military think tank. She wanted a closer relationship to planning as it pertains to rapidly developing terrorist activity, primarily domestic terrorism. She had concluded—during her vice presidency—that it would only grow more intrusive within the U.S. homeland. As she explained it to me, she wanted opinions and suggestions outside the Pentagon chain of command. Actually, we're a slightly different kind of think tank, Mr. President. Each of our officers—and, sir, we actually have a very small full-time staff, eight people, to be exact—has come directly from command of a branch of special forces and has had direct field action experience."

President Snow nodded. "Would that include you, Pug?"

"Yes, Mr. President."

"Didn't you also head a task force for President Eastman regarding the California secession movement? Something about election fraud and militia activity?"

"Yes, sir. I've prepared a full, written after-action report for you on that subject when you feel ready to review it. The secession issue is still very much alive, Mr. President, although we've curtailed the election fraud process. As it stands, California still intends to divide into multiple states, but they haven't rescinded their electoral decision to secede and form their own nation. In fact, as I understand my latest briefing from FBI Director Granata, the movement is actually growing stronger."

Snow nodded. "I'm aware of developments in the west. That problem may overshadow everything else, if we're not careful. I've heard back room chat from my Arizona contacts that the secession movement, at least philosophically, has spread to several other western states. But that discussion can wait for a few days. Let's stick with your current position. What does your task force actually do, Pug?"

"Sir," General Austin interrupted, "may I speak candidly?"

"By all means, General Austin," the president said, turning to look at the older man.

"Sir, General Connor may be too modest to give you the full story. I, on the other hand, don't suffer from that particular genetic abnormality. Washington has cured me of any semblance of humility."

Both President Snow and Pug Connor could not help but laugh at Austin's self-degradation.

"Sir," Austin continued, "for over a decade, first at the National Security Agency and then at the CIA, Pug has served on my staff, most recently as my executive officer. I had to literally drag him out of field command and order him behind the desk. Last year, I recommended him to President Eastman to head the California investigative task force. With some regional assistance from the California Adjutant General and FBI support, the task force broke the ring of corporate moguls that was perpetrating the fraud. But, in light of his current duties—Pug would probably diminish his role—he has an outstanding military record as a combat field commander. America has been involved in two ground wars, but many more covert operations to stop further terrorist attacks. As a captain and then a major, he served as the commanding officer of a Marine Corps Fleet Anti-Terrorist Security Team, which is comprised of a Marine Recon unit assigned as part of a carrier battle group. He has seen direct action in both Afghanistan and Iraq, as well as covert activity in other geographic locations around the world. There's no shortage of trouble spots, Mr. President. This type of assignment can never be openly documented on a military record. Among other decorations, General Connor has a Navy Cross, the citation narrative restricted on a need-to-know basis.

"Mr. President, on the type of missions General Connor used to command, Marines, SEALS or special operation soldiers who did not come home—the media use the phrase 'gave their all'—are generally reported as having died in a training exercise. It's a shadow world, Mr. President. Perhaps that's why it's called 'black ops.' But in summary, with regard to his current command of Trojan—that's the team's designation—once the president designates an action as level 'Troy,', someone from his staff is required to go out into the world, find the worst of our enemies, and either kill or capture them. It's neither pleasant nor easy. And it's terrible on family life. But I submit, sir, that General Connor is eminently qualified to command Trojan and the men who serve under him. Both President Eastman and President Prescott understood this and trusted him. President Prescott gave him his first star at least five years beyond his normal eligibility year date.

"Sir, during the intervening years since your last affiliation with a young Pug Connor, a lot has transpired in his life."

Pug sat quietly through this resume recital, clearly uncomfortable with the disclosure.

"Thank you, General Austin," Snow replied. "Pug, Trojan is quite different from the summer job you had in the law firm, isn't it?"

"It's been a long time since those days, Mr. President. Some days I wish I could go back to that less stressful time."

"Don't we all?" Snow chuckled. "Pug, do you know what President Cumberland's intentions were with relation to your unit's continued operation?"

"No, sir, I don't. I never met President Cumberland," Pug said.

"Understood," Snow said, his tone taking a more defined edge. "And I suppose you'd like to know what I intend to do with your . . . uh, Office of Public Relations . . . what you call 'Trojan'."

"Yes, sir, that's our internal designation. I also have a full operational report for you when you're ready. As General Austin has stated, we do not act without proper authority. Any military action enacted by Trojan requires presidential approval, which we then designate Troy. Within our security network, it's the next level down from an Executive Order."

"I understand. Gentlemen, as I said, I've spoken with President Steadman and, more recently, just about an hour ago, with President Prescott," he said. "She gave me a quick heads-up on Trojan, not much, actually, just a summary. She strongly recommended that I continue the operation, at least until such time as I form my own opinion and judge its worth. General Austin, this morning I also consulted Admiral Barrington, Chairman of the Joint Chiefs. I believe you and he served together some years ago, before you retired from the Air Force. He indicated that he thought you might be considering a second, final retirement."

"That's correct, Mr. President," Austin replied.

"Is that still your intention?" Snow continued.

"I've not made the final decision, Mr. President. I wanted to see General Connor firmly established in his position and the abrupt changes in the White House . . ."

"I understand. General Austin, I won't put you through a long process wondering what's going to happen. I would request that you defer your final retirement and continue to serve your country."

"I serve at your pleasure, Mr. President."

"However," Snow said, "I would like your immediate resignation from the Central Intelligence Agency."

Pug quickly shifted his gaze to Austin, who continued to hold eye contact with President Snow.

"As I said, sir, I serve at your pleasure. You will have my resignation on your desk this afternoon," General Austin said, his voice a bit more formal.

"And then I would like you to take a few days off and go out to Wyoming to spend some time in discussions with former Secretary of Homeland Security, Anthony Weyland. You know Secretary Weyland, of course?"

Austin tilted his head slightly in a questioning mannerism. "Yes, sir. We worked very closely together for several years while he was National Security Advisor to President Eastman."

"So I understand. Again, General, it's not my intention to keep you in the dark. If you serve at my pleasure, as you've indicated, then I would like to obtain your approval to put forth your name as my nominee to serve as Secretary of Homeland Security. Secretary Weyland can bring you up to speed on the nomination hearings."

"Mr. President, I—"

Snow held up his hand. "Take this afternoon to think about the issue and we can talk again tomorrow or the next day. I'm moving very fast on these cabinet appointments, with President Steadman's advice and support, I might add. You come highly recommended by Steadman *and* Prescott, for that matter. And," he said, looking toward Pug, "General Austin, as Secretary of Homeland Security, would continue to be your boss, Pug. Although, as President Prescott has advised, I reserve the right to meet with you and, if I determine necessary, provide direction. Is that suitable to you, General Austin?"

"That would not present a problem, Mr. President. May I assume I would be advised of General Connor's operational orders if they were to come directly from this office?"

"Of course," the president replied. "Effective immediately, consider that Trojan will remain operational. I'll have a memo to that effect delivered to you shortly to enable you to continue to work with the military assets you require. I don't want the Pentagon assuming—or *hoping*—that you've been shut down. I informed Admiral Barrington of that yesterday.

"Pug, I want you to continue to develop the format and mission parameters, and complete your staffing selection. If my intelligence overview is correct, your task force will be needed, and sooner than we would like. Run your written plans past General Austin for his concurrence and then forward them to me. Let's say, thirty days hence."

"Yes, sir," Pug replied.

"General Austin, we still have the secession issue out west. You and General Connor are the most familiar with that problem, so Trojan will continue to assume lead responsibilities on the military repercussions of that issue. We can discuss this further at a later date, but my objective is to retain California as part of our family of states, but I do not, I repeat, do *not* want to use military force to achieve that objective. Are there any questions, gentlemen?"

Pug deferred as Austin spoke first. "It may not be possible to place a damper on the political actions moving forward. The momentum seems insurmountable without military action, which I agree, is absolutely the last thing we should consider. But, absent political or economic pressure, this secession just may become a reality."

"I understand that, General. I hope not, truly, but a military intervention is not morally acceptable. To free the slaves was one thing. To force Californians to follow Washington's lead is another. But I'd like you both to think about it and see what can be done."

The president stood and both men rose. "Pug, it's great to see you again. Congratulations on your promotion and Trojan's future. I look forward to working with you."

"Thank you for your confidence, Mr. President," Pug replied.

"I'll advise Admiral Barrington of this discussion to confirm that he knows Trojan will remain operative and authorized to call on military resources. By the way, General Austin, the admiral was in complete agreement with your selection as Secretary of Homeland Security. Actually, I haven't spoken with anyone who opposes the move, but I've kept the idea pretty closely held so far. That will change next week. We'll announce your nomination, along with several others, next Monday in the Rose Garden."

"Yes, sir," Austin said. "I'm certain you'll find some opposition at that point in time."

"We'll handle the opposition. Well, then, I think that will be all for this initial meeting. Thank you both for coming. General, would you mind if I spoke alone with Pug for a brief moment before he leaves? I'd like him to update me on his parents. "

"Certainly, Mr. President. Pug, I'll meet you over in your office, and you can take me to lunch."

""Why don't you go to the White House cafeteria? Tell them it's on my account," the president said.

"Thank you, Mr. President. I thought I was coming to a pleasant meeting with the president this morning, and in less than thirty minutes, I've lost my current job and added another four years to my working life. My wife is not going to be pleased about that. She was looking forward to a few round-the-world cruises," he said.

Again, the president laughed. "General Austin, have her call *my* wife. She's not happy either, I can assure you."

President William Snow motioned for Pug to be seated again, then he began to speak. "Pug, General Austin seems a fine man. I can see why you've enjoyed working with him these past years. As for you and me, it would seem we've just developed a very different relationship. Who would have thought it those long years ago? Are you pleased with your ability to stay with Trojan?"

"Sir, the assignment presents a rather formidable challenge, but I've discovered that I actually enjoy such opportunity. However, I'm a serving Marine officer, and I go where I'm assigned. In some respects, I'd rather be back in the field, commanding Marines."

"Yes." Snow smiled again. "President Prescott mentioned that as well. That goes for most of the young men who comprise Trojan, doesn't it? You're all warriors at heart. How did that happen, Pug? The transition, I mean. When you were in high school, you wanted to be a veterinarian, if I recall."

Pug leaned back in his chair and smiled. "Wouldn't *that* have been good? Sir," he said, shaking his head slowly, "the change just sort of happened. Probably was assured when my spur-of-the-moment application to the Naval Academy was accepted. I loved my time at the Academy and I love the Marines. But I've asked myself that question many times over the years—how did I become something I never thought about growing up? I can't answer it to my own satisfaction, Mr. President," Pug said. "I know I was caught up in the prestige of being accepted at the Academy. That decision assured the military component. Then after I was married, Cheryl had problems with who I became, as you probably know. That was the primary source of the difficulty leading to our divorce in '01. You knew Cheryl Watkins, didn't you? Her father owned the Ford dealership in Mesa. Well, once we were married, I was just gone on deployment too long and too often, I guess. That wasn't what Cheryl had bargained for, and it certainly wasn't her fault. We never had children, and I guess in retrospect that's a blessing."

"Scott told me about your divorce. I'm sorry, Pug, truly sorry."

"No sorrier than I am, Mr. President. But as I say, it was my own fault. It's almost like I had two angels on my shoulder, one saying '*be a good person,*' and the other one saying, '*kick his ass. Kill him.*'"

"From your job description, I'd say you need to listen to both voices." The president paused for a moment and then spoke more softly. "I've always cared about your family, Pug, and I know that you were aware of how close I became to your father."

President Snow stood up, followed by Pug, preparatory to ending the meeting. "I'm truly glad that you're going to remain with Trojan. I need someone I can fully trust in that position. The advice I seek must come from a trusted source, someone without a personal agenda."

"Thank you, sir."

"I sense you have a deeper conflict than we have time to discuss today. Perhaps we can remedy that over dinner some evening. Helen will demand a reunion."

Snow started toward the door. "Are you eligible to retire from the Corps?"

"Yes, sir. I've got just over twenty year's service, but haven't thought about retirement yet."

"Good. You've made exemplary progress. A one-star general with barely twenty years is unusual, isn't it?"

"I've been fortunate to work with good men . . . and good women, especially President Prescott. They deserve the accolade, not me."

Snow rose again and both men walked toward the doorway. The president wrapped his arm around Pug's shoulder and then turned him so they were facing head on. "I think we'll see one another more frequently if this all comes off as I would like. Please give our regards to your parents. Helen will be thrilled to see that you've come back into our lives. She was the primary culprit in getting your brother together with our daughter. Had you been a few years older, I think she'd have chosen you," Snow chuckled.

"Megan got the best Connor when she got Scott," Pug replied.

"He's a good man. When we all settle in, we'd love to have you over for dinner with both Scott and Megan. He's taken very good care of our daughter and produced some beautiful grandchildren."

"Scott *is* a good man, Mr. President. Much more like our father . . .

and he's home every night," Pug said.

"Don't let your confusion overwhelm you, Pug. Those two angels on your shoulder may indeed have a singular purpose. Will you be in town for the immediate future?"

"No, sir. I actually have a field trip coming up shortly. I should be gone a week, perhaps two."

"A *field trip*. Is that with a briefcase or a weapon?"

Pug smiled and shook his head. "Sometimes *both*, sir."

"It's very good to see you again, Pug. Take care on your field trip, and I'll talk with you again when you get back. Leave those two reports you mentioned with Dixie. I'll find some time to review them before you return."

"Yes, sir. Thank you, sir."

NINE

**SOUTH PACIFIC OCEAN
TIMOR SEA
MARCH**

The Timor Sea, the body of water separating North Australia from Indonesia, was generally peaceful during the summer months. Cameron Rossiter, trim and fit with a yachtsman's tanned complexion, manned the helm as *Rainbow Blue* sailed gracefully through light swells under clear skies. A twelve-meter craft, she'd been built to his specific criteria two years earlier. She had the finest navigational equipment available, including a Global Positioning Satellite system. Referred to as GPS, it was designed to work with a co-ordinated system of military satellites in geo-synchronous orbit. Blue water sailors saw it as the most significant invention since the compass.

Given the vagaries of South Pacific weather, Rossiter had also ordered exceptionally sensitive radar, capable of detecting the smallest squall. Capped off with state-of-the-art automated gear, including self-furling sails, *Rainbow Blue* was designed to enable a one-man crew—although she could hold six—to sail her around the world if desired, racing downwind across the wave tops at speeds up to eighteen knots, and averaging six to eight. After making separate trips to various islands in the Solomons, weathering a force three South Pacific gale during the second trip, the solo skipper was justifiably proud of the sleek yacht's ability.

Five days out of Darwin on a pleasure cruise in the Timor Sea, Cameron Sterling Rossiter, a captain in the Australian Special Air Service Brigade, was sailing alone and enjoying the solitude. Recently returned after a two-year secondment to the 22nd Regiment in England, Rossiter was finally taking a long overdue break. A radio transmission the previous evening had changed his plans considerably and he was now en route to new coordinates, sent from SAS headquarters at Campbell Barracks, Perth.

One hundred and eighty nautical miles northwest of Darwin, Australia, USS *Abraham Lincoln*, CVN 72, and her carrier battle group were on course for deployment in the Persian Gulf. Eighteen hours earlier, *Lincoln* had received orders to divert sixty-two nautical miles south of her intended line of transit and rendezvous with an Australian submarine.

The newest members of *Lincoln's* complement were General Pádraig Connor and Sergeant Major Carlos Castro, USMC, and two unidentified men who accompanied them. The two unknown men were bearded and disheveled, indicating to the *Lincoln* deck crew that they were not military. Probably oil rig workers, one U.S. Navy deck crew yellow-shirt surmised. He was wrong.

The four men had arrived on the daily COD flight, this one returning from Darwin with necessary supplies and the 'pony,' or mail, in transit. Following a change of clothes and storage of some of their personal gear which they would retrieve on their return, Pug, Carlos, and their two companions were lifted off the *Lincoln's* deck on an MH-60R Seahawk and flown about a mile off the port bow to a waiting submarine. It was the closest a foreign—in this case, Allied—submarine had ever gotten to the *Lincoln*, according to her log book. After both ships had received orders to coordinate the rendezvous, with mutual agreement, HMAS *Rankin* had played cat-and-mouse with the *Lincoln's* screening vessels for the past twenty-four hours, with neither side scoring a "kill."

Hovering above the sleek vessel, one by one, encompassed in a rescue strop, each with a small bag of personal and operational gear strapped to his leg, the four transferees exited the open doorway of the Seahawk and were slowly winched onto the stern deck of HMAS *Rankin*, an Australian Collins-class, diesel-powered submarine, where they were met by two crew members who stabilized the twisting cable, grounding the static electricity, and unhooked them from the harness. The second crewman escorted them through the sail and within eight minutes, all four were inside the submarine with the Seahawk en route back to the *Lincoln*. In sixty seconds, the *Rankin* disappeared beneath the waves.

The two 'civilians' immediately went aft, apparently familiar with the submarine. Carlos Castro followed and was shown his quarters. In deference to his flag rank, Pug was met by the executive officer and brought to the captain's small private quarters, where they had a perfunctory chat before Pug went forward for a quick meal, joined by Carlos.

The first visual confirmation that *Rainbow Blue* had reached the proper GPS coordinates was the rippling water behind the periscope, some three hundred meters to the west, off her port beam. In a flurry of compressed air and frothing water, her dark sail bracketed against the fiery globe that was resting on the horizon, the diesel-powered Australian submarine, HMAS *Rankin,* SSG 78, commissioned in 2003, broke the surface, ending the solitude that draws so many yachtsmen to blue water.

Cameron Rossiter lowered the sail, cranked *Rainbow Blue's* small maneuvering engine to life, and made for the submarine. By the time he was leeward of the stealthy vessel, gentle swells nudging his craft against the much larger hull, three male and one female seamen were on deck in blue jumpsuits, dropping protective side buoys and casting mooring lines to Rossiter.

"Captain Rossiter?" a full-bearded man called down.

"That's right."

"Sir, I'm Chief Hensley. Are you prepared to take passengers?"

"Send them over, Chief."

Four men stood behind Chief Hensley on *Rankin*, each clad in a black jumpsuit. When the yacht was secured, they moved to *Rankin's* aft deck, where they tossed several dark green sea bags onto *Rainbow Blue*. Two of the men Rossiter recognized as members of his Offshore Assault Team.

"Permission to come aboard," the unknown, taller man said in an American accent.

"Granted," Rossiter replied, holding tight to the mooring ropes. One by one, the men clutched the Jacob's Ladder and climbed down onto the wooden deck of the yacht.

Immediately the four men were on board, the Chief of the Boat barked orders at the other three seaman on the deck of HMAS *Rankin*. They struggled with two large, rubberized containers as they lowered them over the side of the submarine and onto the yacht. Rossiter's two team members took charge and began to tie them down.

"That'll do it, General," the older Australian seaman shouted down to the deck of *Rainbow Blue*. The chief's face bristled with a full-grown neatly trimmed beard and he had a salty edge to his voice. "That's the full kit."

"Right, Chief. Thanks for your hospitality. See you in two days," Connor replied, giving a loose salute.

"Too right, sir. All the best," the chief replied. Just as quickly as they had appeared, the seamen loosed the mooring lines and dropped through the open hatch on *Rankin's* aft deck. *Rainbow Blue* began to drift away from the hull of the submarine. Rossiter moved to the helm, increased RPMs to the small engine, and motored away from the larger vessel. In less than sixty seconds, the only sign of HMAS *Rankin* was concentric whirls on the ocean's surface. The five men on board *Rainbow Blue* were suddenly alone on the vast ocean, the lower edge of the sun just beginning to disappear beneath the waves.

"Sergeant Macintosh, you and Corporal Jenkins stow your gear in the forward hold," Rossiter directed, cutting the engine and moving to unfurl the mainsail.

The four new passengers went below while the sail took wind. Rossiter brought the yacht about and settled into a port tack, heading north-northwest. In a few moments, the American returned on deck and moved aft, taking a seat on the high port side railing.

"You'd be Captain Rossiter, I believe."

"Yes, sir."

"Good. I'm Brigadier General Pug Connor, American Marines. We turned up some information on the primary subject of our mission, and Whitehall requested your SAS boys to make the insertion. At my request, they invited me and Mr. Castro along for the ride."

Cameron nodded. "Good to have you with us, General. Been on a yacht before?"

Pug nodded. "I know a jib from a spinnaker." He smiled. "I've sailed East Coast intramural competition and crewed twice on the Sydney to Hobart with some of my Kiwi cousins, but that was a few years ago."

"An old salt, eh? I'm coming over on starboard tack, General. Stand by." Cameron stomped his foot on the deck to alert the men below, and then heeled the yacht sharply. The boom swung to the port side of the vessel. Pug ducked beneath the boom and shifted his position to the starboard high side railing. They were quiet for several moments while *Rainbow Blue* settled into her new course.

"You have New Zealand family, you said, General?" Cameron asked.

"My parents live there, and some extended family. My father was born in New Zealand. Captain, we'll make this much less formal if you call me Pug and I call you Cameron. Is that all right with you?"

"Yes, sir. So, you've lived in both America and New Zealand?"

"In my early years." Pug watched the sea for several moments as Cameron brought the yacht through a quick secession of waves. "Have you been briefed on the mission?" Pug asked.

Cameron shook his head. "Limited briefing, I'm afraid. I was already at sea on a short holiday. I was informed by radio of the coordinates for the rendezvous and to expect passengers. I know nothing about the target."

"Then I'll fill you in on the important pieces. You know the two men below, right?"

"Yes, sir, Sean Macintosh and Graham Jenkins. Both are squad leaders from my Offshore Assault Team."

"So I understand," Pug said. "I've worked with other SAS teams before, when I was serving as a Marine Force Recon company commander. First class troops, always ready. We haven't decided if this is a snatch or an elimination. We're headed for East Timor. These are the coordinates." He handed Rossiter a slip of paper. "Two of your other lads are already ashore near the pickup point. They flew commercial to Dili, separately over several days, using full passport and customs control, just like tourists, with false identities, of course, and arriving from separate origins. Let me make my position clear, Cameron. I'm just along for the ride and have no command responsibilities to this team or for the ground squad —you're in command here. If we determine to snatch the target, then I'll assume responsibility for him."

"That'll be fine, Pug. You probably know the SAS are a rather informal lot, officers and men. I mean, at least at the lower ranks."

"Understood. Okay, here's the plan. My other team member, Carlos Castro, will make the actual insertion to the suspect residence. Carlos is deputy director of my office, and a retired Marine Corps Sergeant Major, a very experienced Recon Marine. With everything going well, he'll make the entry tomorrow night, decide the disposition, and, at his discretion, eliminate the man or deliver the target to us on shore. In that case, he'll return to your yacht and we'll transport him to the sub. How long will it take us to get to the northeast coast of Timor?"

"About eighteen to twenty hours, unless we have a wind shift for or against."

"Just before dusk tomorrow, then. That's plenty of time to prepare. Let's get Macintosh up on deck and he can brief you on your shore team." Pug stepped to the cabin entrance and leaned in. "Carlos, Sergeant Macintosh, could you come on deck a moment?"

Macintosh appeared several seconds later, followed by Jenkins and Carlos. Both Aussies stepped aft and sat on the railing. Carlos stood besides Pug, slightly spreading his legs to maintain balance. Full dark had settled over the ocean and the night was silent, broken only by the soft lapping of the waves against *Rainbow Blue's* bow as she cut through the rippled water. Ambient light came from the sky and the muted running lights of the yacht.

"Never get a full holiday, right, sir?" Macintosh asked, grinning.

"The life of a trooper, I suppose," Cameron responded.

Pug spoke up. "Sergeant, I've told Captain Rossiter that you would brief him on the land phase of the operation. His message to meet the *Rankin* was brief and not informative."

"Right, General. Wilson and Gunner went ashore a couple days ago. They've recce'd the place, gave us a sat com call this afternoon on the sub, and said it looks like there are three people holed up in a remote beachfront cabin about four miles from a small village called Tutuala on the eastern tip of the island. The team's got an LUP," he said, referring to a laying up position from which they could observe without being seen, "on a rise about two hundred meters from the cabin. The general said he would coordinate the insertion once we came aboard. When Carlos goes in, Gunner will watch his back and keep the path to the beach clear. The cabin's about a hundred meters from the spot of water where we'll beach. If there's any trouble, or if someone tries to follow Carlos when he leaves, Gunner will top 'em. If it's all gone to hell, our boys will come back in the Zodiac. Then it's just back to the yacht, slip away, and meet up with the *Rankin* again. They'll take it from there, sir. That's about it."

Pug smiled at the casual way in which Macintosh had described the operation, including the possible necessity of killing Wolff's companions.

"What about the kit, Sean?" Cameron asked.

"Basics. We've got four M-4s, didn't see a need for the 203s on this insertion. We've got the Zod for the run to the beach, two re-breathing kits, masks and flippers if we need 'em. That's about it."

"Thank you, Sean. Go below and catch some shut-eye. You'll need it tomorrow."

Both Australian SAS operatives quickly dropped below the deck and left Cameron, Pug, and Carlos topside. "What's the American interest in this, Pug? Was this guy involved in the KLM hijacking?" Cameron asked, turning toward Pug.

"I don't think so. We're just looking for information primarily." Pug nodded toward Castro. "Cameron, let me introduce Carlos Castro." Pug motioned for Carlos to take a seat on the railing. "As I said, he's deputy director of our office. We're essentially a domestic. . . well, primarily domestic," he said, waving his arm outward toward the expanse of the ocean, "anti-terrorism task force within the Homeland Security Department. My source for this operation seems to have been spot-on about this guy. If we can convince the man to talk, he knows quite a lot about terrorist weapons acquisition, and, more to the point, about the buyers. He's been selling to anyone with money for several years, working both sides of the fence and double-crossing most of them along the way. Your Australian SIS intelligence reports show a rapid increase in Indonesian terror cells. This guy just might have something to do with it."

"We're glad to help, General. I've worked with the whole team, including the ground crew. They're experienced operators. Good lads," Cameron said, nodding toward the cabin.

"It would seem so. We didn't talk much—too noisy on the helicopter—but we flew out together on the supply flight to rendezvous with the USS *Abraham Lincoln* a couple of hundred miles northwest of Darwin, and we had a brief chat then." They all sat silently for several moments with Pug taking in his surroundings until Cameron motioned them to stand by while he brought the yacht around to a port tack. When the wind again filled the sail, he continued.

"Quite a firestorm in the States over the KLM shoot-down," he said.

Pug nodded. "Tough choice for a new president. I'm glad it wasn't me."

"Wasn't easy on the Air Force pilot either, I suppose, or his family."

"No. He took some damage from the explosion, lost hydraulic control, and nosed in right after the airliner. He had a full military funeral at Arlington," Pug said, continuing to voice the public story that the pilot's plane had sustained damage when the commercial airliner exploded.

"Deservedly so," Cameron offered. "And the president. What a way to go. His first major decision. With no one to hang it on, your press seems content to lay it all on the new president."

Pug shook his head, looking out over the darkened ocean. "The press is relentless, and they don't care about collateral damage. Worse than a bomb run, sometimes. But how these lifetime politicians formulate their positions and skewer each other has always bothered me. If they're a Democrat, then the Republicans are wrong, no matter what they do. If Republican, the reverse. They never seem to consider whether the action was right or not, just which party label they wear on their sleeve."

"Same thing in Australia, Pug," Cameron said. They sliced through the water for several moments in silence, the distant whine of a breaching whale the only sound on the air." "*Was* the man right to make the call? The president, I mean," Cameron asked.

"From my vantage point, yes. From theirs . . . I'd hate to have to make the call, or worse, to have been the pilot."

"Amen to that. Give me a terrorist with an AK-47 charging at me and I'll take him out . . . or he'll get me. But I don't know if I could blow up a hotel full of people to save the city."

"The enemy has changed color, Cameron. We'll probably never be able to recognize him again. Carlos has seen the dark side of this business as well as the open, traditional combat role. What do you think, Carlos? Has Cameron got it right?"

Carlos didn't reply for a few moments, the creaking of the rigging filling the void. "General, the answer to that is above my pay grade," he replied, "but well within yours. I'll leave those decisions to flag rank."

Pug laughed. "Don't count on it, Mr. Deputy Director. Your new role will take you to heights you never imagined." Pug raised himself off the railing and stepped toward the entrance to the cabin. "Well, if there's a bunk below, I think I'll catch a few hours sleep before final mission planning. See you in the morning, gentlemen."

"Goodnight, General," Carlos said. "I think I'll stay on deck for a bit, get my sea legs back."

Pug went below, and Carlos and Cameron sat quietly for several minutes. "Care to take the helm, Carlos?"

Carlos hesitated for a moment, then rose and slid in alongside Cameron, who released the wheel and took up a position where Carlos had been sitting.

"I've never been on a yacht before. A sub, Gemini, Zodiac, swimmer delivery vehicle, and even a personal flotation device, but no yacht," Carlos said.

"Not much danger of collision out here, Carlos, other than that whale we heard." Cameron laughed. "Have you worked with the general long?"

Again, Carlos was quiet for a few moments. "Not recently. It's a new operation and I've only just retired. But we've worked together before, some years ago."

"I was surprised to see a general officer on this type of mission," Cameron said. "I don't think any of our Australian generals would be out here." The unspoken question seemed to be, '*is he capable of a special operations insertion mission?*'

Carlos looked at the other man for several seconds, then nodded his head. "I understand what you mean, Captain. The first time I actually worked with General Connor was about fifteen years ago. We met early one morning when he came aboard the U.S.S. *Tarawa*. That's a U.S. Navy amphibious vessel specifically designed for Marine Corps operations. The following evening we dropped in to Pakistan, low roping out of a helicopter, and commenced the mission. He was a newly promoted captain and I was a new buck sergeant." Carlos paused, as if recalling the event. "I've not doubted him since. He's an outstanding warrior and he's earned that star on his collar. I could change places with him on this mission and have no doubt it would go off as planned. Don't let his rank fool you, Captain. He's a field operator and only age—or a terrorist bullet—will slow him down."

"High praise," Cameron said.

"Perhaps, but not undeserved."

Ten

**FIFTEEN HUNDRED METERS TO SEAWARD
OFF THE NORTHEAST TIP OF TIMOR—LESTE
MARCH**

Sergeant Macintosh and Carlos Castro inflated the Zodiac and lowered it over the side. Macintosh held it tight against the yacht while Carlos and Corporal Jenkins climbed aboard, then attached a small outboard to the transom. Pug passed two M-4s over the side and Macintosh stored them beneath the seats. Carlos had a small backpack and had elected to carry his own HK pistol, with an attached silencer, in a side holster.

Captain Rossiter spoke down to the small group in the inflatable. "Right then, Sean, we'll anchor nearby and wait for your signal, then we'll relocate back to this GPS coordinate. If Gunner is correct about activity in the house, you should be back before dawn. You know the emergency signal. If something happens, we can motor closer and pick you up near the beach, but if the Zod is operable, you'll get out much faster in that. Good luck."

Once it was full dark, the three men began their run toward shore. Four minutes into the run, the intermittent flashing signal from landward confirmed their contact ashore and indicated that they were on target. Macintosh revved up the engine, and as the rubber inflatable approached the beach, the surf was running low on an outward tide. Ten yards out, Corporal Jenkins and Carlos jumped into the surf, grabbed the side of the raft, and began pulling toward shore.

"Need a hand with that tube, mate?"

The voice out of the darkness startled the three men, and instantly Sean Macintosh had his weapon at the ready until he recognized Gunner striding toward them out of the cover of the brush.

"What's the word, Gunner?" Sean asked softly.

Gunner was wearing a covert communications device with a throat mike, the earpiece in place. "Hold one, I'll check." The stocky, hard-as-nails Aussie faced inland, jabbed the PTT, Push to Talk button, and quietly spoke a few words, waiting for a response. He then turned back to Sean.

"It's 'stand by' at the moment, Sean. Wilson says the place is still dark and quiet."

"Right, then, let's get this raft into the bush and you can show Carlos the way. Gunner, this is Carlos Castro, U.S. Marines. He'll go in alone. You and Wilson are backup, outside security."

"Right, mate."

They pulled the raft up on the sandy beach and dragged it into the cover of a small cluster of scrub brush. Gunner took a few steps back toward Sean and Carlos, who were huddled up near the raft, whispering in the dark.

"Ready to go, Carlos? The LUP is about ten minutes over that hill," he said, nodding in a northwest direction, "and Wilson says 'all clear,'" he added, tapping his earpiece.

"Let's do it," Carlos replied.

Two thousand yards off-shore, *Rainbow Blue* anchored in a calm, outgoing tide. Cameron Rossiter and Pug Connor settled in to wait for the return of the landing party. Cameron went below and retrieved a tin of crackers, diced up a wedge of cheese, and grabbed two plastic bottles of water from the small propane fridge. He returned on deck and handed a bottle of water and a paper napkin with cheese and crackers to Pug. Then he sat on the port railing, and both men began to eat quietly.

Cameron spoke first.

"Have you ever wondered which is worse: waiting for the team to report in, or being part of the team about to go into action?"

Pug nodded his understanding. "You mean, *They also serve who sit and wait.*"

"Something like that," Cameron laughed, then changed the subject. "Carlos said you and he had served together before, some years ago in Pakistan."

"We did. He's an outstanding Marine. I've had my life in his hands more than once."

"Has he always been Muslim?" Cameron asked. "I noticed him in morning prayers earlier, up on deck."

"No, he was raised Catholic. Embraced Islam about ten or twelve years ago."

"Do you know what took him down that path?"

"A woman."

Cameron laughed. "Of course, what else? I've got two Muslims in my outfit as well. I've wondered how they feel about this increasing religious war. It must be tough to fight your own brothers."

"Man has been fighting his religious brothers for centuries, but not always under a religious banner. Carlos has a good understanding of the situation," Pug said, pausing to take a long drink. "He believes the fanatics and their Mullahs have abandoned the faith, perverted their god."

"Is he still with the woman who converted him?"

Pug ate another hunk of cheese, sandwiched between two crackers, looking out over the ocean before he replied. "She's dead. He met her when he was on a black ops mission in the Philippines, acting as an adviser to local forces to identify and eliminate insurgent groups. He met a young Filipina doctor. She was working to vaccinate village children when Carlos's small Philippine army squad took some casualties. They came into the village for medical treatment. Carlos got himself assigned permanently to the local Marine unit. He fell in love with her, they got married, and Carlos spent the next sixteen months in what he calls the best time of his life. Sometimes he'd be in the jungle hunting terrorists. Sometimes she'd be in the villages providing medical assistance. She was a devout Muslim. He came to believe in the faith, and the rest was history."

"How did she die?" Cameron asked.

"The rebel group found out that she was married to Carlos. Seven of them caught her in one of the villages, then tortured, raped, and killed her. She was carrying their first child. Over the next several months, without assistance from his local unit, Carlos found every one of them, one by one. He's been a different man ever since, but still someone I'd trust to have my back in a tough situation."

"Different in what way?" Cameron asked.

Again, Pug was silent, looking out over the vast expanse of the ocean as the yacht gently rolled in the off-shore waves. "He's a natural warrior, an instinctive killer, truth be known, but once this happened, he *looks* for opportunities to kill the bad guys. It's not just another mission—it's a quest, a vocation. I think he believes he can right the world's ills, one terrorist at a time. In twenty years, I've not seen a man I thought could best him up close and personal."

Cameron nodded slowly, finishing his cheese and crackers. "Glad he's on our team."

Carlos, Gunner, and Wilson lay on the hillside until about 10:30 P.M., taking turns watching the cabin, using a telescopic night sight. No entry or exit occurred during that time, but Gunner had informed Carlos that two Indonesians had entered the cabin earlier that morning, remaining inside throughout the day. He showed Carlos two photos on a small electronic device.

"We emailed these images back to SAS HQ. They confirmed these were two of the five terrorists who participated in the Fremantle bombing about eight months ago. They killed nineteen Australians. That's why I'd like to go in with you and kill the bastards."

Carlos nodded. "I'm going in alone. I'll handle it."

Wilson confirmed that all three men had remained in the cabin, two in the front room, with the primary target out of sight toward the back left of the cabin. The three of them watched until the lights went out in the cabin about 11:30 P.M.

At 1:40, the moon cloistered behind a thick bank of low-lying clouds, Carlos pulled his gear together and prepared to leave the observation site, two hundred meters seaward from the cabin. "I'm going down that slight incline over on the right. I'll approach slowly and be in position in about forty minutes," Carlos said. "Before I enter, I'll give you a quick laser beam. Depending on what I find, I'll be out in three minutes, or it might take a half hour. I won't know until I decide if I'm going to snatch or terminate. I'll contact you with a sitrep as soon as the situation is under control. If there's no contact in the first twenty minutes, you can assume I've encountered a problem. Return to the Zodiac and advise General Connor."

"You don't want us to come in and lend a hand?" Gunner asked.

Carlos shook his head. "No. He'll be dead or I will . . . or both. If not, I'll bring him out."

With that, Carlos slipped quietly into the darkness of the foliage, slowly making his way toward the silhouette that represented the cabin. Gunner and Wilson waited on the hillside, Gunner wearing the night vision equipment and watching Carlos for most of his approach. Just before entering the cabin, the Marine lay silently near the front steps, listening for any sound from within. After about ten minutes, he rolled slightly and gave a quick flash from his penlight laser toward Gunner's position.

Carlos donned a gas mask apparatus with night vision capabilities and readied a small aerosol container, then began his approach to the cabin door. He picked the rather primitive lock on the door in seconds. Once inside, Carlos paused beside the entrance for several minutes, listening intently. He could detect the sound of deep breathing and the smell of alcohol and cigarettes.

The cabin was essentially one large room. He could see an L-shaped angle toward the south end where he assumed Wolff was located. The two other men were sleeping, one on the couch, and one on the floor, with several blankets wrapped around his dark form. Carlos pressed the top button on the aerosol device, emitting a slight hissing sound. A colorless, odorless gas escaped into the room, drifting across the body of each of the two sleeping men. Carlos then replaced the can in his side pocket and moved a step at a time toward the nearest man. He unsheathed his six-inch, serrated Fairbairn tactical knife and slowly knelt down beside the body on the couch. The man was turned, face toward the backrest. In one swift, but silent, motion, Carlos placed one hand over the man's mouth and sliced the Fairbairn across his throat, holding him quiet until his body relaxed. He watched the second man as the first bled out, ready to move quickly if he exhibited any sign of awakening.

He then rose quietly and took three stealthy steps to the other man, repeating the process with his Fairbairn until the body was breathless. Sheathing his knife, Carlos waited several long moments, listening intently for any sound of movement coming from the far corner of the cabin. Hearing none, he stood and moved toward the back of the cabin.

Inching along the back wall, one step at a time, waiting at each step and breathing shallow during his transit, Carlos took one more long inhale, retrieved the aerosol can, and then held his breath as he peered around the wall into the room that contained the bed. His night vision goggles reflected the body heat as a green glow of someone lying on the bunk, and there was a slightly stronger odor of alcohol in the air.

Carlos stooped and slowly duck-walked across the floor, keeping his head below the edge of the mattress and expelling the aerosol container as he progressed. The spray drifted over the prostrate form, and in about ninety seconds, Carlos could hear his breathing slow and deepen. At that point, he rose up, replaced the spray can in his side pocket, and withdrew his HK special ops pistol. With the barrel of the weapon, he poked the back of the sleeping man, eliciting no response. Certain the man was under the influence of the gas, he pulled a small leather packet from his side pocket and retrieved a syringe and vial, extracting a few cc's of liquid and injecting it into Wolff's neck. He then placed plastic cuffs on both wrists and ankles, using a longer plastic tie to secure the arms to the legs, essentially binding the man's movement without tying him to the bed. Then he forcefully shook the man, slapping his face several times with no response.

Carlos returned to the front door, pressed his throat microphone button, and gave the "all clear" signal to the SAS troops on the hillside. He then turned on his small flashlight and began to survey the room. In the corner nearest the cooking area, he immediately spotted a briefcase and several sheets of paper strewn about the small dining table. On the floor next to the table was a black canvas case. When he opened it, he saw a laptop contained inside. He removed his backpack and placed all papers and the laptop inside, then slipped the pack over his shoulders again. He then returned to the bedroom. There was slight movement from the sleeping man, but he did not wake.

Carlos approached the bed, pistol in hand, and watched as Wolff began to show signs of awareness. He could see the surprise in the Wolff's eyes as his brain began to register.

"Buenas noches, Señor Wolff," he said. "Comprende?"

Wolff gave no response, appearing not quite coherent. Carlos knelt on the side of the bed and slapped him across the face. "I said, do you understand?"

Wolff nodded.

"I am come to kill you . . . or make you a prisoner. You choose. You have been injected . . . to relax you. You hear, you speak, and you think, even, but only a little movement is possible for many hours. Do you understand?"

Again Wolff nodded.

"Say, '*yes,*' *Señor* Wolff," Carlos said, still holding the pistol in full view of his prisoner.

Wolff nodded and softly said, "Yes."

"Your two visitors today, *Señor* Wolff, who are they?"

Wolff angled his head, a quizzical look on his face.

Carlos rapped the restrained man on the side of the head with his pistol barrel. "*Señor* Wolff, I have your papers and your laptop. I have no need of you. Now choose. Answer my questions and come with me, or you join your friends in the room in front. They have no choice. *Comprende?*"

Wolff slowly nodded again.

Carlos struck the pistol barrel against the side of Wolff's cheek, saying nothing.

"Yes, I understand," Wolff responded.

"*Muy bien*. Now, let us make this decision. Do you want to live, *Señor* Wolff? If I deliver you to the people who want you, it is their choice. But at least you will survive this night. Now, who were your two visitors?"

"Indonesians. Guerillas from the islands."

"What did they want?"

"Just to make contact. They were leaving tomorrow."

Carlos didn't believe him, but stood quiet for a moment, considering his options. He glanced at his watch and then at Wolff again. Both men shared a knowing look. If Wolff was as experienced as Carlos had been led to believe by both British intelligence and General Connor's summary, he knew that on many prior occasions, the roles had been reversed and it had been Wolff deciding whether or not someone would live.

Carlos reached in his pocket again and retrieved the small leather packet, withdrawing another syringe and vial. "You are going on a cruise, *Señor* Wolff. And you will live a while more."

Once he had injected Wolff with a deeper sedative, he pressed his throat microphone and contacted his outside backup. "Coming out with one package. Meet me at the head of the south path."

At the intersection of the paths heading toward the beach, Gunner took the inert body of Wolff from Carlos and carried him to the beach where he was placed in the Zodiac. Both SAS men nodded at Carlos and McIntosh and left without another word, heading inland to return home as tourists.

Sergeant Sean Macintosh cranked the small outboard to life, and the agile Zodiac gathered speed, climbed over the first few swells, and quickly disappeared into the darkness, headed directly off-shore toward *Rainbow Blue*.

In twenty minutes, they reached the yacht. Cameron tossed them a line and held the inflatable fast as they lifted the body onto the deck. Carlos unzipped the body bag to assure Wolff was still breathing. Pug and Cameron lifted the craft out of the water onto the aft deck, and Jenkins triggered the deflation device.

Cameron glanced at his watch. "Right, we've got about two hours till first light. We can be well over the horizon by dawn. Sean, you and

Carlos get our guest below and secure him. I've got some canvas straps beneath the bunk."

"Too right, Captain," Macintosh replied. Both men struggled to lower the immobile body through the small hatch into the cabin.

Cameron moved aft, toward the wheel, passing Pug who was helping Jenkins deflate the raft. "Let's get underway. Pug, pull up the anchor, will you?"

Pug moved to the bow and began pulling on the nylon rope, retrieving the anchor. He stepped to the mast and loosened the halyard securing the mainsail, then joined Cameron at the helm. In a few seconds the sail unfurled, took the off-shore breeze, and *Rainbow Blue* came about, headed away from Timor.

"Pug, why don't you and Carlos get your heads down for a couple of hours. I'll take the helm and the lads will shift off on stag with Wolff."

"Agreed. Carlos said he should sleep till about eight."

"That's fine. If he wakes earlier, Sean or Graham will call us."

Pug nodded and stepped through the hatch, passing Sean Macintosh in the main cabin.

"He's out like a light, General. I'll call you when he comes around."

"Fine, Sean. Thanks," Pug replied, heading forward to the double bunk space where he'd left his gear. Carlos was already lying on the port bunk. Pug lifted his sea bag, dropped it to the floor, and sat on the rack.

"How'd it go?" Pug asked.

"No problems. I put two down, then I sedated Wolff. Drilled him for about ten minutes and decided he might have more information, so I brought him back. Got some documents and a laptop."

"Good, we'll go over them in the morning. Do you think he'll talk?"

"Probably not if he's as much a professional as we've been led to believe, but they should have more luck at Thomson," he said, referring to the Thomson Correctional Facility in Illinois, where all Guantanamo terrorists had been transferred. "If we still had Guantanamo, we'd have more options. With luck, the computer will tell us a lot. It never fails to amaze me how much these guys keep on their laptops, thinking they're secure. But we'll try to get him to open up in the morning. I'll keep him lightly drugged once he wakes up. I spoke English with a thick Spanish accent. Probably should continue using that tomorrow, keep everyone else quiet, and Wolff blindfolded."

"Agreed. Now let's get a few hours' rest." Pug lay back on the bunk, fully clothed, instantly falling sound asleep.

The first sensation Pug felt was Cameron shaking him awake. He sat up on the bunk, rubbing his eyes with the heels of his hands.

"What time is it?"

"Just after seven," Cameron replied, speaking in a whisper since the below decks cabin was so close to where they held their captive. "Wolff's not awake, but he's moving around a bit, so he should be up shortly. Carlos is with him. I brought you some coffee."

Pug reached for the cup. "Thanks."

"What's the plan?" Cameron asked.

"Is he still blindfolded and cuffed?"

"Yeah. The lads taped his eyes shut. Carlos told us to remain quiet in his presence. He won't even know for sure where he is, other than the pitching of the yacht. The particular drug Carlos used leaves people woozy and a bit off balance, not completely alert."

"Fine. You got the video cam set up?"

"Carlos has everything all ready."

"Good, let's get him up and see what we can get out of him while he's disoriented. Carlos will do the talking, just to confuse him with a Mexican accent."

They stepped aft to the main cabin area, which contained a small kitchen and a couple of bunks on either side of the room. Macintosh was reading a paperback novel and sat on the bunk directly across from Wolff. Carlos sat at the small table used for meals. The prisoner lay on his bunk, mumbling incoherently and beginning to shift about.

Pug put his finger to his lips, reminding everyone to be quiet. He motioned to Macintosh to get Wolff up and put him on the small bench in front of the table across from Carlos. Sean lifted Wolff almost bodily, setting him down hard on the bench. Pug took a place on the bunk, just behind the camera, which had been set up to film Wolff over Carlos's shoulder. Cameron sat on the bunk where Wolff had been restrained.

"*Señor* Wolff!" Carlos shouted. "Wake up!"

The confused man mumbled incoherently.

"Shut up and listen, you stay alive. You on ship, near Algeria. I want information. You talk, you live."

Tilting his head toward the sound of the voice, Wolff replied, his speech mumbled. "Algeria? No, . . . Timor."

"I say Algeria," Carlos shouted. You answer or stay here forever. Interpol want you too."

"What do you want? Who are you?" Wolff asked, appearing a bit more rational as the questioning continued.

"I ask questions. You answer. What's your name?"

Wolff paused for a moment, cocking his head to listen to the sounds, adjusting his shoulders to the tautness of his hands cuffed behind his back.

Carlos reached across and slapped Wolff hard across the left cheek, the blow stunning the blindfolded man. "What's your name?"

Wolff struggled against his bonds and shouted an expletive.

Carlos glanced at Pug and shook his head, acknowledging that Wolff appeared as tough as they expected and likely unwilling to talk without more abusive persuasion. "Maybe we loosen your tongue, Wolff, with pliers. We don't care you live or die, you piece of shit. Algerians pay good money for you. Maybe Israelis, Egyptians, but they, how you say, harsh with prisoners. Who we sell you to, Wolff? You talk first, you choose."

Wolff remained quiet as Carlos let him think it through.

After a moment, Carlos leaned across the table and slapped him from the other side, nearly knocking him off his stool. "*What* you doing in Timor?"

Wolff recovered from the blow and sat upright in his chair.

Carlos spun around and released a string of rapid-fire Spanish invective to no one in particular. Then he turned back to face the prisoner.

"Wolff, this is waste of time," Carlos said, his voice now calm and soft. "I told them."

Carlos stood, scraping his chair across the floor for Wolff to hear. He nodded to Pug who began to speak.

"Wolff, I've got a meeting ashore with the Algerians. They'll be more cooperative than you, that's for certain, and when they get their hands on you, they might change the interrogation tactics. You'll wish you could be with me again."

Wolff angled his head again, trying to place the new voice and accent.

Pug continued. "I'll leave you with a couple of my friends and come back in the morning. In the meantime, you can think about what I've said. All we want are some answers and we'll put you ashore. Of course, you have to make your way safely out of North Africa, but then, you grew up here. You know it well. And you've been in and out of here on arms deals to Hamas or Hezbollah for years, haven't you? The choice is yours, Mr. Wolff."

Pug stood, also making sounds of departure, moving about the cabin toward the hatchway. He motioned to Sergeant Macintosh, giving him a 'two minutes with you' signal.

Macintosh stood and stepped in front of Wolff, leaning down to breathe close to his face. "And a good day to yer, Mr. Wolff," he said, rolling his R's and thickening his Scottish brogue. "I'm so pleased we have this time together. Unlike my gentle friend, I don't want any answers," he said, reaching out and grabbing hold of the prisoner's hair, jerking his head closer. "All I want is screams, Mr. Wolff. 'Tis music to me ears."

Wolff didn't respond.

Macintosh tightened his grip on Wolff's hair and twisted his head upward at a steep angle while placing his knee against Wolff's chest, pulling the head against the pressure of his knee.

"I said I don't want answers, or questions, either, Mr. Wolff. I want screams, you see. And we'll get there, I can assure you."

Wolff tilted his head slightly, trying to make sense of the ambient sounds that surrounded his location. Macintosh continued in a softer tone.

"Now that Hispanic lad, he's in charge. Don't know why, since I always get the better results, but still, we all get paid to do our job, ain't that right, Mr. Wolff. He wants answers, I want screams. Funny thing is, Mr. Wolff, you can make the choice, if you know what I mean. Of course, I'm only guessing that you would prefer his way to mine, but still, when all's done I'd like to have a go at my way," he said, pulling even tighter on the blindfolded man's hair.

Wolff grunted in response to the physical assault, but remained silent. Carlos nodded at Macintosh, who knocked Wolff back against his chair, then stepped away.

All was silent for several moments as Carlos once again scraped the stool on the deck and resumed his seat across the small table from Wolff. "You tough man, *Señor* Wolff. I am tougher. This is last chance, asshole. Talk or die."

"Go to hell," Wolff replied. Finally Pug motioned to Carlos and mimed injecting a syringe. Carlos nodded and stepped behind Wolff, retrieved a prepared syringe from the counter top, and jabbed it into Wolff's neck.

By early afternoon, with some satellite phone help from Washington, Pug had entered restricted files on Wolff's computer and performed a cursory review of data without much success in deciphering any of it. Late that afternoon, he downloaded the video of the interrogation onto his laptop computer, hooked up his sat com telephone, and connected with his DHS contact, transmitting his written report and the full video, plus the contents of Wolff's laptop by secure encrypted satellite link to General Austin. Thirty minutes later, Pug, Carlos, and Cameron sat on deck as *Rainbow Blue* made for the next contact with the Australian submarine.

Just before dark, the rendezvous with HMAS *Rankin* was accomplished, and Wolff, still drugged and unconscious, was transferred for delivery to Australian authorities who had already made arrangements for his transfer to the Americans who would fly him out of Australia.

With *Rainbow Blue* secured against the hull of the submarine, Carlos scrambled aboard and Pug tossed his bag to the waiting Aussie seaman. The two SAS troopers also boarded *Rankin*. Pug then turned toward Cameron and reached to shake his hand. "Captain Rossiter, it's been a pleasure. Maybe we'll meet again some time. I figure I owe you a good dinner for this South Pacific cruise."

"My pleasure, General. I just might pop over and take you up on that meal."

"You're on. Have a good trip home. It should be quiet out here for the next few days without us. I doubt it will be quiet where I'm going. And it won't be comfortable for Wolff, either."

"I like it quiet, Pug," Cameron said, loosening the lines, "and I've got a few days left on my original plans. Won't be surprised, however, to get another message from the colonel to report in. Vacation's over, I'm afraid."

Pug accepted a hand up from the chief of the boat, stepped back onto the steel deck grating of HMAS *Rankin,* and watched for a few moments as *Rainbow Blue* drifted away from the sub. He gave a quick salute toward Cameron and then slipped through the hatch and down the ladder.

Nine hours later, at dawn, a helicopter once again appeared on the horizon, and both Carlos and Pug were hoisted up and transported to USS *Abraham Lincoln*, now two hundred miles further west. They caught the COD again the following morning, headed for Jakarta, where they transferred to commercial aircraft, and returned to Washington D.C.

Eleven

**RUMSEY VALLEY
YOLO COUNTY CALIFORNIA
MARCH**

Following the convocation of legislators in Las Vegas, Dan and Nicole Rawlings had spent another three days in the neon city, attending several shows and just enjoying time away from the pressures of Dan's legislative duties in Sacramento. Although the trip had been to discuss the prospect of other states joining with California in forming a new nation, it had also served as a brief extension to the abbreviated honeymoon Dan and Nicole had taken to Mazatlan after their marriage in January.

Their wedding had certainly not been every girls' dream. A New Year's Day decision, a quick trip to Reno, a Friday, Saturday, and Sunday in Mexico, and then they came home as Mr. and Mrs. Daniel Rawlings, with Dan returning to his state capitol office the following Tuesday, spending the next two months behind closed doors in California Assembly and Senate workshops on constitutional development.

Nicole's retirement from the FBI, confirmed shortly before Christmas, had been a blow to the young woman, changing the course of her life even more dramatically than her decision to marry Dan Rawlings. They had moved into Dan's condo in Davis, about twenty miles west of Sacramento. As he had promised, they contracted to build a new home slightly northwest of Davis, up Rumsey Canyon, where Dan's family had settled shortly after the Civil War. It was to be the fourth Rumsey / Rawlings home in one hundred and forty-five years. Jack and Ellen Rumsey had been the last to build, in 1946.

On a bright Sunday morning, the last day of March, Dan suggested they drive up Highway 16 toward the new home site to view the work that had been accomplished in their absence. Fifteen miles from Woodland, just west of the tiny village of Esparto, Dan took a slight detour off the main road. Nicole knew immediately where he was going: the Esparto Cemetery to visit Jack Rumsey's final resting ground.

Jack Rumsey had been the patriarch of the family through most of the second half of the twentieth century. He had died at age 89 of a heart attack the previous August. His death had occurred one day before the insertion of federal troops into Sacramento and the brief gun fight between the 82nd Airborne Division and the California State Reserve that the press had dubbed The Battle of Capitol Mall. Dan had commented several times that he was grateful that Jack had been spared the necessity of seeing his beloved California party to an armed conflict between California and military forces of the United States of America. Even Dan found it hard to believe.

As they pulled into the small, well-maintained cemetery, Dan parked on a side road and they exited the vehicle, slowly walking toward the Rumsey and Rawlings' family plot. Dan's older brother, Tom, who had died during birth, lay in a row with Ellen and Jack Rumsey and several earlier generations of Dan's family. Now, with a new home, the prospect of a new state, and even the possible advent of a new nation, Dan found himself wondering if Jack Rumsey would lay buried on "foreign" soil.

"The roses are starting to bloom," Nicole said, pointing toward the row of bushes that surrounded the family plot. Dan looked in their direction, taking Nicole's hand and strolling past several headstones. Jack and Ellen's ornate marker had an asymmetrical appearance, with Jack's engraving fresh and bold, compared to Ellen's inscription, which had tarnished a bit in the decade since her death. It gave the marble edifice a visual, compelling, and heartfelt story without the need for explanation. In most respects, it was a traditional family plot, with headstones reflecting that some members had spent merely hours on their earthly sojourn, others nearly a century.

"My mother told me that her mother, Grandma Ellen, planted those roses almost fifty years ago. Mom's been caring for them ever since she was a teenager, when Grandma would bring her here to tell her about our early pioneer family."

"They're lovely," Nicole replied. "We never had flowers so early in Connecticut. That's one reason I love California. Did you have much to do with your grandmother?" she asked. "I know you and your grandfather were very close, but how old were you when Ellen died?"

"Late teens. Yeah, Grandma and I often just strolled through the orchard in the evenings." Dan chuckled a bit as they walked, a quick memory flashing through his mind.

"What?" Nicole said.

"I was just remembering. When I was younger, I'd often spend the weekend here in the valley with Jack and Grandma. I'd go out in the orchard with Jack before twilight. We couldn't pass two almond trees before Jack would say, '*pick up that bit of brush, would you, and toss it on the pile over there.*' We could never just 'take a walk.' There was always something that needed to be done in the orchard. But with Grandma, we would walk, talk, often sing a song together, and she'd teach me about the squirrels and various birds that fluttered through the grove. As the sun would begin to set, we'd often see a few deer come down from the hills to forage through the trees, looking for immature almonds or tender, low-hanging branches. I really loved Grandma."

As they walked, Nicole stepped a bit closer to Dan, slipping her arm in the crook of his elbow. "And Jack," she said.

Dan stopped walking, considered her comment, then turned and kissed her on the cheek. "Yes, and Jack." He looked up at the massive oak trees that bordered the cemetery, the afternoon wind rustling through their leaves. "This is where the voices in my blood live," he said softly. The previous year, Dan had achieved publication of his first novel, a fictional family saga of his ancestors who lived in America for twelve generations and settled this part of California five generations earlier. He had named the novel "*Voices in My Blood*" after the feelings he had for those ancestors.

They walked a bit further and Dan stopped to pick a few weeds from his Uncle James' plot, bending down and brushing dirt off the engraving. "I never really knew Uncle James. He was my mother's younger brother, but he died early. As you can see from the dates, he was barely thirty."

Dan rose, brushed some dirt and grass off his knees, and headed for the car. "Let's get moving up the valley. I suppose you're anxious to see the progress on our new home," he said.

As they walked toward the vehicle, they were silent until Dan exited the cemetery and headed northwest toward Highway 16 a few miles up the side road. This time Nicole started to laugh softly.

"Okay, share the humor," Dan said.

"I was just thinking about this new house we're building. Is our address going to be 224 Pioneer Drive, Rumsey, California? Or 224 Pioneer Drive, Rumsey, *North* California? Or maybe 224 Pioneer Drive, Rumsey, North California, *Republic of Western America*? Or just, 224 Pioneer Drive, *Anytown, Anywhere*?"

Dan looked at her as he pulled on to the main highway, a broad grin crossing his face.

"How about Mr. and Mrs. Rawlings, Pioneer Lane, Tent City, West Coast? There wasn't much more than that when my great-great-grandfather first drove up this canyon in his Conestoga."

Nicole shook her head. "Nope, I want running water. *Hot* running water. And besides, anyone who hopes to be the governor of a new state shouldn't live in a tent. A log cabin, maybe, but not a tent."

**RANCHO MURIETA COUNTRY CLUB
SOUTHEAST OF SACRAMENTO
MARCH**

California Governor Walter Dewhirst won the honors on the first hole with a flip of his tee. As he addressed the ball, Lieutenant General Robert Del Valle stood quietly off to one side, waiting his turn. Their wives, who were playing as partners in the Sunday morning match play against the men, sat in their golf cart, waiting to drive forward to the ladies' tees.

Despite having received no formal communication, Dewhirst knew what was coming. Del Valle was finally going to resign his position as Adjutant General for the State of California, as well as his position as Commander, California National Guard. He'd been increasingly distraught at the direction of the secession. The collective failure of the military and the California legislature to stop the movement had brought him to the end of his patience. Truth be known, Governor Dewhirst felt the same way, but had decided to serve out his term—another twenty-one months—and be the last governor of the state of California before it became an independent nation.

Del Valle's turn came and he pushed his drive, coming to rest a few paces off the fairway some twenty yards behind Dewhirst's ball. The two carts drove forward about thirty yards, and the ladies stepped on to their tee while the men remained seated.

"Monday morning sound about right, with an effective date of July 1st?" Governor Dewhirst said.

Del Valle stared quietly at his partner, a man with whom he'd been playing golf for most of the past ten years. "I'd swear you're clairvoyant, Walt."

Dewhirst laughed, then quickly went silent as his wife shot him a disapproving look. Her partner, Jean Del Valle, was addressing her ball, and she was a stickler for the etiquette of golf. She sent a nice drive down the fairway about one eighty, and the ladies walked back toward their cart. Dewhirst drove forward toward the resting place of his wife's drive, resuming his humorous chuckle.

"I'm not so much clairvoyant, Bob, as you are transparent. You wear your feelings on your sleeve, at least as they pertain to the secession."

"You're right, as usual. In the modern-day, California vernacular, it *sucks*, Walt. It just plain *sucks*."

Again, Dewhirst started to laugh. "You've begun to make the transition to civilian life already. When you finally get frustrated enough, you can start saying, '*whatever,*' and fit right in. But you're right. It does suck. The whole damn thing has gotten to this point on a fraudulent basis, yet here we are. Have you decided what you're going to do?" As Jean Del Valle prepared to hit her second shot, Dewhirst parked some distance away so they could continue to whisper. "Or are you really going to retire?"

"Confidential, right?" Del Valle asked.

"Of course, Bob."

"I've accepted appointment as the chief executive officer of The Montclair Advocacy."

Dewhirst's eyes grew larger and he nodded his head. "Very prestigious appointment, Bob, and no better man for the job. Heading the nation's premier conservative think tank is an outstanding opportunity. They've already come out against the secession, no matter how far down the pike the political process. Do you think Montclair can turn it around?"

"I don't know, Walt, I truly don't," he said as they started forward again, pausing as Jean Del Valle took her second shot. "But we're damn sure going to lobby against it. The Board was adamant when they offered the appointment that they did not want to surrender to the 'ragged mob,' as they called it."

"Isn't Dan Rawlings using Montclair Advocacy as his consulting firm for preparation of the constitutional document?"

Del Valle nodded as Walter Dewhirst drove toward his partner's ball. "He is. In fact, he's contracted with Montclair to meet with his larger, multi-state group in Mexico next month to discuss the bigger picture. He doesn't know I'm going to be there to try to dissuade them from pursuing the idea."

"I read in your monthly National Guard newsletter that you promoted him to major earlier this month."

Del Valle nodded acknowledgement, stepping out of the cart and choosing his seven iron. "He's gotten on the bandwagon for secession for some foolhardy reason, but I had to recognize his contribution to the whole Shasta Brigade and election fiasco. General Connor advised me that the president—Prescott, actually—suggested he receive some commendation, so we gave him a Bronze Star and a promotion to major."

"It's not undeserved, Bob," Dewhirst said.

Del Valle looked toward the first green, sized up his shot, and hit the ball about five feet onto the front surface of the green, leaving a forty-foot, two putt for par. He replaced his club and stepped back into the cart. "You're right, Walt. Rawlings is a good and capable man, but I just can't get my head around why he's shifted his political positioning on this issue."

"Well, I can tell you one thing," Walter Dewhirst said as they drove toward his tee shot, "depending on where they set the minimum age for governor in the new constitution, Daniel Rawlings may damn well be my replacement as governor of California, whatever the state is called at that time."

Del Valle was quiet for several long moments as the governor took his approach shot, placing it inside all three balls that were on or just off the putting surface, then driving toward the cart path which circled the elevated green. Then, as they retrieved their putters, he commented again.

"If it has to happen, he's probably a good man for the job, Walt. He doesn't have your experience or flair for compromise solutions that satisfies all parties, but I have to admit, Major Rawlings is a good officer, and now he has an equally good woman as his wife. Nicole Rawlings is a capable force in her own right. A man can go far with such a woman at his side."

"Shhh," Dewhirst whispered, "don't let the women hear you say that, or we'll be on the hook for another Mediterranean cruise."

TWELVE

**EISENHOWER EXECUTIVE OFFICE BUILDING
OFFICE OF INFORMATION & PUBLIC RELATIONS
DEPARTMENT OF HOMELAND SECURITY
WASHINGTON, D.C.
MARCH**

Brigadier Sir Colin McIntyre, military attaché to the British Embassy in Washington, sat on the far side of the long, oval table, accompanied by Major Trevor Hampton, Executive Officer of the British Special Air Service 22nd Regiment, Lieutenant Colonel Harold Armstrong, commanding officer of the Australian SAS Regiment, and Captain Cameron Rossiter, commanding officer of OAT, the Offshore Assault Team, part of Australia's SAS counter-terrorism effort.

On the near side sat General Pádraig Connor in his capacity as Director of the Office of Information and Public Relations, Department of Homeland Security, known to the men around the table as Trojan. To his right sat Carlos Castro, his Deputy Director and recently retired Sergeant Major, United States Marine Corps. Other participants included Clark Webb, FBI counterterrorism liaison, and John Blanchard, CIA. They had been joined by Theodore Cannidy, the president's newly appointed National Security Advisor, who had served President Steadman as Secretary of Defense.

At the far end of the table sat William Austin, newly confirmed as Secretary, Department of Homeland Security. Following his meeting with President Snow several weeks earlier, Austin was quickly confirmed by the United States Senate to his new cabinet post in the unprecedented time of nine days. General Austin chaired the meeting. Standing at the opposite end of the table in front of the projection screen stood Lars Johansson, a member of Homeland Security's domestic threat analysis directorate.

"Gentleman, thank you for coming on such short notice," Secretary Austin said. "With respect to our joint international terrorist efforts, the past few days have forced us to consider a complete revision of our thinking as regards what level of threat was posed against us. The information obtained by General Connor, Mr. Castro, and Captain Rossiter from their exploits in the South Pacific have stirred the proverbial hornet's nest, to say the least. When our friend, Mr. Wolff, arrived at the Thomson Correction Facility, he was greeted with the usual procedure and isolated from all outside contact. From the filmed interview we have just seen, both the short clip from the yacht and his initial interrogation at Thomson, you can see that he was not cooperative, even though he was threatened with placement into the general population, which he was told included a group of Middle Eastern captives. He will remain at Thomson until the Department of Justice determines how to handle his case. In the present environment of terrorist judicial rights, I'm afraid he might go free. We actually have no evidence of any specific crime to which we can tie Mr. Wolff."

"I don't concur. We have the testimony of those involved in the California secession movement and the Shasta Brigade attacks. Mr. Secretary," Pug said, turning to look at Austin, "there are several witnesses and some testimony that has implicated Wolff."

"Most of those principals are dead or easily impeachable," Austin replied. He looked down the table at Carlos. "Mr. Castro, I concur that you made the correct decision to bring him out, rather than the alternative, despite the fact that he might be set free. But I'm curious. Why did you make that decision?"

Carlos considered his response for a few seconds, then nodded and replied. "Mr. Secretary, General Connor left that determination to my discretion. Earlier in the evening, prior to my entry, the lookout team had observed two Indonesian or Filipino men who were present in his quarters. They had been identified by Australian SAS as part of a terrorist assault three months earlier, resulting in Australian deaths. After eliminating those terrorists and subduing Mr. Wolff, my initial questioning, under sedation, indicated to me that he was preparing an upcoming operation, perhaps involving the Filipino group. Then, upon observing the written notes in his possession—notes I could not fully comprehend, since they were in French—I was able to decipher enough to feel that he would have information of additional importance which I did not have the time to extract. NSA has since removed and translated all the relevant information from his laptop."

"It appears your judgment was correct. In any event," Austin continued, "we're faced with an international dilemma somewhat different than we've been anticipating. The impending threat, while less spectacular, is much more dangerous. If the information from his computer is correct, and much of it has already been corroborated, then Australia, Britain, and the United States can look forward to a blood bath in the streets throughout our three countries. Raising the threat level, at least in America, will only exacerbate the situation, since we don't have any definition of target location. Lars, give us a rundown of what we know and why this situation is so different. Unfortunately, gentlemen, as is often the case, what we know is far exceeded by what we *don't* know. Lars."

"Thank you, Mr. Secretary. Gentlemen, we got very little information from the video-taped interrogation we've just seen, part of which was taken at sea on the yacht. But, as you've also seen, the Thomson interrogation was a bit more informative. Then, we've acquired additional information from the data contained on his laptop. British and American intelligence agencies have been able to ferret out specifics about arms sales Wolff made, through his subsidiaries, to individual groups in England and Australia. In total, about two hundred hunting rifles of various caliber, scopes, an equal number of pistols and dozens of silencers, along with a couple hundred pounds of Semtex. But the sales, as small as they are, are not as important as the *delivery* information we obtained. Unfortunately, all weapons had been delivered *prior* to

Wolff's capture in Timor, and although we know where and when they were delivered, we have no idea where the weapons are now or, more specifically, who has them."

Major Hampton, the British SAS officer, spoke first. "Mr. Johansson, you said sales to England and Australia. What about America?"

Secretary Austin answered. "As the gun control groups are always telling anyone who will listen, we already have plenty of those in every household, Major, we don't need to buy them overseas or from clandestine arms dealers. You can buy them on nearly any street corner in the larger cities, or in gun shops, for that matter, with fake ID. But you can be certain they've added a few pounds of Semtex to their inventory as well."

The CIA representative leaned forward in his chair and turned toward the briefer. "Mr. Johansson, from the written statement we received prior to this conference, all we're talking about are a couple hundred rifles and handguns. What's the particular flap about that level of weapons sales? Why is it important enough to involve Trojan?"

Lars continued the presentation. "Mr. Blanchard, as Secretary Austin indicated, this is not the type of threat for which we've planned. It's not the amount or type of weapon that concerns us. It's the delivery system for the attack. For years, we've focused on the interception or prevention of airline hijackers, despite our lack of complete control over foreign airports, as the recent KLM incident has shown." He paused for a moment as those present reflected for a moment.

"We watch for weapons of mass destruction brought onto our shores, or even bio-chemical weapons. That level of threat perpetrated in a single, spectacular event, has been our greatest concern."

Secretary Austin interrupted. "And those concerns still exist, and we have to be prepared to deal with them."

"Exactly, but small arms . . . ?" Blanchard queried, holding out both hands, palm up, in a "so what?" gesture.

"Mr. Blanchard," Secretary Austin continued, "if the information from Wolff is correct, the terrorist groups—and it should be noted we cannot confirm this is a Middle-East Al Qaida operation, it could be another of the Islamic splinter groups from Indonesia—have determined to go 'low-tech' for their next phase of operations. They learned one very significant fact from 9/11. They hurt us with over 3,000 deaths, and infuriated our nation. We brought down two Middle Eastern governments as a result. And they learned even more from the KLM incident: we'll kill 300 to save 3,000, however distasteful it is. Afghanistan and Iraq, plus the Nobel Eagle Air Force action, demonstrated that we won't stand for that kind of attack. But they also learned that the economic damage from 9/11 was far greater in the long run. After the KLM incident two months ago, the airline industry has once again nearly shut down. Two major companies are on the brink of bankruptcy after having barely recovered from the events of 9/11. It took over three years for the stock market to right itself again. No guesses on how long it will take us if this plan succeeds. The public furor over President Cumberland's decision to take down the airliner, and the congressional demand to be notified immediately about future incidents before they're enacted, is ridiculous, but it's served to further lower confidence in our government. The stock market is always a victim of such public discord."

Austin paused, scratched his chin, and looked around the table. "While these large-scale operations like the Twin Towers are disastrous, they can only be accomplished infrequently and they depend on a lapse in security. But these terrorist groups are not stupid, gentlemen. We do ourselves a disfavor to make that assumption. Terrorists have learned even more from watching our evening news. Let me ask the group a question. About ten years ago, what single event caused the most internal disruption to our citizens, albeit on a local scale, around Washington D.C.? A disruption, I remind you, that could be repeated quite easily in any environment with little risk attached? And a disruption, gentlemen, against which we have very little, if any, defense?"

The small group of men was silent for several long seconds.

"Urban snipers," Captain Rossiter said.

"Excuse me?" the CIA's Blanchard said, leaning further forward.

"Urban snipers, Mr. Blanchard, as General Connor projected in his written report," the young Australian said more confidently. "One man and a rifle. Two men, referred to as the Beltway Sniper, stopped most retail business, disrupted social outings and personal shopping, and even cancelled school sports events in Virginia and the surrounding area for nearly two months over ten years ago."

Again the room was quiet for several seconds. Secretary Austin broke the silence. "Captain Rossiter is right on the money. We're not talking about hijacking, or dirty bombs, or chemical or even biological weapons in our water, for that matter. From Wolff's laptop, we've learned the basics of the operational plan, or at least, we've pieced it together from several sources of information, since Wolff only knew the types of weapons sold. We're talking about dozens—perhaps hundreds—of two-man hit squads who will scare our citizens to death, forcing them into seclusion . . . and do the same to our friends in England and Australia, if the analysis is correct. And that, gentlemen, is a threat which will render the strongest army in the world completely impotent. The only defense is aggressive local law enforcement, and, of course, civilian militia groups acting as vigilantes who will cause us yet another type of problem all by themselves. Carry on with your briefing, Lars. Let's distribute the specifics of what we know. Then I suggest we go home, get with our respective intelligence agencies, wring our hands a bit more, and then decide how we can counteract this new dimension of grass roots terrorism we face."

"Mr. Secretary," Pug interjected, "as important as it was to us to obtain this information, doesn't it strike you as peculiar that an operator like Wolff was scraping the barrel, being used as procurement officer for small arms? Something doesn't ring true about this whole scenario."

"Are you saying this is beneath him?" Austin asked.

"Sir, what I'm saying is that I think there's more. That we don't know the whole story yet."

Forty-five minutes later when the meeting broke up, Carlos Castro slipped alongside Cameron Rossiter as they walked down the hallway. "I was surprised to see you here this morning. Going straight to another meeting?"

"No, we're going to reconvene at the British Embassy at two."

"How about some lunch?"

"Great. Your boss owes me dinner for a yacht charter, right?" Cameron smiled. "I'll happily let you pay."

Carlos laughed. "It was a short cruise, part of it in a rubber dingy.

You'll have to settle for a hot dog and a Coke in the park."

"What, field rations? And here I always thought the American military had the finest kit available."

"We do. That's why I'm offering you a hot dog from a corner vendor. Or would you rather have an MRE?"

Seated on a bench near the Vietnam Memorial Wall, Carlos and Cameron watched quietly as dozens of people strolled past the glistening, reflective edifice, stopping occasionally to read the names or to place a small token at the base of a particular panel.

"You'd think the visitors would taper off. It's been forty years since that war ended, and people still come. Some of them never even met or knew the relative or friend they come to honor," Carlos said.

"A tribute to man, if not to war," Cameron replied.

"So how'd you get this assignment?" Carlos queried. "I thought you were just out for a summer cruise."

"Natural fit. I'm commander of the OAT section of our SAS counter-terrorism group. Off-shore assault team. Because I'd been in on the snatch, our CO agreed that I could carry on."

"Well, you were smack on the money about the sniper routine."

"That was General Connor's call. But it's how to deal with it that's going to be the problem," Cameron added.

"We're going to be hard-pressed to find a way to interdict that kind of operation," Carlos said. "The D.C. snipers showed us that, and they were only two guys without much planning. These hit squads, if indeed that's what this is all about, will be much more organized, probably even mobile throughout the countryside. What do your boys think? Did they concur with what the interrogation turned up? Will Australia get hit?"

"We're taking precautions. Australia's on the Al Qaida hit list, that's for sure. The attacks at Bali and Fremantle confirmed that."

"Well," Carlos said, "the Aussies deserve a lot of credit, especially in your part of the world. They've fronted up every time this terrorist activity has risen, and they've been firm in supporting both the UK and the U.S. General Connor figures they'll be targeted for sure."

"We've just elected a new government," Cameron added. "Much more conservative. That should keep us in the fight, maybe even allow us to fight back."

Carlos glanced at his watch. "Hey, I'd better run. General Connor will be looking for some answers. You in town long?"

"No. We meet this afternoon with Brigadier McIntyre at the British Embassy, and then take the night flight to LA, and on to Sydney. And congratulations on your retirement and appointment as deputy director of, what do you call it, Trojan? At least, I *think* I should congratulate you."

Carlos stood, followed by Cameron. "Take care, Cameron. I think we'll be seeing more of each other." He offered his hand. "Good to be working with you again."

"I hope it will be good, Carlos. These fanatics can make everyday life miserable if we can't find a way to stop them. And I've been in the Indonesian jungle before. If we have to find some of them, it's not a nice environment."

"If this threat assessment is correct, we'll spend more time on the streets of Sydney and Washington than the jungle. Keep in touch," Carlos said and took off across the park.

Thirteen

**OVAL OFFICE
THE WHITE HOUSE
WASHINGTON D.C.
MARCH**

Since leaving the CIA and accepting his appointment to Homeland Security, General Austin had been directed by President Snow to locate his primary office within the west wing of the White House, where both he and the National Security Advisor were immediately available as required.

Across the street, in the Eisenhower Executive Office Building which housed Trojan, Pug Connor returned from a luncheon with two of the Joint Chiefs to find a voice mail requesting his appearance in Secretary Austin's office at 3 P.M. He glanced at his watch, which read 2:40. He grabbed his notes and briefing papers from the morning meeting and walked briskly down the stairs and across the street, entering the White House grounds. As he cleared security and entered the corridor, he met General Austin just coming out of his office. Austin inclined his head, signaling Pug to follow.

"Good timing. We're headed down the hall," Austin said.

"Are we going where I *think* we're going?"

"We are. Dixie called and said the president has squeezed twenty minutes into his schedule and asked us to join him. We'll just play it by ear. I think Admiral Barrington will be there too, along with Patrick Collins, the president's choice for Secretary of Defense."

Admiral Barrington was outside the president's office when they arrived, and Defense Secretary Designate Patrick Collins and newly confirmed Vice President Hank Tiarks were already in the Oval Office. Dixie, the president's secretary, stood and motioned them through the doorway. Inside, President Snow rose to greet them.

"Good morning, gentlemen. Let me introduce Vice President Hank Tiarks and Patrick Collins, soon to be the Secretary of Defense," the president said. As the men shook hands, the president motioned the group to a small cluster of chairs and a large, deep burgundy leather couch. The president gave a nod to Pug, then took his seat. "I've read the brief on the interrogation transcripts and the overview of the attack plan. We're short on time this afternoon, so let's hear your analysis, Secretary Austin," he said. "What unwelcome visitors can we expect?"

"Mr. President, we've compiled a fairly confident picture that several of the various terrorist groups have concentrated their objectives and plan to hit us—and our allies, I might add—where we are most vulnerable, on our own soil again."

"Are you telling me we know the target this time?"

"No, sir. The target is America—everywhere. But this time, as you saw from the summary, no airplanes, no plagues, no dirty bombs, and no chemical contamination of water supply or anything like we've considered, although those possibilities are always on our watch list. No, this time, Mr. President, we have reason to believe that the various terrorist groups, we don't really know which one, intend to infiltrate America. If there is one central command, they possibly already have the people in place—small teams of snipers—in America, Australia, and England. From our experience this past couple of years, I wouldn't be surprised if we didn't have native-born Americans mingled in with the infiltrators."

"Snipers? And *Americans*, too, you say?" Snow repeated.

"Yes, sir. Hit teams. Religious zealots, primarily. Mr. President, if you recall, there were two snipers a decade back who brought the D.C. and Virginia areas to a standstill. That's what we believe they intend to do, but on a much larger scale. Hit us at the local level, a killing here, a killing there, a drive-by shooting in a mall parking lot, with this scenario replicated across the country every day or every week. From what we can gather, there is no large objective, no catastrophic disaster. The only possible objective of a small-scale operation like this is to terrorize neighborhoods and communities. Make our people believe that their government can't protect them."

"You mean throughout the country? Random killings?"

"Yes, Mr. President. That's how we see it."

"Do you concur, Admiral Barrington?"

"I do, Mr. President. The body count will probably not be high, statistically speaking—in fact, far less than from automobile accidents every weekend—but once the media gets on to it, we can certainly expect that as these groups take credit and try to obtain publicity for their terror tactics, the public fear will be rampant."

"And the Aussies and the Brits as well?"

"Yes, sir. Our intelligence leads us to believe they're also on the list."

"Issuing a higher domestic threat alert won't do any good, will it, General Austin?"

"No, sir. What could we tell the public? Stay home because there may be a gunman waiting on the grassy knoll? I personally think that would just fuel the panic. And that's exactly what these people want to create."

The president nodded his understanding. "Then they're correct. The government *can't* protect their citizens. How do you suggest we deal with this type of threat? Pat," he said to the designated Secretary of Defense, "How could the military be applied? Martial law? Occupy our own cities? If this shooting starts soon, similar questions are bound to come up in your confirmation hearings."

"Mr. President, I think Secretary Austin and Admiral Barrington have laid out the problem to the extent we understand it. In the end, if it turns out that we're right and we see multiple sniper teams in our cities, then it will be a matter of vigilance on the part of local law enforcement, rather than the military. It's not the kind of threat that can be repulsed by a squad of soldiers. Heaven forbid it should come to armed National Guard patrols on our streets like they had in northern

Ireland in the seventies and eighties, but a public panic could eventually require exactly that."

"That's drastic, isn't it?" the president asked.

"I hope it's not necessary, Mr. President," Collins said.

"More likely, various armed militia groups, especially in the western states, will try to take the lead with uncoordinated, locally directed patrols. Roving bands of citizens, like the Minutemen who manned the Arizona and Texas border against illegal immigrants a few years ago," General Austin added.

"What do you mean, General? *American* militia?" President Snow asked.

"Primarily the western militia groups, Mr. President. They'd find it their patriotic duty to defend their homeland, to search out and destroy the infiltrators. And they won't be particular about the evidence they need to convict someone. The wrong skin color or foreign accent will suit their purpose. Any ethnic group different from the basic Anglo-Saxon European will be as afraid of the militia as they are the terrorists. They would *both* become terrorists, essentially."

The president leaned back in his chair, his face a mask of discontent. "That's all we need—a few hundred self-directed posses with the hanging rope in the back of the pickup. Do we have a contingency plan?"

General Austin answered. "Mr. President, we're not completely helpless, but the lack of knowledge about targets, cities, or even timing is the worst problem. We can't ask local law enforcement to go on to double shifts in a constant state of alert. They're complaining already about the cost of overtime and man-hours. But we're working on it. These snipers will need to communicate, to contact their central command, if there is one. We've asked the NSA to focus their electronic intercept search patterns for communication in that area."

The president rose and walked back toward his desk. "Okay, gentlemen. I appreciate your briefing. Keep me informed. Oh, by the way, General, I need to get my cabinet nominees through the Senate quickly, if we're to deal with this threat. If these, uh, snipers are coming to America, what are the possibilities you could direct a couple of them to the Hill before the confirmation hearings get started?"

Austin smiled broadly as he stood. "Well, Mr. President—"

President Snow waved off the reply. "I didn't say that, General. I *really* didn't." He continued, "Secretary Austin, if you have time, I would like you and General Connor to remain for my next meeting. Pug, this is relative to your prior assignment in California, and Secretary Austin should be brought up to speed. Joyce Jefferson served as my lieutenant governor, then she was elected governor of Arizona. She called a few days ago and asked to meet with me. She's a wonderful person and an outstanding leader, but I don't have a good feeling about her agenda."

"Yes, sir," Austin replied.

As the Oval Office cleared of participants from the prior meeting, Dixie stood in the doorway and guided several people into the room. "Mr. President," his secretary said, "Governor Jefferson is here for her appointment."

The first person through the door was an attractive, well-dressed black woman, followed by three men. Pug immediately recognized one of them as Dan Rawlings, the California legislator with whom he had worked on the secession investigation. The other three, including Governor Jefferson, he did not know. President Snow rose to greet the group.

"Joyce, how lovely to see you again," the president said, kissing her cheek.

"And you, Mr. President. May I introduce my associates. Donald Tompkins is currently serving as attorney general for the State of Utah, Harry Phillips is mayor of Eugene, Oregon, and Dan Rawlings represents the 8th District in the California legislature. Gentlemen, may I introduce the president of the United States, William Snow, former governor of Arizona and my dear friend."

All shook hands, and President Snow introduced Homeland Security Secretary Austin and General Connor.

"Good to see you again, Dan," Pug said, warmly shaking his hand.

"You two know each other?" the president asked.

"Yes, sir," Pug replied. "Mr. Rawlings and I worked together on the California secession investigation. He provided the key bit of information that led to the breakthrough."

Pug smiled as Dan shook his head in disagreement. "Sorry, Mr. President, it was actually *Mrs.* Rawlings who provided that information. But at that time, she was Nicole Bentley, an active duty FBI agent. She was medically retired after being shot during that investigation and has since married Mr. Rawlings."

"I'm pleased to meet you, Mr. Rawlings, and welcome, everyone. Please, find a seat and then, Joyce, you can tell me what brings you to Washington."

The group sat around the small conference area in the Oval Office and Joyce Jefferson opened the discussion.

"Mr. President, we're grateful for your time this afternoon. We know you're extremely busy forming a new government and trying to put your team in place." Jefferson hesitated just slightly, pausing to gather her thoughts. "Sir, the four of us represent a contingent of politicians from the western states. *Conservative* and *moderate* politicians," she emphasized. "We've come out of respect for your office . . ." she paused again, and smiled at the president. "No, Bill, that's not exactly true. We've come out of respect for *you*, to give you advance notice of our intentions."

"Joyce, we've been friends for a long time, haven't we? I know that quirky way you have of buttering the bread before you slice up the sandwich."

Jefferson issued a slight chuckle. "Touché, Mr. President. I'll get right to the point. Next Monday, the 25th of March, a consortium of states will be holding a press conference in Las Vegas to announce our intention to join California in seceding from the United States of America and to form the Republic of Western America. As brusque as that notion is, that's our message in a nutshell," she said in her well-known, no-nonsense manner.

Silence followed, with the president slowly nodding his head. "So it's true," he said. "I've heard rumors. It's hard to keep a movement this important quiet for long. I'm surprised the press hasn't blown it wide open. How many states do you represent?"

"Nearly everything west of the Mississippi has a movement, Mr. President. We've been in contact with supportive elected officials in all nineteen states. By no means are they all in agreement, and we're not even certain that all will pass the various secession referendum in each state, but we're quite certain of about ten states, roughly eighty million people, about twenty-six percent of the U.S. population. The other nine states would add another thirty million, or thirty-five percent. California and Texas intend to divide into three states each. Once the announcement is made, I fully expect the idea to jump the Mississippi and run across the midwest red state belt." She paused for a moment while the group considered her remarks.

"Mr. President, we've even had inquiry from British Columbia and several northern Mexican states, notably Baja and Sinaloa."

"Why, Joyce?" the president asked. "Why now?"

"Mr. President, as you know, Mr. Rawlings here was one of the most staunch opponents of the California secession movement when it started nearly two years ago. We were all opposed," she said, sweeping her arm to include her three associates. "But Congress has continued to press forward with their government intervention, their *'government knows best'* philosophy. The legislation they've passed, the legal action against Arizona, where the federal government has failed miserably to protect its citizens, I might add, has only served to fuel this rebellion. When you and I served together in Arizona, Bill, we often spoke of the growing federal intervention. It's been so incremental that most people just take it for granted. The federal government today bears no resemblance to the last generation, much less to the early twentieth century. But this past five to ten years has been a great leap . . . backward, in our opinion. It's not progress we oppose, but centralized government control. In short, that's not American."

"Vote the bastards out, Joyce," the president said, his tone clearly exasperated. "Then elect those you think will restore sanity."

"You know as well as I, Mr. President, that's not as easy as it seems, even within constitutional grounds. With a media biased against anything traditional and plenty of money to fuel the campaigns of progressives, the public is overwhelmed with competing ideas. When one candidate promises to buy their groceries, and the other candidate tells them they need to 'tighten their belt,' they'll vote for the one who promises the gravy train. It's inevitable. But we haven't come prepared to discuss the details of our new government functional operation or the organizational structure. As to the basics, the Republic will be founded around the original intentions of America's Founding Fathers. States' rights, extremely limited federal authority, especially judicial activism, and a strong restriction on the length, process, and *cost* of election campaigns. We want to restore the America of our parents and our grandparents. We're calling a halt to the incremental march toward socialism. We don't care if people are sensitive to that word. That's what America is becoming—a socialist nation—and it's not what we want. We're confident it's not what the majority of Americans want, either. In a decade or two, people will relocate to whichever nation and government structure fulfills their personal beliefs. When that occurs, the liberal nation will have to tell the 'takers' that the "givers" have moved away and there's no more gravy.

"I predict here and now, Mr. President, that within five years, the Republic of Western America will be a larger, more populous nation than the United States. It's what the people want, despite the liberal media that trumpets a cradle-to-grave, entitlement utopia."

"Do you see no room for reconciliation?" the president asked.

"Certainly. Congress can join us in our restoration of original principles. They can listen to the majority consensus, not the special interests or favored few. As I said a moment ago, Congress can tell the thirty percent who contribute nothing that the thirty percent who contribute nearly everything have gone. I don't see that happening, Mr. President. Historically, few men with such power, or women, for that matter, have ever given it up voluntarily. And that brings me to my secondary point and one reason for our advance visit. We do *not* want bloodshed, Mr. President. We want your word that you will not use the military to force these states to remain loyal. There is no issue of morality, slavery, or insurrection here. You would not be fighting for a just cause like Lincoln. We represent a large percentage of Americans who feel they've been betrayed. You're an Arizonian, Mr. President. I *know* you understand, and likely sympathize, at least privately."

"It's been years since my term of office in Arizona, Joyce. I've assumed the office of the presidency with its national perspective. My oath is to the Constitution, to hold this nation together."

"Yes, sir," she nodded, "and so is the congressional oath to protect and defend the Constitution, not to reinterpret it every time it stands in the way of some new-found idea. Elected and appointed federal officials have ignored the Constitution for two damn long, repudiating their oath to defend it. They've ignored or even destroyed the very principles upon which this nation was founded. Tell me, Mr. President," she said, her righteous anger beginning to increase, "who in their right mind believes that James Madison thought free speech meant nude dancing? Who thought that freedom of religion meant that religious icons could not be viewed in the public square or that prayer would be outlawed in schools? And who, by the grace of God, thought that saving a baby seal was more important than saving a baby human? My heavens, Bill, we don't even come *close* to representing what our founders believed. The legal and semantic distortion of the Constitution and English common law is so impractical as to boggle the mind. We'll answer any questions we can, Mr. President, but this movement has risen quickly and gained credibility and momentum. Next Monday we will present it to the nation. We expect overwhelming agreement from the people, if not from those who are likely to lose their power base."

Secretary Austin and General Connor had remained absolutely silent during this exchange, as had the three men with Joyce Jefferson. Now President Snow turned to Austin. "Mr. Secretary, in light of our prior meeting, I guess that old saying is true—when it rains, it pours?"

"That, sir, is an understatement," Austin replied.

Fourteen

**CAPITOL MALL
SACRAMENTO, CALIFORNIA
MARCH**

Walter Dewhirst, governor of California, stood on the same west-facing steps where he had stood only six months earlier when he had formally announced the formation of the independent Republic of California and called for international recognition. The result that day had been nearly a dozen deaths from rifle fire between the 82nd Airborne Division, which had been inserted by the president, and the California State Military Reserve, which had been formed from the former California National Guard and California Highway Patrol. More accurately stated, it was the public's perception that the shots had originated from those sources.

The actual shots had initially come from several well-placed members of the Shasta Brigade, a northern California militia group that had been instructed to turn the insertion of federal troops—essentially martial law—into an open battle. The fire-fight had lasted less than ninety seconds before the president was on the phone to the 82nd commander, telling him to immediately withdraw his troops.

Today, standing on the same steps, behind the same podium, stood many of the same characters: California Governor Walter Dewhirst,

Assemblyman Daniel Rawlings, and General Robert Del Valle, Adjutant General for the State of California, who had already announced his retirement, originally scheduled for July, as being effective May 1st.

New attendees included Joyce Jefferson, former governor of Arizona, Donald Tompkins, attorney general for Utah, Harry Phillips, mayor of Eugene, Oregon, and about fifty other elected officials from every state west of the Mississippi River. Today was the day for the big unveiling. The Republic of Western America was about to be born, or, more factually, the conception and gestation period was about to be announced. Originally planned for Las Vegas, the public announcement had been changed to California in honor of the Golden State's position as first in line to secede.

As with other significant political announcements, the news media had been relentless in their quest to scoop the story and to publicly proclaim the event, including details, well before the official announcement. The evening before, Glenn Beck had made the historical pronouncement the highlight of his show, bringing three leading elected officials, one each from New Mexico, Colorado, and Montana, as guests on his show. These officials, two men and one woman, confirmed that many states west of the Mississippi River had aligned with California in their desire to sever relations with the United States of America.

"Why choose separation from the United States?" Beck asked. "Why not work from within?"

"You of all people should know the answer to that, Glenn. Your chalk board talks have iterated most of our primary points over the past couple of years. Look," the majority leader from the Montana legislature said, "We want to return to an earlier America, where principles meant more than they do today, when they were not fleeting, based on the emotion of the moment. We use the old anecdotes about a contract being just a shake of the hand, someone's word being worth gold in the bank. Those are fallacious on their own merit, although I believe such people existed, perhaps even exist today. But most of the change that has come to America—philosophical change, I mean, not planes instead of horses, or electricity instead of wood stoves—has diminished our freedom to act as we choose. The federal government—and states are not immune to this overburdening quest for power, either—has inserted itself into all aspects of the human condition. In a misguided attempt to foster good health, they regulate how much fat can be in food, how much salt restaurants can serve, and how much exercise our children should have. But this is the same government that continues to subsidize the tobacco farmer, to permit 'medical' use of marijuana. There is no rhyme or reason to their actions. They are all taken in self-interest. Which corporate entity contributes the most is the driving force behind many of their decisions. We want to start over, Glenn, to restore our basic freedom. And that means the freedom to fail, for the individual farmer, for the small business entrepreneur, and the right to tell the guy who hasn't had a job in fifteen years, one who *isn't* disabled, that it's time to get off the gravy train. But it also means the right to fail for the banker who invests our money unwisely and still wants his profit margin when he loses, and for the labor union who forces wages and benefits so high that their industry can't compete on the international market. We've had enough of the "privatize gain and socialize loss' philosophy."

"So," the host said, leaning toward the table and speaking directly into the camera, "I could not have predicted that this might be the result, but America is on the verge of division . . . yet again. Hopefully, if this action, this national divorce takes place, it will be accomplished peacefully and without the need for military intervention. We do not want another Civil War," Beck added.

In his closing remarks, Beck summarized that during the prior six months, a small, growing populist unease had expanded and the proposed formation of the Republic of California had grown to become the Republic of Western America, or *would* become such, as soon as the various states' voters approved the national referendum, set for Tuesday, November 5th, 2013. For the states which were in agreement, the Montana spokesman said, the new nation would become effective January 1st, 2015.

Today, in Sacramento, the first step was becoming reality. As hordes of reporters, television cameras, and dozens of legislative officials seeking to climb on the bandwagon convened on the steps of the Sacramento Capitol, Governor Dewhirst stood behind the lectern, with Joyce Jefferson to one side and Daniel Rawlings to the other.

Rawlings was in just as much awe as the legislators that had appeared on the Glenn Beck show. A year earlier, he had been the county administrator in Yolo County, immediately northwest of Sacramento. When the California secession was only political hyperbole, he had been opposed. A recent widower and new author—*Voices in My Blood* having become a national bestseller in the first few weeks after release—Dan had been elected to the California Assembly. He was then chosen by Governor Dewhirst and the Speaker of the California Assembly to draft the constitution for the proposed new Republic of California. He had also been coerced into serving with a presidential task force, headed by Colonel Pug Connor, to investigate the origins of the secessionist movement. Within the following year, he was part of the team that uncovered the election fraud, had fallen in love with and married the investigating officer, FBI agent Nicole Bentley, became a bestselling author, and, as demonstrated by his presence today, became a proponent of the secession. Reviewing all that had transpired during that year as he stood alongside former Arizona Governor Jefferson on the California capitol steps, he found it hard to believe. Then Governor Dewhirst began to speak.

"Ladies and gentlemen, may I have your attention please. This briefing will be short, but it will be followed immediately by a full press conference in the legislative conference chambers. It is my pleasure to introduce the former governor of Arizona, Joyce Jefferson. Governor Jefferson has been selected by her colleagues to speak for the elected officers assembled here today. Governor," he said, stepping aside to allow Jefferson to stand behind the microphone.

"Good morning," Jefferson said. "I have a brief announcement to make, and, as Governor Dewhirst has stated, my statement will be followed in one hour by an open press conference inside. Those here today represent political movements within twenty-three states of our union. As our press conference convenes, representatives from each of these states will simultaneously hold a press gathering in their respective capital cities." Jefferson paused for a moment, looking briefly at Dan Rawlings, who stood to her side. He nodded and gave her a gentle smile.

"My fellow citizens, it is with a degree of sadness and a deep humility that I announce the intention of the twenty-three states west of the Mississippi River to hold a special election, set for November 5th, 2013.

The purpose of this election is to establish the level of public support for the legal separation of those sovereign states from the United States of America. All states approving the formation of a new, independent nation will commence the developmental process to implement the Republic of Western America, effective January 1st, 2015. Those states defeating the motion will remain with the United States, regardless of their geographic or non-contiguous location.

"May I further state, as clearly as I can, that it is our commitment to our citizens that this political action will be done without any use of military force, and our goal will be to accomplish the separation with a minimum of dissension. We have briefed the president of the United States and have obtained President Snow's commitment to that peaceful objective. In fairness, I must acknowledge that President Snow is decidedly opposed to this movement, but he is also committed to avoiding military confrontation.

"I call upon all nations of the world to assist us in assuring a peaceful and productive transition. We commit to those nations that the Republic of Western America is dedicated to assuming her place in world affairs without guile and without expansionary intentions. A further press conference will begin, inside, at 10 A.M. Thank you for your attention."

President William Snow sat in front of the large screen television in the residential quarters of the White House and watched the scene from Sacramento unfold before his eyes. The past two months, since the untimely death of President Clay Cumberland, had left him bereft of understanding as to how things had happened so fast. On one front, America was expecting terrorism on the home streets at any moment, unknown, of course, to the general public. On this latest front, if the western politicians had their way, America was about to be split down the middle, half of the country going its own way. In three hours, the National Security Council was going to convene to discuss this latest crisis, and Snow was certain several of the members would be calling for insertion of federal troops into the capital cities of those states that voted to secede, or at the very least, arrest and detention of those politicians who advocated for secession, an act of treason, as some called it.

The political pundits, airing on every channel this morning, were all certain of one thing: the president was going to have to take action to prevent this national divorce. They were unanimous on one point: they were uncertain how best to accomplish that feat of magic without military or law enforcement authority being enacted. So, in fact, were his closest professional advisors. Even *that* was unusual. Pollsters, Monday Morning Quarterbacks, and most political supporters were confident about what the president *should* do in any given situation. Their confusion over this newest threat to the continuity of America only added to his chagrin. It appeared that his college political science professor's adage, '*the easiest problem to solve is someone else's,*' was true.

He didn't hear her approach, so the soft, warm hand on his neck surprised him. He turned to look back over his left shoulder to find his wife, Helen, leaning down to kiss him.

"Got time for a sandwich before you meet the wolves?" she asked.

"That would be great," he said, clicking off the TV and rising to follow her to the sitting area at the other end of the room. Knowing what some of his NSC cohorts were likely to request, he had decided to cut them off at the knees and hold a pre-emptive press conference as soon as the 'wolves' had had sufficient time to digest the Sacramento announcement and the various states' press statements. The presidential conference would begin in just over an hour. He sat in a leather chair and Helen handed him a roast beef sandwich with mayonnaise and pickles, wrapped in a paper napkin.

"Where would I be without you, lady?" he joked.

"Probably still practicing law in Phoenix," she replied.

"Wouldn't *that* be nice." He took a bite of the sandwich and leaned back in the chair, resting his head on the rear cushion for several moments as he chewed and swallowed. "Where *did* the road divide?" he said as Helen sat across from him on the couch.

"Excuse me?" she said, tilting her head.

"At what point did we change direction? Why aren't we *still* in Phoenix, and why am I not still practicing law, or better yet, playing golf?"

Helen smiled and nodded. "I can tell you the *exact* moment, Mr. President," she said. "Do you remember Clarence Henshaw?"

"The city councilman from Mesa?"

"That's him. You were doing what you referred to as 'community involvement' and serving on the Phoenix city council. Do you remember when Clarence announced that he was going to run for governor of Arizona? We were sitting at our breakfast table and you read his announcement in the paper. Do you recall what you did then?" Helen asked.

Bill Snow laughed, shaking his head. "I do, actually. I think I said, 'heaven help us if such fools take charge of our lives.'"

"That's right. At that exact moment, I knew you were going to run for governor of Arizona. The rest is history."

"Are you kidding me? I didn't even know myself for about three months."

"*I* knew," she replied.

"How?" he said, a bit more serious in his query.

"Because I knew *you*, Bill. We were making pretty good money in those days, but that was never your goal. You used to teach the kids, 'We each have to take a turn standing on the wall to defend America. It's not someone else's duty, it's ours.'"

"I said that?"

"You did. That morning, at that moment, our lives changed direction. And Councilman Clarence Henshaw lost his next election for the Mesa city council, and you ran for governor and won."

Snow rose from his chair and came to sit beside his wife on the couch. "Any regrets, sweetheart?"

"Not for a moment, Mr. President. Most people will never know this job isn't at all what it's perceived to be. Sure, there's lots of power, lots of prestige, everyone stands up when you enter a room, and, if you eventually write a book and enter the speaking circuit, there's recovery of the money you forego in your government service. I don't make light of that. But in fact, it's a sacrifice, clear and simple. A personal sacrifice for those who hold the office. It certainly is a sacrifice for their families. Personal lives and privacy are sacrificed to the nation. And half the nation, or more, disagrees with everything you do. And the political opposition will impugn your every motive."

"And if we go home after one term, having never been elected?" he asked, holding her hand and looking into her eyes.

"You won't be the first, and besides, I've always wanted to learn to play golf with you. We'd have plenty of time for each other, wouldn't we?"

President Snow looked at his wife for several long moments, then cupped her chin in his hand and kissed her lips. "I love you more than my own life, Helen. Thank you for always standing beside me." He continued to look at her, knowing that she was always uncomfortable with praise or, in this case, adoration.

"Well," she said, rising and brushing off her dress, her face flushed. "Finish your sandwich and go meet the press. This promises to be an adventurous day. What will you do? Have you formulated your plans?"

"Lots to consider, but I know what I *won't* do. I will *not* go to war over the secession. I'll do everything in my power, short of military intervention, to try to stop this break-up of our nation, but I will not use the military to oppose it. And that's what I intend to tell the press before I meet with the Security Council. That should put a kink in their plans."

Helen stepped toward the door and paused, looking back at her husband. "I love you too, Mr. President. Do what needs to be done, and if the nation doesn't agree, then you can take me home to a beautiful Arizona sunset, probably in the Republic of Western America," she added. "By then, it will be time for someone else to stand on the wall."

Fifteen

**HMAS *NORTH LAKES*
BRISBANE RIVER
QUEENSLAND, AUSTRALIA
EASTER SUNDAY, MARCH, 2013**

From the bridge of Her Majesty's Australian Ship, *HMAS North Lakes,* an *Armidale* class patrol boat, Lieutenant Commander Kate Cartwright, Royal Australian Navy, sat in the captain's chair, watching the wharf facility at the Brisbane Bulk Sugar operation pass by on their starboard quarter, while Midshipman Barker, a JOUT, or Junior Officer Under Training, nervously took his first attempt at pilotage under the watchful eye of Lieutenant Jones, ship's navigator. Very little activity was apparent in the commercial sugar facility, not surprising for a Sunday morning, especially in light of the long four-day Easter weekend. Most people had, in fact, turned their attention to the celebrations planned from Brisbane to Coolangatta, in concert with the Australian University Games along the Gold Coast. Many were simply taking one last weekend away before summer ended.

As *North Lakes* ploughed steadily forward, the imposing Gateway Bridge drew closer, then loomed overhead. They passed beneath the graceful arch on their way east down the Brisbane River toward the rendezvous with *HMAS Defiance,* an *ANZAC* class frigate, scheduled for half an hour later in Moreton Bay. Both ships were newly commissioned, the most recent of their respective classes to be built.

As a patrol boat commander, depending on the daily work load, Cartwright crossed beneath the bridge several times a week, yet there was always something exciting—satisfying, even—about sailing under the graceful overhead span, either entering or leaving the river basin.

Opened for traffic in 1986, the bridge had originally presented a design problem. Due to the proximity of the Brisbane International Airport, the bridge was restricted in overall height to a total of 80 meters, but to accommodate the passage of bulk container vessels, it needed a minimum lower elevation of 55 meters. The result was a nearly flat profile, with a gently sloping arch in the center, the design problem having been transformed into an aesthetically pleasing engineering and architectural solution.

Commissioned in 2008, *HMAS North Lakes* was a Royal Australian Navy Patrol boat, one of two on temporary assignment to patrol South Queensland waters. Built in Henderson, Western Australia, the ten *Armidale* class boats had nearly replaced the *Fremantle* class, only two of which remained in service. *Armidale* patrol boats, like the *Fremantle* before them, were more than the traditional river gunboats operated by navies around the world. With some functional improvements since the original HMAS *Armidale* had been commissioned in 2005, *North Lakes,* a twin screw capable of more than twenty-five knots, was fifty-seven meters in length with a crew of twenty-one and capable of handling two to three meter seas as she performed various coastal duties around Australia.

At twenty-nine and an honors graduate of the Australian Defence Force Academy in Canberra, class of '05, Lieutenant Commander Cartwright was justifiably proud of the sleek lines of her new ship, and, understandably proud also of her new posting as captain of the *North Lakes.*

In twenty-five minutes, they entered the western stretch of Moreton Bay, the original location of Brisbane, which, when founded in 1824, was the home of a penal colony to house the truly incorrigible who were formerly incarcerated in Sydney as part of the 19th century British determination to colonize Australia.

Later, during WWII, Moreton Bay had been the home of a contingent of the United States Navy's Task Force 72, more specifically designated Navy 134, U.S. submarine headquarters for the eastern half the South Pacific. Another U.S. submarine operation, responsible for the Indian Ocean, had been headquartered in Fremantle, Western Australia. Both bases had been commanded by General Douglas MacArthur, Supreme Commander of the Pacific Theater of operations, who was based in Darwin after his evacuation from the Philippines.

Nearly two hours earlier, near Mooloolaba at the mouth of the estuary through which all ships entering Brisbane had to pass, north of Bribie Island, *HMAS Defiance* had taken on her harbor pilot for the two-hour transit into Brisbane's port facilities.

Two of the most imposing harbor entrances in the world are San Francisco, California, and Sydney, Australia. Each harbor is entered directly from the open waters of the Pacific Ocean and each has a magnificent bridge guarding its entrance. In a centuries-old custom the Americans called "Man the Rails," or, as the Australians call it, "Procedure Alpha," sailors line the railings of the vessel as it passes under the arch. Brisbane was a less imposing entry point.

Being further inland, entry to Brisbane was a circuitous route, requiring a roughly two-hour passage through a maze of channels, Northwest, Spitfire, and Main among them, before actually entering the broader reaches of Moreton Bay. *HMAS Defiance* had traversed this route through the morning and was due to meet *North Lakes* at the western edge of the bay, just short of where both vessels had been directed to conduct a ceremonial run up the Brisbane River.

As *North Lakes* left the river proper and entered the more open waters of the bay where navigation was confined to a series of well-marked channels imposed by the limited depth of parts of the bay, Lieutenant Commander Cartwright lifted her binoculars and immediately could see *Defiance* making her way toward them.

Several other vessels, including two VLCC crude oil tankers and one ULCC tanker, were also navigating their way back to sea. By the time ultra-large crude carriers had come on the scene in the late 1990s, some drawing as much as fifteen meters, sections of Moreton Bay were reduced to clearance of only a single meter between seabed and the ship's keel, making the pilot's job all the more demanding.

At 0920 hours, *North Lakes* and *Defiance* commenced their run into the Brisbane River system. Both ships' companies were dressed in S3s, or ceremonials—the Australian Navy's dress white uniforms for formal occasions. *Defiance* was in the lead with *North Lakes* in line astern, a by-the-book procedural 500 meters separating the ships. Ships' crew not on specific duty elsewhere lined the rails as the vessels made their way upriver. A few spectators were beginning to appear at various vantage points along the bank.

The two-ship parade passed the Port of Brisbane on their left side, and, off to the north, on their right, or starboard side, Lieutenant Commander Cartwright noticed three commercial aircraft spaced out on their final approach to the Brisbane International Airport. The channel began to narrow slightly as the ships entered the actual entrance of the Brisbane River and more commercial facilities began to appear, predominately on the north shore. Passing the BP Products oil refinery and then Cement Australia, despite the fact that the requirement to maintain proper separation from *Defiance* required constant attention, Cartwright had continued to allow Midshipman Barker to con the ship. She could detect growing tension in his commands as the procedural formalities increased and the ship's maneuvering room decreased.

Directly over the port bow about two miles distant, Cartwright observed a small aircraft flying northeasterly, coming low over the Bulimba Creek tributary and turning toward their vessels. Casually, she lifted her binoculars to get a better look. It was a two-engine Beechcraft with what appeared to be a single pilot in the cockpit, flying low and fast at about 200 meters. Cartwright thought this peculiar, given the speed and the flight path to Brisbane International, plus the direction of the morning wind. The commercial airliner's approach pattern had indicated an approach from the east. But on an otherwise calm Sunday morning, the small anomaly registered no alarm in her mind. She had seen her share of show-off pilots buzzing the local beaches. The small aircraft flew directly over the gap between *Defiance* and *North Lakes* on a course for the north shore and, as Cartwright assumed, was probably destined for the airport or for a trip to impress early sunbathers.

Without signs of distress or a change in engine sounds, the aircraft banked slightly and dove directly into a cluster of fuel tanks located along the river shoreline. A huge oil tank exploded on impact. Orange and yellow flames burst forth into the bright morning sky, thick black smoke curling upwards. Several surrounding tanks immediately exploded, flying debris having penetrated their structure. Lieutenant Commander Cartwright was instantly off her chair, moving to the starboard side of the bridge.

"I have the con, navigator has the ship," Cartwright commanded, thereby relieving Midshipman Barker from his training duties. "Slow ahead both engines," Cartwright immediately added.

"Captain has the con, slow ahead both engines," the helmsman repeated while transferring the order to the engine room.

Over the next several moments, all eyes were on the blazing inferno to starboard, which was growing exponentially as surrounding fuel tanks succumbed to the heat and exploding debris. Lieutenant Christensen, the Executive Officer, appeared on the bridge, and Cartwright gave him a terse nod. Cartwright quickly ascertained that *Defiance* had also slowed her progress. As the full complement on the bridge of both vessels practiced an involuntary 'eyes right,' neither ship noticed the second Beechcraft approaching from the port side along the same path as the earlier aircraft until it was only about 500 meters from *Defiance*.

Five seconds later, the twin engine aircraft slammed into the bridge structure of *Defiance*, causing the entire ship to shudder. A tremendous explosion followed, ripping through the center of the ship and scattering crew and shards of flying metal in all directions. Flames and thick black smoke rose from the *Defiance*. After a moment of disbelief, complete bedlam ensued.

Aboard the *North Lakes*, Cartwright commanded, "Slow astern both engines." The helmsman repeated the order to the engine room. The captain then picked up the main broadcast microphone. "Hands to emergency stations. *Hands to emergency stations!*" she directed, her voice excited, yet steady and tempered. She exchanged an apprehensive look with her XO.

"Dick . . ." she began.

"I'll take care of it," he replied, unspoken understanding passing between them as he left the bridge to assume command of the damage control party.

For some inexplicable reason, in the growing emergency her mind flashed to an incident some months earlier when she had first assumed command and had been on a quiet inspection through the ship. Outside the junior sailor's recreation space, she overheard several of the sailors talking.

"She'll run us aground one day, she will. How'd we come up with a bloody Sheila for a cap'n? She don't belong here."

"Don't be flapping yer gums with me, mate. She'll be right, just wait and see. She'll come 'round."

Cartwright had been tempted to exercise her command authority and reprimand the offender, but had refrained, allowing the remark to go unaddressed. Still, it had remained in her thoughts over the next few months. Now, without warning, in an unforeseen emergency, it was time for her to 'come 'round'."

Ship's sirens were going off on the *Defiance,* reverberating across the gap between both vessels. *Defiance* was dead in the water, flames leaping from the foredeck and superstructure. Sailors were in the water directly in front of *North Lakes,* having either been blown off the deck or jumping in to avoid the spreading flames.

Lieutenant Commander Cartwright knew the men and women in the water, if not badly injured, could make it to shore, just over a hundred meters on the starboard side of the ship. Many were swimming toward the *North Lakes* or the opposite shore, over two hundred meters distant, determined to avoid the inferno in the fuel storage facility on the north bank. She could see the sailors remaining on *Defiance* trying to organize to fight the fire, appearing on deck in protective clothing and rushing to the forward section of the ship.

"Nav, take the con," she commanded. "Bring us close alongside, slowly now."

"Ma'am, she's fully ablaze. We can't get any closer," Lieutenant Canidy, the navigator who had assumed control from Midshipman Barker, responded.

"I said bring us alongside, Mr. Canidy," she confirmed, her voice remaining controlled, but directive. Barker stood rooted to his spot on the far side of the bridge, unsure of his responsibilities or how to respond to the growing crisis.

"Aye, ma'am, coming alongside," Canidy responded, taking a measure of courage from his commander's confident tone and demeanor.

The heat became intense as *North Lakes* slowly crept up on the port beam of *Defiance,* her once-proud superstructure now a mangled inferno of twisted steel. Lieutenant Commander Cartwright surveyed the chaotic scene. White uniformed sailors, both men and women, were strewn across the deck, some motionless, others struggling to escape the conflagration, many already having gone over the side into the water. At both ends of the *Defiance,* damage control teams were feverishly attempting to slow the fire's advance.

Her own damage control team, directed by Lieutenant Christensen, the XO, were standing by their railings, hoses in hand, the spouting water already beginning to arch across the gap as the two newly commissioned warships, their military designation now more than simple definition, drew closer together. Other *North Lakes* crew were on their port side, lowering the Jacob's ladder, single ropes, and tossing life preservers into the water, beginning to assist with retrieving *Defiance* sailors from the river. Several of the *North Lakes* crew had already jumped overboard in full dress uniform to save injured and burned sailors from going under.

Ashore, the activity increased dramatically over the next several minutes with the sounds of the Brisbane fire brigade racing to the scene of the fire. What had started to be a dress white ceremonial day, an easy day of public relations and naval pride in support of the Queensland celebrations, had quickly turned into an inferno of immense proportions. Cartwright knew that sailors had died, that more might yet die under her orders. It was the classic lesson in command that had been reviewed at the Naval College at HMAS *Creswell.* Her instructor's words rang clear in her mind. *'Command isn't a question of whether or not you're prepared to die for your crew, but whether you're prepared to order some of your crew to die for everyone else.'*

In only moments, on a clear Easter Sunday morning, in the tight confines of the Brisbane River, Lieutenant Commander Kate Cartwright, commanding officer of *HMAS North Lakes,* had joined with the proud heritage of Australian naval officers who had taken their place in a long line of naval engagements, stretching back through Guadalcanal, Coral

Sea, and the Battle of Matapan, and even further back to Gallipoli in WWI, almost one hundred years earlier.

Today's astonishing actions were not so public, not so openly declared, not so clearly defined, and came from a far more cowardly enemy, but from this morning's opening attack, Australia had unceremoniously been put on notice: they were about to reap the rewards of defying the terrorists of the world.

While not a classic naval battle in the traditional sense, Lieutenant Commander Kate Cartwright had exercised her command authority during the initial encounter of what would prove to be a long and costly domestic terrorist conflict. As later honors commending her bravery and that of her crew—two of whom, including Lieutenant Christensen, her executive officer, had died fighting the inferno—would demonstrate, the young commanding officer, as her equally young junior sailor had predicted that day months earlier, had indeed "come 'round."

In 2001, the Royal Australian Navy had stopped and boarded the MV *Tampa* in the Indian Ocean, some 140 kilometers north of Christmas Island. The ship had been bound for Australia and was loaded with refugees, mostly from Afghanistan. After a period of detention on Nauru, with some immigrants being admitted to New Zealand, Australian immigrant visas were granted to many of the former refugees, including two brothers who were eight and eleven years old at the time of their admission to Australia. The family had settled in northern Queensland.

Twelve years later, on a warm fall day, the temperature hovering just below 28º Celsius, both brothers, now in their twenties, strolled along the beach front in Surfer's Paradise. They were about to reward their adopted country with the full measure of their devotion to Al Qaida, Islam, and the World Jihad movement.

Situated seventy-five miles south of the Brisbane River, Surfer's Paradise is one of the most populated recreational destinations on the Gold Coast in Queensland, Australia. On a beautiful Easter Sunday, the Strand was jammed with enthusiastic people. Nearly every nationality could usually be found in the cosmopolitan crowd at this popular Gold

Coast tourist spot, and today was no exception. Close to eight thousand people jammed Cavill Avenue, the distinctly commercial tourist area at Surfer's.

Millions of tourists and locals frequented the area annually, plying its outstanding beaches, trendy shops, and multiple restaurants with food from many cultures available within two or three blocks. Increasingly over the recent ten years, high-rise hotels and resort facilities had dotted the horizon, making the Gold Coast an international, yet affordable, playground.

The Easter weekend provided yet another opportunity—for many, the last before winter—to yet again enjoy the fruits of living in one of the most beautiful places on earth. The two clean-shaven, young, and highly fit Afghani brothers jostled their way through the boisterous crowd, rounding the corner near O'Malley's Irish Pub and heading west down Cavill Mall. Within moments, they were immersed in the throng, elbow to elbow with people from all walks of life. Carrying a beach towel wrapped around his arm, the younger of the brothers concealed a silenced weapon and found it easy to place several shots in quick succession as they pushed their way through the milling people. Both men were several meters away before the victims even had time to realize they had been shot. Only when the victims had fallen to the pathway did the multitude react. For most of the tourists, the reaction was to simply step over or around the prostrate bodies.

Within moments, dozens, perhaps hundreds, of people had pushed and shoved their way past the three people who were lying on the footpath directly across the street from McDonald's. Their jumbled bodies seemed to be the result of a collective trip and fall accident. With passersby unable to even see the confusion until they were right on top of it, medical help was not summoned until someone finally stopped to render assistance and saw the blood pooling beneath the first person they tried to help to their feet. The cry for police and ambulance then traveled swiftly through the crowd until one of the shop owners placed a call for help. Even the emergency medical personnel had difficulty pressing their way through the crowd, and by the time they reached the injured people, all three were dead from small-caliber gunshot wounds, inflicted at close range. Two had died from damaged internal organs—

one had simply bled out while waiting for help.

Long before medical help arrived, the two gunmen, unseen and, in the din of the crowd, unheard by anyone, had made their way further west to where Cavill Mall turns into Cavill Avenue, and vehicular traffic began to compound the crowd control issue. The brothers passed throngs of people, various restaurants, shops, and entertainment buskers who had gathered even more people to watch their show.

In front of the statue of Matey, a mixed-breed dog who became a fixture on Cavill Avenue in the fifties with his wandering and friendly nature, a large assembly had gathered to watch a swagger man as he, and his trained dog Molly, entertained the crowd. By the time Molly completed her act, jumping up and standing on the soles of the busker's boots while he lay on his back on the ground, his feet propped up in the air, four additional people had suffered bullet wounds, one of them dying immediately, dropping toward the ground to hang over the single-strand cable that separated the people from the grass-enclosed park area in front of the RSL Club and the Veteran's Memorial.

Further up the avenue, near the Tiki Village resort, the two men entered their rental car, made the ten-minute drive inland, and pulled in to the parking facility at Pacific Fair Shopping Centre, the largest indoor/outdoor mall in the area, packed with thousands of tourists and sightseers. In the next hour, nine more people would die from gunshot wounds in the mall or parking area, one of whom was not discovered until the following morning, slumped in the back of her van.

Although the three attacks—at Cavill Mall, Pacific Fair Shopping Centre, and the morning's air assault on the Royal Australian Navy vessels in the Brisbane River—were coordinated within an hour of each other, they escaped the immediate recognition by authorities, at least as far as public announcements were concerned, that they were possibly related. It was not until later that evening, when the news stations received a recorded message from an organization calling itself World Jihad, that the Office of the Prime Minister publicly acknowledged the relationship of the attacks.

From the sketchy and unsubstantiated attack plans that had been outlined by the captured weapons dealer, Wolff, and the conclusions drawn by Trojan in their analysis of impending disaster, Queensland,

Australia, fourteen hours ahead of Washington D.C., was the first to learn about the validity of the threat.

As Easter Sunday rolled around the world, the fear of further terrorist attacks took on new meaning as Muslim extremists unleashed a new order of terror against predominately Christian populations in the Commonwealth nations and the United States of America. Innocent Australian citizens were the first to shed blood in the latest round of terrorism. Great Britain would follow some ten hours later. And America was to be next, but on a far broader scale.

Sixteen

TURNER FIELD
ATLANTA GEORGIA
EASTER SUNDAY, MARCH
(THE NEXT DAY, USA TIME)

The Atlanta Braves took the Sunday afternoon game 6–3 against the Los Angeles Dodgers in a nearly packed house. William Foster and his wife, Shari, made their way down the exit ramps on the west side of Turner Field, along with nearly 36,000 other happy Braves' supporters. Another winning season was underway, and the Damn Yankees had better get ready for the next World Series.

The owner of a miniature golf course and driving range about twenty miles north, Foster had lived in or near Atlanta all of his forty-four years. He'd met and married Shari eighteen years earlier, and they had three children, all of whom were distraught that they hadn't been allowed to attend the game, but Foster had been adamant: "*The Easter Sunday game is traditional for me and Mom.*"

Easing through the exit, shoulder-to-shoulder with several hundred other patrons headed for the west parking area, Foster was at first confused by what appeared to be his wife's stumble. He tried to grab her elbow to keep her from falling, but he was unable to support her weight and she dropped to the pavement, with the crowd trying to step around her rather than halting their progress. He knelt to speak to her as people continued to jostle around them as they pressed ahead. He spoke to her, but her eyes appeared confused, disoriented. The fans continued their relentless surge to get to their cars and to head home.

At Safeco Stadium, Seattle, Washington, the story repeated itself. Not to be outdone by his Ford Motor Company competition's "Employee Appreciation Day" the previous month—a chartered fishing vessel into Puget Sound with 125 employees on board—Ralph Tunston, owner of four Toyota dealerships located along I-5 from Seattle to Portland, had purchased 136 tickets to the Easter Sunday game, pitting the Seattle Mariners against the visiting California Angels. There was to be a picnic dinner following the game at Northwest Fantasy, the new theme park developed west of Puyallup.

Three chartered buses were waiting at the southern entrance of Safeco Stadium and everyone had been advised to be on their bus by 4:15 or find their own way to the picnic. The only person to not make the bus was the boss, Ralph Tunston. As the buses pulled away from the stadium, Ralph was being lifted into an emergency vehicle for transport to Seattle's Emergency Trauma Center, one of the finest in the nation if the victim arrived within the 'golden hour.' But no trauma team on earth could have saved Mr. Tunston, who was shot in the back. He was pronounced dead on arrival. Cause of death: a gunshot wound through the rib cage, entering from the back and exiting the chest, after tearing a hole through the heart.

Helen Clark was essentially a 'plank owner' in Busch Stadium, St. Louis, Missouri, having attended the first game, a twelve-inning marathon against the Atlanta Braves, after completion of the new stadium in 1966. She'd attended hundreds of games since. Her ten-year-old niece, Shelly Liston, and their German Shepherd, Gus, remained in their vehicle in the parking area of Busch Stadium for over an hour after the stadium had emptied out. One shot to the head of each of the women and one to the chest of the dog had left them quietly in their van until later that afternoon, when the clean-up sweepers began to scour the lot.

America's favorite pastime had taken on a new dimension, and a lazy afternoon at the ballpark had forever changed.

Seventeen

**RESTON, VIRGINIA
EASTER SUNDAY, MARCH**

Pug Connor sat near the open door of the balcony of his three-bedroom, three-storied townhouse in the suburban community of Reston, Virginia, a slight breeze playing against the curtain on the first truly warm day of the late arriving spring.

Pug nibbled at the second slice of homemade pizza from the previous evening as the fourth and final round of the Honda Classic Golf Tournament was being broadcast on ESPN. Chad Sorensen, a thirty-one-year-old club pro from Southern California, who had regained his touring card the previous year, was leading the event by two strokes. Immediately after Sorensen teed off on the fifteenth, the Breaking News logo scrolled across the bottom of the screen.

11 dead or wounded in multiple shooting incidents at sports arenas throughout the nation. Further information to follow.

Off and on throughout the day, highlights of the burning frigate in Brisbane and the shootings in Surfer's Paradise had been reported on network television. Pug felt as if he were waiting for the other shoe to drop, but as yet, nothing had transpired in America, and he'd received no notice of action related to a response directed at Australian terrorists.

Pug clicked the remote and shifted channels to Fox News. Weekend anchors Jonathan Sharp and Leslie McWilliams sat behind the joint presentation desk, their normally well-groomed appearance and calm demeanor disrupted by what appeared to be slight tension. Leslie was speaking.

" . . . not only that, Jonathan, but literally moments before the top of the hour, the Fox News desk received an unidentified claim that the shootings were planned and directed by . . ." she paused, looking at a small slip of paper in her hand, " . . . by a group calling themselves World Jihad. For those of you who have just joined us following announcements on other networks, throughout the past ninety minutes we have been receiving reports of multiple gunshot injuries at various locations throughout America. At last report, thirty-seven people have been shot in nineteen separate locations, primarily at professional baseball stadiums after the close of the games when crowds were leaving the grounds. There are eleven confirmed dead at this time, with reports still coming in."

Pug was up and grabbing his keys by the time the audio shifted to Jonathan Sharp.

"This is unprecedented . . ." he heard Jonathan say as he clicked off the TV.

"You got that right, buddy," Pug said as he bounded down the stairs, two at a time, to his ground-level garage.

Pug's cell phone rang just as he exited the Eisenhower Executive Office Building elevator and headed for his office. The name on the caller ID was not unexpected.

"Good evening, Mr. Secretary."

"You've seen the news?"

"Yes, sir. I'm just entering my office."

"Good. I assume you've alerted the team and have arranged to assemble Trojan. I'll be there in twenty minutes," General Austin said.

"They're on the way, sir." When Pug reached his desk, his mobile rang again, with no name visible.

"General Connor."

"Pug, it's Colin McIntyre."

"Good afternoon, Brigadier. You've been watching the news, I presume."

"Indeed, and receiving initial reports from Whitehall. We've had several incidents at home as well, it would seem. Add that to the bombing and shooting incidents in Brisbane yesterday, and it would appear the war has started."

"Yes, sir, it would appear so. I've advised Secretary Austin that I am convening Trojan to discuss our next step."

"And what *is* the next step, Pug? How will you seek to curtail these not-so-random attacks?"

"Brigadier, as we said at our last gathering, this is not a question of using Delta Force, SAS, or Seal teams. Even the Marines or British Para's can't storm this beach. There are no easy answers."

"Correct, indeed. General, would you be willing to allow an outsider under the tent flap at your meeting?"

"Sir, there will be nothing discussed that would not benefit from your presence. We're gathering at the EEOB conference room immediately."

"Thank you, Pug. I'll be there as quickly as I can."

By 1630, seven of the eight Trojan members were assembled, plus Brigadier Colin McIntyre, military attaché to the British Embassy. In the short history of their tenure, they had used existing staff for a couple of covert missions, but increasingly it was certain they would need to call on outside military assets.

General Pug Connor and Carlos Castro made up the command structure. The remainder of the team included two Army Rangers, Captain Ted Prince and Lieutenant Carlyle Sanderson, Navy Lieutenant Roger Steppes, a SEAL team leader, and two experienced FBI Hostage Rescue Team members. One man each from the CIA and FBI were assigned as liaison, although not designated as part of Trojan. The JCS tried a politically correct attack and had criticized Connor for not appointing any women to the team, but he had stood fast in his decision, and their end run failed.

One of the attributes that all Trojan team members had in common was that each of the men seated around the table would rather have been at the pointed end of the stick—all had actually been there on more than one occasion—commanding the action team, rather than sitting around this table discussing options. As Director, Pug used the training he had received from General Austin, that most intelligence operations were won or lost in the planning stages. None of the team agreed, but they all followed their orders and had begun to coalesce as an operational team.

When General Austin and then Brigadier McIntyre arrived, Trojan assembled in the conference room. On a large monitor on the far wall, the Fox News live feed continued to update the casualty lists. Forty-seven people had been shot, most at close range in crowded conditions. Thirty-four were confirmed dead, including seven children. Most importantly, the group calling itself World Jihad had issued a statement to Fox News via a taped message. Pug had already called the television station to request a copy of the electronic version of the tape be relayed to the White House, which was then transmitted to his office. The Trojan team sat around the room listening to the surprisingly well-spoken male voice deliver his tirade in excellent, British-accented English.

"Allah be praised. This is the voice of World Jihad. We have struck at the heart of your country. This is only the beginning. Hundreds of Allah's warriors have been placed throughout America, England, and Australia. No longer will your people be safe from Allah's justice. No longer will you have free access to violate the homeland of those who follow the true faith. We can strike wherever and whenever we choose. You believe your government has created homeland security. You have no security. Your families are not safe, your children are not safe, your homes are not safe, your schools are not safe, your communities are not safe. Now you will know what the oppressed people of the world have suffered for many years at the hands of the Great Satan. You will feel our pain. You will suffer as we have suffered. Prepare to die. This is the voice of World Jihad. Allah be praised."

Those around the conference table were silent, the boldness of the message disturbing to the core. Pug turned off the tape player and General Austin sat quietly for several seconds, his fingers steepled in front of his chin, his face impassive. Finally he spoke.

"There we have it. Open, declared war, with no enemy in sight.

I'll confess to you, gentlemen, I cannot recall a time when I've felt more helpless, more . . . more unable to respond. Across the river, our Pentagon counterparts are putting together every contingency plan you can imagine, including further invasions of those countries we think are behind this. Most of that will be to show the public that we are responding, doing something . . . *anything*. But I don't believe that's the answer, nor do I believe it will solve the problem. And I'll tell you one more thing that's very disturbing to me. When we get to the bottom of this, I think we'll find that some, if not most, of these current attacks are home-grown."

"*Americans?*" Brigadier McIntyre asked.

"I believe so, Brigadier. You've had similar British nationals attack your public transportation system. Increasingly, we've seen more and more Americans buy into this 'America done us wrong' philosophy. The common thread seems to be attendance at a local mosque and occasionally some out-of-country training. Religion is a strong persuader of what's right and what's wrong."

McIntyre nodded. "That certainly has been the case in Britain."

"In which case, if they *are* Americans, even racial profiling would be insufficient to identify them," Pug said.

"That's right. These cells are small and widely scattered. It's probably the same in Britain and Australia. Many British Muslims are second and even third generation. They've been coming to Britain since the end of the nineteenth century. We should not discount overseas directions, and most likely they're funded from countries that hate the U.S., but ideology has no geographical boundaries. We would be fooling ourselves if we think we're looking for a car with two Middle Eastern men, with full facial hair, turbans prominently displayed, driving around with rifles hanging out the window."

Austin continued. "So, let's take this one step at a time. General Connor, for the purposes of this meeting, you now command the infiltration force. How would you set them up? How would you communicate?"

Before assuming command of Trojan, Pug had worked for General Austin for a bit over five years at the NSA and CIA, and was familiar with his method of dumping a hypothetical problem on the table and letting those present sort it out. Assigning the role of the enemy commander was one of his favorite mechanisms to accomplish the objectives.

"Mr. Secretary, I'd rather play the good guy this time," Pug said.

"I bet you would, General, but that's my role tonight. Get on with it," Austin said, his normal humor absent in the face of the unfolding crisis.

Pug was silent for about ten seconds. "They would use the 21st century 'dead-drop,' Mr. Secretary. An Internet café and e-mail."

"Agreed. How would you set it up?"

Just as Pug was formulating his thoughts, preparing his initial answer, the door was opened by a Secret Service agent who glanced around the room. He stepped back into the hallway to make room for President Snow, who immediately entered the conference room. Everyone came to their feet.

"Please, gentlemen, be seated," the president said. "May I join you for a few moments, Mr. Secretary?"

"Certainly, Mr. President. Sit right here," Austin said, drawing up one of the second-row chairs next to his. "We were just beginning to formulate our thoughts."

"That's what I came about, actually," the president said, taking his seat. "I've just spoken to British Prime Minister Winters. They've had eleven shooting incidents with fourteen people dead. Yesterday evening, I spoke with Australian Prime Minister Hunter from Canberra. Seventeen Australian sailors died on the *Defiance* and two on the rescue ship. Seven people were shot in the melee at Surfer's Paradise. Five have since died." The president looked around the table briefly, his gaze stopping on McIntyre. "I presume that you are Brigadier Colin McIntyre."

"I am, sir."

"Good. Glad to see you here. General Austin, if you have no objections, Prime Minister Winters has asked if we could include Brigadier McIntyre in the Trojan strategy meetings. He has asked our military attaché in London to participate with his response team."

"I would be pleased to have the brigadier's expertise on our side, Mr. President. Consider it done."

"Good," the president said. "Now, just before coming over here, I signed a presidential order designating this situation as 'Troy,' authorizing full authority to Trojan to call upon any and all assets necessary to counter this new form of attack. General, while there is still some coordination to arrange with governors and, in some cases, mayors, those assets will include local law enforcement as well as military. Full federal funding for local law enforcement will stand behind that directive. I'll deal with Congress later. We're not yet considering declaring martial law, but the idea has been raised by several senators. Congressional leaders are meeting tonight to discuss emergency measures to remove all restrictions from the Patriot Act and to grant far broader discretion to law enforcement and the military. Since we're dealing with a domestic issue, that expansion of the Patriot Act will open a whole new debate among the liberally minded. You and General Connor will have a copy of my memorandum within the hour. The JCS and the secretary of defense will receive copies this evening as well. I know you're only just starting your meeting, but are there any initial thoughts or response to today's attacks?"

"We're not surprised, Mr. President, only perplexed at the moment as to how to best counter an unidentified, widely dispersed enemy who can freely choose his place and time of attack. General Connor was just about to assume the role of a terrorist and take us through operational planning as if he were the group leader."

The president tilted his head and smiled grimly. "I hope for our team's sake, General, that you will remain on *our* side in this fight."

Pug smiled briefly. "They have to obtain communication from somewhere, Mr. President," he said. "Perhaps we can think of a way to get inside that communication network, maybe even identify at least when, if not where, they'll strike next."

"That may be, General Connor, but we can't discount that they may already know what they're supposed to do, that they don't need constant direction. For all of their technical know-how, we're still dealing with a medieval mentality. In those days, the warriors were just told to go and kill, with overall objectives established and plenty of discretion for the field commanders. Well," the president said, rising, "I won't keep you from your meeting." The officers around the room also stood. President Snow paused as he headed for the doorway.

"Thank you, Brigadier, for working with us on this problem. My condolences for the losses your British citizens have suffered today. As usual in times of crises, the British and American people are hand-in-hand against an enemy. Mr. Secretary, please assure that I'm briefed on what actions General Connor's team determines to implement?"

"Certainly, Mr. President. Thank you for meeting with us this evening."

When the president left, Secretary Austin picked up where he had left off, once more asking about communication between the terrorists. "A 21st century dead-drop, you said, General?"

Pug did not respond, and for several seconds silence filled the room.

"General *Connor*," General Austin said, his voice more emphatic. "Your thoughts, please?"

"Sorry, Mr. Secretary, I was, uh . . . I—"

"You were drifting, General. Get focused. Communication. That's the subject. Stay on topic."

"Yes, sir. My apology. It was something the president said that got me thinking," Pug said, pausing for a long moment. "General, they may not need *any* communication."

"What? How could they operate such a widespread, coordinated attack without communication?"

"Consider this, sir. They're all suicide bombers, in a sense. They may have received a very simple instruction before they left wherever they came from. Go kill Americans until you're captured or killed."

"No, the opening attacks were too well-planned. All sports arenas, all baseball games."

"Understood, sir, but they may already have several predetermined places, times, and dates for coordinated attacks for maximum impact, the rest to be selected at random. They may also have a website where they can check in occasionally to receive a change of orders. Mr. Secretary, it doesn't matter if they shoot two people in Chicago or Atlanta, Modesto, California, or Ashland, Oregon. Public fear of the unknown is their greatest weapon. At first, everyone will think it will happen somewhere else. Sort of like the random freeway shootings in Los Angeles a few years ago. But if shootings occur in small town America, in our backyard, so to speak, as well as the larger cities, all our citizens will be terrified."

"You don't paint a very bright picture, General," Brigadier McIntyre said.

"No, sir, I don't. But it's only one thought. And I *am* the enemy commander."

"It's not a pleasant thought, Pug, not pleasant at all," Secretary Austin added. "But you're still the terrorist commander for the evening. Let's brainstorm around the table for a few moments, based on your idea that these individual terrorist cells may act as free agents. Any reasoned idea, or unreasoned for that matter, should be entertained. Captain Prince, your thoughts, please."

Eighteen

FOREST ROAD # 245
NORTH OF MISSOULA, MONTANA
APRIL

Dressed in camouflage BDU's, a thick, silvery beard covering the lower half of his face, Thorton Campbell, known to his associates as Thor, sat quietly at the head of the rough wooden table. Two men sat on his right and one on his left while a large group of men filed into the room. Fifty-five years old, with piercing blue eyes, closely cropped gray hair and a steely gaze that covered the room in a slow, calculated sweep, all that was lacking to fulfill the image of a highland warrior was a crested shield, a breastplate of stiffened leather, and a green, black, and blue tartan kilt.

Six generations after the original Scottish immigrant, Angus Campbell, had cleared a hundred and sixty acres, Thor had abandoned the original Campbell family farm in Minnesota. Five years earlier, when Thor had retired from the Army after twenty-eight years of service and two major wars, Vietnam and Gulf I, he had settled in northern Montana.

Always aware he wasn't cut out to be a farmer like his ancestors, the former Army Ranger had graduated from the Virginia Military Institute, entered active duty, and had retired as a lieutenant colonel. Two negative efficiency reports and a formal charge of negligence had stopped his rise to full colonel. In 2004, twice-divorced and uncertain of what to do after the Army, he had purchased a fishing and hunting supply store about ten miles north of Missoula and quickly found common ground with the local militia unit, becoming their small-arms instructor. Elevation to command of the platoon-sized membership came quickly by virtue of his natural leadership skills and the fact that he was the only one among the group who had held a valid military commission. No one else in the unit had more than eight years' enlisted service, two of those becoming NCO's. Only two had seen combat, and about half had never served on active duty beyond the initial stint in boot camp. The Blackfoot Brigade, about forty-two strong at its core, with additional members in various levels of activity, ranged in age from seventeen to sixty-eight. Campbell had invited only three of his command staff to attend this gathering, including both of the combat veterans who now served as unit NCO's.

All in all, during the past two days, about eighty staff officers had arrived from over a dozen militia units, settling into the stark accommodations at Camp Brockton, so named after a popular local youth who had excelled at football in the 60's, and then won the Silver Star posthumously in Vietnam in 1967 at the age of nineteen. The gathering of unrelated units was unprecedented. They represented the broader western region—north to Washington state, south to Arizona, northwest along Idaho's panhandle to the Canadian border, and east to Colorado—with most of the states in-between represented. Campbell had driven to each region, contacting the top leadership of these separate militia groups, requesting them to meet and discuss the new terrorist threat facing America. The terrorist attack throughout the nation, coming on the heels of Campbell's invitation, had been fortuitous, raising the group to a fever pitch and giving Campbell status as someone who was knowledgeable. *Someone* had to deal with these rag-heads, was the prevailing outcry.

Traditionally, paramilitary groups preferred to act alone, content to battle the government with words and small acts of rebellion, tax avoidance, or inflammatory statements aimed at showing their neighbors that the authorities were not as invulnerable as they seemed. The occasional stand-off with local law enforcement was usually more bluster than substance. Truth be known, some of the militia ranks came from the same law enforcement officers who ringed their training camps holding them, ostensibly, under siege. The call for a general gathering of unit leadership was the result of the growing domestic terrorist threat they had all long-predicted would be forthcoming. The time had come.

Campbell sat at the front of the room, not because he was seen to be, or had been selected as, the leader, although he did command his particular group, known locally as the Blackfoot Boys, but it was his invitation that had been delivered, and his camp that had been selected to host the gathering.

When the last man was seated, without preamble the room grew quiet. Campbell rose, and for several long seconds scanned the room, nodding to several personal acquaintances. Most were dressed as he was, in camouflage BDU's, field jackets, or blue jeans and down vests. They had one obvious thing in common: to a man, they were Caucasian, of European ethnic origins. Although April had arrived and spring was in the air, a brisk Montana mountain chill still permeated the room. In a deep, sonorous voice, Campbell began to speak, softly at first.

"America is under attack. For nearly fifteen years, we've been under attack by foreign terrorists. Now, three weeks ago, there was the opening barrage with the shootings at the baseball parks, courtesy of World Jihad. We all heard the taped message night after night on the news. Then there was the rash of drive-by shootings in mall parking lots a couple of weeks ago, again, claimed by World Jihad. Last week, people in nine cars were shot across the nation's highways, causing several multiple car pile-ups and over a dozen deaths. And what is our government doing about it? *Nothing*!" he shouted, pounding his fist on the wooden table. "Sure, they sent APB warnings, eventually found one of the vehicles on the highway and blew the rag-heads to hell, but Washington is impotent to prevent these attacks. This gathering," he said, making a sweeping motion with his arm to include all in the room, "is long overdue." A few heads nodded around the room.

"Even the military will not be able to deal with this invasion," he continued. "It's not a war for frontal assault, military tactics, or set piece battles. The cops will be hamstrung by politically correct, ethnically restricted, no-profiling laws that have no bearing on this threat and will totally disable their effort to protect honest Americans. There's not one damn thing wrong with racial profiling. If you're looking to kill a snake, you avoid the animals with legs and look for something that slithers. *That's* profiling, it's not racist, and it's appropriate in this instance.

"The Pentagon will claim we need to invade another foreign country. Politicians will claim it's a law enforcement problem. But even if the cops make some headway, whenever they appear to be successful, the liberal court judges will reverse their actions. If any of the invaders are actually caught, the ACLU will defend them and the courts will turn them loose to kill again. The politicians are genetically spineless and physically timid—if not cowardly—always sniffing the wind before they make a decision. They'll fear the loss of power more than they fear the loss of liberty." More heads nodded and some verbal assents rumbled throughout the room.

"*We*," Campbell said, again sweeping his arm from left to right, "America's *true* patriots, are *not* so restricted. *We* will defend America, beginning right here, right now, in this room. *We* will seek out and destroy the rag-heads, the invaders, those who think they can come here and kill our women and children. *We* are America's first line of defense. *We* are the leadership cadre. We will patrol the highways, protect our cities, and hunt down these vermin. *We* will kill these animals wherever we find them. Our numbers are few, but once the word is out, we'll grow. Many of you served on the Arizona border with the Minutemen. Other like-minded patriots will flock to *our* banner. Americans will finally listen to *our* call. And we, the American Brigade Command … we *will* be ready."

Shouts of agreement rose, some men took to their feet and began clapping and within two minutes, Thor Campbell, commander of the Blackfoot Brigade, had pulled the disparate cluster of disgruntled men together through common cause. The American Brigade Command, quickly dubbed the ABC, had been formed.

Nineteen

**JOINT SENATE & HOUSE CONGRESSIONAL
INTELLIGENCE COMMITTEE
WASHINGTON, D.C.
APRIL**

Senator Andrew Forrest Culpepper, Democrat from Tennessee and a direct descendent of Nathan Bedford Forrest, the infamous Civil War Confederate general, was attired in his trademark white linen suit, a thick mane of curly silver hair offset by long, bushy sideburns and eyebrows. To most, his presentation was a century out of date. His fleshy jowls and rotund bulk betrayed a lack of physical exercise, but his well-known propensity for penetrating intellectual debate overrode the physical shortcomings which caused the uninformed to dismiss the man.

Culpepper sat at the center of the assembled committee members and began to bang his gavel, calling the meeting to order. In total, ten men and three women, senators and representatives from their respective committees, sat around the green, felt cloth-covered dais which had been arranged into a semi-circle. In front of their raised platform was a standard, rectangular witness table, also green felt-covered and equipped with three microphones. Three additional men, each in civilian clothes, sat quietly before the committee members; Secretary of Homeland

Security William Austin, Brigadier General Pádraig Connor, and White House legal counsel Adam Brooks. The witness table was clear of any documents or books, the three men sitting in silence, their hands folded on the table. In contrast to standard congressional committees, most of which were open to the public, the room had been sealed and no viewers sat in the audience. Two uniformed guards stood outside the doors, barring admission to the curious passerby or determined reporter seeking an inside scoop.

Senator Culpepper cleared his throat, looked left and right down the line of committee members, and began his oratory, his well-known Deep-South drawl stretching out the words and displaying his flamboyant propensity for southern articulation.

"Good morning, ladies and gentlemen. Thank y'all for coming. We should not have to detain y'all too long, if my understanding of the facts is correct. They are, of course, indisputable. We're here this morning to investigate the complete and utter failure of this president and his lackluster administration to protect the American people. The terrible tragedies that have befallen innocent Americans these past several weeks are despicable, and our failure to apprehend those cowards who perpetrated these actions leaves no room for equivocation in our investigation. The American people demand nothing less than a total change in the administrative structure that has failed to protect them. This committee has a solemn duty, a clear and definable task laid out before us. Because of the failures of this administration, failures, I might add, that would not have happened if we had a competent president…"

Without speaking a word to his two companions, Secretary Austin pushed away from the table, rose from his chair, and began to exit the room. He was followed immediately by General Connor and Adam Brooks.

"Mr. Secretary, Mr. *Secretary*," Culpepper boomed, "may I ask what you are doing, sir? We have only just begun our meeting."

Austin paused, stepping back to grasp the riser behind his chair. "Mr. Chairman, as much as I respect this committee and the congress that authorized its charter, we have far more important issues at stake than a partisan campaign to assess how one political party may gain public acclaim over the purported inaction of another political party. If you will excuse us, Senator, we shall leave to carry on with our duties."

Culpepper banged his gavel again, looking to his committee members for support. "You will do no such thing, Mr. Secretary. You will sit down immediately and will respond to the formal inquiry of this legally constituted committee."

Austin began to walk toward the back of the room and Culpepper resumed banging his gavel. "This committee, sir, has the authority to *compel* your presence, and it shall do so forthwith."

Austin stopped once again, turning back to face the committee. Pug Connor and Adam Brooks stood quietly at his side. "Mr. Chairman," Austin replied, "you have every right to compel my presence if this bi-partisan committee, in *consensus*," he said, sweeping his hand to reflect the entire committee, "agrees with your request." He paused to look at the remaining committee members, each of whom had been silent throughout this unusual opening gambit. "However, Senator, I believe that the majority of the members on this committee are aware that America is under attack by a foreign..." he paused a moment, considering his words, "... and, unfortunately, even a domestic enemy. They are aware that the safety and security of our people hangs in the balance. And they are aware, Senator, that political grandstanding to exacerbate the discomfort of our national leaders, including my commander-in-chief, is not in the best interest of our national security. And I, sir, have little time for political posturing or blatant misuse of elected power. Now, if you will excuse me, I have other duties to perform." Austin turned to head for the door, Culpepper resorting once again to banging his gavel.

Before Austin reached the committee room door, a soft, feminine voice rose from behind the dais, her microphone amplifying her smooth contralto tones. Her voice was stark in respect to the chairman's raspy bleating. "Secretary Austin, if you will grant me a moment of your time, please," she said.

Austin stopped immediately and turned to face his questioner. "Senator McKenzie," he said, his voice conciliatory and a gentle smile playing across his face, "it would be my honor to answer your question."

Senator Rachel McKenzie, Republican from Kansas and a strikingly attractive woman in her late thirties—early forties, when she admitted it—turned toward the chairman of the committee and addressed him directly. "Mr. Chairman, if I may have the floor for just a moment."

Culpepper leaned back in his chair. "If you can do something, *anything* to bring this meeting to order, Senator McKenzie, the Chair will be most grateful."

"Thank you, sir," she replied. "Mr. Secretary, please understand that we—this bi-partisan committee—are, as you have indicated, highly aware of the gravity of the current status of our nation. I concur with you, sir, that this is not the time for political divisiveness or party politics. This is the time for American unity. For political cohesiveness. For cooperation, indeed *joint* action against what seems to be an impenetrable cadre of terrorists who are wreaking havoc with our national sense of security. And I can also assure you, Mr. Secretary, that this committee, comprised of *both* houses of our Congress and representing *all* political spectrums contained therein…" she paused, looking up and down the row of her fellow members, "…seeks answers to the difficult problems we face."

Her smile grew broader and her face softened as her body language appealed to the man standing before her. "Mr. Secretary, we *need* you here today. America needs you here today. *I* need you here today. I honor your selfless service to our country over the past four decades and perhaps more importantly, I have learned—*personally* learned in difficult times—to trust your word. If you would give us your valuable time this morning, I assure you that we will cease any semblance of partisan bickering and together, as Americans, we will strive to find a defensive solution to our current problems. Speaking personally, General, I blame no one person, no particular party, and certainly not the president of the United States. It is the enemy we should despise, and, with all due respect to our esteemed chairman, it is not our political opposition that is on trial this morning. Will you grant me that simple request, General, and remain with us?"

Throughout her brief comments, General Austin had recalled with clarity the moment in 1971 when Air Force Major James Thompson, Senator McKenzie's father, flying as Captain Austin's squadron commander with Austin as wingman over the DMZ in Vietnam, had transmitted a warning that he had spotted two Russian SAM missiles rising from behind their flight formation. The memory was no less clear then on the day it had happened, and seldom had been far from his thoughts over the past forty years. The fireball that engulfed Major Thompson's F-4 Phantom had literally disintegrated the aircraft, destroying his ejection seat and any hope of egress for the pilot.

And then Austin thought of the years of friendship he and his wife, Christine, had shared with Thompson's widow, Charlotte Thompson, as she struggled to raise their only child, a one-year-old daughter named Rachel. The Austins had served as grandparents to the young girl, watching as Charlotte, thirty-two at the time of her husband's death, had never remarried, struggling to rise from the devastation of such an early life tragedy.

Eventually, young Rachel had grown to maturity, completed law school, married Richard McKenzie, also a lawyer, and borne two daughters of her own. Then, in a twist of nature's irony, four years earlier, Richard had been killed by an IED in Iraq while he was serving on deployment as a company commander with his National Guard unit. And now here Rachel sat, a United States Senator from her home state of Kansas. Austin had carried the weight of this knowledge for many years, a young woman bereft of father and husband, both killed in war three decades apart.

Austin replied. "Senator McKenzie, out of my understanding of the importance of our present objectives and my heartfelt respect for your personal sacrifice to this country, we will consent to remain and respond to the inquiries of this committee. I fully appreciate the importance of our task. But if the remaining committee members would please understand, I will not waste our precious time or resources in defending unwarranted accusations against my commander-in-chief. I serve at the pleasure of the president of the United States. He is tasked with the defense of our nation. His administration requires the support of both houses of Congress, and both political parties, to accomplish that mission. An attack on our nation is not the president's personal fault, but a unified response to that attack is certainly within the definition of his job duties, as it is within mine. I intend, to the best of my ability, to fulfill that responsibility. As I see it, regardless of party affiliation, we are here to help him, not to hinder him, in the achievement of that objective. If that can be agreed, then my colleagues and I are at your disposal." Austin turned his eyes toward the chairman of the committee. "Senator Culpepper, is that an agreeable premise?"

The scowl on Culpepper's face was evident even from the distance where Austin stood. "Mr. Secretary, as a member of this august body for nearly thirty years, I will not be gagged and bound by any rules you deem to place upon this committee. We have difficult and pertinent questions to ask of you this morning. I will say and ask what I feel is in the best interest of the American people."

Austin nodded. "Agreed, Mr. Chairman. By all means, please ask your most difficult questions, extract from us anything necessary to help us reach acceptable measures to counter this attack. But Senator, I submit, notwithstanding your long years of dedicated service, that we can press the inquiry without hyperbole. We need not denigrate anyone to achieve these objectives." Austin paused, lowered his head, and contemplated his next thoughts for several long, quiet moments, during which Senator Culpepper held his gavel, appearing prepared to interject, then Austin began to speak in a soft, almost humble, tone.

"Senator, I am not a politician. I was a serving Air Force officer for thirty-five years, then served with our civilian intelligence community, but I have only recently entered these hallowed halls in my present incarnation. I plead guilty to ignorance of the diplomacy required to initiate an inquiry such as we pursue this morning, but innately, I believe it can be done honorably and without guile. Can we not seek joint solutions without casting individual aspersions? Can we not work together as Americans, not as Democrats or Republicans? I can assure you, sir, the task at hand is difficult enough without our being internally divisive."

The scowl slowly left Senator Culpepper's face, replaced by the beginnings of a campaign smile. "Mr. Secretary, if you and your colleagues would please have a seat, I believe we can proceed as intended. You may not like all that I have to say or where I point the finger... or at whom... but, sir, I admire your stance, and, begrudgingly perhaps, I will remove the partisan cloak I must often wear. As you request, I will try to remember that I am an American first, a Democrat second."

"That, sir," Austin said as he moved back toward the witness table, "is all that I can ask of any man... or woman," he added, glancing at

Senator McKenzie.

Three hours later, after all committee members had, in turn, taken their moment of private glory in the questioning process, all parties filed out into the corridor. General Austin took a few moments to wait until Senator McKenzie left the dais, approaching her in the hallway. Pug followed close behind.

As the senator approached, Austin proffered a broad grin. "Rachel, how very nice to see you again. How are your girls?" Senator McKenzie stood about five foot nine, trim with exceptionally healthy looking skin and facial features. Her clear blue eyes, framed by loose-hanging shoulder-length dark hair, projected an aura of intelligence along with a sincere warmth. She quickly closed the gap, obviously pleased to see Austin. "Uncle Bill, it's so nice to see you again."

Rachel stepped close to the general and was immediately enveloped into a warm embrace. She then stepped back, his hands still on her shoulders. "You should come and see my girls for yourself. We've all missed your visits since you retired from the Air Force. Congratulations on your new appointment. I knew President Snow would make good choices."

"I'm grateful for his confidence," Austin replied. "Christine was talking about you the other day," he said, speaking of his wife. "She said something about your daughter, Charlotte, getting married. She also thinks I'm too busy and that perhaps it's time we *really* retired and headed somewhere warm . . . and peaceful." He laughed. "Rachel, let me introduce General Pádraig Connor. Pug and I worked together for the past several years. He's now the Director of Homeland Security's Office of Information and Public Relations."

Rachel extended her hand, holding Pug's eye contact. "My pleasure, General. I was impressed with your testimony this morning. And of course, yours too, Uncle Bill," she added. "It was a bit testy at first." She chuckled. "But Senator Culpepper has his own inimitable style."

Austin grunted. "So I noticed. In fact, one of his aides handed me a note just as we broke up. We've been invited to his office for an *informal* chat."

Rachel nodded her understanding. "The *real* meeting, I would guess. Well, please try to find some time to visit us, Bill. And Christine is correct. Charlotte is twenty-three and getting married next week. Allison is twenty-four and just about to finish law school at Georgetown. They grow up fast, don't they?"

"So did you, *Senator*. I miss the days when I could take you on my knee or scare the wits out of you on the roller coaster." He laughed.

"Yes, well," she blushed slightly, "we shouldn't burden General Connor with *those* stories now, should we?"

Austin smiled warmly and put his hands on Rachel's shoulders once again. "It's *so* good to talk with you again, Rachel. Christine and I will make it a point to call and come for a visit one weekend soon. I promise. Be sure to send us a wedding invitation. And thank you for an excellent compromise solution this morning. The meeting could have gone very badly without your assistance."

"All in the line of duty, Uncle Bill. It was my pleasure to meet you, General Connor," she said, turning to face Pug once again and offering her hand. She then embraced General Austin, kissing him on the cheek.

Austin and Pug walked in the opposite direction from Rachel McKenzie, heading for Culpepper's office.

"General, is Senator McKenzie part of your extended family? She sounded like you and she had a lengthy history."

"I'm an honorary uncle. But she's as much a member of our family as the children we never had. A surrogate daughter, I would say. I flew in Vietnam with her father the day he was shot down and killed. She was about one at the time. My wife and I stayed in touch with the family over the years. I attended her wedding about twenty-five years ago. She already had two children before she graduated from law school. A very organized and determined woman. Then, several years ago, her husband was killed and history repeated itself."

"Her father and her husband *both* killed in combat. What a tragedy." Pug glanced back down the hallway just in time to see Rachel McKenzie stepping into the elevator.

"Indeed. Now, let's see what General Nathan Bedford Forrest's triple great-grandson has to say to us."

Twenty

**OFFICE OF SENATOR ANDREW F. CULPEPPER
HART SENATE OFFICE BUILDING
WASHINGTON, D.C.
APRIL**

Reaching Senator Culpepper's office, they were shown in immediately, and the senator came out from behind his desk, all smiles and southern hospitality.

"That hearing didn't turn out so bad now, did it, Mr. Secretary?" Culpepper smiled.

"I've faced worse," Austin said, his demeanor relaxed, but his political antennae vibrating. The quietly offered invitation from one of Culpepper's low level staffers had not been anticipated. Austin had sent Brooks back to the White House to report to the president, but directed Pug to remain with him.

Despite his 'I'm new at this' charade in the committee room, former Lieutenant General William Austin had spent countless hours with behind-the-scenes congressional committees over the years and knew the ropes quite well. Staging a walkout had been a ploy that worked to establish his reluctance to impugn the president or others of the Republican persuasion and had resulted in the committee members toning down their verbal assault.

"To employ an oft-used phrase, 'I was just doin' my duty,' General, satisfying my constituents and party adherents. Nothing personal, of course. Actually, I find I rather like our new president. He's more approachable than Cumberland would have been, God rest his soul."

"I understand the need for theater, Senator. Now, how can we help you further?" Austin asked, still wary of the senior senator's intentions. Culpepper motioned for both men to take seats.

Senator Culpepper had decorated his office, in which he had been firmly ensconced since the Hart Senate Office Building had been built thirty years earlier in 1982, with primarily antebellum and Civil War themes, most of them reflecting his home state of Tennessee. A half-dozen limited editions and two excellent originals of Civil War battles lined his walls, all done by the famous military historian and artist, Don Stivers. Both the original paintings depicted stages of the Civil War in which Confederate General Nathan Bedford Forrest led his cavalry regiment.

Bronze statutes rested on several bookcases and a nearly life-size statue of Andrew "Old Hickory" Jackson, another famous Tennessean and the seventh president, stood just outside the entrance to his private office. On the front of the senator's desk was an engraved sign, "Git thar fust with the most men!", which was the famous quote from General Forrest, noted for his use of quick mobility in battle.

"General, I know you're not as naïve about political matters as you pretended this morning, but I'm not as curmudgeonly as I might appear, either. I just might surprise you with my, shall we say, *private* beliefs regarding the current situation. I thought it would help if we could get together, out of the public eye, and discuss the matter." Culpepper reached into a drawer to the side of his desk and retrieved a clear plastic document protector, about a half-inch thick with documents, placing it on his desk top.

"Let me try to sum up why I asked you to meet with me this afternoon. As is the case in any war in world history, there are devious factions in society that would use any crisis, our current predicament included, to enhance their own objectives. Translated, that means 'build their bank accounts,' General. War profiteers. Scum of the earth, if you ask me, and dishonorable to their respective nations in time of crisis. As we both know, there are some Iraqis who are more wealthy today than Saddam was before the war. The same thing will happen in America with this latest invasion of our shores. I hope, General Austin, that you and I can form an alliance against them, but my opening gambit this morning was necessary to renew my well-established 'anti-administration' bona fides. The people we're dealing with are concerned, with good reason, that the current administration will not favor their plans for increased profitability. From what I've seen of President Snow and some of his cabinet-level appointments, yourself included," he chuckled, "they're probably right. Oh, they shield their plans with verbiage of patriotism, honor, security for the nation, etcetera, but it's all . . . what did you call my harangue this morning? *Hyperbole?*"

The crusty old senator, a veteran of many such clandestine political conspiracies, chuckled for several moments. "Perhaps I laid it on a bit thick in my opening monologue, and, given my history in the Senate, I've already confirmed my anti-administration stance. Your walk-out disrupted that plan rather quickly, but we can both thank Senator McKenzie for saving the day. A very astute woman. As to my true intentions, perhaps you should ask President Snow to have a quiet word with President Steadman, my Democratic cohort in many a clandestine battle, before condemning me completely."

Austin nodded his understanding. "Perhaps we both were grandstanding a bit this morning, Senator. *'Public performance often belies private action,'*" he said, quoting a phrase from Senator Culpepper's recent political treatise.

Culpepper grinned at the reference. "Now *that's* what I'm talking about. You're smarter, politically speaking, than you pretend." He then turned his attention to Pug Connor. "Son, it speaks highly that General Austin brought you with him to this private meeting, and I'm going to infer from his decision that he trusts both your integrity and your confidentiality. Unless informed otherwise," he said, glancing toward Austin, "I'm going to proceed on that assumption. I'm playing a dangerous game here, General Connor. Perhaps not as life-threatening as some of the missions I've learned you've undertaken, but potentially as damaging, politically speaking."

Noticing Pug's surprised look, Culpepper laughed. "Yes, son, I try to learn as much about those appearing before my committee as I can, and I'm certainly impressed with your military exploits before you landed behind a desk. I read your complete file when your name came before the Senate for confirmation as a general officer. Despite the . . . *hyperbole* . . . we are careful who we promote to flag officer rank.

"The Navy Cross doesn't display as prominently when the recipient is attired in civilian clothing, but believe me, I'm highly impressed with what I know about you. Our common enemy, General Connor—and I'm speaking of the war profiteers, not the terrorists—don't fight in the same way as your former opponents. Even the current terrorists, as cowardly as they are to be shooting innocent civilians, are more prepared to do battle than the culprits I'm talking about. Terrorists are prepared to die for their cause. These greedy insiders are only prepared to kill, not to die. Be that as it may, I trust I can rely on your discretion regarding this discussion? We must keep it between just the three of us."

"I'm learning by the minute, Senator," Pug said with a smile, "and I believe I'm under the tutelage of another master teacher this morning. I've learned that being under General Austin's command carries a different kind of danger, but I'm finding it can be more intimidating than facing an AK-47, if you understand what I mean."

Culpepper laughed boldly, a bit more vocal in his outburst. "I do indeed, son, I do indeed. My committee has massacred many a person across a green felt tablecloth. Now, General, before we get to the meat of our discussion, tell me what you know about PSC's, private security companies."

Austin hesitated only a moment. "I know they've taken on an increasingly larger role in our overseas government operations, especially what used to be referred to as BG, or bodyguard security work. Beyond that, if you're referring to any covert military operations, domestic or international, I've not queried into that area, not in the short time I've served in Homeland Security. I gather from your comments that I better open my eyes a bit."

"Wide open, General, wide open. They're making inroads that would astonish the most ardent follower of our military posture. And, to be fair, they serve a very important purpose to meet our security needs, especially with the all-volunteer military we've had since we ended the draft. However, for about the past ten years, they've been seeking to change the dynamics and especially the scope of that relationship. Are you familiar with a firm called SI? Strategic Initiatives is the formal name. John Harford is the principal owner, a West Point graduate and former Army Ranger."

"Absolutely. I've met with Harford and some of his key staff. The State Department and Homeland Security have a long-standing contract with them to provide security for traveling diplomats, especially for overseas meetings in hazardous countries."

"Exactly. But they don't limit their involvement to personal security missions. They're much more involved in operational elements than meets the eye, covert as well as publicly bid contract work. I meet on a regular basis with two of the principals of SI. They now account for nearly twenty percent of duties that used to be performed exclusively by the military. Bit by bit, they've been reducing their reporting relationship to the Pentagon and cultivating a direct link with Congress. Simply stated, they want to work for the people they can buy. That does not usually include the Joint Chiefs of Staff or senior generals and admirals at the Pentagon. These officers are not *all* innocent, however, since SI fills their command structure with retired flag officers and generals, some colonels, most of whom were favorably disposed to SI when awarding prior contracts. But again, I suspect that you're more aware of this development than you've let on."

"Let's just say the entire military concept has changed dramatically during my thirty-eight-year tenure, Senator," Austin replied.

Culpepper again looked at Connor. "Pardon us, son, while the general and I go down memory lane for a few moments. You might actually learn something yourself in the process. General, you joined the Air Force in what, the late sixties?"

"1964, actually. Air Force Academy, class of 1968," Austin replied.

"Do you have any idea how many AFSC's, Air Force Specialty Codes, or career fields, existed in the active duty cadre at that time?"

"Actually, I don't, Senator, but I think I know where this is going. Over the intervening forty years, the military has moved nearly fifty percent of those job classifications to civilian contractors who perform the job. We have far fewer military job designations today than we did in the sixties."

"Exactly, and the same has happened in each of the other armed services. If the military were called upon today to be self-sufficient, they'd lack the experienced troops to perform all these support functions. During my brief stint in the Army . . . back in the 'old' days, General Connor, I was told it takes about four and half support troops to keep one combat soldier on the front lines. The Air Force is closer to eight support people for every flight crew member. And yes, General Connor, I know that *every* Marine is a rifleman first," he said, allowing another small laugh to escape. "But as regards the force structure, do my statistics conform to your understanding, Mr. Secretary?"

"You're correct, Senator," Austin replied. "By the very nature of the Air Force mission, they probably have the highest ratio of support personnel to operational pilots. Even some of the pilots are support, ferrying supplies and freight and not fronting the enemy. But we both know all these people are essential to the overall mission and the military services are interrelated. The Air Force flies the Army where it needs to go, the Navy transports the Marines, etcetera."

"But the public really doesn't understand all that, General. When the media complains that we had 300,000 troops in Iraq at one point, we probably had less than 75,000 combat troops available, soldiers with rifles out on patrol. These front line troops all have to eat, clean their clothes, receive mail, work the computers, fix the airplanes, do the myriad jobs that keep things working. PSC's, or their less dramatic counterpart, the contract vendor, have assumed many of these roles, rendering us, at least in my opinion and that of many of my colleagues, less responsive and more subject to a breakdown in the system, should the contracts be called into question."

Culpepper continued his review. "Enter PSC's, private security companies. The British hired the Prussian and German mercenaries to fight with them against the colonies during the Revolutionary War. The practice has been going on for centuries. America is now doing it with home-grown security firms. For the most part, they're staffed with former military troopers, but that's not the end of the story. The important point to consider is that they're now performed by private firms, run by civilians, responsible to no single nation, corporation, or entity. They're responsible to shareholders. They have, in fact, become extremely multi-national in their make-up, especially at the senior levels. Their bottom line is the quarterly profit and loss statement, not the security of the nation. Certainly, I don't mean to impugn the majority of their staff any more than I meant to discredit the president this morning. They have various types of associates, as I believe their staff members are called, who are loyal to their American oath, but PSC's have begun to do business with many nations and that fact cannot be overlooked. The question becomes, when push comes to shove, to whom do they owe their loyalty? We all know that today's international ally is tomorrow's opposition. How many Asian or Middle Eastern wars have been fought where America had armed *both* sides over the previous decades?"

Austin nodded his understanding. "You're suggesting that for some of the corporate executives, their primary loyalty is to the bank account, to shareholder profits?"

"I am, General, I am indeed. With this latest iteration of terrorism, which you, among others, have tried to convince us for several years was coming to American soil, PSC's are presented with another great opportunity to expand their opportunities to become America's surrogate military, and—this is the important part—another branch of domestic law enforcement. Believe me when I say, General, that every security provision we now encounter in our airports could, with the flick of a presidential pen, very well be present in public shopping malls, schools, and sports arenas. Our citizens could be subject to search and seizure at the whim of the local law enforcement officials. That's the extent to which PSC's would like to extend their authority. And Congress—my esteemed colleagues—are fast moving to become their staunch ally, all in the name of public safety and security."

"You don't paint a rosy picture, Senator," Austin stated.

"Paint it anyway you see fit, General, it's a fact, and to quote a marketing phrase, '*it's coming soon to a theater near you.*' The quintessential question of our time is fast becoming '*How much freedom will our people surrender in order to increase their personal security?*' Who would have believed twenty years ago that we would have armed guards with automatic weapons strolling casually through our airports, that it would take over thirty minutes to an hour just to clear your way through to the departure gate, that older people with knee and hip replacements would need to practically undress because they will *never* be able to pass the metal screener, and that the most common practice for people flying would be to be dropped off at the curb by their family since sitting at the departure gate with a loved one is no longer permitted? And what man doesn't go to the public restroom in the airport and check the briefcase or package standing beside a urinal, wondering if it was left twenty minutes ago, or belongs to someone currently using the facility?"

Austin shook his head. "Again, not a rosy picture of the America we all know, or *knew*, and loved."

Culpepper stood and walked around to the front of his desk. He reached back and picked up the clear plastic folder and handed it to Austin. "When you have a few moments, General, please review this proposal from SI to *enhance* their services to our nation. I think it will open your eyes. SI calls it Domestic Tranquility. And this is *very* close to achieving approval by the congressional committee structure, in both houses, and the military hasn't even been given the opportunity to review it. At least not openly. I personally gave a copy to Admiral Barrington about ten days ago. He was astonished at the content."

Culpepper retraced his steps to the window, gazed down at the view of Washington D.C., and stood silent for several minutes while General Austin quickly scanned through the folder. Then Culpepper came back behind his desk and resumed his seat.

"We've been talking for twenty minutes and haven't even mentioned the terrorist attack on our citizens. I don't take this threat lightly, General, as I stated in committee this morning, but I am absolutely certain, even more so with you at the helm of HSD, that we will defeat, or at least find a way to live with, this level of domestic terrorism. Despite its public image, the media hype, and the fear of our citizens, the actual impact on our people is minimal. The causalities so far have been equated to less than ten percent of our weekly traffic fatality toll. But what I am *most* concerned about, which I will admit only in private meetings, mind you, is the end result and what type of security arrangements America will have at the other end of this current crisis. If we give the PSC's carte blanche and allow them to run roughshod over our legal protections, habeas corpus, etc., heaven help us in our attempt to withdraw such blanket authority when the crisis ends. Declaring martial law would be easier to rescind. A greatly enhanced authority provision, called Domestic Tranquility, will live forever.

"Gentlemen, at this very moment, with the full knowledge of the president, Congress is working on a dramatic extension and broadening of the Patriot Act. The changes will authorize almost free reign to law enforcement to seize and hold suspected terrorists *or their suspected supporters*, for unlimited time. Some are pushing for a ten-day limit, without recourse to legal counsel. A national Guantanamo, so to speak. These are tougher restrictions than Abraham Lincoln enacted during the Civil War. The fear among my colleagues is palpable, reflected by their constituents and the national panic. They feel bound to do something to counter the terror in the streets. And we haven't even addressed the internal, self-proclaimed militia, the unrestrained, white-supremacist based groups that love to kill anything not Anglo-Saxon."

Austin nodded to acknowledge his agreement. "You're absolutely right, Senator, but none of this was discussed this morning. What restrains your colleagues from speaking openly about their fears of repealing too much of our freedom?"

"Fear, plain and simple. Fear of exacerbating the public panic. Fear of being called soft on the war on terrorism, or *'man-made disasters,'* as our esteemed Speaker of the House likes to call it. The congressional need to do something is much broader than you might imagine, especially on the House side, where they're all up for election every two years. Perhaps unknown to you, some of my colleagues in the Senate, and perhaps the House, have been in discussions with the Chief Justice of the Supreme Court. If legislation is enacted and upheld by the courts, America will change to an extent never even considered by the founders. General Connor," Culpepper said, once again directing his comments at Pug, "I'd like to speak directly to you for a moment, in a most candid manner, if you please. Notwithstanding your reporting relationship to Secretary Austin, I understand you have a special relationship with President Snow."

Connor glanced at General Austin, who nodded his assent. "I have a historical relationship, Senator, outside of politics or the military. But it does not provide either favor or obligation in my current assignment."

Culpepper smiled. "Well stated, young man, and true to your responsibility to General Austin. But you can talk to the man, can't you? Straight up, I mean. Your father was his law partner for many years. Your family and his associated? Am I right?"

"You are, Senator, but I will not infringe upon that relationship. My line of authority is to Secretary Austin."

"Again, commendable, but short-sighted. I'm sure Secretary Austin would agree. A close, even trusted relationship is important, son. Don't underestimate the importance of access. In this town, it means *everything*."

Pug squirmed slightly in his chair, becoming very uncomfortable with the request being presented. Secretary Austin remained silent, to Pug's chagrin. Culpepper continued.

"What I'm contending, General, is that we are entering dangerous waters right now, in this present crisis. If the Congress enacts restrictive legislation on American citizens, gives law enforcement free reign, and remember my inclusion in that definition of law enforcement any PSC's serving in that capacity, and then the courts, through coordinated agreement, uphold those changes, we may well be giving away our inherent freedoms to corporate executives who are responsible only to a small body of elected officials whom they helped, through financial contributions, into office. Not a pretty thought, General. We need to be certain the president understands that concept."

"Perhaps you underestimate President Snow, Senator," Pug replied. "And what about the liberal groups? Won't they and their constituency oppose such a police state?"

"With every fiber of their being, I would assume. I'm not saying it's a done deal, but if approved and supported by judicial fiat, how would they continue to oppose? No, the danger exists and it's closer than any of us would like to think. Son, with Secretary Austin's permission, I'm going to ask you to deliver a message to our president. Eventually I'll speak with him myself, but for now, I need to stay publicly *opposed* to his policies to sustain my relationship with those proposing these changes. Succinctly stated, General Connor, I would like you to tell the president that I believe that if this new legislation, Domestic Tranquility, is passed, the Constitution will be in desperate trouble. Tell him that Senator

Culpepper believes it's time for him to recognize the danger and to move to retain the American freedoms that we all love. It's time for our president to step up, to be a leader and not a pollster. That's not meant in any fashion to be an accusation. From what I can see, President Snow has made an excellent start by avoiding all commitments that belonged to his predecessor. He's shown himself to be his own man. If he comes out and opposes these proposed changes, both sides of the aisle will condemn him in the strongest terms as a weakling, soft on terrorism. He will likely become one of the most vilified presidents in American history, his name will be associated with lack of strength to defeat terrorism and an unwillingness to fight this invasion, a man reluctant to place in effect the tough measures necessary to fight internal terrorism because of his fear of the people. They'll call him soft-natured, not tough enough to face an enemy in mortal combat. In truth, if he rises to the challenge, he has the opportunity to literally save America as we know it. If not, I don't know where it will all lead, but I don't like the prognosis. That's all I'm asking you to tell him, privately and confidentially, since I can't, at this time, approach him personally."

"Senator," Pug said quietly, "I do not meet directly with the president without his request or direction from Secretary Austin."

"Mr. Secretary," Culpepper said, his exasperation visually apparent, "do you concur with my request of General Connor?"

Austin sat quiet for several long seconds, his face unreadable. Finally he spoke. "I sincerely hope that the picture you paint is not forthcoming, but I concede that you're far better positioned than I to know of the developing issues. As to your request of General Connor, I will seek a meeting with President Snow and assure that Pug accompanies me. But Senator, and you too, Pug, don't be surprised if President Snow already has the situation well in hand."

"My thanks for this impromptu meeting, gentleman, and Godspeed to both of you," Culpepper said, rising to escort them to the doorway. "And let me know what you think of the SI proposal, Mr. Secretary. Jennie will give you my direct number. Call me anytime. Very nice to have met you, General Connor. I wish you the best in your regular job of curtailing these wandering terrorists. Your Trojan team has its work cut out for it."

TWENTY-ONE

KENSINGTON, MARYLAND
APRIL

The following Saturday afternoon, Pug had finally agreed to leave his office where he had been in virtual residence since the Trojan team had convened the night of the shootings. Each member of the team had been dispersed to various sections of the country to work with local law enforcement to ascertain requirements for surveillance where federal intervention could be of assistance.

After much cajoling by his brother and a directive from Secretary Austin to ". . . get out of here and recharge your batteries," Pug had consented to attend his sister-in-law's birthday dinner. The day expanded to an early morning round of golf with his youngest brother, Scott.

At 6:30 A.M. Saturday morning, Scott, Pug, and Scott's oldest daughter, Ally, had been on the first tee of the Kenwood Golf and Country Club, where Scott had been a member for several years. In their traditional match play format, Pug beat Scott three and two. To the pleasure of both men, at fourteen, Ally was a natural athlete and had shot an impressive eighty-one, with one OB. On the drive home, Pug complimented the young girl on her solid game.

"She's my retirement plan," Scott jested. "When I turn fifty, I'll caddy for her on the LPGA."

"I might want a younger caddy, Dad," the young girl had teased.

"And certainly a better-looking one, Ally," Pug added.

Throughout the round, as Ally rode in the cart with her father, Pug had a non-playing driver in his cart and a third cart had followed the group. Once they were in the car on the drive home, with a black Cadillac Escalade following, Pug commented on the escort.

"Seems you have a permanent addition to your family," he said, nodding toward the trailing vehicle.

"Something we've had to get used to. Dad was firm about it," he said, referring to his father-in-law, President William Snow.

"Better you than me, brother," Pug laughed. "Do they go everywhere with you?"

Scott nodded assent. "It's not all bad. We get preferential parking at the mall and we don't have to line up for movie tickets." He laughed. "You still on for Sunday dinner? Megan probably has another of her exercise buddies lined up for you to meet."

Pug shook his head, a soft moan escaping his lips. "I love your wife, Scott, but she needs to get off the band wagon. When I'm ready, I'll shop for myself, thank you very much."

Scott released the wheel momentarily and raised both arms in surrender. "Hey, it's not *my* doing. Part of the price we pay for family love. You've got to know that you're a special needs project for all the sisters-in-law. The rest of our brothers couldn't care if you remained single the rest of your life. In fact, the way your golf handicap has dropped to single digits, they're jealous of your free time. So," he said as they pulled into the driveway of their home in Kensington, "let's see what needs to be done before we go out for our birthday dinner. Megan's not happy with turning thirty-eight."

"Poor old lady," Pug said.

Two hours later as they arrived at the Cheesecake Factory in Kensington, Scott, Megan, and their three children all walked toward the entrance. Pug had followed in his car so he could leave as needed and had parked several slots down from Scott's vehicle. As he walked to join their group, he remembered that he had left his camera in the car. A few feet from the family, he waved and started to turn around, calling out to Scott.

"You go ahead, I forgot my camera. I'll be right back." Walking back to his vehicle, a cluster of people was gathering in the parking lot and caught his attention. There were a dozen or more people in formal dress, heading for the restaurant. As Pug drew near his car, he came face-to-face with a woman walking to join the larger group. He recognized her instantly as Senator Rachel McKenzie. Her smile indicated that she recognized him as well.

"General Connor. How very nice to see you."

"Thank you, Senator. I can't say as I expected to run into you again so quickly."

"Nor I, but it's nice to see you. We've just been to a photography session at the park. That beautiful bride over there is my youngest daughter, Charlotte. She'll be married next Wednesday. The bridesmaid standing next to her is my older daughter, Allison, who has not yet found the right guy."

"My advice: don't push her. It'll happen," Pug said. "My brother just told me that all my sisters-in-law are on the lookout for that *special lady* for me. I told them to lay off." He smiled. "Congratulations on the wedding. Do you know the young man well?"

"The families have been friends for several years. He just finished his degree at Kansas State. They've dated steadily for about a year."

"The younger sister getting married first. How does that go down with Allison?"

Rachel laughed. "She says she doesn't care, that she's happy for Charlotte. Well, I better hurry over and do the Mom thing. Nice to see you again."

"And you too, Senator. Please enjoy the happy day."

"I'd like it if you would call me Rachel."

"My pleasure, Rachel. Take care now," he said, starting to walk toward his car again.

After taking two steps, Rachel stopped and turned back. "General?"

"Yes?"

"Our reception will be held Wednesday evening at the Bridal Veil Centre. I think Uncle Bill and Christine will be there. If you aren't busy, I'd be pleased if you could drop by. I know it's short notice, but…"

Pug thought for a quick second before replying. "I'd be pleased to come, Rachel, if you can consent to calling me Pug."

"Of course. Great. It starts around seven and it's just come and go. And please, don't even think about a wedding gift. This is very informal. We'd love to have you attend. Uncle Bill will probably feel more comfortable with close friends besides my mother and me." "Well then, I better mind my manners. I'll see you Wednesday and thanks for the invitation."

TWENTY-TWO

PUEBLO BONITO EMERALD BAY
MAZATLAN, SINALOA, MEXICO
MAY

Fifteen miles north of downtown Mazatlan, Mexico, the five-star accommodations surrounding the Pueblo Bonito Emerald Bay Resort and Spa shimmered in the setting sun. Palm trees, multiple pools, an oceanfront restaurant, a lush, green eighteen-hole golf course, and the peaceful calm of a warm Mexican night greeted the guests as they arrived. For most of the day, the shuttle had run between the airport south of town on the forty-five minute drive to the area called Nuevo Mazatlan, bringing the Americans from various arriving flights. At seven P.M., the group was supposed to assemble for the opening dinner in an area on the outside portico reserved for the fourteen guests and their wives, husbands, or partners.

In preparation for the upcoming election, which the inevitable polls said was viewed favorably by at least six points in eighteen of the twenty-three states, each state had appointed two members to serve on what was called the Structural Committee. This committee numbered forty-six members, plus three appointed staff with specific expertise in federal, state, and local government. That committee, in turn, had appointed eight members to what they referred to as the Constitutional

Sub-Committee. In light of his recent work with the California draft constitution, Dan Rawlings was selected to chair this sub-committee.

Dan had retained the Montclair Advocacy, as he had for the California research, to work with the committee to develop the basic goals and objectives of the formative nation. Six staff members—PhD's, lawyers, and one noted economist—were appointed by Montclair to attend this first gathering. To Dan's surprise and great pleasure, the new chief executive officer of Montclair Advocacy, Major General Robert Del Valle, Dan's former commanding officer in the California National Guard, was also coming. When the secession had been announced, Del Valle, strongly opposed to the intended divorce, had resigned as Adjutant General of California, and retired. Two months ago, Montclair had announced his appointment as chief executive, effective May 1st.

All in all, twenty-eight people were expected to arrive by dinnertime. The Montclair team, four men and two women, were all of moderate to conservative persuasion, in line with the philosophy of the emerging political leaders.

The decision to meet outside the United States, and, if possible, in confidence, was driven by the committee's desire to keep the press at bay, at least until they had developed a basic outline of intent. Since Governor Jefferson's announcement, every member of the leadership of the secession movement had been besieged by press. It was not expected to decline, and a meeting such as the one planned in Mexico—essentially to lay out the foundational format for the Republic of Western America—would draw media like flies.

The working seminar was scheduled to last five days. The male and female spouses or partners who accompanied the delegates knew that their respective companions would be involved every day. When selected by the group to chair the committee, Dan Rawlings had quipped that during the original American constitutional convention, John Adams might have survived on letters from Abigail, but he preferred that each attendee have someone to whom they could personally complain each night after a long day's debate. The partners knew they'd see nothing of their companions for most of the working day, but once they arrived at Emerald Bay, the beauty of the resort facility quickly convinced them that being on their own wasn't such a bad deal, especially those who enjoyed basking in the sun, lying by the pool, playing golf, or just being waited on hand and foot.

Dinner the first evening started the process. With a soft Sea of Cortez breeze wafting through the portico of *La Cordeliere*, the oceanside dining facility at Emerald Bay, Dan Rawlings rose to welcome the guests as the bevy of waiters scurried around the room, displaying their finest Mexican hospitality.

"Good evening to everyone. My name is Daniel Rawlings. I'm a state legislator from northern California and have been appointed to chair this sub-committee. This is my wife, Nicole, who tells me that after five days in the Mexican sun, I won't recognize her when we leave to go home. I hope everyone here who will not be sequestered indoors for the next few days will take advantage of the beautiful Mazatlan community. We have arranged several optional tours and activities for non-delegates, so please, enjoy yourself, either in the community or around the pool.

"I don't think everyone knows everyone else, so please take some time this evening to at least meet those at your respective tables. By the time we leave here, I suspect we will have made some new friends, and, if history is any guide, some new enemies," Dan said to a response of laughter. "So, enjoy the evening and I'll see everyone in the morning, 9 A.M., in the Cardenas Conference Center. With any luck, we will manage at least the first few days without the press getting wind of our gathering."

As the dinner concluded and attendees began to filter out to their rooms, General Del Valle and his wife met Dan and Nicole Rawlings outside on the walkway leading to the cabanas.

"Dan, how very nice to see you again. I wasn't certain you would be part of the delegation to this committee. Nicole, from the zest in your smile and the energy you project, one would assume that you've recovered well from your injuries at the hands of the Shasta Brigade."

"Thank you, General. Perhaps getting married was the key," Nicole said, holding tight to Dan's arm. Dan pulled her closer.

"General," Dan said, "are you here for the entire five days, or just to kick off the seminar? I admit to being surprised at your presence, given your earlier opposing stance on the issue."

Del Valle nodded. "You were opposed too, Dan, as I recall. What changed your mind?"

Dan thought for a moment, looking toward the moonlight reflecting off the Sea of Cortez. "No single event, General. But the momentum generated by several other states inviting me to meet with them regarding our progress in California had significant impact on my thinking. The concept is far more broadly accepted than I thought. And my earlier meetings with Dr. Chambers from your Montclair staff opened my eyes to how far we've actually distanced ourselves from the Founding Fathers."

"I understand," Del Valle responded. "America certainly has come a long way from those initial concepts of freedom. Dan, my role with Montclair puts me in a precarious position. It's possible that my opening remarks tomorrow may seem offensive, both to you and to your other delegates. I don't mean them that way, but there are some things that need to be said. I hope you'll hear me out before you form any conclusions. Why don't we all have a good night's rest and discuss the issues tomorrow."

"General Del Valle, there are no opinions I respect more than yours, sir. I'll give full consideration to any thought you have to deliver. That's why we invited Montclair to moderate this forum. Now that you're the director of the Advocacy, it will bear even more weight. Thanks for the heads-up. Mrs. Del Valle, please enjoy your stay. Till tomorrow, General," Dan said, slipping his hand in Nicole's as they departed.

At 8:45 A.M. the following morning, eight delegates and six consultants from the Montclair Advocacy had gathered in the conference room. A beautiful Mexican breakfast was set out on the sideboard and the participants were enjoying *huevos rancheros*, which was a combination of scrambled eggs and potatoes; *chorizo*, a spicy pork sausage, and a wide assortment of fresh fruit including pineapple, oranges, bananas, and kiwi fruit, or, for the more healthy minded, a simple continental breakfast of sweet roll, plus orange, mango, or pineapple juice, and coffee.

The room was arranged with a large, semi-circular table, open at one end, with a full-sized white board to the front and both sides. A stand-alone podium was placed in the opening of the table arrangement.

At 9:00 A.M. sharp, Dan Rawlings rose from his seat and took a position behind the podium. The room grew quiet, and the few Emerald Bay staff who had been cleaning up the breakfast items left the room.

"*Buenos dias, compadres,*" Dan said, mimicking his limited Spanish ability. "And that's it for my Spanish, except I have actually learned '*Donde esta los baños,*' because we all need to be able to find the toilet. I would assume that three months ago, not one person in this room was thinking of spending a week in Mazatlan. Yet here we are, on the brink of forming a new nation and, for the majority of us, I would think, quite sad at the realization that we are considering leaving the nation of our birth. I join you in that confusion.

"My family has been in America for twelve generations, since 1620, and in California for five, moving west after the Civil War. I love America. I love what America stands for, how it has acquired its place in the world, and how it has historically respected individual and even the regional freedom of other nations. We've all seen the e-mail chain letters that show America's contribution to the world, how the only land we ever kept after our wars was sufficient ground to bury our dead. All of that is true. A visit to Europe and the allied cemeteries will demonstrate America's commitment. What has been referred to as America's 'nation building' has been to the good of the country involved. We never assumed ownership or even governmental control of those nations, certainly not beyond the time required for the formation of their own government. The bustling economies of Japan and Germany for the past quarter century are two prime examples. We're attempting it again now, in the Middle East, in a region of kings, princes, dictators, and religious autocrats who see no merit in allowing the general populace to elect their leaders. It has always been a strongman rule in that region of the world, and America is having difficulty getting the residents to accept a change which their leaders do not want." Dan paused for several seconds, took a sip of his juice, then continued.

"We did not come here for a history lesson, but before I turn the time over to our Montclair Advocacy colleagues, let me remind everyone of one more fact of history. The last time America tried this—to draft and enact a constitution—it took them over seven years from the end of the Revolutionary War to get the individual states to agree. We are committed to having no war, but we are also committed to having a constitution. Toward that end, let's set aside the traditional methods of negotiating, of bargaining for our pet interests. Let's see if we can reach accord on principles in which we all believe. Once our initial job is accomplished, our final product has to pass the scrutiny of our forty-six state representatives and then the further examination of the legislatures in each of the respective states, however many that turns out to be. As it currently stands, we have twenty-three states set to hold an election to determine approval for the formation of the Republic of Western America. Within those elections, both Texas and California each have separate issues on the ballot to divide themselves into three separate states. If approved by each state, the initial RWA will include twenty-seven states. At last count, multiple polls have predicted that nineteen of the twenty-three states will pass this referendum, including Texas and California. Individual primaries have been, and will continue to be, held around the west, leading up to the national election in November."

A spontaneous round of applause rose from the assembled delegates and just as quickly ceased.

"With that in mind, let's begin the process. I am very pleased that General Robert Del Valle has joined us for this seminar. It has been my privilege to work with the general over the past several years, both as a National Guard attorney, under his command, and as a member of the California state legislature, working with Governor Dewhirst and General Del Valle in the formative aspects of California's future. I trust and respect General Del Valle more than any other single individual I know. We should listen carefully to what he has to say.

"I am also pleased to introduce Dr. Roslyn Chambers from the Montclair Advocacy. I have worked with her this past six months on the California constitution development. Dr. Chambers holds a J.D. from Yale Law and a Ph.D. from Stanford, specializing in the economics of constitutional taxation. She comes from a solid background in governmental law, including twelve years as a professor at the Pepperdine University School of Law before accepting appointment at Director of State and Local Government at Montclair. As a graduate of Yale, she somehow escaped the liberal slant that so often accrues to those from the Ivy League legal fraternity, but we should all understand, Dr. Chambers is not a dedicated conservative thinker, ignoring all information contrary to that point of view. To quote her own bio," Dan said, looking down to read from a prepared script, "she is not '. . . *afraid to access, analyze, adapt, or even implement the positive elements of liberal thinking.*'

"I stand in awe of her understanding of the meaning of these formative and historically important documents and have been led to appreciate her judgment on more than one occasion. Ladies and gentlemen, I give you Dr. Roslyn Chambers."

Chambers rose from her seat to the left of the podium and came to stand in front of the group. She was dressed in a lightweight, two-piece business suit, burgundy in color, an off-white silk blouse, and a matching forest green and burgundy scarf tied around her neck. She was about fifty, had short dark hair, expressive hazel eyes, and stood about five feet, five inches tall.

"Thank you, Mr. Rawlings. It is a pleasure to be with you this morning. Our opening comments will likely be surprising to this assembly, given the nature of our assignment to help you form a new nation. We ask you to give us today, and perhaps a bit of tomorrow, before you reach any conclusions.

"We understand that you have allocated five days to form the foundational documents for a new nation, or at least the principle philosophical components of those documents. That time frame, in and of itself, speaks volumes about the nature of the task you have asked us to perform. It's very quick. Almost impetuous. Democracy involves what has been termed a pluralistic, incremental society. Significant movement is slow, painstaking, and often painful for those involved. Along the way, many citizens do not like the direction, the encroaching philosophy which varies from their vision of the future. One single, important issue will turn someone against a philosophy that otherwise is completely in accord with their beliefs. But, if a democratic nation has *any* future, it will lie within the foundation of its core values. The most significant aspect of American democracy, as it has been practiced for over two hundred years, is that it is changeable, reversible in application, but, and this is my key point this morning, *irreversible in principle.*

"The Montclair Advocacy's director, General Robert Del Valle, will address this point after my opening remarks, but from my perspective, please understand that if America is to maintain those core values, I firmly believe we must *use* the system in order to *change* the system. I ask you to keep an open mind this first day and allow us to present the issues as we see them. Perhaps, in the process, you may see a different path from the one you have chosen.

"So," she said, pausing a moment and taking a sip of her orange juice she had brought from her table, "in considering the foundation for a government structure, let's consider what we already have. The Constitution of the United States of America has served us well for two hundred and twenty-four years, with only twenty-seven amendments. Ten of those were added immediately. Some of them were to rescind earlier amendments, basically social experiments that failed. There are also concepts that the founders knew should have been included initially. '*All men are created equal*' springs to mind, but was politically unpalatable and required postponement. That correction did not occur until the thirteenth amendment in 1865.

"Essentially, there have been very few changes in this seminal document that founded the United States of America. It would seem that the 'old boys' got it right, didn't they? And this time, in our modern, collegial atmosphere, we've added the 'old girls,' so the decisions we reach in this century should be a *far* better product."

Again, laughter and a smattering of applause filled the room.

"I have created an agenda, at least for the first four sessions, morning and afternoon, today and tomorrow. We will take it from there as we jointly see fit. After General Del Valle's remarks, we will discuss the structure of our government, the three branches of government, and the primary functions of the federal system, as originally intended. I'm quite sure the founders didn't intend for your six-year-old to learn about sex from an action video.

"I'd like to establish one basic premise: if the 'old guys,'" whom we lovingly call the Founding Fathers, got it right, why should we deviate? I propose that we review and analyze what's in the original documents, at least philosophically, and see how they apply to us today. Two hundred years of judicial interpretation has certainly changed the meaning, or the apparent meaning, the politically *acceptable* meaning, but perhaps that is the crux of where we stand as regards the need for change.

"And please, throughout the day, this is a *seminar*, not a single-voiced lecture, so speak up at any time and let's have an actual discussion. Let's see how long it takes us to get into an argument. Perhaps the first thing I should do is to introduce our team. We'll learn more about the rest of the staff—some of whom suggested that they should wait by the pool until their turn on the agenda—over the next several days, but for today, our primary moderators will be myself and Major General Robert Del Valle, who will address us now, and continue his comments after lunch. General Del Valle, as has been stated, is the new Executive Director of The Montclair Advocacy. Formerly, he was the Adjutant General of the State of California. He is a graduate of West Point, holds a Masters degree from the National War College, and took his Ph.D. in public policy from the University of Southern California. His doctoral dissertation was 'Honor in Public Service: Roosevelt to Roosevelt, The Early Twentieth Century.'"

Del Valle took the floor at 9:25 A.M. "Good morning, ladies and gentleman," Del Valle said. "I believe it important for me to establish some understanding with each of you from the outset. In the planning stages of any military exercise, we employ what is called the OPFOR. It stands for opposition or opposing force. I stand here with you today to represent the OPFOR. If, in my assumed role as OPFOR commander, you determine that Montclair's advice and counsel is not what you expected, there will be no consulting fee. I am *that* determined to represent the opposing force.

"I won't mince words this morning. Here is the executive summary, the bottom line and the underlying principle of our presentation to this committee: under my direction and with the concurrence of my colleagues here today, The Montclair Advocacy is opposed to the establishment of the Republic of Western America. We are opposed to the singular secession of California and always have been. Secession of several states of our union, a division of the nation of states we have formed, goes against the basic mission statement of The Montclair Advocacy: *Strength through Unity of Purpose*.

"Look around the room. Of the eight delegates, not one of you is over fifty. Perhaps only two are over forty. And from our former association, I know that Mr. Rawlings is under thirty. Compare that with the Montclair staff. We average fifty-seven. Certainly age is not the criteria by which we should judge people or their accomplishments. Some of my staff, myself included, envy your youth, your vitality. The future is in the palms of your hands. All of the delegates here today are smart. You're well educated. And you're well intentioned. But you are not wise. That, ladies and gentlemen, is something that *does* come with age.

"Over the next two days, as we examine America's governing documents, her process of change, even her failures over the past century, I hope to be able to convince you of the error of your ways, and at the same time, demonstrate to you how you may bring about the change that you desire. Valid change. *Dramatic* change. But honorable change that results in a stronger, more capable and more vibrant United States of America. Do you want a more conservative America? Do you want not only a nation, but a nation *under God*? We can show you how to achieve that end. And I will make one further statement: beginning next week, The Montclair Advocacy will begin a public campaign against voter approval of the formation of the Republic of Western America. Obviously, if we cannot reach accord this week in our discussions here in Mexico, then Montclair will necessarily withdraw from participation in the process.

"Now, our remarks today are not what you were expecting to hear and you need a few moments to consider your reaction. Therefore, my colleagues and I will remove ourselves from the room and allow you to deliberate on whether or not you prefer to continue this discussion. If you choose to do so, and I sincerely hope that you will give us a chance to fully explain our position, we will return and I shall present the thesis for our argument against secession. Mr. Rawlings, as chair of this committee, is that acceptable to you?"

Dan glanced around the room and received a few affirmative nods from his associates, then turned back to look at General Del Valle.

"General, I think we *all* could use a twenty-minute break. But I hope I'm speaking for the remainder of my colleagues when I say we will be privileged to hear your opinion and conclusions when we return. Sir, thank you for your candor this morning. As you mentioned last evening, it was not what we were expecting, but, with this twenty minutes to reflect, I think we will probably all agree that your position is not all that unexpected. Let's meet back here at 10:45."

During the break, Dan pulled up a chair next to Nicole, who was reclining on a sun lounger besides a sparkling, blue-water pool, a cool drink on her table and several towels, beach bag, and sun tan lotion beneath the table. A copy of Governor Jefferson's *A Colored Cowboy* was lying open across her stomach. A *signed* copy, she would have said, had anyone deemed to ask.

"I've only got a few minutes on this break, Nicole, but I think the week is not going to progress as we originally thought. I'm going to text Governor Jefferson, but the general has just dressed us down like school children. Montclair, I mean Del Valle and the whole staff, are opposed to the formation of the Republic and are determined to spend the next couple of days convincing us of that fact. It's an end run, or a sneak pass, or any other sports analogy that fits. I'm really surprised, and maybe a bit disappointed," Dan said.

Nicole sat up in her chair and pushed her sunglasses back on top of her dark hair. "Are *you* surprised?"

"Are you kidding? I'm astonished. The general was opposed to the California issue, but to bring his team down here and try to reverse our purpose? That's brazen. I respect the man, but good grief, he's gone off the deep end. He said if we didn't like what his group said, there would be no consulting fee. Amazing."

Nicole smiled and lifted her drink, taking a sip and offering one to Dan, who shook his head. She replaced the glass on the small, round table, and took his hand. "How much time do you have?" she asked.

"About five minutes. I have to, uh, '¿donde esta los banos?'" he said.

"Okay, let's put this together. General Del Valle knows Pug Connor, right?"

"Yes," Dan said, a quizzical look appearing on his face.

"And Pug Connor knows President Snow . . ."

Dan hesitated. "Yes," he said, a bit softer, the wheels clicking in his head before Nicole continued.

". . . and Pug knows that General Del Valle was opposed to secession and he probably knows that Montclair was retained to provide consulting advice to our movement, and . . . he also probably knows that the general resigned as Adjutant General of California because he did not want to be part of the secession."

Dan was silent for several seconds. "He's here on presidential orders," he concluded.

"That might be a bit strong. I think he's here on his own business, his own initiative. But his interests and those of the president coincide. Dan," Nicole said, raising his hand to her lips and kissing him. "Pure and simple, he's here for America. He's the same man you've always known and admired. What else could you expect from him? I tried to tell you in Las Vegas, but it's hard to tell your new husband that he's wrong about such an important issue, especially when you're still on your honeymoon. I think you've gotten carried away with pride. Please don't take that wrong," she said, pulling his hand closer to her. "You're all fired up about this new movement and what part you can play in its formation, but you've forgotten why you got here in the first place. You've forgotten the voices in your blood," she said, echoing the title of Dan's successful novel from the previous year. "And you've forgotten Jack's admonition," she said, referring to Dan's recently deceased grandfather, who had told Dan that if he didn't stand up against the militias and the secession nuts, his ancestors would rise up out of their graves and stomp all over him.

"How did I get such a smart wife?" Dan said, his smile now returned.

"Well, first, you got her shot while she was rescuing you, and second, you got her medically retired from the FBI, and third . . . you got her to fall in love with you. Go back in there and listen to General Del Valle. If he doesn't make sense, go ahead and build a new nation. Who needs a unified America, anyway?" she said, lying back down on her sun lounger. "Oh, and don't forget the *baños*, or the rest of the meeting will be uncomfortable."

"I am going to open and close my comments," Del Valle began, "with quotes from my favorite statesman, Winston Churchill. No other politician had his gift for either content or delivery. In light of my message this morning, one which none of you were prepared to hear, my request to you follows Sir Winston's thoughts on courage. To me, Churchill was a man who admired, and personified, courage. He said: *'Courage is what it takes to stand up and speak; courage is also what it takes to sit down and listen.'* I ask you to do just that for the next short period of time.

"For forty-two years, ever since my graduation from West Point, I have endeavored to honor my oath to defend and protect the Constitution, from foreign and *domestic* enemies. What has been proposed makes your group essentially a domestic enemy. I would not go so far as to say it's treasonous, because you are calling for a public referendum, a national vote. If this were Britain, it would be a vote of confidence in the government that might just result in a change of leadership. We have no such system, so for some of you, and your associates in the states, you have chosen what you perceive to be the only legitimate alternative: form your own nation and leave the USA.

"Over the past sixty years, America has become the strongest nation on earth economically speaking, although that is waning quite early in our history. Our military strength has been amply demonstrated around the world—no standing army can successfully oppose us. Instead, we face a man with a suitcase bomb or a civilian army in residential neighborhoods. No army in history can defeat such enemies, willing to sacrifice their lives in exchange for a few dozen of us. But far more important, America has always been the strongest nation on earth morally. Many would find that hard to believe, given the trash Hollywood and television puts out as everyday life, but it's true collectively, if not individually. We combine moral behavior with freedom of choice to a far greater extent than any other nation that has ever existed.

"Here is the simple fact: America, as we know her, cannot survive this secession movement. If that's the basis of our political position, then why, you might ask, has Montclair accepted your commission to moderate the seminar and help develop a governmental structure for the new nation? I can answer that distinctly, ladies and gentlemen: we didn't accept the commission to form the structure for a new nation. We came to help *you* examine the structure of our present nation, and see how we can apply it to our advantage. We are decidedly opposed to cradle-to-grave socialism. We are opposed to government in the state to which it has evolved. In that, we can agree. America is moving much too far in the wrong direction and removing freedom of choice in the process. That road leads to slavery.

"Montclair is conservative in philosophy. We *do* believe in free enterprise. We *are* opposed to the growth of government, excessive debt that even our grandchildren won't be able to repay. But we are also opposed to running away from America's troubles and finding our own little Utopia. For the sake of our discussion this morning, let's examine the facts. Two Americas, no matter how closely aligned and coordinated their intent, will quickly become disparate in philosophy. *One* American is already disparate. The president can barely achieve fifty-two per cent of the vote in a national election. That means almost half of the country did not want him . . . or her. Within twenty or thirty years, there will be *four*, if not *six* Americas, philosophically, if not legislatively.

"But if America were divided and no longer the strongest force for good on earth—and, by heaven, I hope we can all agree that America has consistently been the primary force for good in the world this past century—but if we surrendered that title, that obligation to our role in history, who would replace us. China? Russia? A Pan-Arab confederation with government by Sharia law? Would *any* of those nations have the best interest of the world as their primary goal? Would they reach out to protect their neighbor if they were in trouble? Or would they join the invaders and take control over yet another country?

"These are all global considerations. Those of you in the room, I dare say, have not given much thought, education, or concern to global issues. Replace America with *any* of those countries, and within fifty, probably twenty-five years, there wouldn't even be a history book to laud the twentieth-century efforts of the United States of America. We would have ceased to exist. And the Evil Empire would have won.

"You are all very young. Frankly, you're ignorant. You see America locally, not internationally. You see America's drift to the left, a more liberal society, taxation run rampant, a system of takers and givers, and each of you is tired of giving. I understand that. But consider this, ladies and gentlemen: you are all selfish."

Del Valle remained quiet for a long moment as the insult hung in the air.

"You ask, how can we be selfish when we are the *givers*? The ones who pay taxes. The ones *not* on welfare. The ones the takers look to for sustenance. I can answer that. The takers are easy to figure out. They're greedy. They're the ones de Tocqueville spoke about when he said America would fail economically when her citizens found out they could pay themselves from the public purse. But the givers are selfish because they believe that they've *earned* what they have through hard work, industry, free enterprise, smart thinking, and they want it all right now. How many of you live in a home nicer than your parents had? How many drive a 'name brand' car?

"Selfishness takes many forms. We constantly hear that America is actually a 'center right' country. If so, why do the left-leaning always turn out to put their candidates in office? I can answer that also—to assure their continued entitlement check. The 'givers', as we have called them this morning, are so engaged in pursuit of their personal fortune that they do not vote, they do not participate in community, they do not 'give' what the country needs, so we have elected people who will 'take' what they have and 'give' it to those who they promised to feed. Selfish? Yes, too damned concerned with 'self' to put in the time and effort necessary to keep the horde at bay.

"Don't misunderstand me. Individual industry is what created America and without it, America will fail as surely as it will if the secession is implemented. America has gone off the rails. As surely as the sun rises in the east and sets in the west, the fifty percent of citizens who pay tax cannot sustain the fifty percent of citizens who don't. But as greedy as those non-paying citizens might be, it's not totally their fault.

"Let me give you an example. If I said that if you would come and listen to me speak for thirty minutes every Saturday night, I would put one thousand dollars in your bank every Monday, how long would you come and listen? Forever, I would predict. Politicians have been promising everything to everyone for over one hundred years. It's the way to acquire public office. We call these people leaders. I call them loaders. Freeloaders. They take from you to give to them so they can stay in power, and then they claim to be benevolent. It's a shell game, and you provide the pea."

Del Valle ceased speaking and looked around the room, pausing to hold eye contact with each person in the room, nodding, smiling to ease the tense atmosphere and gauging the reaction.

"If you will give us three days, we will show you how to change America . . . the *United* States of America, the one and only nation in the history of the earth that guarantees, or used to guarantee, the right to teach correct principles. We must remain one nation. One nation dedicated to the core values established by our Founding Fathers. One nation standing as a beacon of light to the world. One nation under God.

"I said I would close with another Winston Churchill quote. What we are proposing to discuss these next several days is not really difficult. It closely follows, in my opinion, Churchill's greatest and most important quote: '*All the great things are simple, and many can be expressed in a single word: freedom, justice, honor, duty, mercy, hope.*'

"May God guide our hand in this endeavor."

Four days later, as Dan and Nicole waited at the Mazatlan airport for their Alaska Airlines flight to San Francisco, Dan received a text on his Blackberry from Joyce Jefferson.

President Snow has invited us to Camp David next Monday. Call this evening when you return. Joyce

Dan showed it to Nicole. "The plot thickens," he said.

"Or the first team has taken the field," she replied.

TWENTY-TWO

FRANKLIN COUNTY SHERIFF'S SUB-STATION
RICHLAND, WASHINGTON
MAY

Franklin County Sheriff's Lieutenant Rex Clinton departed the Richland Sub-Station where he had conducted his shift briefing, having advised the six deputy sheriff patrol officers of the operational orders for the upcoming twelve-hour patrol. At 6:20 PM on a cool May evening, he began to traverse his route, signaling his on-duty status with the joint dispatch center which controlled operations for the police and sheriff for the Tri-Cities area of Richland, Kennewick, and Pasco, Washington.

A few miles west of the Tri-Cities was the Department of Energy's Hanford Site, a nuclear research and waste disposal facility, one of the original sites from which the World War II Manhattan Project had derived some of its plutonium. The Hanover nuclear facility was on the government's critical watch list in the current crisis. Since the terrorist attacks had started, Lieutenant Clinton had made it a point to patrol the facility several times on each shift.

Four weeks earlier in Spokane, along with about two hundred law enforcement officers from the northwestern states, Clinton had attended a briefing by the Homeland Security Department. A man named Pádraig

Connor and several other personnel from HSD had spent the entire day informing the gathering of what little was known of the terrorists that now roamed America. Most of the law enforcement officers were unimpressed with the lack of intelligence and felt the federal government had done little to prevent the current situation. The further up the chain of command the police and sheriff's officers were, with some holding responsibility for budget considerations, the more mollified they were when Connor announced that the federal government would pick up the tab for overtime and extra patrols. At the end of the meeting, most left with a feeling of helplessness, having gained little actual information from which to formulate a plan of action.

The one bright spot on the horizon was the impact of the congressionally approved enhancements to the Patriot Act, which authorized search of suspicious persons without the need for reasonable cause—a long-standing requirement of liberals opposed to any authority for the police—and retention of those who were deemed persons of interest, both of which gave law enforcement a far broader ability to investigate. A detention period of 96 hours had been agreed to by the joint House and Senate Intelligence committee as part of the temporary revisions to the Patriot Act.

Taking up a favorite spot along State Highway 240, a strategic position which allowed observation of traffic flow near the entrance to the DOE Hanford Site facility, yet kept his cruiser out of public view, Lieutenant Clinton settled down to watch the evening commuter traffic heading west from the Tri-Cities. By eight, it was full dark, although the passing vehicles were required to traverse under a bright set of highway lamp posts placed near the entrance and were easily visible from his vantage point.

A muted gray Toyota Corolla with two men in the front seat drew no particular attention until the third time Clinton saw it. Using a pair of Zeis binoculars, he read the Oregon license plate number and ran a registration, bringing up a Budget Car Rental ownership. The two male occupants and the rental status brought to mind two of the criteria Homeland Security had listed as watch points.

When the vehicle appeared a fourth time about twenty minutes later, Clinton pulled out onto the highway and from a loose tail, followed it. He notified dispatch of his observation, citing the license number again, and maintained a distant vigil. After about ten minutes, the vehicle left the rural highway and headed up Highway 395 to the north, toward Spokane. Clinton did not pursue and gave it no further thought, returning to his normal evening routine.

At 1:15 AM, after four traffic violations, two drunken drivers, and a domestic dispute, Clinton met with two of his fellow officers at the local Denny's to break for dinner. Chicken fried steak, mashed potatoes, and corn, followed by a piece of German chocolate cake, completed the stop. Good-natured ribbing from his fellow officers regarding the amount of food he had consumed at dinner was not unusual, but was offset by the fact that he remained trim and fit at six feet, one inch, and 195 pounds, and had recently won, at the age of 41, the department-wide physical readiness profile which included five physical agility and endurance tests, plus a body fat analysis where he had scored less than 8 percent. As a result, Lieutenant Clinton was easily able to take such ribbing in good stead.

As the trio exited Denny's toward their respective patrol cars, Clinton glanced across the street at the 7-11 convenience store. Parked to the front of the building in the end slot, he saw the gray Toyota Corolla, the Oregon license plate matching his earlier query. The driver was in the car, but the other man was either in the store or using the restroom facility. Clinton quickly walked to his closest fellow officer's vehicle and motioned for the third officer to join them. He explained the situation, including the two matching profile issues, the vehicle's previous proximity to Hanford, and advised that he was going across the street to speak with the occupants of the vehicle, but that he was going to time it to coincide with the return of the passenger. He instructed the other two officers to pull around behind Denny's to take their patrol cars out of view and to watch as the situation developed.

Clinton pulled his vehicle into the entrance to the 7-11, holding place to the far right of the parking area, near the air pump and away from either the suspect vehicle or the several cars that were being fueled near the pump islands. Simultaneous with his arrival, the Toyota's passenger exited the convenience store, and Clinton could see that the man was startled by the sheriff's vehicle parked nearby. His step quickened toward the Toyota and he averted his eyes. In that instant, fifteen years of law enforcement instinct told Clinton that his suspicions were correct. Terrorist or not, the two individuals had reason to fear the law. Clinton stepped out of his vehicle and slowly approached the Toyota. Before he had taken three steps, the man who had exited the store ran around the front of his car, pulled a small caliber pistol, and fired a shot at Clinton, missing and hitting the patrol vehicle, shattering the windshield. Lieutenant Clinton retreated behind his driver's side door and pulled his primary weapon, a 9mm Glock. Careful not to fire and risk injury to someone inside the store, he held fire as the passenger quickly entered the car and the driver reversed out of the parking spot, tires squealing as they began to flee the area. Clinton stood, taking careful aim over the top of his driver's side door, and fired one round, striking the driver of the vehicle. The man slumped over the steering wheel and the Toyota impacted a Ford that was fueling at the nearest island. The passenger jumped out of the Toyota, gun in hand, and began to run for the darker area behind the 7-11, loosing off another wild shot toward Clinton. With a carefully aimed shot, Clinton brought the man down, causing him to drop his weapon, which went skidding along the pavement. Both sheriff's deputies arrived on the scene with their weapons at the ready, having run across the street. One of them kicked the assailant's weapon further from his hand and knelt down to place handcuffs on the prostrate man, who now was screaming in pain from his gunshot wound.

Clinton approached the driver's side of the Toyota, backed by Officer Talmadge, and slowly opened the door, observing the head wound of the driver. He reached in and felt for a carotid pulse.

"He's dead," Clinton reported to his two companions.

"This one took it in the shoulder, Lieutenant," the second officer said.

Two additional people existed the 7-11, and a small crowd of what Clinton had come to call 'night people,' because of their unusual dress and aberrant behavior, began to gather to see what had happened. Clinton returned to his vehicle and called dispatch, reporting the incident and calling for an ambulance. He then returned to the crashed vehicle and began to examine the interior, retrieving the keys from the ignition and opening the trunk, where he visually observed an assortment of small-arms weapons, including a rifle equipped with a scope. A box of flares and a plastic-wrapped block of what appeared to be individual lumps of clay were also visible. From prior training, Clinton recognized it as plastic explosive material. Lieutenant Clinton was careful not to disturb any of the physical evidence and assured that no one else had access to the subject vehicle.

Deputy Talmadge, at Clinton's direction, began to cordon off the area with yellow plastic crime scene tape and to initiate crowd control. Two additional sheriff's vehicles arrived, and a City of Richland police cruiser. Within thirty minutes, Augustus County Sheriff William Huntley was on the scene and assumed command. By 6:00 AM, the normal time for the end of Clinton's shift, two FBI agents from Spokane had arrived and assumed command and control from Sheriff Huntley. The wounded gunman had been taken to a nearby hospital, under armed guard, and was undergoing surgery as the FBI arrived on scene.

At 1:30 PM, Lieutenant Clinton was still on duty, having completed a debriefing with the FBI and was working on his written reports. Just after 2:00, an Air Force helicopter landed in the sheriff's sub-station parking area and General Pádraig Connor and Carlos Castro, dressed in civilian clothes with Homeland Security badges prominent, arrived on scene, having flown directly from Andrews AFB, Maryland, to Fairchild AFB, west of Spokane, where they transferred to an Air Force helicopter for the ride southwest to the Tri-Cities area.

Upon initial investigation, the dead suspect was unidentifiable but was assumed from his physical characteristics to be either an Indonesian or from the Philippines. From the documents found in the luggage in the vehicle, the wounded suspect was determined to be an American from the Seattle area.

The first break in the national tragedy had been obtained as a result of Franklin County Sheriff's Lieutenant, Rex Clinton, and his astute observation of the recurrent visits of the gray Toyota. The limited result of the investigation would prove that tracking the remaining terrorist teams was as difficult as General Austin had assumed, with one exception. The American terrorist had a Blackberry concealed among his luggage found at the Motel 6 where the two men had booked a room for the night. The Blackberry, with Internet history recorded internally, provided some clue as to the method of communication, but as quickly as the primary website was discovered, it had closed down.

PRESIDENTIAL RETREAT
CAMP DAVID, MARYLAND
JUNE

Neither Dan Rawlings nor Joyce Jefferson had ever been to Camp David, the presidential retreat in Maryland, a short helicopter flight from the White House. It was President Snow's second trip, the first having been Easter Sunday weekend when he had been interrupted by the events in Australia and the shootings at American baseball stadiums. His wife, Helen, had remained with her daughter and grandchildren, while President Snow had returned to immediately meet with Secretary Austin and the Trojan team.

Today's meeting was about the other war in America, the secessionist movement in the west. Following the president's briefing on the meeting in Mexico, provided by General Robert Del Valle, Snow was determined to make a further attempt to dissuade his former associate, Joyce Jefferson, and the younger legislator, Daniel Rawlings, from continuing down that path.

When Dan and Joyce entered the largest of the cabins, it was not a conference room at all, but set up in the form of a large living room, with couches, overstuffed leather chairs, and a homey atmosphere. Homey, if you didn't take into consideration the stern faces of those seated around the room. It was evident that the earlier meeting had been ongoing for some time before they arrived.

Dan recognized the principals in the room. In a large, brown leather chair with an ottoman to the side sat President William Snow. To his right, moving counter-clockwise around the room, was Secretary of Homeland Security, William Austin. Next sat General Pug Connor. The next person was personally unknown to Dan, but he recognized him as Patrick Collins, newly confirmed Secretary of Defense. Closest to Dan as they entered the room was his former National Guard commanding officer, Lieutenant General Robert Del Valle. Two empty chairs remained. President Snow motioned to the one on his left and smiled at Joyce Jefferson.

"Joyce, very glad you could join us. Have a seat, please," the president said. "Mr. Rawlings, have a seat beside Governor Jefferson. Welcome to Camp David. I think everyone knows everyone else. If not, we can get further acquainted during lunch break. We've been meeting since eight this morning. I have to return to Washington about three this afternoon, so we have a short time frame to reach some resolution of our differences, if, in fact that can be accomplished. Joyce, are you and Mr. Rawlings prepared to speak for your constituents? Your political allies, I mean, not the general public."

"Mr. President," Joyce replied, "as much as any single politician can speak for another, we have an understanding with those members of the coalition."

"Good, then let's get straight into it. I don't have time this morning for the niceties of diplomacy. American is at war, Joyce, pure and simple. We have armed conflict in the Middle East and we have roving bands of terrorists in middle America. I simply do not have time for a political insurrection at home. This whole secession thing started off as a complete and utter fraud and you know that. You, Mr. Rawlings, know it better than anyone else in this room. The supposed support for secession was fraudulent, the elections were bogus, and the perpetrators are all either dead or disbanded. Why the hell are we still dealing with it?"

Joyce Jefferson did not hesitate or equivocate. "Pure and simple, Mr. President, the public warmed to the idea and found it attractive. We were unable to get anyone east of the Mississippi to listen to our grievances. True, it may have started with a charade to get Senator Malcolm Turner re-elected against a younger, better-financed opponent, but the message he delivered began to take root."

"Did the message General Del Valle delivered in Mexico not give you pause, Mr. Rawlings? Did you not take his comments to heart?"

Dan appeared less willing to take on the president of the United States, but after a slight pause, he nonetheless spoke boldly. "Mr. President, I have complete respect for General Del Valle. His warning of possible harm to America as a result of our actions, was not taken lightly. But affording the general my respect does not mean I find myself in agreement with him on all counts."

"You've vacillated on this issue, haven't you, Mr. Rawlings?"

"No, sir. I believe in political parlance the term would be 'flip-flopped.' I have not returned to my earlier stance in opposition. Once my research—most of which came from the Montclair Advocacy, I might add—was completed, I gained a deeper understanding of just how far America has drifted, and continues to drift, from the original intentions of our Founding Fathers. Sir, I would say that *America* has vacillated. For half a century, devious politicians have found every opportunity to revise the meaning of our constitution in order to achieve their objectives, the primary one being retention of power. As a conservative, Mr. President, surely you understand that argument, even if you don't agree with it."

President Snow leaned forward in his chair, his face stern and unflinching. "What I agree with, Mr. Rawlings, is none of your concern. I represent the United States of America and part of our nation is in treasonous rebellion. Do *you* understand *that*? I would be fully within my rights to have both of you arrested. As a serving major in the United States Army, Mr. Rawlings, I could have you called to active duty and ship your ass to Greenland."

"Mr. President—" Joyce interrupted.

President Snow held up his hand for Joyce to remain silent. "What do you have to say, Mr. Rawlings?"

Dan paused again, glancing momentarily at General Del Valle. "Mr. President, Governor Jefferson and I came to this meeting at your request. I, personally, have left a written statement with my wife to be delivered to the press should I not return from this meeting. I have tried to place myself in your shoes, sir, but your words only serve to confirm the essence of our grievance against a dismissive administrative and legislative body that does not care what the public feels is right. You may indeed arrest me for treason, but the public trial that would ensue would not serve your interest, or that of our nation . . . or nations, as it were. As to my military status, I resigned my commission in the United States Army last August and accepted a commission in the California State Reserve, an independent militia under the authority of the governor of

California.

"Mr. President," Dan said, slowing his breathing and trying hard to soften his message, "we did not come here to be contentious. But we also did not come here to acquiesce to the demands of a government that has, to date, failed to listen to our heartfelt concerns. Do you think arresting Governor Jefferson or myself will ease that situation? Are you prepared to arrest and incarcerate every elected official west of the Mississippi who has taken up the banner of secession?"

President Snow took several deep breaths and settled against the back of his chair. "You're an arrogant bastard, Rawlings," he stated, his voice now calm and detached.

"Guilty, Mr. President. By no means do I intend to be disrespectful, but as I said regarding General Del Valle's advice, respect and agreement are not mutually inclusive. We disagree with Washington, Mr. President. We have had enough of roughshod legislation, judicial fiat, and liberal revision of America's long-standing principles. There *is* still room for reconciliation, and I'm certain Governor Jefferson would agree with me, but there is no room for retreat on our need to call a halt to the liberal move toward socialism. Certainly not all of the residents out west will agree with us. I think it will take a generation or more for families to decide where they want to live and under what banner. Eventually, we'll have a very divided nation, philosophically speaking. I wish that were not true, but it's increasingly obvious that the growing social divide in America cannot be surmounted by forced obedience to a liberal point of view. I am prepared to accept the outcome of the democratic process and let the electorate decide."

"Joyce," the president said, turning to his old associate, "are you in agreement with Mr. Rawlings?"

"One hundred percent, Mr. President. I could not have phrased it any more clearly. May I ask a question of our participants this morning?"

"Certainly," the president replied.

"Gentlemen, I will assume that you are all in agreement that what we are proposing out west is wrong. But can any one of you say that you do not agree with what we are *saying*? Are we wrong in our charges against the nature of intrusive political interference this past quarter century?"

Several of the men seated around the room looked to the president for response, but he remained quiet in his seat and slightly raised his hand in a gesture signifying approval for anyone who desired to do so, to speak.

Secretary Austin spoke first. "Governor Jefferson, I can't fault your logic. But simply put, the game isn't going your way, so you intend to pick up your marbles and go home. That's the coward's way out. The Montclair Advocacy, under General Del Valle's leadership, has initiated a most appealing campaign against secession, citing a failure of the American citizen to make the necessary changes. Apathy is the enemy of democracy, not judicial fiat. Individual greed is the cause behind liberal politicians being elected, not a failure of the system. America became complacent. Our people found it easier to take a hand-out from the government than to suffer through tough times. Once those running for office promised ice cream, people forgot about the nutritional value of cabbage soup. They forgot that ice cream melts, but cabbage soup sticks to your ribs. If your group puts as much effort into getting people to the polls as they are doing in moving this national divorce forward, you just might have an impact.

"Throw the bastards out, Governor. Find a couple of hundred truly honest men and women, stand them behind the pulpit, and throw the corrupt bastards out of office. If you go down this path, there will be the euphoria of change, of a brand new start, of resurrected principles, but once you open the door to this division, you will find many who are strongly opposed to the actions of your new federal government. But you'll have already opened the door. In twenty or thirty years, you'll have the Republic of Northwestern America splitting off from you. And on and on it will go. We already have the system in place in the Constitution. We just need to find the courage to use it again and to pull the plug on those who need to hang on to Mama's tit." Austin paused for a moment, a sheepish smile coming across his face. "My apology, Governor. A poor analogy and disrespectful."

Joyce Jefferson laughed. "Rather appropriate, I would say, Mr. Secretary. If only I thought we could cut through the morass of the *we only want to help the poor'* crap that flows like water in Washington under the guise of a caring, benevolent government, I'd have hope. But to date, nothing seems to be able to change the system and the drift away from who we were supposed to be. Every four years we vote for 'change and hope,' only to find out that we're further down the road to institutionalized economic slavery."

"What do your latest polls say, Joyce?" the president said.

"In six weeks, Mr. President, as the individual primaries occur throughout the west, and, notwithstanding the Montclair Advocacy's oppositional campaign, we are going to see an overwhelming approval in twenty-one of the twenty-three states who have the issue on the ballot. The other two are neck-and-neck. Are you willing to let the public decide this issue?"

"No, Joyce, I'm not. I'm going to pull out all the stops, short of military insertion, to bring a halt to this divorce. We just can't afford two Americas at this time in our history. Maybe we could never afford it. I'll throw a court-ordered injunction in every state court I can to stop this nonsense."

Joyce Jefferson stood her ground. "And *that* statement, Mr. President, is proof positive of what we are trying to say. The courts will vote their *political* beliefs, their *personal* values, not the constitutional principle. They will judicially decide whatever is required to retain their philosophy in power. The same with Congress, and the hell with the people who want it the other way."

"I understand your point, Joyce. You know I do. Still, I will retain our nation under one flag by any means at my disposal."

"Well, Mr. President, unless Mr. Rawlings and I are under arrest, I think it best that we leave it at that and return home."

The president remained quiet for several moments, then stood up, followed by all in the room. "Joyce," he said, smiling and stepping forward to reach out and hold her by both shoulders, "I admire you, as I always have. Your personal story is nothing short of astonishing. Your entire family history demonstrates what America stands for, despite the cruel way they were brought to our shores. I wish there were some way we could reach accord and end this marital spat."

"As do I, Mr. President."

Snow kissed her on the cheek and turned to Dan Rawlings. "Mr. Rawlings, you are still one arrogant bastard, but I admire your stance as well."

"Thank you, Mr. President. My grandfather, who was also a California legislator in the fifties and sixties, once told me a little story about arrogance. He was an enlisted man in World War II, in the Navy. He told me that the exact same characteristic in a human is seen differently in the military and also in politics. An officer with a strong opinion was generally seen as a self-confident individual, destined for higher office. An enlisted man who stood his ground was an arrogant son-of-a-bitch."

President Snow laughed loudly. "I know more officers than I do enlisted men, Mr. Rawlings, but I can tell you that's not true. Most of the officers I know are also arrogant bastards. Have a safe trip home. And gird your loins, son, because the full power and authority of the United States government is going to come down on you like a ton of bricks. And this time, General Del Valle is not going to arrive with the cavalry in the nick of time."

"That's what I'm afraid of, Mr. President."

Twenty-Three

HART SENATE OFFICE BUILDING
WASHINGTON, D.C.
JUNE

Two weeks following his first appearance before the Senate subcommittee on intelligence, General Austin was back at the witness table, accompanied by General Connor. He came at the invitation of Senator Culpepper after the two had determined this was a proper forum to address the contents of the draft Domestic Tranquility bill. Culpepper gaveled the meeting to order.

"Senators, Secretary Austin, General Connor, welcome this morning to our weekly committee meeting. The subject this morning, ladies and gentlemen, is Secretary Austin's summary analysis of the draft Domestic Tranquility proposal as put forth by Strategic Initiatives. We are also here to review the supporting analysis, recommending approval, prepared by General Wainscott, Deputy Chief of Staff of the Army. I provided Secretary Austin a copy of the proposal several weeks ago and have invited him to present his findings."

He paused for a moment, shuffling some papers on the table in front of him.

"Are there any initial questions or inquiries that need to be addressed before we turn the time over to Secretary Austin?"

On the far left end of the table, Senator Wright, Democrat from Arkansas, leaned forward and spoke into his microphone. "Mr. Chairman, I have a quick question, if you would indulge me."

"Certainly, Senator Wright. Please proceed."

"Mr. Secretary," Wright began, "in preparing for our hearing today, I read several of your earlier memos to this committee. My question this morning stems from that reading. You indicate that the State Department and diplomatic efforts will bear little fruit with these terrorists and those who support them. Could I ask you to further explain that statement?"

Secretary Austin looked toward Senator Wright and thought for just a moment. "Senator, do you believe in God?"

A startled look on his face, the senator responded. "What does my spiritual leaning have to do with my question, Mr. Secretary," he said, his voice now challenging.

"Everything, Senator. May I ask the question again? Do you believe in God? Any god?"

"Let's assume for the sake of our conversation that I do not. How would you answer the question?" Wright asked.

"Given the content of our meeting today, and the time frame, I'll try to provide a summary answer. Diplomats, including those in our State Department, believe that any two reasonable parties can sit down and find mutual agreement about some, if not all, of the issues on the table. Compromise is the result. But my theory about our current adversary varies from that premise. If the diplomat in question is not a man of faith, and by faith, I mean someone who believes in God, he will never understand this particular enemy. Our jihadist enemy is not seeking more land, more gold, or more power. He is seeking one thing: for every living human on earth to confess that Mohammed is the prophet and Islam is the only way to heaven. He will not compromise with us, or anyone, because, from his perspective, there is no compromise with God's commandments. God has told him to convert everyone to Islam or kill him. It doesn't matter if we believe that God said no such thing—the jihadist *does* believe it. No equivocation. A man, or a diplomat, who is not a man of faith will not understand that. It is not a logical or rational issue which can be negotiated. For that reason, diplomacy really doesn't matter, because our jihadist enemy is not seeking to compromise. Even another man of faith is doomed to failure because, again in the eyes of the jihadist, the other man's faith is misplaced. But at least another man of faith will *understand* the enemy, whereas someone who has no faith in God cannot."

Wright was silent for a moment, and then spoke. "Thank you, Mr. Secretary. That's all I have this morning. Thank you, Mr. Chairman."

"Are there any other questions for Secretary Austin before we begin? Hearing none, the floor is yours, Mr. Secretary."

Speaking without notes or prepared text, Austin took a drink of water and began. "Thank you, Mr. Chairman. Members of the committee, I offer my appreciation for your invitation this morning to present my thoughts on the proposal currently under review by this committee. My comments today are not in written form and are delivered to your committee '*in camera.*' They are not for publication, merely for consideration as you ponder the merits of this proposal. In addition, I would like to state initially that my thoughts will differ significantly from those of General Wainscott, who has recommended approval. However, I understand his position and his advocacy of this proposal. He is tasked with defending America, domestically and internationally. I cannot fault his position, but merely point out some of the inherent difficulties that would be associated with adoption of the SI proposal in its domestic application.

"Winston Churchill once said, '*America will always do the right thing, but only after exhausting all other options.*' I think we are once again in that position. We are sorting through the options and, hopefully, it will not take us too long, or be too late, when we finally arrive at the right decision. Another of history's leaders, closer to home, made more succinct remarks when he addressed the military's propensity to 'fight the last war' again. In 1961, President John Kennedy was preparing to establish the special operations force that became the famous Green Berets. He chastised the military leadership, reminding them that we faced '. . . *another type of war, new in its intensity, ancient in its origin— war by guerrillas, subversives, insurgents, assassins, war by ambush instead of combat, by infiltration instead of aggression, seeking victory by evading and exhausting the enemy instead of engaging him.*'

"Most military flag officers continue to prepare to fight the last war again. That is a well-known concept. The outstanding land battle victory in Iraq in 1991 and again in 2003 seemed to confirm the validity of that preparation, a fixed piece, open field army on army. However, in the latter example, we were absolutely unprepared for the insurgency that followed. That failure was uncalled for, since there was plenty of historical precedent. The French underground after German occupation, aided by the US and British Jedburgh teams. The Norwegian underground which worked with the British. They each were successful to the extent they were willing to have innocent civilians executed for their attacks.

"There isn't an army in the world that thinks it can stand up to the USA on the traditional battlefield. But they also know that we have no defense against one man and a suitcase bomb. With that premise, let me address the merits of the proposal before this committee.

"As a career military man only recently entering the political arena, I can see much merit in the proposal before the committee, especially in light of the roving band of terrorists ravaging America at present. Indeed, had some of the law enforcement retention authority been available to our troops in Iraq or Afghanistan, we might have made quicker strides."

Austin paused for a moment, looking briefly at Senator McKenzie, who was sitting on the far left of the dais.

"America is often accused of being populated by a soft, weak people. Granted, we do not foster the Spartan lifestyle. Few of us are in daily training for the Olympics. And we tend to be self-indulgent in peaceful times. Yet in every instance where America has been in peril, our young men, and now even our young women, have risen to the occasion. They have become tougher, more prepared, and equal to the challenge. They have learned, as my Marine associate, General Connor, has quoted on more than one occasion, that true toughness is more mental than physical. Our young people find the way to acquire that mental strength and to persevere.

"We have demonstrated in adequate historical example that we do not need to raise Hitler Youth from the cradle in order to have a strong defensive force. Yet our personal indulgence, as it is often called, is not prohibitive of strength. I will grant you that many in our society would prefer that someone else's son stand on the wall and protect us. Not all are willing to share the burden. But our volunteer military has proven that many accept their duty to America, despite the multiple combat tours they must endure to fill the requirement others have forsaken.

"Our people also know that if they disagree strongly enough with our national policies, they can throw all of you out of office at the next election. We usually don't," he chuckled," but we can if we so choose."

Senator Culpepper leaned forward in his seat and smiled at Austin. "We are glad this morning, Mr. Secretary, that your testimony is in closed session and will *not* be provided to the press," he quipped to laughter around the dais.

"Thank you, Senator. I was not, of course, speaking of anyone on this particularly astute and illustrious committee." More laughter.

"History is replete with authoritarian and permissive societies. Which ones have been successful and which have succumbed? As we might imagine, the answer is not all of one and none of the other. When foreign nations threaten the interest of the United States, many say diplomacy is the answer. 'Peace with Honor' in 1939 England resulted in World War II. Leninist and Stalinist Russia led to three quarters of a century of repression, fratricide, economic failure and eventual collapse. Hitlerian Germany brought the world to the brink of doom in search of the master race, nearly eliminating another culture they considered inferior.

"Most democratically minded governments, which are generally consensual and incremental in nature, are slow to confront an enemy, but, once aroused, they have been very successful in defeating them. And now the enemy has come to our shores. Since the end of the War of 1812, America has been fortunate to fight our enemies abroad, yet now we are faced with an invasion of terrorists. How do we deal with that? How shall we restrain these terrorists without reducing the freedoms our people enjoy? Are the restrictive measures curtailing personal freedoms that are contained in the proposal before you the answer? And where will Americans stand on this most monumental question? Those are the questions you have to decide."

"Mr. Chairman, might I ask Secretary Austin a question?" Senator McKenzie asked.

"Mr. Secretary, will you accept an interruption from Senator McKenzie?"

"Certainly, Mr. Chairman, with pleasure."

"Thank you, General Austin. Many of my colleagues in the Senate, beyond this committee, are concerned about the duration of these measures and how long the American people might be subjected to these restrictions. Do you have any advice for this committee as regards the longevity of our emergency and, perhaps more importantly, the proposed preventative measures?"

"Senator, that is the quintessential question, isn't it? Let me address the issue this way, given the confidentiality and non-public setting of the committee. In light of Senator McCain's 'hundred years' war' comment, and the attendant press ridicule, I hesitate to reveal my thoughts, but you are entitled to my honest opinion.

"In 1934, the Chinese communists, under the leadership of Mao, were all but defeated by the Nationalist government. They began an 8,000 mile retreat which took just over a year. It came to be called The Long March, and was the standard for sacrifice which Mao used to unify his people. General Mao saved his army and lived to triumph in history's greatest reversal of military defeat.

"I have begun to think of our war on terrorism as The Long War. Our citizens, including those on this committee, don't want to hear such talk. We want to win—tomorrow. But I firmly believe that there are children not yet in high school who will serve in Iraq, Iran, or Afghanistan. The citizens who will continue to fight this war, and to fund its expenditure, are not yet even born. Senator, this is not simply a battle with black and white victory. We are in a battle for our way of life. I believe in the depths of my soul that it is the battle of good and evil."

"That's a very depressing scenario, Mr. Secretary," Senator McKenzie said. "Do you see no light on the horizon, some way to counteract the longevity you describe? How can our citizens face up to the issues of our generation?"

"Now *that* is what I find depressing, Senator. This prognosis is *politically* unacceptable, not inaccurate. Our leaders cannot tell the public the truth. We tell them tomorrow will be fine. We've become a society of instant gratification. For many of our citizens, beyond next week, beyond *tomorrow*, is too long to wait for anything. When people shop, they don't ask, 'how much does it cost?' they ask, 'how much does it cost *per month?*' They want it *now*. The great French philosopher and parliamentarian, Alex de Tocqueville, said that a democratic America would likely fail from within, not through external conquest. By those words, he meant that our freedom, our liberal attitude toward the rights of the individual, would bring about our demise. Once the people found out they could vote themselves a constant income, that the public purse was open to politicians who promised its unequal distribution, the economy of such a society would fail. And how much better it is to buy what we want, and know that someone else will have to foot the bill. That someone else is our children, grandchildren, great-grandchildren. But inclusive in de Tocqueville's analysis was the right to expect freedom without restraint. Will the security measures contained in this proposal reverse that premise?

"Was de Tocqueville right? Or is Domestic Tranquility a total reversal of two hundred years of personal freedom which will abrogate the liberty ensured by the Constitution? These are the questions before this committee. At the core of my experience, I have come to believe one basic principle: there is no freedom without security, but conversely, there is no security without freedom. It is a dichotomy America has wrestled with since our Founding Fathers laid down the basic tenants of our nation."

Pug sat quietly to the general's right side, occasionally making eye contact with Rachel, but no expression of personal acquaintance was exchanged. She was taking notes, intently listening to General Austin. Senator McKenzie had been very understanding when Pug had called to advise that he would be unable to attend the wedding reception due to work commitments. As Secretary Austin had delivered his comments, Pug could see several of the senators nodding in agreement with the general, others more stoic and reserved in their visible response, reluctant to reveal their position.

Austin continued. "In preparation for this morning, I wrestled with presenting examples of history wherein one nation or another sacrificed either liberty or security in pursuit of peace. Many nations have felt the strongest military assured them of prosperity and invincibility, but a well-armed battalion is no match for two terrorists in a car with a rifle or a bomb. Other societies have determined that having *no* military assured them that the outside world would not see them as a threat, thereby eliminating the need for conquest. Both examples were right ... and wrong.

"America has had growing international influence since the end of World War I and has been a world power since World War II. We have often assumed the role of world policeman, trying to right the perceived wrongs of other governments, to impose our democratic values on sovereign nations. Bluntly stated, we have stuck our nose in where it was not wanted, even by those we were trying to protect. One persistent question of the day is whether or not democracy is acceptable in a region of the world where the law of Sharia—the religious law of the Koran—has been the way of life for centuries. Sharia is far more repressive of personal choice than the freedom American's enjoy, but to many, including millions of Americans not of the Islamic persuasion, the principles espoused under Sharia are preferable to the 'anything goes' law of a permissive society. As America has raced around the world seeking to impose our democracy, we have often resorted to doing so at the point of a gun.

"I began my military career in Vietnam. I know that hearts and minds are not won by force. By these statements, please do not misunderstand me. It's my opinion that America has brought far more good to the world this last century than they have bad. But we have not always been right. We have not always honored our commitment to our founders that we would be both honorable and benevolent. The fact that something is less repulsive than its alternative is not sufficient reason to choose either.

"Members of this committee will recall the words of a former president, Bill Clinton, when he addressed his party's national convention. He said '*we should lead the world by the power of example, not by the example of power.*' Strong words, motivational words, true words. Commensurate with that philosophy is the political concept bandied about by everyone who thinks diplomacy is the answer to everything. They shout, 'military might should be the last resort.' But inherent in that statement is the concept that military power *must* be a resort at some point or it loses its validity.

"So," he said, looking at each senator individually for one or two seconds, "where does that leave us in deciding the relative merits of Domestic Tranquility? I will leave you with these parting thoughts and then I am available for questions on specific aspects of the program. If Domestic Tranquility becomes the law of the land in America, our Constitution will become simply an historical document, its principles abrogated by the removal of the freedoms inherent in its overriding philosophy. There will be no retreat from that posture short of another revolution. A *domestic* revolution, I might add. And as we all know, we already have such a revolution brewing out west. Will we be strong against terrorism? Yes, to the extent that terrorists will find it much harder to enter America, circulate freely and terrorize our citizens. Will we be weaker? Yes, in the sense that step by step, innocent Americans will be detained for days, even weeks. Our citizens will be afraid to leave their homes, afraid to criticize the government, afraid to oppose policy. The next step would be the restriction of a free press on the grounds of national security. Everyone in this room knows that the media abuses their right to publish anything they find newsworthy. They have even degraded professional journalism to the point where they present their opinion as news. Yet, as distasteful as it has become, we must learn to live with that hypocrisy. America would not be a free country without a free press.

"I implore you to give strong consideration to the lasting implications contained in the basic philosophical change that this program will bring to America. Its ramifications will reverberate far beyond our shores. And do not delude yourselves into assuming that these changes are short-term, designed to counteract the *current* threat. They will become irreversible. They will become the American model. And they will change the America in which we each grew to maturity, free to change our residence, free to approach Congress and demand change, free to print articles critical of the government, free to live unencumbered by repression and restraint.

"I would add one more thought for your further consideration. What has been termed politically correct speech, to include tolerance for the views and actions of others, has expanded so far in our country that we are no longer able to speak out against values that are intrinsically opposed to those upon which our country was founded. We have gone from 'freedom of religion' to 'freedom *from* religion.' What were once core values are now unacceptable. We are not allowed to pray in school, post religious value statements in public places, observe religious symbols on public grounds. We cannot voice opposition to those whose views are so antithetical to the American notion of a free country that we allow the most abhorrent crime, the most egregious personal lifestyle, or the most restrictive philosophy to be presented as the norm. Our tolerance has devolved to the point where anyone can perform any aberrant act, but *no one* is allowed to say they don't like it. At the same time, we have allowed those same advocacy groups to demand elimination of speech which proposes the opposite point of view. Free speech is allowed *only* as it supports their point of view. And we, those of us in this room, the leaders of this nation, have not only tolerated such restrictive notions, we have advocated them ourselves, we have enacted them into legislation, forced obedience, dismantled programs deemed offensive, including supposed religious education, especially creation science, and required elimination of any reference to the Ten Commandments or God, all under the guise of tolerance and separation of church and state. Separate their requirements for adherence, by all means, but understand that you cannot separate one's belief from their actions simply because you want it so. The sky is blue, snow is white, the grass is green. It cannot be otherwise because you want it to be so. Congress seeks judges who have *no* demonstrable values so that they can opine objectively. We seek to eliminate them from consideration simply because they *have* values. How foolish have we become? And now we seek to implement Domestic Tranquility, which, if enacted, Senators, will be anything but tranquil.

"I thank you for your time this morning and the opportunity to speak to you on this critical issue. General Connor and I will be pleased to remain as long as required to answer your questions."

Twenty-Four

WHITE HOUSE OVAL OFFICE
WASHINGTON, D.C.
JUNE

Secretary of Homeland Security William Austin sat quietly as Marine General Pádraig 'Pug' Connor completed his briefing to the president of the United States and the newly confirmed Secretary of Defense, Patrick Collins. The meeting had lasted forty minutes and was about to break up, after which Pug had been invited for a family dinner in the White House residence, along with his brother, Scott, and Scott's wife, Megan.

"To summarize, Mr. President, the Australians have continued to have sporadic shootings, mostly at public venues, on the beaches, malls, and sporting events. The same thing has happened in England, but to a lesser degree. In the U.S., highway shootings have increased this past two weeks, but we consider that to be a passing phase, with other venues likely to be added. Some shootings have happened outside factory or industrial settings where people have been shot as thousands of workers leave at the end of their shift. Most of these have taken place in the parking lots. We have a confirmed death toll in America of 327, with over 600 additional wounded."

"And the first time we've gotten close to any of the perpetrators was this sheriff's incident in eastern Washington a week ago?" the president asked.

"Yes, sir," Pug responded. "The ABC, that's the joint western militia cover name for the American Brigade Command, claims to have killed several of the shooters, but all we can confirm from law enforcement is that in Wyoming, three illegal Mexican workers were hanged by unknown criminals. It has all the earmarks of the militia."

"So," the president said, "the only real thing we confirmed from the Richland arrest by the Sheriff's Department was that Americans are also involved in this terrorist activity and that the wandering teams have a website they can access to get the latest updates. And since these two caught in the Richland shootout with police have not reported in, they've closed that website and apparently moved to another one."

"Yes, sir," Pug nodded, "and we also know that they appear to be completely free to choose their targets or their method of operation. It's much as we discussed that first night when General Austin assembled Trojan after the opening gambit at the baseball stadiums. Communication is not essential. The teams are all expendable, it appears, and act independently. They have demonstrated no command and control procedure."

"It would appear, General Connor, that they don't really need one. Where do you go from here, Mr. Secretary?" the president asked, turning his attention to Austin.

"We're only getting bits and pieces, Mr. President, but we're not as ignorant as we were several weeks ago. As you know from your daily reports and the news broadcasts, these guys claim everything they do as part of the World Jihad movement. The recent shootings along a several-hundred-mile corridor of I-70, from St. Louis to Denver, killing nine, wounding three more, and resulting in a seven-car pileup outside Salina, Kansas, had to have been coordinated, at least part of the overall plan. NSA is checking every new website added to the World Wide Web in the past thirty days. That would be millions, by the way, but they can at least sort them by creation date. We'll keep working on it, Mr. President. We also need to get a closer look at the militia action. That has the potential to become almost as dangerous as the actual terrorists, since they are not as discerning about their targets as our police officials."

President Snow stood up, coming around to the front of his desk. "Thank you all for coming. I've got a quick meeting—hopefully it will be quick—with the Speaker of the House. I suspect we will gather again in the immediate future. Any updates, please, each of you keep the others informed."

The small cluster of men began to leave the Oval Office and the president walked besides Pug, speaking quietly. "I'll see you upstairs, Pug. I think your brother and my daughter have already arrived. Helen invited Senator McKenzie also, perhaps just to round out the numbers, or maybe it's her way of getting you two acquainted." He smiled.

Pug nodded. "Thank you, Mr. President. I've got a few sisters-in-law on the same wavelength. I dodge them all the time."

"I understand." The president laughed. "Helen is just like them, I'm sure. They can't stand to see a good man stay single."

By the time President William Snow arrived at the First Family residential quarters, the First Lady, Helen Snow, had everyone seated around the dinner table. Scott and Megan Connor, their three children, Alicia, fourteen, Morgan, eight and baby Bill, named after his presidential grandfather. Also in attendance were Pug Connor and Han Chou Lee, President and CEO of Teak Wood Products, a large Taiwanese furniture export company headquartered in Kaohsiung. Seated directly across from Pug sat Senator Rachel McKenzie, looking radiant in a burnt orange pantsuit, and a crème-colored blouse.

The meal was just about to be served when the president arrived. He circled the table, kissing his wife on the cheek, ruffling young Ted's hair and also kissing his daughter, Megan, and his granddaughter, Alicia.

"I offer my apologies to everyone. Lee, *nee how*," he said in Mandarin Chinese, "thank you for coming on such short notice, but when I heard you were going to be in town and leaving so quickly, tonight was my only opportunity to invite you."

"Thank you, Mr. President. I'm honored to be in your home, especially with your family," the elderly Chinese man said.

President Snow took his seat at the head of the table and unfolded his napkin, then the waiter began to serve the first course. "For those of you who don't know Lee, he's the president and founder of an international furniture export company in Taiwan. Our association dates from the late seventies when I represented his firm on their purchase of a large warehousing facility in Phoenix. After we closed the deal, he invited me to vacation with him in Kaohsiung, in southern Taiwan. It's a beautiful country. We've maintained contact ever since. He's here at the direction of the Taiwanese government on business with the State Department. I'm honored to have him here tonight. Unfortunately, he has to leave directly after dinner to catch a flight back to Taiwan. Lee, you need to let me know a bit sooner the next time you're coming to Washington. You're the only one I would be willing to practice my Mandarin on without feeling foolish."

"Once again, I am honored, Mr. President," Lee replied. The elderly Chinese man spoke excellent English, but with a slight British accent.

The president turned his attention to his other guest. "Rachel, very nice of you to come also. Is the Senate keeping you busy?"

"As a freshman senator, they keep me confused *and* busy, Mr. President," she responded.

"Get used to it." He laughed. "Lee, do you remember the Chen family? They owned the small electronics store in Tsoying and contracted with the American military servicemen to buy their appliances when they rotated back to the states?'

"Yes, of course. Wonderful people. They still live in Kaohsiung."

"I feel sort of like them now," President Snow said. "I'm the guy who lives *above* the shop."

Lee chuckled and nodded his head, pausing to take a drink of water. "I suppose that's right, Mr. President. An honorable Chinese tradition."

President Snow shook his head from side to side. "Does everyone think that just for dinner, they could call me Bill? I'd be very grateful for just a moment to be *out* of the office and *above* the shop."

"Can I still call you Grandpa?" Alicia asked, a glint in her eye, confirming she'd been paying attention to the grown-up talk.

"My little darling, you can call me anything you want, as long as you sit in my lap and hug my neck every time you come to visit. I know you're fourteen, but you'll never be too old to sit in my lap," he said, smiling at his granddaughter.

After the dessert round of coconut custard had been served and consumed, Helen Snow stood and moved toward the doorway. "Grandma is headed for the theater downstairs, where, as I am told, the pre-release version of *Far World: Fire Keep* is just waiting for some children to come and see it. I also understand that we have the choice of snow cones or popcorn, or both. Do I have any takers?"

Both children jumped up immediately and ran to join Grandma as she walked toward the door. "Oh, Grandma, my school friends will be *so* jealous. *Fire Keep*'s not even in the movies yet. I can't believe it," Alicia cried.

"Count me in too, Mom," Megan said, "I have a feeling Dad is going to bore Pug and Rachel to death with more business. If it's a question of watching Scott Savage's creatures save the universe, or Dad's political discussion, well, just count me in the movie group. Dad may have joked about being the "man above the shop," but he meant every word of it. When he's awake, the *shop* is open. Scott," she said to her husband, "movies or politics?"

"Movies for me too, Megan. My contribution to politics was fulfilled when I voted for your father. Good luck, Pug," he said to his brother.

The president said his goodbyes to Lee as the elderly gentleman left with a Secret Service escort to drive him to the airport. Then President Snow, Pug, and Rachel moved into the living area and took seats around the fireplace, which in the advent of warmer weather had been filled with a beautiful bouquet of flowers.

"I asked Helen to take the kids downstairs so we could have a bit of time to discuss a few things. Not a strategy session, of course, but the three of us are going to become increasingly involved in the decisions about how to proceed. I also wanted to ask you, Rachel, about the proposal that has come before your intelligence sub-committee, specifically Domestic Tranquility. The SI proposal to beef up our private security options throughout America. Pug, have you had a chance to read that proposal?"

"Yes, sir. General Austin was given a copy by Senator Culpepper the day we visited in his office. Absolutely astonishing, especially the measures suggested if we need to reach Phase III. Basically, it calls for the suspension of habeas corpus, elimination of a citizens' right to an attorney for anyone whom they see fit to detain, *without criminal charge*, for seven days. For all intents and purposes, they're proposing a police state."

"Exactly. That's my understanding as well. Rachel, how does the committee see it?"

"Mr. President—"

"Nope, it's Bill for this evening, Rachel."

She smiled briefly and nodded. "Not part of my protocol training, Bill. How does my committee see it, you ask? I'm sorry to report that this piece of Gestapo legislation has garnered more support than I would have thought. There are many who feel it's justified in light of the attacks on our people in public places. Oh, they voice concern about suspension of rights, constitutional privileges, etcetera, but they end up affirming support, certainly for the early phases which are not quite so restrictive."

" How do *you* see it, Rachel?"

Senator McKenzie was quiet for several moments, looking for some seconds toward Pug and then turning back to the president. "Sir, I've not been very popular in my opposition. I fear that if I'm too vocal, I'll lose credibility, and be of no use to you or those who oppose this police state action."

"I understand that, Rachel, but if everyone who opposes it takes that cautionary position, it will simply slip through. Who are the major proponents?"

"Senator Culpepper for one, although I sometimes think he is playing a devil's advocate role, trying to extract the thinking of the others."

Pug interjected. "Rachel, when General Austin and I met with Senator Culpepper in his office the day we appeared before your committee, he was much more negative about the SI proposal. That was why he gave it to the general to review. He voiced skepticism, but said he needed to take a supportive position publicly to ensure he was approachable by the SI principals. Either way, he can talk to people from both sides of the argument. And of course, sir, the message he had me deliver to you the other day reveals his thinking."

"Maybe it does, Pug, maybe not. It wouldn't be beyond him to try to stand me against this so he had an adversary to challenge. And avoiding publicly revealing his position is his standard political ploy," the president said. "Senator Culpepper is a master at playing his cards close to the chest. I don't think we'll know where he truly stands until the proposal is brought to a vote. Maybe not even then. If he's certain it will pass the full Senate, then he would probably vote for it just to shield his opposition and curry favors from the other supporters."

Rachel continued. "There's a new wrinkle to the proposal, Mr. . . . Bill. It was discussed today, actually. John Harford, president of SI, testified before our committee in closed session, and while I can't divulge the content of that meeting, I *can* say he proposed that SI demonstrate some of the security measures live, in a multi-city pilot program. He suggested that they implement the program in two or three local areas, cities with a large military presence and therefore potential targets. He said some of these attacks have been directed at such places because it heightens the public's perception that even our military can't protect itself. Several people who were shot, as you know, were soldiers or civilian contractors working on military bases. They've even killed two CIA analysts while they were driving to work in Langley. Harford suggested a pilot program in San Antonio, Colorado Springs, and the environs of Washington D.C."

"What is he proposing, Rachel?" Pug asked.

"Marked and unmarked vehicles, aerial drones with visual—but not attack—capability, mobile command and control vehicles in semi-articulated trucks, uniformed and *armed* guards in the malls, at public sporting events, and a list of smaller measures," she replied. "The committee reacted very favorably."

"I guess we can be grateful he didn't ask for Hellfire missiles on the drones. Who else testified?" the president asked.

"General Wainscott, Army Deputy Chief of Staff, who recommended approval of the proposal. He's the one who wrote the Army's position paper on the inability of National Guard troops to meet this kind of domestic police challenge, constitutionally and manpower-wise. At least, on a long-term basis."

The president made a note on a small pad by the side of his chair. "Pug, does Secretary Austin have a position on this SI proposal?"

"Sir, as a career military man, General Austin can see merit to much of what is proposed, but he drew a clear distinction between governing an occupied country after a war and governing a democracy within our domestic borders. Security measures for the former are not conducive to the freedoms inherent in the latter. He said this is more than the proverbial slippery slope. He thinks implementation of such a program will never be able to be reversed. If we add legislative revision to the measures undertaken, essentially suspending constitutional rights, the Constitution will die a natural death, or so he thinks, and will never be recovered. I would suggest you speak with him yourself, sir. For all the protection it might afford, the measures proposed will curtail innocent citizens from enjoying their freedoms."

"I understand," President Snow said, nodding and making another note. "I think I need to have another meeting with Admiral Barrington, Secretary Austin, yourself, and a couple of the House and Senate leaders, and perhaps even Senator Culpepper, to draw the old fox out. Rachel, when is your committee's next meeting?"

"Day after tomorrow, Mr. President."

Snow smiled, stood up and stretched his arms above his head. "I think perhaps I should consider a joint House and Senate fact-finding committee, with a couple of military minds and even Homeland Security personnel assigned to participate. I see two people who could serve and have my full confidence," he said, smiling at both Rachel and Pug.

"Mr. President—" Rachel began when the president raised his hand to stop her.

"No, Senator, I think it's a good idea, and I'll request implementation this week. But now that we've reverted to 'Mr. President,' I think it's time for a snow cone and to see if *Far World* is any safer than Earth. You both coming downstairs with me?"

Rachel and Pug rose from their chairs, Rachel speaking first. "Mr. President, I have an early meeting on the Hill in the morning. If I might beg off, I came here straight from the office tonight, so I think I'll catch a taxi and head home. I have to read the background material before closing my eyes tonight, although the stimulating reading material in this farm subsidy package might just accomplish both objectives."

"I'm heading toward Reston, Rachel. May I offer you a ride home?" Pug said.

Rachel thought for a moment, gathered her purse, and replied. "I live near Mclean, just off the George Washington Parkway, so not too far away. I appreciate the offer, Pug, and I'll take you up on it."

The president headed for the door. "Well, then, thank you both for coming tonight. I hope we get a chance to do it again," he said.

As they exited the room, Rachel in the lead, President Snow winked at Pug and whispered in his ear. "I'll tell Helen she can be proud of you. No motherly interference necessary."

Twenty minutes later, pulling off the Parkway toward Rachel's home, general discussion about Pug's brother's and younger sister having filled the journey, Pug stared at Rachel for several long moments as they waited at an intersection.

"Maybe we could do this sometime on our own, have dinner, I mean, without chaperones."

Rachel didn't respond immediately, reaching in her purse for her cell phone. She keyed a Speed Dial number and then closed the phone. The stop light had turned green and Pug was underway again.

"Just turning on my house lights and the outside security lights," she said.

"Wow, a high-tech woman."

"No, just a single woman living alone in a dangerous city," she said. "Besides, America is under attack, or haven't you heard? Turn left at the next light, then right on Patrick Henry Lane. Third house on the right."

Pug followed as directed and pulled up in Rachel's driveway, shutting off his engine. "Beautiful view of the Potomac," he said, admiring her home. "About that dinner on our own sometime," he repeated.

Rachel turned to face him and leaned against the car door, her face intense, focused on his, but her eyes warm and inviting.

"I don't think we should go down that road."

"What road?" Pug replied.

A slight grin crossed Rachel's face, but she didn't immediately respond, causing Pug to anxiously shift in his seat. "We're not twenty-two-year-old college students, Pug. You know what road I'm talking about, so drop the gamesmanship, please."

He laughed softly, nodding his head. "Okay, consider me duly chastened. May I ask why not? Is there someone you're currently dating?"

She ignored the second question. "I like you, Pug. That's why not."

"Reverse logic?"

"Not at all. Basic female logic. I do like you. I really like you, and I can see that you like me. I *could* say I don't date younger men," she said, a broader smile crossing her face.

"Forty-two and forty-four does not place me in the category of a Toy Boy," he said.

Rachel laughed out loud. "I guess not. It would appear that we've both done our homework on the other's biography. And it's forty-*three*, not forty-four."

"Guilty again. I looked up Senator Rachel Ann McKenzie's congressional stats and life history. I'm assuming you've done the same. But am I entitled to any other explanation? I mean, let's face it. Two single people our age, both educated, both involved in government, favorable toward the military, involved in similar political issues—at least, at present. What are the odds that we could find someone else who had the same values, same interests, card-carrying conservatives, so to speak."

"Very low odds, I would say, Pug."

"And you say you like me."

"Yes, I do, and that is exactly why I don't want to go down this road."

Pug shook his head. "You told the president that the Senate confused *you*. I can only imagine what *you* do to *them*," he responded.

Again, silence for several moments. Then, "Okay, here it is in a nutshell, General Connor. My father was an Air Force pilot who was killed in aerial combat in Vietnam before my second birthday. My husband was a National Guard company commander and was killed, also in combat, in Afghanistan just over five years ago. Now, I've just met another military guy who is a Marine general with an outstanding combat record with a Bronze Star *and* a Navy Cross for covert actions that are not public information. While that makes you a brave and competent officer, a leader of men from your peer's perspective, and the nation has expressed its gratitude, it makes you a poor risk for a romantic relationship with a woman who has more than paid her dues to America. Is that clear enough?"

Pug stared into Rachel's eyes, holding his tongue, absorbing the rhetoric she had just delivered. She had succinctly confirmed everything General Austin had told him that day in the Capitol. Her face was stoic and her demeanor quite serious.

"A *romantic* relationship, you say? That sounds good to me, Senator," he said, keeping a straight face.

After about ten seconds of silence, both of them started laughing out loud.

"Why don't we just start with dinner sometime, Rachel? Sometime soon. Maybe I chew nosily, or pick my teeth. Maybe I'll make you share the bill. You may not want to go down that road because it's full of pot holes, not because the destination is unclear. . . or dangerous. Maybe I just want recreational sex. Maybe *you* just want recreational sex. Let's not jump to conclusions too soon."

"Goodnight, Pug," she said, opening the car door. "Thank you for a lovely evening and a ride home. See you . . . when I see you," she said. "It sounds as if the president is going to put us in the same room together rather quickly. And I think we'll both be too busy for *any* recreation."

"Goodnight, Rachel. And by the way, I like you too, Senator," he said.

TWENTY-FIVE

OFFICE OF STRATEGIC INITIATIVES
WASHINGTON D.C.
JUNE

"I want that pilot program approved now, General, not next month or next week. *Now!*"

"I understand, Mr. Harford. I make the final presentation to Senator Culpepper's sub-committee tomorrow. I see no reason for delay. I can assure you, we'll get it done. I already have assets in the 4th Army command at Fort Sam Houston ready to implement. San Antonio will be the Army's staging area for the pilot."

"The Army is in a supporting role, *not* the primary agency. Remember that. A lot's riding on this, General Wainscott. I'm sure you understand. If we can prove the merits of our surveillance techniques in San Antonio, Colorado Springs, and even here in D.C., then the program will go national. I need experienced men to command that program. You're about to retire and I'm counting on you to fill one of those roles. Do we understand each other?"

"We do, sir. Just leave it to me."

Harcourt rose and started to walk toward the door of his office, a signal that the meeting was over. "Call me the minute the meeting ends and I'll get things started. Remember, your Army cohorts are in an observation role only, to report on the results. By your own comments, this is not a program for the Army or the National Guard. I'll take care of the tactical implementation. SI has that covered."

"I understand. I'll call you tomorrow," the general said, departing Harford's office.

Several seconds after Wainscott left, a side door opened and another man entered without comment. Harford looked at him briefly and returned to his seat behind the desk. The man assumed the seat occupied moments earlier by General Wainscott.

"It would seem that your time has come, my Irish friend," Harford said. "Did you ever envision the day when you would ply your trade on American soil?"

At five ten, with reddish-brown, thick hair, and a skin darkened by years of outdoor living, the new visitor to Harford's office did not present the appearance of an accountant or any other business professional.

"I did, John. It's not the first time I've been here on . . . business. I could see it coming as far back as 9/11. Those conspiracy fools who blamed their own government for those actions have only made it easier. And you certainly had that general dancing on a string."

"The world's a funny place, Devlin. If I had stayed in the Army, I would have been a lieutenant colonel or perhaps a full bird, but I would also have been getting Wainscott's coffee. Now, a four-star general is sitting in that chair, saying 'yes, sir,' and kissing my ass."

"Grab it by the bollocks, my pa used to say. When do we commence operations?"

"Saturday, if all goes well tomorrow in the closed Senate committee meeting. Wainscott will testify and call me after the vote. Have you lined up both operations?"

"Six men in Kansas City, random shootings at the mall, followed within an hour by a half-pound of Semtex in four separate locations at the Marriott, including the lobby. There's a convention of city managers who will be in the adjacent grand ballroom. Our actions will be successful, barring an unexpected law enforcement presence or unusually alert hotel security. This attack will cause international news, John."

"That's what we're counting on."

"Some four hours later, with your pilot program already operative, the unmanned aerial surveillance over San Antonio will spot a suspicious van, and quick response alert forces manned by SI Troopers will capture or kill the six men inside as they attempt to initiate random shootings along the River Walk, thereby proving the merit of close surveillance. The attacking force in San Antonio is expendable, John. Primarily Middle Eastern, all with Muslim ties. Most, if not all of them, will die in the ensuing firefight with our security forces on the ground. The resident commander will see to that. I've worked with him before and he understands the importance of succeeding based on the intelligence I'll provide."

Harford nodded. "Better if they're all dead, Devlin. And by the following week, with media coverage rampant and legislative demand growing, the pilot program will be expanded to several hundred cities across the nation as quickly as we can gear up. How much do your 'terrorists' in San Antonio know? And the Troopers, especially the team leader?"

Devlin Hegarty smiled. "They know where San Antonio is, John. Nothing more."

It was John Harford's turn to smile.

To the untrained eye, Devlin Hegarty would have appeared to be nothing more than a rugged-appearing businessman in an Armani suit. But beneath the tailored cloth, the fifty-four-year-old former IRA bomber had maintained the physical fitness of an Olympian. To the practiced eye, his face betrayed even more. His piercing eyes, beneath the reassuring nature of their deep blue, were hard and unflinching, reflective of years of close-in work during the heyday of IRA action in Northern Ireland. Those days were over, but despite the growing peace accords in Ireland, Hegarty had found ample work throughout the world. It had not taken him long to discover that there was never a lack of would-be leaders who thought that the opposition, or in some cases, the incumbent government, needed to change. Working alone for the most part, he occasionally tapped into the netherworld of mercenaries and soldiers of fortune as he had on this occasion for John Harford. Hegarty had been on SI's black ops payroll on many occasions over the past decade, and John Harford had learned to trust the man, at least to the extent that Harford trusted anyone.

"Well," Harford said, "get your field teams in place and I'll give the word by Thursday afternoon at the latest. This is only the start, Devlin. We have a lot to do these next few months to prove the success of our internal security program."

"Do you want the rovers to continue?"

"I do. These impromptu shootings around the nation have succeeded beyond my expectations, instilling fear in every locale they visit. Retail sales are down nationwide, high school sports are poorly attended, if not cancelled. Politicians and law enforcement are impotent. We don't want to ease the pressure in the rest of the country. How many teams do you still have operating?"

"Forty-three two-man teams, at last count. Two have not reported in for over 48 hours, but that's not unusual. They're both in remote areas of Nevada or Arizona."

"What about the team captured in Richland, Washington?" Harford asked.

"One's dead, of course, and the other knows nothing. In fact, he was a last-minute recruit, brought along by his brother. I didn't put them together for this exact reason. If he'd been with his brother and the older man had been killed, the young kid might have talked, at least as much as he knew and his brother might have told him more than he needed to know."

"*Will* he talk?"

"Of course. He's just a teenager and scared. But he knows nothing except that his brother is also part of the operation. That will give Homeland Security something to think about. Two Muslim Americans, not just Middle-Eastern infiltrators. Most of them have ethnic ties to the Middle East, but they were born here. The American intelligence agencies must be very confused by now, and the politicians who know the latest facts will be reluctant to admit to the public that their own people are perpetrating these shootings."

"He'll certainly tell them how you communicate," Harford said.

"Probably, but they already knew we'd use e-mail or the Internet. Don't worry, John, we're safe."

"Well, keep them operating, and as soon as July arrives, start the forest fires in the Northwest, moving east to North Dakota. We'll move into Oregon and California in mid-July. Just be sure the media continues to receive notice that World Jihad is taking credit for the actions. And have some World Jihad material in the car with the San Antonio terrorists. They're a mix of Arab and American, right?"

Hegarty rose and nodded. "Mostly Arab, just as you directed. And nothing will show success better than dead terrorists *before* they commence operations, right?"

"Exactly."

"One more thing, Devlin. In a few weeks, after these two operations, I want you to scout out the federal prison facility near Chicago where they house the terrorists that were moved from Guantanamo. See if you can find a vulnerability."

"For a prison break?"

"Perhaps, but more for a snatch during transfer. There's someone in there who will be brought to court. I want him free . . . or dead."

"I'll look into it," Devlin replied.

HART SENATE OFFICE BUILDING
WASHINGTON D.C.
JUNE

With General Austin at a western European security conference in Brussels, Pug Connor attended the Senate intelligence committee hearing in his place, specifically invited by Senator Culpepper. The subcommittee was comprised of only eight bi-partisan senators, including Rachel McKenzie. Pug and two other non-committee members, both on General Wainscott's staff, made up the limited audience. Army Deputy Chief of Staff General Wainscott was the only witness seated at the forward table prepared for his presentation.

Senator Culpepper gaveled the meeting to order. "Welcome, General Wainscott. The committee members have reviewed your presentation report and are prepared this morning to hear final argument on the implementation of the pilot program in the selected cities. Are you convinced, General, that this is the appropriate way to increase security for Americans?"

"I am, Mr. Chairman. The Army has always fought—and won—America's overseas conflicts. On home ground, it's quite different. It's paramount that we find a method to detect and capture these terrorists, preferably before they attack. A para-military force, bridging the gap between military and law enforcement, is the answer. Americans have suffered enough, from the Army's point of view, and we need to end this chaos."

"You'll find no disagreement on that score, General. However," the older senator said, "We must not forget the liberties that our people take for granted. This pilot program does not include expansion of the Patriot Act, nor does it permit unrestricted detention of citizens as requested in SI's proposal. Those components of the full program are still under debate. Do you understand those restrictions?"

"We do, Senator."

"The Senate will not condone increasing our security at the expense of freedom for our residents or the terrorists will have won."

"Senator, it's a thin line we walk, for both the Army, who has been called upon to provide internal security, and law enforcement officers in these communities. In order to protect our citizens, the people are going to have to accept some inconvenience. I for one would sacrifice some of my freedom to assure that my family could live and move about more safely. Haven't we already done that in our airports, in our federal, state, and local government buildings where we now have metal detectors and personal search criteria? Domestic Tranquility has been designed to increase our safety with the least measure of intrusion into our daily lives. Most people will never even notice the aerial camera surveillance the same way we drive through an intersection or visit a bank and never even think about the cameras recording our presence. Think about it, Senator, when did you last consider that your picture was being taken every time you came through the halls of Congress, visited an ATM, walked through a metal detector or entered your bank lobby? We take it for granted now, when once it was non-existent. The White House was open to the public every Wednesday for cheese-tasting during Andrew Jackson's presidency. Could we do that today? No, Senator, we have to deal with our times in the most secure, yet non-invasive way. Domestic

Tranquility is designed for just that purpose."

"And presuming we move to the next phase, how do you defend the arrest and detention or suspension of habeas corpus without legal assistance?"

General Wainscott nodded his understanding of the question. "An unfortunate departure from our history, Senator, but not unwarranted. The pilot program will show the merit of the proposal. It's a rare law enforcement officer who would use the arrest power beyond its intended scope. These men and women are dedicated to our safety. You personally have met with principals of Strategic Initiatives. You know they have America's best interest at heart. John Harford is dedicated to protecting America, as is the United States Army. I'm only sorry that for the first time in my career, we have to do so on our home shores. I recommend that we give Strategic Initiatives a chance to prove their mettle, to show how they can increase our security and enable us to practice the freedom we've come to expect."

The questioning went around the dais with several senators, those who had already determined their vote, conceding their question time to other committee members.

"Mr. Chairman," Senator McKenzie said from her seat, three positions to the left of Senator Culpepper, "may I have a few moments for questions?"

"Certainly, Senator McKenzie. The floor is yours."

"Thank you, Mr. Chairman. General Wainscott, I read your endorsement of the Strategic Initiatives proposal for Domestic Tranquility over the past several days. Several points come to mind, but the one that concerns me the most is the lack of a sunset clause, or an end-result timetable. Can you please explain the anticipated duration of these extreme measures and how long our citizens can expect to have to live under these restrictions?"

From his seat several rows behind the table at which General Wainscott was sitting, Pug smiled to himself, knowing full well that Rachel was plucking at straws. Approval for the pilot program was a done deal. She had told him as much when he had dropped in to her office shortly before the meeting to invite her to lunch. To his surprise, she had readily accepted. She just wanted the general to go on record as having voiced his support for a program that had no end date. She had even acknowledged to Pug that it was unfair to ask the question, given the nature of the emergency and the intelligence community's complete inability to estimate the duration of the attacks perpetrated by the mobile bands of shooters that the press had dubbed The Wild Bunch.

"Senator McKenzie, I can appreciate your hesitancy to vote for a program that has restrictive components which will affect our citizens without full awareness of the duration, but I also know that you understand the nature of our enemy. He is relentless and does not seem to work on a timetable. The fact that the enemy is comprised to some degree of native-born Americans who have attacked their fellow citizens only exacerbates the situation. For all we know, these shooters have been directed to kill Americans until they themselves are killed or captured. This program will help to bring that about. As to the end date for the pilot program, in all candor, I would hope for the opposite. I would hope, would predict, actually, that this pilot will succeed and the program will be expanded. A successful demonstration of intervention should allow this committee to recommend expansion throughout America until we have eradicated these vermin."

Rachel McKenzie pushed her point. "Then, General, you are saying that the Army expects this program to become standard practice in our nation, with all citizens required to adhere to its tenants? To be subject to search and seizure, detention and interrogation, all without benefit of counsel?"

"As abhorrent as that seems at present, I'm afraid so, Senator. With proper precautions, of course. As I stated earlier, I cannot envision law enforcement officers using the right to detain citizens unless they have just cause. We are not seeking a totalitarian state or the overriding authoritarian nature of some of the repressive governments of history."

"And the security guards who will be far less trained than our career law enforcement officers?" she asked. "Who will assure they exercise their authority judiciously? Who will control their actions?"

"An excellent question, Senator. You are correct that most of the Domestic Tranquility personnel will be new to the field and will require close supervision. We have anticipated that aspect and have prepared for it with trained personnel in leadership positions. As in the Army, the strong middle management, our experienced NCO's, actually run the daily operations of our Corps. The same will be true with SI's field operators, drawing from the vast array of experienced law enforcement officers and even retired military officers and NCO's."

"And these newer, lower-level officers. Will they be armed as well?"

"Without a viable means of defense, Senator, these men and women would be unable to perform their responsibilities, and should they encounter suspects, we would see our personnel impotent to stop the carnage. Historically, security forces in our public settings, such as a shopping mall, are visual deterrents to petty theft or vandalism, not physically capable of stopping an actual attack. To use the correct parlance, they 'observe and report.'

"As a young lieutenant, I fought in one war where the Army was required to requisition ammunition and to operate in the field with very restrictive rules of engagement. It was not a pretty sight. Yes, Senator McKenzie, all field personnel will be armed, but they will receive the proper training before being placed on the street in that capacity."

"I have no further questions, Mr. Chairman," Rachel said, closing her folder. "With your concurrence, Mr. Chairman, I call the question."

Culpepper banged his gavel again, looking both ways on the dais. "Are there any further questions before the committee votes this morning?" he asked. "Hearing none, I call the question. All in favor of granting General Wainscott approval to award a contract to Strategic Initiatives to initiate a pilot program in San Antonio, Texas, Colorado Springs, Colorado, and the District of Columbia, say aye."

The proposal passed without opposition and Senator Culpepper closed the session with one comment. "Please be reminded that the location of the pilot cities is a highly classified piece of information which the press would love to have for publication, but premature release of this information would simply sentence the program to failure, since the terrorists could avoid these cities. Senators representing each of these states are present on this committee. I trust you understand the burden placed upon you for confidentiality."

Before leaving the building, General Wainscott made a brief cell phone call. John Harford answered the private line himself.

"Unanimous approval, Mr. Harford. Domestic Tranquility is a go."

"Well done, General. Alert your command structure in San Antonio and we'll commence our operation within 48 hours."

Simultaneous with Wainscott's phone call, Pug sent a Blackberry email to General Austin in Brussels. 'Wainscott successful. DT begins Friday. Vote unanimous."

Within moments, Austin's reply came. "The dance has started. Choose your partner."

TWENTY-SIX

CAPITOL GROUNDS
WASHINGTON D.C.
JUNE

The May temperatures were still in the mid-70's as Pug and Rachel walked across the Capitol grounds toward Union Station, the central train depot in Washington D.C. A fixture in the Capitol since before the Civil War, it had been expanded into a retail shopping mall with stores on several levels, all extending down. In the central foyer, a restaurant had been built on a small mezzanine overlooking the main entrance. Pug asked the young woman at the entrance for a setting for two. They were escorted to the small table near the railing in the rear. As soon as the waiter came, he smiled as he held the chair for Rachel.

"How very nice to see you again, Senator McKenzie. A pleasure that you joined us for lunch."

Pug shook his head as the man filled their water glasses and then departed.

"I'm with a celebrity, it seems," he said.

"Everyone in the surrounding area who makes their living in service, food, or otherwise, quickly learns the elected representatives. I sometimes think they have a picture board in the kitchen or the employee lounge." She chuckled.

Pug took a sip of water and spread his napkin on his lap. He looked—stared, actually—at Rachel for several moments before speaking. She did not rise to the bait and open the conversation. She just smiled in return.

"I was surprised," Pug said, "pleasantly surprised, I might add, when you agreed to have lunch today. Is lunch safer than dinner?"

"I knew I'd be hungry after a long meeting with General Wainscott," she replied. "Besides, I was curious whether you really do pick your teeth at the table."

"Ouch! I'll have to be careful what I reveal around you, it seems. But Wainscott was well prepared, wasn't he?" Pug added.

"I expected nothing less. This is a big proposal, and an important departure from our personal liberty. I'm sure the general did not make the recommendation without long consideration. And it probably was hard for him and his colleagues to admit that the Army is not prepared for a domestic security role. They've been doing it for several years in Iraq, of course, but to have to patrol American cities, American streets, and to restrain American citizens—that would leave a bad taste in the military psyche, I would assume, and I can only imagine what it would do to the public image of our military. I have no reason to question his motives, nor his intent."

Pug grew serious, his facial expression transparent. "Rachel, why *are* so many elected officials in support of these measures? What's to be gained from clamping a lid on free movement of our citizens and subjecting them to search and seizure? The chances of actually preventing one of these random attacks is minimal at best."

Rachel looked away for a long moment, watching the people transiting the lobby floor, about ten to twelve feet below their position. Just as she was about to speak, the waiter returned. "Will you have your usual, Senator?"

"Yes, Henri, a Caesar salad please, and water," she replied.

"And you, sir?" the waiter asked.

"I'll have the corn chowder soup, please. And iced tea."

"Yes, sir, right away."

Rachel returned to the question. "Pug, I don't know if there is a simple answer. I agree with you that this program is questionable in its objectives. Perhaps not the objectives, but the projected results. Still, you're not surprised to hear that across the nation, our constituents are writing, calling, e-mailing, and actually visiting our offices to ask what we intend to do about this internal threat. The government's primary mission is to protect the American people. I'm not trying to teach civics to you, by any means, but most elected officials realize that we have to do *something*. We have to show the people that we're sensitive to the problem and are seeking remedies. We have to be *seen* to be doing something, is perhaps a better way to state it."

"Then it's all for show."

"Much of politics is for show, Pug," she said, a bit terse. "If you don't know that, you haven't been watching the polls."

"I'm sorry if I offended you, Rachel. I don't mean to, but the answers to this thing have me puzzled. I have to admit that Trojan is no closer to finding resolution. Probably less, but we don't care about the polls. For what it's worth, I don't think SI has the answer. Wainscott made it seem like they were the answer to a prayer."

"You sound like an Old Testament prophet," Rachel said.

Realizing that he had been preaching, Pug remained silent for several moments, then laughed softly. "Marines don't have beards."

Just as the waiter was returning with their lunch, Pug's cell phone vibrated. He checked the Caller ID and flipped the phone open. "General Connor," he answered.

"Please hold for the president," the clear feminine voice said. In several seconds, President Snow came on the line.

"Are you still in the Senate hearings, Pug?"

"No, Mr. President. We finished about thirty minutes ago. I'm at Union Station with Senator McKenzie, having lunch."

"I'll have a car outside in five minutes, Pug. If Senator McKenzie is not otherwise engaged, please ask her to join us."

"Sir, do I need to advise Trojan to assemble?"

"Not yet. We'll discuss it when you arrive. This is not pleasant news, Pug. There was a car bombing in Brussels just a few moments ago. The Dutch Deputy Director of Security and General Austin were both in the car. I'm sorry, Pug, but both men, along with the driver and the security agent, are all dead. The report will be on the news momentarily.

I'd like you to meet with us immediately. Defense Secretary Collins and the vice president will also be here."

Pug was silent, but his face was once again transparent and he could see that Rachel was anxious to know the content of the call.

"One moment, Mr. President." Pug redirected his comments at Rachel. "Can you join me for a meeting with the president? Right now?"

Rachel nodded.

"Mr. President, we'll be there as quickly as your transport arrives. We'll be outside the main entrance to Union Station."

"I'm very sorry, Pug. I know how much you admired General Austin."

"Thank you, sir," Pug replied and closed his phone. Rachel looked at Pug, waiting.

"There was a car bombing in Brussels. General Austin is dead."

Rachel reached across the table and quickly squeezed his hand. Then she removed two twenty-dollar bills from her purse, placed them on the table, and stood.

"Let's go, Pug. I'll call my office from the car."

TWENTY-SEVEN

WHITE HOUSE OVAL OFFICE
WASHINGTON D.C.
JUNE

"One man in a taxi crashed into the vehicle, which contained Per Van Brocklin, Deputy Director of Dutch Intelligence, and Secretary Austin, who were riding together in the rear. The taxi exploded. The driver and bodyguard, both of whom were U.S. Secret Service agents, were also killed in the explosion. No group has claimed responsibility as yet, but we expect World Jihad to step forward through the European news agencies soon."

The briefer was Thomas Kincade, Director of the Central Intelligence Agency. To his left sat George Granata, Director of the FBI, who was also Pug's neighbor, and across the table, on the divan in the Oval Office, sat both Senator Rachel McKenzie and General Pádraig Connor. The president sat in a chair at the head of the group, with Vice President Tiarks to his left. The room remained silent for several seconds after the briefing was completed. General Austin's Assistant Secretary of Homeland Security, Lillian Stromberg, completed the group.

The president was the first to speak. "Lillian, this is a terrible burden for Homeland Security. I know the general depended on you for daily operations and that the two of you had only begun to formulate your plan of action and division of authority. I know he would want you to carry on in his stead. Are you comfortable assuming the Acting Secretary role in his absence?"

"Mr. President, we will do our utmost to press forward. Sir, Mrs. Austin is . . ."

"I've spoken to her already, Lillian. I plan to visit with her as soon as I make a public statement. She's been the wife of a general officer for many years. From her comments just before we convened this meeting, I believe the general had explained to her the nature of his new job and the dangers inherent in traveling abroad. She's quite a brave woman herself. General Connor, you're a friend of the family, are you not? And Senator McKenzie, your family has known the Austins your entire life, I'm told."

"That's correct, Mr. President," Rachel answered. "The general served as my surrogate father on more than one occasion. They had no children of their own."

"Would you and General Connor be comfortable coming with me to see Mrs. Austin?"

"Yes, Mr. President," Rachel continued. "It was my plan to go to see her immediately after this meeting. Thank you for asking."

"General Connor?" the president said.

"Yes, sir. It would be an honor to accompany you."

The president turned again to the new Acting Secretary of Homeland Security. "Lillian, I am going to have General Connor's operation report directly to me for the immediate future. Can you see that he has the full support of Homeland Security until we sort out the reporting line?"

"Certainly, Mr. President. We'll give the general all the support he needs."

"Thank you. Now, do either the CIA or the FBI think this was anything more than an opportunity taken by the terrorists, or is there the possibility that it's more wide-spread and we need to increase security around key government officials?"

Kincade spoke for the CIA. "Mr. President, we have no intelligence to indicate that this action was part of a larger event, other than the continuing threat we face every day. I believe Al Qaida targeted the security conference in Brussels, and Secretary Austin's vehicle was convenient. We don't even know that they targeted a U.S. diplomat, considering all those in attendance from the several European countries."

The president nodded, then turned to Vice President Tiarks. "Hank, will you see to the return of Secretary Austin's remains, please? All military protocol and honors."

"Already underway, Mr. President."

"Thank you, Hank. We will ask Mrs. Austin about her wishes and intentions for burial and advise you immediately. If there's nothing further, perhaps we should conclude our meeting. The story will be on the news outlets by now and I need to prepare a statement before we leave. Pug, perhaps you and Senator McKenzie could move to the press room. I'll need to address the public immediately, but I don't want to delay our visit to Mrs. Austin."

Sitting in the press secretary's office foyer, Pug and Rachel waited as the White House staff scurried about, preparing for the impromptu press conference. Fox News, CNN, and each of the major networks had interrupted their regular programming to present the limited facts that were known. Al Qaida had struck again. A U.S. cabinet officer was dead. There seemed no end in sight to the tragedy a small group of dedicated terrorists could inflict on the most powerful nation in the world. But immense power had no recourse against one man—or woman—determined to give their life in the furtherance of their beliefs.

"Pug, I'm going to call my office and then my mother. She'll want to know about Uncle Bill's death and then she'll want to phone Christine. I'll be right back," Rachel said, walking quickly out of the small anteroom.

Pug sat alone for a moment, the silence allowing him to reflect on General Austin's sudden death. The president would address the nation. Tell them about the cowardly murder of one of America's leaders. Lament the loss of a friend, a decorated hero, a needless death. But General Austin would see it differently. He had taught Pug many things, especially in his attempt to convince the young Marine that working behind a desk to plan the operations was every bit as important as leading a team of Marines in a frontal assault. And what did his death prove? He'd had no chance to shoot back. He died at the hands of an assassin, not an enemy charging him or shooting a missile at his aircraft from three miles distant. General Austin had faced those dangers, had proven his courage under fire, had defeated the enemy. But America always had enemies. If one saw the world in terms of good and evil, good *always* had enemies.

General Austin had paid the price for his beliefs and he did so from behind a desk. Pug found it hard to fathom, having earned his stripes in the hard crucible of battle, he and the enemy each having a weapon. Pug had also earned his stripes through the loss of his men in combat. Perhaps the greatest lesson about leadership General Austin had taught his young Marine officer, while trying to convince him that the battle is fought not only from the trenches, but from the offices of leadership, was the proven adage of senior military leaders. It was the same lesson Lieutenant Commander Cartwright, Royal Australian Navy, had learned at the RAN academy: ordering subordinates, both men and women, to a surety of death, was far more difficult than facing the enemy yourself, one-on-one, in combat.

Following the president's press conference, Pug would accompany him to Mrs. Austin's home in Bethesda. The thought brought back unwelcome memories. Memories of Afghanistan.

It was in the Hindu Kush, in 1991, when Captain Pádraig Connor, Sergeant Carlos Castro, and six Force Recon Marines had sat on the hillside of the mountainous range awaiting extraction. Two Marines rested beneath the shelter of their ponchos, the battle the previous night having taken their lives. The deaths were Lieutenant Connor's first combat loss, and Sergeant Castro had understood the isolation brought on by the loss of men under your command. As a corporal, Carlos Castro had been part of Gulf I, in 1990, when two of his platoon had been killed in action. Castro had not been in overall command, but he understood combat-related death up close and personal.

Six, and then eight days after returning from Pakistan, Lieutenant Connor and Sergeant Castro attended each funeral, having met with the families, in the first instance, a mother and father, plus three siblings. In the second, a grieving nineteen-year-old widow with an eight-month-old son. Pug had told Castro later, as they flew back to Pendleton, that he would rather face an armed enemy than a grieving widow.

Sitting in the press office of the White House, the feeling had not abated. While the president would be the primary person to brief Mrs. Austin, Pug knew her, had dined at her home, had been treated as a son. And, unrecognized until this moment, Pug had come to respect, admire, and after nearly ten years serving under his command and partaking of his paternal advice, even love, his former commanding officer.

Rachel walked back into the room and sat beside Pug. "You okay?" she asked.

"Just remembering," he replied softly. "How did your mom respond?"

"She's calling Christine right now, and my office is arranging for her to fly out this evening from Kansas City. I'll fly back with her on Friday night, unless General Austin's funeral delays her return. I've got to go, since I'm scheduled to address a convention of city managers in Kansas City on Saturday morning."

"For a few moments back in the car, I forgot that your family was such close friends with the Austins," Pug said.

Rachel nodded. "We've known each other for over forty years. After all this time, the roles are reversed. Christine Austin was the first person to call my mother after the military notified Mom of my father's death in Vietnam. They've been close ever since."

Pug reached for Rachel's hand, gently stroking the back of her fingers. "I know you understand the nature of such loss better than most, Rachel, but it took me a bit longer. General Austin said as much while he was trying to convince me that working in military intelligence had just as much value in the war on terror as field operations. He said 'It's not the warrior who suffers the real agony, Pug, it's the wife, the mother, the children, the remaining family who live to regret his absence, the daughter who walks up the aisle without presence of her father, the wife who raises the child without the father to share the love.'"

Slowly tears began to form in Rachel's eyes and Pug stopped talking, content to hold her hand. "I'm sorry, Rachel. I didn't mean to open old wounds."

She nodded, placing her hand over his.

Abruptly, a White House aide stepped into the doorway. "Senator, General, if you'll follow me, please, the president is about to enter the press room. I have two seats set aside for you."

Pug and Rachel stood and silently followed the young man down the corridor. They were engulfed by a bevy of reporters and White House staffers. As soon as they sat, another staff person came through the door and announced the arrival of the president. Pug and Rachel stood along with the occupants of the room as the president mounted the dais and took his position behind the lectern.

"At 11:20 this morning, local time, Homeland Security Secretary William Austin was killed in a car bomb attack in Brussels. Secretary Austin was attending a conference of security leaders from European nations seeking ways to confront terrorism. Once again, it has been demonstrated that terrorists do not want peaceful solutions to the ills of the world. Secretary Austin served this nation for four decades, both in war and in peace. He was seeking further methods to assure peace when he was needlessly killed. The United States puts these terrorists on notice that we will follow every path to find and kill or capture those who planned this murder. I personally offer my sincere condolences to Mrs. Austin. The general was . . ."

Twenty-Eight

DULLES INTERNATIONAL AIRPORT
WASHINGTON, D.C.
JUNE

Sometime after 10:00 PM, Pug drove Rachel to Dulles International Airport to meet her mother's plane. The president's visit to the Austin household had been difficult, to say the least, but Pug recognized in President Snow the gentle hand of a compassionate man, belying the weight of his office. Mrs. Austin was a remarkable woman, her strength resilient, her expression of gratitude to the president sincere. Despite the many other occasions when Pug had met her, his admiration for the woman took on a new dimension during the president's visit. Shortly before they had left, Christine Austin's sister had arrived to fill the absence of family. With no children of their own, Rachel had been concerned that the older woman would be alone for the night and had offered to stay, but Mrs. Austin had declined, grateful that Rachel's mother would be coming to visit tomorrow.

As they waited near the luggage carousel at Dulles, Pug held Rachel close, his arm around her shoulder.

"These are not the circumstances that I envisioned for us to become friends, Rachel. I'm truly sorry for this loss and the memories it fosters."

Rachel raised her hand to her shoulder, covering Pug's hand. "The circumstances are not important, Pug. I'm grateful you were with me. Uncle Bill was like a father to me and I know he was fond of you, trusted you, and that his feelings were reciprocated. It's your loss, too. I feel numb, actually. I might—"

Suddenly, Rachel leaned to the right, scanning the passengers coming down the escalator. "There she is," she said, quickly walking forward and embracing her mother as she stepped away from the moving throng of people. Pug remained quietly behind. After a few moments of tears and hugging, they approached him together.

"Mom, this is General Pug Connor. Pug worked with Uncle Bill for the past several years. They became very close."

Mrs. Thompson extended her hand and showed the briefest hint of a smile. "I'm pleased to meet you, General. Thank you for meeting me."

"My pleasure, ma'am. Your luggage will be on carousel eight. I already have a trolley."

"I only brought one bag. I have some of my things at Rachel's home." She turned to Rachel as they walked toward the luggage carousel. "Do you know when the funeral will be held?"

"Yes, Mom. Friday morning at Arlington. Christine did not want any public ceremony, but agreed to the president's request that Bill be buried in the national cemetery. I have us both booked back to Kansas City on Friday night."

Mrs. Thompson nodded. "That's my bag, General," she said, pointing to a light gray case which Pug retrieved.

Thirty minutes later, Pug placed the suitcase just inside the front door of Rachel's home.

"Rachel, if I can be of any assistance over the next several days, please phone. I've called a meeting of my team tomorrow morning to discuss several items, but mostly to deal with our new reporting line to the president's office. Please, do call if I can help."

Rachel looked up at Pug for several seconds, then stepped close to him, placing her hands on his shoulders. She then kissed him lightly on the cheek, pulled back, and looked into his eyes. "You've already been helpful, Pug, perhaps more than you know. Thank you."

"If I don't see you beforehand, I hope to see you at the funeral on Friday," Pug said.

"I'll arrange it, Pug. My staff will organize seats for us."
"Good night, Rachel."

Twenty-Nine

OFFICE OF STRATEGIC INITIATIVES
WASHINGTON D.C.
JUNE

Wednesday morning, Devlin Hegarty sat in John Harford's office, discussing the latest turn of events and the final plans for the Saturday events in San Antonio and Kansas City.

"Who could have envisioned that Homeland Security would lose their secretary so quickly? General Austin was one of the staunchest opponents of Domestic Tranquility, or so my inside sources tell me. We're well-rid of the bastard," Harford said.

Hegarty wondered silently whether Harford had other teams working on such events, or if it was truly a coincidence and Al Qaida was behind the attack.

"One more thing, Devlin. It's come to my attention that Senator McKenzie of Kansas will be at the Marriott on Saturday morning, giving an address to the city managers who are holding a convention. That's actually a stroke of luck."

"Do you want the explosion timed to her address?" Hegarty asked.

"Absolutely not. That's what I'm saying. She'll speak at 11:00 AM, giving the keynote. I want the explosion no earlier than 2:00 PM. She sits on Culpepper's intelligence committee and I think she can be swayed in favor of Domestic Tranquility. A close brush with death will help convince her. I need her vote."

"They reconvene at 1:30 after lunch, so 2:00 PM it will be," Hegarty replied. "The Overland Park mall will be hit earlier in the morning, followed by the Marriott. San Antonio will take place about 4:00 PM. Texas is in the same time zone, so about two hours after the Marriott explosion. Saturday will be a busy day for Fox News and CNN, not to mention emergency services."

"Yes, well, if this doesn't wake up America, I don't know what will. Are you sure the San Antonio SI security team is prepared to intervene successfully?"

"Absolutely. The team leader of the SI defense squad is ready. I've worked with him before. Sean Kilpatrick. A good man. His great-grandfather trained my father in Belfast in the old days."

Harford gave a quick chuckle. "No matter the cause, there always seems to be work for enterprising young men, eh? How *are* things in Ireland these days?"

"Too peaceful," Hegarty replied.

"Well, we can thank our lucky stars for Al Qaida then, right? Catholic or Protestant, Muslim or Christian. Some religious group always wants to kill another religious group. It's a good thing we have all these men of *faith*, or there might not be any wars to prosecute."

Hegarty nodded assent. "And some financial wolf is always ready to help them through the process with no religious compunctions."

"I'm sure you've noticed that your Swiss account has increased substantially. Be certain you share some of those proceeds with your key players. I don't want any disgruntled employees complaining and drawing attention because they weren't paid."

"Not to worry. Everyone is taken care of. Everyone who will live to spend it, that is," Hegarty replied.

THIRTY

MARRIOTT HOTEL
KANSAS CITY, MISSOURI
JUNE

Senator Rachel McKenzie, Republican, Kansas, finished her address to the International City & County Manager's Association gathered at the Marriott Hotel in Kansas City about ten minutes to noon. 377 municipal administrators had gathered for the annual conference and were just breaking for lunch prior to the welcoming speech by the mayor of Kansas City, scheduled for 1:30 PM.

At her invitation, Rachel's mother had attended her speech. She met Rachel in the foyer as they made their way toward the front entrance, but were stopped by several police officers who asked her to wait just a moment.

"What's the problem, Officer?" Rachel asked.

"Ma'am, there's no danger at the moment, but there has been a shooting at the mall in Overland Park. Quite a large shooting, with multiple injuries. Your staff director, Mr. Halversen, asked us to assure your safe arrival at the airport, so we've arranged for alternate transportation with a police escort."

Rachel and her mother took seats in the foyer for a moment while they waited. "Do you want to come back to Virginia with me, Mom?

Just while they sort this out?"

"No, of course not, dear. I can take a taxi home. Don't worry about me."

"No way, Mom. Ted will see that you get home safely." Ted Halversen was director of Senator McKenzie's Kansas City office. "Are you sure you wouldn't rather that I stay for a few days?"

"Rachel, as terrible as these events are becoming, we need to carry on with our lives. You have work to do, I have a Sunday school lesson to teach tomorrow, and I refuse to let these people disrupt my life or make me live in fear."

Rachel smiled momentarily as her mom bristled at the intrusion into her life. The police officer stepped in to the seating area and said, "It will be just a few minutes, Senator. They're bringing up an unmarked van to transport you. Why don't you step into the lounge while you wait? The news is broadcasting the shooting on TV and you can watch what's happening."

Indeed, Fox News had a live feed from an overhead helicopter, and the parking lot near the main entrance to the mall was crowded with police vehicles, including the SWAT van. Heavily armed officers were located at every position outside the mall entrance, and some were already on the roof of the building. As Rachel watched, she thought about how many times she had entered through that same revolving door into the Overland Park Mall, how often her mother had used the entrance, and she wondered whether any of their friends were there this morning.

Sheppard Smith, a Fox News commentator, was voicing over the camera shot from the helicopter, conversing in a split-screen shot with Megyn Kelly, who was on the scene having quickly departed another assignment she was covering across the Missouri River.

"It's our understanding, Megyn, that an alert security officer assigned to the mall, but unarmed, notified police of the first shooting before he himself was shot and presumably killed. His body is just inside the doorway and emergency rescue has been unable to reach him to ascertain his condition. At least two of the perpetrators have also been shot, along with a wounded police officer who has been taken to the hospital. We don't know yet how many people inside the mall, if any, have also been shot, but we have to assume that injuries have taken place. This is not the usual shooting we've come to expect, or to learn about after the fact, with one or two shooters killing silently and then disappearing. It's also the first attack we've been able to see live, where police were on the scene before the shooters departed. By first reports, there are at least four, perhaps five armed men who entered the mall and began shooting at random, starting with the security guard."

Megyn adjusted her microphone and turned to look at the camera. "Shep, police officials on the ground have just informed me that contact with retail shop personnel inside the mall, who have taken shelter in the back of their stores, has alerted them to the fact that at least two men are barricaded inside the front entrance. They have numerous customers seated around the large flower planter you can see through the door. They're using them as a shield against a police assault. This is a very dangerous situation and far from over. Hold on, Shep, the police spokesman is making a further comment . . ."

The live shot of the parking lot continued while Shep contributed a voiceover, reiterating all that had been learned about the opening events in the shooting. Shortly, Megyn returned.

"Shep, the police spokeswoman just informed us that four alleged terrorists have already made their departure, and the police, assisted by the Kansas Highway Patrol, are involved in a high-speed chase heading west on I-70. It would appear that there were six terrorists in this assault, an usually brazen attack, with, presumably, two men still inside with hostages."

At the moment Megyn made her final comment, the picture being broadcast of the mall parking lot and entrance erupted in a large explosion, smoke and flames pouring out of the mall entrance, reaching the closest police vehicles. Megyn was standing about sixty yards away and the picture of the scene skewed violently as the helicopter carrying the camera veered away from the rising blast, steadying several seconds later as the pilot gained control.

"Are you still with us, Megyn?" Shep said, his voice rising.

With a shaky picture, the camera again focused on the disheveled reporter, her hair and clothing in disarray. "I'm here, Shep," she said, regaining control. "There has been an explosion. Someone inside the mall has triggered a bomb and one can only imagine that those closest to the blast have been severely injured. We could see at least a dozen or more people seated around the planter inside the front door. Hold it, Shep," she said, even more intense. "The police are rushing the front door. SWAT is storming the entrance, Shep."

Senator Rachel McKenzie and her mother stood transfixed in the Marriott Hotel as they watched the dramatic scene play out in front of their eyes. Rachel stepped outside into the foyer and motioned to the officer who had spoken to them.

"Officer, I want to go to my local office. I won't be returning to Washington today. Can you arrange that?"

"Yes, ma'am. The van is arriving now. If you would like to come with me, we'll see that you and your party are transported safely."

By 1:30 PM, just under 300 city and county managers had reconvened in the Grand Ballroom where the mayor of Kansas City was to address them. The remaining seventy-seven registered attendees had presumably remained in the lounge or their rooms, watching the horrific event unfold on their televisions. At 1:36, just as the deputy mayor was advising the attendees that the mayor had been called away to deal with the terrible developing disaster in Overland Park, the first explosion erupted in the room, midway through the seated crowd. Over the next four minutes, three other explosions blasted various areas of the Marriott Hotel, including the lounge, the main foyer, and the circular entrance to the hotel, bringing down the overhanging balcony and balustrade. Over 175 people died in what became known as the Kansas City Massacre and made news headlines around the world.

In Tel Aviv, two cabinet ministers seated in a local café watched CNN coverage when one remarked, "I wonder if American politicians will ask themselves to use restraint in their response as they have always asked us to tread lightly."

"One thing is for certain," his companion replied, "they can no longer be neutral."

It was 2:54 PM in San Antonio, Texas.

Rachel's cell phone rang just as she entered her private office in downtown Kansas City. Her staff was absent, other than a couple of key members who were present during the ICMA speech.

"Senator McKenzie," she answered.

"Rachel, it's Pug."

"Pug, I didn't recognize the number."

"I'm calling from the anteroom outside the Oval Office. I'm about to speak with the president." He paused. "Rachel, I'm so thankful to hear your voice. I knew you were speaking at the Marriott this morning."

"I left about an hour before the explosion."

"Are you staying to see what you can do?"

"I am. Don't know when I'll return."

"May I call you again?" Pug asked.

"I'd be grateful, Pug. And thank you."

"I'd better go. The president will be available in a moment. Stay safe, Rachel, and give your mother my regards."

"Pug," Rachel said.

"Yes?"

"I'll probably be back mid-week, perhaps a few days later. Will you do something for me?"

"Anything I can, Rachel, you know that."

"Will you meet me at the airport? I . . . I just . . ."

"Let me know when. I'll be there, Rachel, and thank you," Pug replied.

As he ended the call, the door to the Oval Office opened and FBI Director Granata exited, nodding to Pug as he left. The president's secretary stepped toward Pug.

"General, the president can see you now. He has three minutes before his next meeting."

"Hopefully I'll need less than two. Thank you." Pug stepped into the office and stood before the president's desk. President Snow said a few quick words into the phone and hung up. "Pug, this has not been a good day."

"No, sir. Mr. President, I just spoke with Senator McKenzie. She delivered an address at the Kansas City Marriott this morning, but was out of the hotel about an hour before the explosion. She is safe and in her local office."

The president just nodded. "I'm a bit rushed, Pug. I presume you're looking for a Troy designation for this event today?"

"Yes, sir. At the moment, the Kansas Highway Patrol and Kansas City police are still pursuing the terrorists west on I-70. The police are not equipped or trained to deal with this type of emergency or this type of enemy, Mr. President. They will continue to pursue until they can contain the situation. The terrorists will seek additional hostages somewhere and more people will die."

"What do you recommend?"

"Mr. President, I want to get an Army Blackhawk up from Fort Leavenworth, block the interstate in both directions, and take this vehicle out as if it were an enemy troop transport. This is a military enemy, Mr. President. We have ample means to stop them, but we need your approval, or a Troy designation, following which I will issue the authority to fire on the vehicle."

The president observed Pug for several seconds and then voiced his approval. "Jennie will have your written Troy designation in hand in five minutes. Just wait for it by her desk. And Pug, General Austin trained you well. Such situations permit no equivocation. You're the right man in the right place."

"I'll see to the Army, Mr. President. Thank you, sir."

THIRTY-ONE

STRATEGIC INITIATIVES
WASHINGTON, D.C.
JUNE

John Harford's office at Strategic Initiatives was busier than usual, with multiple people, including many in uniform, coming and going. It had been like that since Saturday afternoon, after the first episode in Kansas City. By Monday, the bee hive of activity had not settled down.

"Senator Winchester, thank you for coming to see me this afternoon. I know that your Mondays are very busy, but this is highly important. It's been a terrible weekend for America," John Harford said, taking a seat next to the senator from Connecticut.

For the past forty-eight hours, every major news station had run the endless, repetitive loop of the Kansas City bombing, and with live coverage, the Fox News helicopter had been on scene about seventy-five miles west of Kansas City on I-70 when the Army Blackhawk helicopter had fired a missile at the black van as it raced along the interstate. Only one occupant had survived and he did not last through the trip to the hospital.

Coverage of the San Antonio intervention was, of course, less dramatic, since only six terrorists and one Strategic Initiatives trooper had been killed. Still, high praise was voiced from all quarters on the successful event, and when SI released the film clip from the Predator drone that had initially spotted the six men outside of San Antonio, preparing their weapons for the attack, the coverage quickly gained acclaim and calls were already forthcoming for extension of the pilot program. Two newscasters and the city council in Kansas City had stated that if only such a program had been in place nationwide, the tragedy at Overland Park Mall could have been prevented. Even traditional liberal groups were clamoring for more protection, while conservative groups screamed that had liberals not stood in the way historically, such events could have been prevented long ago. Some hard-core conservatives even went so far as to indicate that although the death toll was horrendous and unacceptable, liberally supported abortion clinics had killed more people in the past few months than the entire attack had killed. There was no meeting of the minds on philosophy.

In the well-appointed confines of Strategic Initiatives, Chairman of the Board and CEO John Harford continued to address his congressional visitor.

"Our small success in San Antonio was completely overshadowed by the brazenness of the terrible events in Kansas City and the senseless deaths. I'm sure you agree. Still, the pilot program for Domestic Tranquility has begun to show its merit and you are certainly aware that the press is lauding our success. And they're right. Imagine if we'd only had a few Predators flying over Kansas City. How many people might be alive this morning?"

Sensing the fervor behind Harford's monologue, Winchester readily agreed. "John, you're absolutely correct. How can I help?"

"How long have you been in Congress, Augustus?"

"Four years in the House and nine in the Senate. Halfway through my second senate term."

Harford clasped his hands together, steepling his fingers in front of his face, thankful he did not have to raise the specter of past financial contributions in a veiled threat. "Augustus, it's time for you to leave your mark on Congress. You've done some excellent work for our nation, but this bill will be your crowning achievement. Something to be a lasting tribute."

"And what would that be, John?" Winchester asked.

Harford rose from his seat, walked behind his desk, and picked up a slim, spiral bound document, about thirty pages in all. "This, Senator Winchester, is the Domestic Tranquility Act. It has been prepared by the finest legal minds in the country. Once passed and signed by the president, it will supplant The Patriot Act and will become the guiding force for American domestic security for the next decade. The provisions of this bill will assure that law enforcement officers, military national guard, and even privately contracted security forces, such as those on duty in San Antonio this past weekend, will have the necessary authority and resources to combat these terrorists who dare to invade our country. Think of it, Augustus. With the barest minimum of personal intrusion, certainly nothing to bother the law-abiding citizens of our country, we can enact and oversee the measures to protect our people on a daily basis. Why should Americans be in fear of going to Sears and ending up dead? Why should we be afraid to attend a convention in a five-star hotel and worry about being blown to bits? No, sir! Through the effective representation of Senator Augustus Winchester of Connecticut, once again New England will be at the forefront of defending America. With this bill to your credit—and I can line up two opposition party senators to co-sponsor with you—you will likely represent the people of Connecticut, perhaps even the American people nationally, for years to come. Certainly until you're ready to hoist a jib and spend the remaining days of your life on your beautiful yacht off the coast of Newport. Are you ready for that challenge, Augustus? Are you ready for immortality?"

Unspoken by the chairman, but not unnoticed by Winchester, was the part Harford had played in his campaign financing over the years, especially the last campaign for the Senate when the Republicans had overplayed their hand with a bright, young lieutenant governor whom they had run against him. All in all, Harford had contributed nearly six million dollars to Augustus Winchester in his congressional campaigns. Failing to respond to Harford's direct appeal was suicidal, politically and financially speaking, since he would surely switch his financial alliance to someone more malleable.

"Of course, as I said, you won't be alone in this campaign, Augustus. Every congressman or congresswoman I have ever helped to finance, every senator, and every lobbyist who has ever worked for me will get behind this bill completely. Even the normally liberal media will be in support if we play our cards right. It will be a full court press, Augustus. Domestic Tranquility will become the law of the land within sixty days if I have anything to say about it, and I *do* have something to say about it. Are you ready to lead the charge, Senator Winchester?"

"Do you have the necessary votes on Senator Culpepper's committee to get the bill on the floor for a vote?" Winchester asked.

"Leave that to me. With the narrow escape Senator McKenzie had on Saturday, I would think she would be leading your supporters to recommend a full Senate vote immediately."

"John," Winchester said as he rose from his seat, "the Founding Fathers had it right. I think it's time that we restored domestic tranquility in America, don't you?"

"Now you're talking, Senator. Now you're talking."

As Senator Winchester left, Harford sat behind his desk for several minutes until his secretary buzzed his intercom.

"Sir, Mr. Hegarty has arrived, and security called to advise that a Mr. Campbell is downstairs, obtaining clearance to enter the building."

"Fine. Confirm to security that Campbell may enter, and when he arrives, send both men in."

Harford stood behind his desk and gazed out the window toward Capitol Mall. The two men coming to his office had never met. In fact, Harford had never met Campbell either, but before his disappearance several weeks earlier, Jean Wolff had praised his ability to, how did he put it, "do what was necessary without remorse." Putting these two men together would complete the liaison between the east and west coast efforts to foment the plan. And if Devlin could find a way to get Wolff out of federal custody, he would be the right man to deal with the western militia units.

Before his untimely death last year, John Henry Franklin had possessed the election resources and Harford had the political connections to make everything work. Or so he had thought. Franklin was gone now, as was the phony election process, but adaptation was a hallmark of Strategic Initiatives, and SI *was* John Harford.

A small knock on his door broke his reverie, and as his secretary opened the door, both men came into the spacious office.

"Gentlemen, welcome," Harford said, stepping forward into the room to greet them. "Thank you, Laurie. No calls, please. And let Captain Jenkins know his guests will be at the marina in about forty-five minutes."

"Yes, sir," she said, closing the door behind her.

Campbell stood just under six feet, was casually dressed in slacks and an open-necked shirt, and sported a full beard, with a thick head of unruly hair.

"Mr. Campbell, I've not had the pleasure," Harford said, extending his hand, "but Jean Wolff had nothing but praise for your dedication to America. I'm pleased to meet you. And Devlin," he said, turning toward the slightly older man, "good to see you again. Dev, this is Angus Campbell, commander of the burgeoning American Brigade Command, a western patriot movement. Mr. Campbell, allow me to introduce Devlin Hegarty. Devlin is director of field operations for Strategic Initiatives. Please, take a seat."

Both men took seats in plush, chocolate-brown leather chairs in front of the burnished oak desk and Harford returned to his swivel chair. With a full view of the United States Capitol Building in the background, the office was designed to exude power and project an inference of access to U.S. government officials, sufficient to make visiting foreign dignitaries sign on the dotted line to obtain SI services.

"Now, let's get the show on the road. No time for pleasantries. Mr. Campbell, are you geared up for the western campaign? Subordinate unit resources in place, the Brigade ready to act?"

Campbell glanced briefly at Hegarty, who had maintained a stoic expression and, thus far, had not said a word. Looking back at Harford, Campbell nodded slightly, but seemed hesitant to speak openly.

"Mr. Campbell, have no concerns about security of information in this office. Mr. Hegarty is aware of the overall scope of the plan. The takedown of the terrorists in San Antonio was his operational plan and has proven to U.S. government officials that SI can deliver. We need your group to further our aims out west. So, again I ask, is the Brigade ready to find and kill these terrorists and protect our nation?"

"We are, Mr. Harford. We don't have the equipment or resources at our disposal that SI offers, but we have the manpower and zeal necessary to get the job done."

"That's all we ask. Mr. Hegarty will provide everything else you need. Your Brigade is critical out west. We both know what will happen if law enforcement catches these guys. They'll spend decades costing us fifty grand a year, then another few million to provide them lawyers and color television. Your brand of justice will see that never happens. And not underserved, I might add."

"As I said, we'll get the job done."

"Excellent. Now Devlin, I've arranged for you and Mr. Campbell to have a lunch cruise on the Potomac to discuss our mutual objectives. You'll have total privacy out on the water. Mr. Campbell understands his role in the *western* theater of operations. You can fill him in on the rest."

Harford stood up, smiling as he did so. "I trust you gentlemen will find ample amenities on the *Rosewood*. Just let Captain Jenkins know if you need anything further," he said. "Oh, Mr. Campbell, give me a private moment with Devlin before he leaves. You can wait momentarily in the foyer. Nice to have met you."

Campbell stepped out of the office and Harford waited just a moment as the door closed. "Dev, remember the limitations of Campbell's role. He has to believe that SI is chasing these terrorists and that's all. He can bring a lot of manpower to bear, but more importantly, these guys will do most anything we ask of them. Their involvement will serve to further inflame law enforcement and our military, so convince him how he can be of service. I don't expect you'll get any resistance to a suggestion that he find and kill these roving shooters. If he kills a few innocent, non-European people along the way, so much the better for our needs."

"I understand, John. I'll handle it."

"And one more thing, Dev," Harford continued, "when you sort things out with Campbell, it's becoming forest fire season in the northwest. Direct one of your rover teams to a forested area in Montana with orders to start a fire. But after you do, give Campbell a heads up intelligence briefing about where to locate and ambush them. Tell him to make a public example of them. Display the bodies so law enforcement will find them. But at the same time, direct a half-dozen or more of your teams to start forest fires throughout the northwest, of their own choosing. Don't tell Campbell about them."

"Consider it done, John."

"And last, in about a week—I'll confirm the timing later—I want you to go to Copenhagen and supervise a container shipment to the states."

"More weapons?" Hegarty asked.

"A small nuclear package, being delivered from another source in Chechnya."

"*Nuclear?*" Hegarty said, his face betraying his shock.

Harford nodded, but grinned. "We're not going to *use* it, Dev, SI troopers are going to *find* it and once again, save America. That will absolutely confirm our dependability and insure the growth of support forces for Domestic Tranquility." He paused for several moments and added, "But if we *have* to use it to show Americans the dangers we face . . . well, we'll face that prospect later. Just see that it gets here in one piece. The gentleman who set this up is the one who's now in federal custody in Illinois, but I have the Danish contact information you can use. The shipping arrangements have already been made. It's *machinery* for a new plant in Ohio. Then you're going to find a way to get Mr. Wolff out of federal prison. Can you accomplish that assignment, Devlin?"

"I can damn sure try."

"I'll give you further details next week. Now go have a pleasant lunch with your new team member. Don't think I'd enjoy a lunch with Campbell. These hard core militiamen are interesting, aren't they?"

"Not *my* kind of life," Hegarty responded. "We did some rough stuff in my day, but we always stayed in top hotels when not on operations. These guys *like* to sleep in the mud."

THIRTY-TWO

SENATOR RACHEL MCKENZIE'S HOME
MCLEAN, VIRGINIA
JULY

The following Thursday evening, Pug drove to Rachel's home. She had arrived the previous evening and spent all day Thursday in her senatorial office, preparing responses to constituents calling for immediate passage of the new bill submitted only 48 hours before by Senator Augustus Winchester, Democrat from Connecticut. She also sent several letters of sympathy to families that had lost relatives in the Overland Park Mall shooting. She spent the rest of the afternoon reading the text of the draft Domestic Tranquility Act in preparation for the sub-committee hearings scheduled for Monday morning.

Pug had called that morning to ask her to dinner, and she was ready when he rang the doorbell. They stepped out onto the terrace where they both paused for several moments, gazing out over the Potomac River.

"You look tired, Rachel," he said.

"I'm exhausted, Pug. Bone weary. It's emotional fatigue, I know, since I've not had any time to exercise, jog, or do anything physical. I'm just physically drained."

"Why don't we just sit here for a bit before we leave? I think you need some time to unwind."

Rachel nodded her agreement. "That sounds wonderful. Let me get us a couple of glasses of iced tea."

"Sit down, Rachel." Pug said. "With your permission, I'll get them."

"There's a pitcher in the fridge, with glasses in the second cupboard to the right of the stove," she said.

When Pug returned, Rachel had moved the deck umbrella to shield them from the setting sun and placed two chairs near the small table. Pug placed both glasses on the table and slid his chair next to hers, both facing the river.

"I could get used to being served," Rachel said.

Pug smiled. "Living alone can become rather selfish," he admitted, "but one has to fend for one's self. Serving each other is part of the human contract, isn't it?"

"Are you selfish, Pug?" she asked, a softer tone appearing in her voice.

"Sometimes, I probably am. No one to answer to, time commitments only to myself. Yes, I suppose I am."

"That's why I try to convince my daughters to come home as often as possible. The 'mom' takes over and I become the servant, rather than selfish."

"I could drop by occasionally if you need someone to cook for, or to serve."

Rachel looked at Pug, her eyes bright and suddenly cheerful. "You *are* good for me, Pug, but I meant what I said before. That road is full of potholes."

"I beg your pardon, madam. Are you calling me a pothole?"

Rachel laughed out loud, the first time in over a week. "What's the old country music expression, five miles of bad road?"

Pug reached for Rachel's hand, pulling it closer to his lips and kissing it. "Why don't we just consider me a 'detour' road for awhile? Maybe we'll find out that you can get where you're going without dropping into one of those pot-holes."

"Why don't we just finish our tea, watch the sunset over the river, and drive to the restaurant? I've had too many potholes already this week."

They sat silently for nearly five minutes, sipping their drinks before

Rachel spoke again. "I think I've let my sorrow overwhelm me. Three of the people in the mall attack, two women with whom I'd served when my girls were in Brownies, were killed. The father and one son who had gone to a basketball game that Saturday were devastated. I attended church with Mom on Sunday, the day after the attack, and the pastor asked me, and Mom, since she's in the women's organization, to go with him that evening to visit the family. I knew this woman, Pug. I loved her and her family. These people were not constituents, they were like sisters. So very close to my heart. My mother's strength pulled me through it. I could see that even the pastor admired my mother for her strength. Joan's — that's her name, by the way, the woman who was killed — husband was virtually speechless. The boy, he's about fifteen, was in tears the whole time, but silent too. I'm not a psychologist, but he seemed to be in shock. They couldn't understand how this could happen in America. I can't either, Pug. On the flight back, I even asked myself how God could let this happen."

"That's understandable, Rachel. You've already had more than your share of tragedy in your own life. It's too close to the surface every time you see someone else struck by tragedy. When I was young and something terrible would happen, and I would question why, the answer my father always gave me was that we all had to remember the basic premise of free choice. *We* choose, not God. He gave us that right. And good people often suffer the consequences of the evil decisions of others. We can only see *this* life, but if someone believes in an afterlife, then the eternities will hold the answers for us. We may eventually see our mortality as but a weekend with respect to eternity. A tough weekend sometimes, but comparatively short. It's not pleasant to contemplate, Rachel, but life comes with many types of potholes."

Again they were silent for several minutes before Rachel broke the silence. "I'm hungry. Are you ready to go?"

Pug gathered up the glasses, walked into the kitchen and rinsed them in the sink, placed them in the dishwasher, then returned to find Rachel standing on the front steps. As he closed the front door, they descended several steps off the porch and walked toward Pug's car, and once inside, Rachel pressed a Speed Dial number on her cell phone."

"Activating the security system in your house?" he said, remembering the first night he had driven her home.

"You learn fast. No wonder they made you a general," she said.

Three hours later, as they arrived at Rachel's home, it was nearly midnight. Pug walked her to the front door, where they paused near the railing on the porch to view the moon reflecting off the Potomac.

"Thank you for tonight, Pug," Rachel said. "I needed this tranquility." She hesitated, her face turning grim. "I may grow to *hate* that word, given its new affiliation with the bill Senator Winchester introduced on Tuesday. It would be a shame to lose such a peaceful word because of association with more distressful events."

"Will it pass?" Pug asked.

"In a heartbeat. Any representative or senator opposed will be vilified and ostracized by his or her peers. It will cross party lines better than any legislation in memory."

"I must admit, Rachel, that it contains some measures that will make my job a lot easier to perform. Arrest and detention, I mean. And interrogation, search and seizure of property."

"Is that the America you envisioned when you were a child, when you entered the Naval Academy? Is a police state your idea of freedom?"

Pug shook his head. "Of course not, but we're faced with a terrible situation, Rachel. I don't have to explain that to you, of all people. At some point, we have to rely on our guardians to have our best interest at heart. We have to trust the police and the military."

"And what about others who are less restrained or honest then you are, Pug? Who will curtail their actions? Who will stop them from abusing those rights? Probably some politician in South America, maybe even a well-meaning person, said it was good for their country too, then hundreds of people began to disappear and were never seen again. If you think that can't happen in America, you underestimate the nature of people who demand to have their own way. Power is an addictive thing, Pug. Those who hold it come to believe their vision is the only one worth pursuing and violating the rights of a few people—or a few thousand—is worth the sacrifice. Not *their* sacrifice, of course, but those who disagree. Dissent will become a thing of the past. I've already seen the symptoms in the Senate. People who ran for office for honorable reasons convince themselves that their ideas are the only right ones. In some countries, they convince themselves and others that a few hundred or a few thousand people killed is little to ask for the salvation of tens of thousands of others. And it grows incrementally. People become afraid to speak against the government."

He nodded. "I understand the concerns. It will be a balancing act and law enforcement, military or civilian, will need to police their own house to assure civil rights are not trampled in the process."

"As I said, it hasn't worked in many countries that we came to call 'banana republics.' Their citizens are oppressed, or killed, by those intent on retaining power."

"Granted," Pug said. "But we can rise above that."

"I hope so, Pug. I truly hope so."

"Thank you for tonight, Rachel. I'm very grateful you accepted my invitation."

"For me too, Pug," she said, stepping in close. Without comment, she leaned even closer and lifted her chin, placing her hand behind Pug's head and pulling him close enough to kiss. He reacted by putting his arms around her, wrapping her in a full embrace. When she withdrew, Rachel leaned back and smiled up at him. "I know we need to face our potholes, Pug, and can't run away from them, even if they seem dark and dangerous."

"Are you suggesting that you're willing to 'patch' my pot-holes, Rachel?"

"I'm suggesting that I don't want to be alone tonight. I'm suggesting that this is *not* recreational sex, but that it's an emotional need. I *do* care for you Pug, and it may not sound romantic, but I need you on duty tonight, General Connor."

"Yes, ma'am," Pug said, pulling her closer once again. "The Marine Corps is honored to be of service."

THIRTY-THREE

EISENHOWER EXECUTIVE OFFICE BUILDING
WASHINGTON D.C.
JULY

When Pug walked into the EEOB on Friday morning, he was met in the corridor by Carlos Castro. "Seen the morning papers?" Carlos asked.

Pug raised his copy of the *Washington Post* from under his arm and motioned toward Carlos's office. Once inside, Pug dropped the paper onto the table top and took a seat in front of Carlos's desk. The headline read:

> *Domestic Tranquility Law of the Land*
> *Individual Citizen Rights Restricted*

"It gives us carte blanche," Carlos said, "but it certainly ties the hands of ordinary citizens if they happen to be stopped for trespassing."

Pug nodded. "Senator Winchester has been quoted on every talk show since last night. He's today's hero. Truth is, it will make our job a lot easier, with no restrictions and ten-day retention without charges being filed."

Carlos exhaled and took a chair behind his desk. "General, America is headed down a path that may be impossible to retrace. I'm trying to see the bright side of this, but as a lawyer, even a non-practicing lawyer, I find this infringement on citizen rights troubling. Don't you?"

Pug was still standing and retrieved his newspaper from the table, re-reading the headline. "I haven't decided, Carlos. Anything that helps us catch the Wild Bunch . . . I just don't know. We'll see."

"What I'm concerned about, General, is that we'll see the fallacies of this course of action too late to reverse course."

"I understand that. Well, let's see what the day brings," he said, leaving Carlos's office. As Pug entered his office, his telephone voice mail light was flashing. Three messages were identified and he pressed the play button. The lilt of an Irish accent in the first message took his complete interest and he quickly listened to the next two, neither of which was important and both were deleted. He replayed the first message.

"Good day to yer, General Connor. If you've time for a stroll with a friend of the old sod, be at the Washington Memorial, Friday morning at 11:00."

Pug quickly glanced at his watch, which read 7:45. He had just enough time to finish reading the Domestic Tranquility analysis paper Carlos had prepared and to meet with the Trojan team to discuss the pros and cons of the analysis. He pressed the intercom button.

"Carlos, just got an interesting phone message. Could you join me for a few moments, please?"

"On the way, General," Castro replied.

As soon as Castro stepped into Pug's office, Lieutenant Holcomb followed him. Pug smiled as both men entered the room. Holcomb deferred to Carlos at the doorway, a sure sign that the junior officers were accepting a former enlisted man in a senior position.

"Two Marines and a Naval Lieutenant in the same room. What should we make of that, Mr. Deputy Director?" Pug quipped. Holcomb had often been the foil in the service rivalry in the office.

Without the slightest hesitation, Castro puffed his chest and lowered his voice several decibels, replicating the Marine drill instructor's soft warning that was often delivered just before the in-your-face, spit-flecked tirade. He assumed the third-person personae, so familiar with drill instructors. "General, the Deputy Director, with Marine green blood still flowing in his veins, believes that the Naval officer in question has experienced an epiphany and deeply regrets his choice of military service. It is my opinion, sir, that he has come to request an immediate transfer to the Corps," Castro replied.

Pug laughed out loud while Lieutenant Holcomb stared silently at Castro. In the first few weeks of operation, each of the officers selected to be part of Trojan had responded well to the presence of a former enlisted man serving as Deputy Director. On several occasions, some of the team had privately shared with General Connor their admiration for the new deputy and his ability to grasp the most abstract concept of their operation.

"Hardly, Mr. Castro," Holcomb added. "Despite your transition to the civilian world, where your co-workers have tried to teach you the protocol for the use of a knife and fork and more importantly, a napkin, this Naval lieutenant thinks it's more likely that with two Marines in one location, and in recognition of said Naval lieutenant's responsibility to the Naval Service, which includes the *subordinate* service commonly referred to as the Marine Corps, said Naval officer was required to assure protocol was observed and he felt it his duty to prevent any disparaging behavior and protect the image of the *Naval* service. With all due respect to our Marine commander, of course, General," he said, a sly smile on his face.

"Okay, "Pug said, "the obligatory inter-service rivalry having been accomplished for today, two petulant Marines having been properly chastened, shall we proceed with the nation's business? I've had a voice mail contact from an old Irish associate. Carlos, it's your new friend from Dublin, Mr. Donahue. He wants to meet with me at eleven hundred hours near the Washington Memorial. Carlos, can you arrange perimeter security, please, and keep it low-keyed? But I want a shooter within range."

"Aye, aye, sir."

"And Jim, I'll want you in the van to monitor the conversation. I'll be wired, although my contact will assume that and likely not speak plainly."

"Will do, General. Can you tell us what this man wants?"

"I'm not certain. He's a former brigade commander in the IRA. I've known him for about six years, met with him twice, in Ireland and Brussels. I sent Carlos to meet with him in January."

"Do you know the subject of today's meeting, sir?" the lieutenant asked.

"No. But this is the man who put us on to Wolff and the domestic shooters. Maybe he's opened a new link."

"We'll be ready, General," Castro said.

"Right then. Hop to it," Pug said. "I expect everyone to be up to speed on Domestic Tranquility and Trojan's analysis by our staff meeting at 9:00. I'll keep it short, about thirty minutes, so we can get ready for the following meeting with our Irish friend."

The Washington monument was a central icon in downtown Washington D.C. Thousands of tourists visited the site every day of the year. Ironically, in the nearly three months that random shootings had dominated the American landscape, none had occurred anywhere near D.C.

Trojan had considered that intentional and determined it was not an oversight, but perhaps preparatory to the D.C. area being the target of a much larger, coordinated attack similar to the nationwide baseball park shootings which had kicked off the Wild Bunch. An attack such as the Overland Park Mall or the aborted attack in San Antonio was imminent and was a constant threat. The absence of shootings, however, had not lessened the presence of security. Capitol police had been augmented by regular Army forces and BDU-clad soldiers were visible on every street in the downtown area. The outside mall from the Capitol Building to the Lincoln Memorial reminded him, as Lieutenant Holcomb had once exclaimed, of the penalty quad at Annapolis after a particularly rough weekend of miscreant behavior by midshipmen, with dozens of uniformed personnel walking punishment tours. Holcomb admitted that he had been among the throng during his first year at the Naval Academy. Pug had admitted to a few laps himself during his academy days.

At 10:30, Pug strolled casually from his office toward the needle-shaped obelisk—some called it missile-shaped—pausing on the corner to buy a hot dog and a Sprite. As he approached the monument, he sat down on a bench and began to eat, watching the tourists stroll by, or enter and leave the monument. It was a brave soul who ventured forth to climb the 897 stairs to the pinnacle, which, some years earlier had been closed due to safety concerns. In about ten minutes, Kevin Donahue quietly slid into the seat next to Pug.

"Top 'o the morning to you, General."

"Good morning, Kevin. Did you come in through customs, or slip across from Canada or Mexico with the illegals?"

"Which method will allow me to stay and draw retirement pay?" Donahue asked.

Pug laughed. "The latter, I think. Both are entitled to health care and are safe from politically incorrect ethnic jokes. So, what brings you to America . . . this time, Kevin?"

"From the news broadcasts, the information I gave you in Ireland seems to have been accurate."

Pug nodded. "And it was appreciated. You called, I came, and I'm here listening. You didn't make the trip to confirm earlier information. What's up?"

"Given our friendly, cooperative association, I thought some of the *facts* needed to be corrected. I may have left you with the wrong impression and I didn't want you to think I misled you, at least not intentionally."

Pug raised an eyebrow, turning to look directly at Donahue. The older man continued.

"We've *both* been misled, lad, and I don't want to leave that impression."

"I'm listening," Pug repeated.

"Did I ever tell you about me sister, General? A beautiful lass she is. But a bit obstinate. Never would listen. She married a fellow from Donegal. Kilpatrick was his name. Sure now the Kilpatricks are a sturdy lot, but a bit inclined to skite, if you know what I mean. They shoot off their mouths too often, taking the mickey out of anyone they think less fortunate."

Pug knew enough to keep quiet. Donahue would get to the point soon enough, but in his own Irish, literary way.

"Anyways, Maureen, that's me sister's name, by the way. Maureen and Kilpatrick had a young lad named Sean. Sean was too young to become involved in the 'business,' if you get my meaning. He didn't have the benefit of years of experience. And when my lot, the old timers, smoked the peace pipe with the bloody Brits, Sean was unable to find local work, so he had to find suitable outsource work, so to speak. Do ya understand, General?"

"I'm with you, Kevin. The IRA was no longer recruiting disaffected lads, but other causes were always in the market."

"True enough. Such lads are needed in many places. Young Sean and some of his mates have worked with another of me associates from the old days, Devlin Hegarty."

Pug was familiar with Hegarty's name. "*He* didn't lack experience from the old days, did he?"

"Right you are, General. Top marks. Anyway, Hegarty took young Sean under his wing and they've been working far and yonder, North Africa mostly, sometimes among the Islamic radicals, working both sides, if you know what I mean. My generation called them wild geese. Soldiers of fortune, I think the Americans call them. Mercenaries by any name perform the same function, regardless the paymaster."

"Is this going somewhere, Kevin?" Pug asked, his patience growing a bit thin.

"Ah, General," Donahue said, removing his pipe from his side coat pocket and knocking it against the sole of his shoe, then beginning to fill the bowl, "sure now you should have been born and raised where your grandfather was so you could understand the Irish way. There's no need to rush a good story. The ending is just as satisfying with a bit of learnin' along the way. With peaceful joy running rampant on the old sod, what else have I got to occupy my time?"

Pug smiled and nodded his assent. "Sorry, Kevin. In your own time, then."

"That's a good lad," the older man said, putting a match to his pipe. "For the past few years, Devlin Hegarty has been doing the odd job for a private security firm, an *American* firm, called Strategic Initiatives."

Pug sat up straighter, his attention now riveted.

Donahue nodded. "Thought that might be of interest. Here's the kicker, General, darlin'. Some of my old associates tell me that Hegarty has been recruiting from among our younger lot, forming a para-military squad. But he has *also* been recruiting some of the disaffected Islamic lot in North Africa, promising them the pot o' gold and a chance to meet Allah. And to meet him on *American* soil after having dispatched Satan's followers first. If ye get my meaning."

"How do the two tie in?" Pug asked.

"Well, my sister is attending a funeral in Derry this week, seeing to her oldest son, the aforementioned young Sean Kilpatrick, after his body was returned from . . . San Antonio. He was the Strategic Initiatives team leader who brought down the terrorist squad. He caught the unfortunate bullet in the head. But from what the grapevine in Ireland says, General, the terrorist lot *also* worked for Strategic Initiatives. Sean worked for Hegarty, Hegarty worked for Strategic Initiatives. Hegarty also recruited the Islamic lot, both North Africans *and* American Muslims. Tight little family group it seems."

Pug was absolutely silent, his mental gears working overtime.

"You mean—"

"I mean, General, that you may be chasing the wrong fox. There's another point to clarify. The asshole you captured in Indonesia, the illustrious Mr. Wolff—it seems I was *supposed* to find out about him and to relay the information to the Americans. Someone *wanted* you to know they were coming. And I was the fool in the middle. Not proud of that, lad, not proud at all."

Pug remained silent for several seconds, his thoughts ruminating. "You're saying the terror teams that hit on American soil, even the larger mall attacks, might have been recruited and planned by Strategic Initiatives? That both attackers *and* defenders were planned by the same group?" he asked, seeking to clarify his thoughts.

"It wouldn't be the first time in history, lad. Al Qaida is certainly having a field day around the world, but are they the *real* culprit here in America? Even Al Qaida may not know who set this up. They probably don't care. Americans are getting killed. Allah is being praised. And World Jihad is getting the credit. Remember, for the most part, these disaffected groups work in independent cells. They might have been duped as well, since the objective meets with their stated goals. But who stands to benefit from this new American legislation? As these attacks on American soil increase, and they *will*, General, who will provide the tens of thousands of security forces and surveillance equipment throughout America? Who was on the scene immediately when the San Antonio terrorist lot were, uh, *coincidentally* observed in preparation and then overcome by an attack of lead poisoning? And that's not the end of the issue, lad. From what I've been told, there's lots more to come, what your military calls 'blue-on-blue' engagements."

Pug thought about the dreaded military term for friendly fire, considering for a moment what Donahue could mean.

"Are you saying some of our own military is going to turn rogue? Attack other units?"

"Probably not active duty military forces. I don't know the details, but my source seems to feel that some of your federal agencies are in danger of internal attack, most likely from the western militia units. It's all tied into this growing secession mania out west. And they *did* attack federal agencies last year in California, didn't they? He says the militia is also going to start cracking down on illegal aliens, not only Mexicans, but those who they think are of Middle Eastern origin. They feel the growing public support for the secession of western states gives them legitimacy. If they kill a few hundred Mexicans, it will make border crossings a bit more risky."

Pug thought about that for a moment, accepting the possibility. "You're confident of your sources in this, Kevin?"

Donahue shook his head. "No, it's a secret world we deal in, lad, and information is always suspect. I've just admitted the fallacy of my prior information, but my source this time —an Irishman well-placed *inside* Washington, I might add—had no reason to exaggerate or mislead. He's been accurate in the past. That's the first story I've got for you this morning, my friend. Proving it's up to you. I wouldn't want you to think I'd misled you or put you on the wrong track. Wolff seems to have been a pawn to point in the wrong direction. They probably thought you'd kill him rather than take him prisoner. They wanted it to have the look of foreign origin. Al Qaida *is* your enemy and they probably *are* behind much of the turmoil, but someone else, someone *here*, in America, has taken it to new heights. Unless I read it wrong, Strategic Initiatives has simply tapped in to some of the netherworld of terrorist groups and used them to achieve *their* objectives, *and* SI's objectives. Until I received this information, I had no reason to suspect that someone in America was working both sides of the street, so to speak."

"Nor did I," Pug replied. "You said that was the *first* story you had for me?" he added, standing up.

"The second story is shorter. I don't know much. In fact, I know nothing of the details, but," Donahue hesitated, again knocking his pipe on the heel of his shoe before standing up to face Pug. "Word is that someone from America has procured a nuclear device. A small, portable nuclear device, according to my source."

"*Has* procured, or *will* procure?"

"Sorry, lad, has *already* procured," Donahue repeated.

"Is it in America yet?" Pug asked.

Donahue shook his head. "I don't know."

"Thank you, Kevin. It's certainly not good news, but thank you."

"When this is all over, General, *if* it's ever over, come home and see the old sod the proper way. No business, no intrigue. I'll personally take you down the Ring of Kerry, we'll play a few rounds of golf, and you can see what your ancestors left when they ran away toward the American dream. God's blessings on ya, lad. And sorry for the bad news. It seems that double dealing was not limited to Wolff. You're damn lucky that Wolff is behind bars. You've got some ferrets under your own umbrella, it would seem. Given the furor over this new legislation, and what my inside source intimated, the links may go deeper than the security firm, even into the venerable halls of Congress or even the president's cabinet. It would seem that all Americans are not . . .well, *American*."

Donahue watched the younger man for a few moments, then smiled broadly and his voice grew lighter. "You remember how things turned out between our two Irish compatriots, Michael Collins and Èamon de Valera. Politicians switching sides or looking out for number one is nothing new. Never assume the enemy is over the *other* side of the barbed wire. He might be on *your* side of the barricade. Oh, and give my regards to your young associate, Carlos. If he's listening," he nodded toward the white van parked in the restricted zone about a hundred yards distant, "top 'o the morning to you, Carlos." Donahue grinned and gave a gentle wave.

Pug reached to shake Donahue's hand. "Thank you, Kevin. I owe you another one. A *big* one, it would seem. Safe trip home."

THIRTY-FOUR

EISENHOWER EXECUTIVE OFFICE BUILDING
TROJAN HEADQUARTERS
JULY

Pug reached to turn off the tape and the men in the room sat silent as they contemplated the information that had been provided in the audio and written transcript. Around the table were Pug Connor, Carlos Castro, George Granata, Director of the FBI, Paul Duffield, Deputy Director of the CIA, and President William Snow. The president spoke first.

"When was this meeting, Pug?" the president asked.

Pug glanced at his watch. "Seven hours ago, Mr. President."

"George, have you or Paul uncovered any corroborative evidence to support this information?"

"No, sir," Granata responded, "but we can't afford to ignore it."

"Granted," the president nodded. "I want this given top priority, gentlemen. Pug, how confident are you about Strategic Initiative's connection to the domestic attacks?"

"Mr. President, it's all speculation at this point, but we can draw some valid assumptions. If only three cities were selected for the Domestic Tranquility pilot program, it seems coincidental that one of the ground attacks took place in one of those cities, San Antonio, and was thwarted, with *no* survivors among the terrorists. However, that's pretty thin evidence to confirm their involvement. Mr. Castro has put two Trojan operatives on it and they're checking with former military associates who now work for SI, supervising some of the troopers they have in the field. No information yet."

"Do we have any reason to believe, I mean *any* reason, that the transfer of a nuclear weapon into the U.S. has occurred?" the president pressed.

The CIA director responded. "We've not had any intelligence to that effect, but again, we can't afford not to take it seriously, Mr. President."

'Agreed. Take every measure you have to assure we cover every entry point. I know the difficulty. Thousands of containers arriving every day, tens of thousands of trucks on the road across the nation. Just find it, gentlemen. If it's here, find it."

"It may take care of itself, Mr. President," Pug said.

The group went silent. Then the president nodded his understanding. "If SI *is* involved, they may *find* it like they uncovered the San Antonio attack to prove how well their program is working?"

"Yes, sir. But I agree with Mr. Duffield—we can't afford to make any mistakes."

"That will do it, gentlemen. I need to stay with Pug for a few moments."

The other department heads left the room and the president took his seat again at the head of the EEOB conference table.

"Pug, I've had a heads up from DOJ about some court-ordered action that will transpire tomorrow. As you predicted, without any hard evidence of terrorist involvement, Jean Wolff is going to be released on Monday morning in Illinois."

"I thought that might happen. I'll handle it, Mr. President."

"Do you need any further authorization?"

"No, sir. The Troy designation you gave for the initial capture covered all contingencies. We just need to be a bit more careful here in America."

"Do you think he'll leave the country immediately?"

Pug hesitated for a moment before answering. "No, sir. If he knows he was betrayed by Strategic Initiatives, he'll be looking for payback.

He's not a foolish man, but he just might feel obligated to take revenge."

"That's in our favor, right?"

"I don't know, Mr. President. It's always helpful if two of our enemies decide to kill each other, but it's rare. I'll discuss it with Mr. Castro and my staff. But rest assured, sir, we'll watch it closely."

THIRTY-FIVE

UNITED STATES DISTRICT COURT
NORTHERN DISTRICT OF ILLINOIS
WESTERN DIVISION
ROCKFORD, ILLINOIS
JULY

United States attorney Gail Masterton slid several manila folders into her briefcase, rose from her table in front of the judicial bench, and stepped through the waist-high swinging gate, departing the court room. Judge Marshall Alfred had just ordered the release of a federal prisoner, Jean Minards, AKA Jean Wolff, from his detention at Thomson Federal Correctional Facility, Thomson, Illinois.

The hearing, held in the United States Courthouse on South Court Street in Rockford, had lasted less than twenty minutes. Despite the federal government's case for retention of a man whom Ms. Masterton claimed was a direct threat to the United States of America, Judge Alfred rejected all arguments, citing lack of substantial evidence and accusing the government of having detained Mr. Minards illegally. Ms. Masterton was grateful the judge had declined to address the method of Wolff's capture.

Less than five minutes following the judge's ruling, Wolff, dressed in a solid black suit, white shirt and red tie, had departed the courthouse, entered a black limousine, Illinois license plate VIP 6, and immediately disappeared.

Almost disappeared.

On the east side of the courthouse, Carlos Castro sat in the passenger seat of a black Suburban with Lieutenant Holcomb behind the wheel. Two other Trojan vehicles of different make and color, call sign Baker 2 and Baker 3, enveloped the courthouse, parked against the curb, one of them double-parked. As the limo pulled away from the front steps of the building, Castro's vehicle fell in behind, radioing instructions to the two other pursuit vehicles who moved to parallel streets to enable switching of their chase vehicle as the limo proceeded.

Six blocks west, VIP 6 pulled into a large parking facility, driving up the ramp to the fourth level. Only one switch had been made in the prior six blocks, placing Baker 3 in close pursuit while Baker 1 fell two blocks behind. Baker 3 entered the garage slightly behind the limo.

At the next-to-top level, a parking attendant stood beside several orange cones, blocking further entrance. As VIP 6 approached, he removed two cones and the car swiftly entered the circular ramp, heading to the top level. The attendant waved off Baker 3, placing a No Entry sign in front of the up-ramp. Baker 3 immediately turned left, stopping in front of the stairwell where Lieutenant JG Gomez, a Navy Seal, exited the passenger side and raced up the stairs. As he arrived and opened the door leading out onto the uncovered parking area, he spotted seven limos parked side by side. VIP 6 pulled into an empty space, second from the end.

Immediately a medium-height male in a plain dark suit, white shirt, and red tie exited each vehicle. They all wore a black balaclava over their heads, and in an orchestrated move, they clustered together, then swiftly jostled between vehicles, one man entering a separate limo, which then departed the top floor, entering the down ramp and heading for the street. Gomez noted that the license plates each read a non-sequential pattern consisting of VIP 3, 5, 6, 9, 12, 13, and 15. All of the vehicles were black with heavily tinted windows.

Lieutenant Gomez raced back down one flight of stairs to Baker 3, entering the vehicle and transmitting to Baker 1 and 2.

"Subject vehicle is exiting the parking facility accompanied by six other limos of identical appearance. Target has switched vehicles with six other men, similarly dressed. Impossible to ascertain which vehicle contains target. Baker 3 will continue to shadow VIP 6."

Carlos listened to the message from his vantage point in Baker 1, across the street. He watched as all seven limousines exited the parking facility, turning alternately left and right into the flow of traffic. "Baker 2, follow VIP 3 east, Baker 1 will take VIP 13 west. It's the luck of the draw, guys. Report destination as determined." Baker 2 and 3 acknowledged Castro's direction and began pursuit.

In VIP 9 with his balaclava removed, Jean Wolff lost sight of the remaining VIP vehicles as his driver merged onto the highway, heading south on I-39. Six hours later, with several switchbacks and detours, including retracing about twenty miles north on I-39, VIP 9 crossed through Springfield, Illinois. In Springfield's White Oaks Mall parking lot, Wolff changed vehicles to a dark gray Ford Taurus. As he entered the passenger side of the vehicle, the man behind the wheel nodded to him, started the engine, and immediately left the parking area.

"Welcome back to the world, Mr. Wolff. We've got about four hours ahead, including a few detours, then your flight from St. Louis to Spokane. Devlin Hegarty is my name. I'm SI's field operations director. Mr. Harford sends his regards and said to tell you he arranged for your release. You'll find ample funds, passport, ID documents and plane tickets in the briefcase in the back seat. Additional funds have been placed in your usual account. Mr. Harford also said to tell you that Bright Point is fully operational. Anything else you think you might need, I'm here to help."

Wolff was silent for several moments, glancing in the back seat at the briefcase. "What's the status on the package from Holland?"

Hegarty nodded. "All taken care of. I saw to the shipment myself in Amsterdam. It should cross the border into eastern Washington state in about thirty-six hours."

"Any problems?"

"None. As I said, Bright Point is still on track. The full details are in your briefcase. They'll come in from Canada on a routine agricultural run, switch trucks at a rural farm north of Spokane, transfer the case, and then leave the new truck in a prearranged location. There's a Montana militia guy named Campbell who will make the pickup and keep the truck under wraps until either you or I contact him. Then he'll leave the truck where we tell him and SI troopers will just happen to find it. They'll become instant heroes, and SI, the flavor of the month. Contact phone numbers and a cell phone, plus your ID call sign, are also in the briefcase. And Harford wants you to contact him ASAP." Hegarty went silent for a moment, content to drive as dusk turned into night. He glanced at Wolff before speaking again.

"Personally, Wolff, I don't like this deal. Bringing a nuclear weapon onto American soil is too damn risky. I haven't liked it since Harford put me on to it when you went missing, and I told him so. I've got plenty of other things to do to keep these rovers scouring the country, so I'd just as soon that you take Bright Point back under your control. I've got two men who will meet you at the Spokane airport when you arrive about midnight."

"Weapons?" Wolff asked.

"They'll have them for you in Spokane. There's a pistol in the glove box in case we run into trouble, but you're going to be boarding your flight shortly, so there are no weapons in your briefcase."

Wolff stared at Hegarty for a moment, took the pistol out of the glove box, checked the magazine and load, replaced it, and then leaned back against the headrest, closing his eyes and going silent.

THIRTY-FIVE

**LAMBERT—ST. LOUIS INTERNATIONAL AIRPORT
ST. LOUIS, MISSOURI
JULY**

At eight A.M. the following morning, presenting a Virginia driver's license identifying him as Clark Westinghouse, Wolff cleared security at Lambert-St. Louis International airport after arriving in the Marriott shuttle from downtown St. Louis. His luggage consisted of a single wheeled carry-on bag procured from a twenty-four hour Walmart, complete with essential toiletries and a few items of cheap clothing.

The gray Taurus Devlin Hegarty had driven in Springfield was parked on a side street in East St. Louis, Illinois, just across the Mississippi River from the city, with both front tires flat to discourage instant theft. Devlin Hegarty remained with the Taurus, folded double into the trunk, his brain two ounces heavier.

Wolff responded to the call for American flight 581, non-stop for Los Angeles, connecting to Aero Mexicana for Cabo San Lucas. Just before boarding, he sent a short text message to John Harford.

Bright point on horizon

When he stepped off the plane in Los Angeles, he received an equally terse answer.

Meet PSC conference August to select horizon

Departing the American Airlines terminal, Wolff discarded the cell phone in a communal trash bin, shedding himself of all electronic ties to Harford or SI.

**EISENHOWER EXECUTIVE OFFICE BUILDING
OFFICE OF INFORMATION & PUBLIC RELATIONS
DEPARTMENT OF HOMELAND SECURITY
WASHINGTON, D.C.
JULY**

Carlos Castro sat to the right of the end seat as the rest of the Trojan team filed into the room, taking seats around the long, rectangular table. It was the same table where the full team had met the night the roving band of shooters had started their terrorist attack and they had listened to the recorded message from World Jihad. It was three days since Jean Wolff had given them the slip in Illinois. The entire team had a dejected appearance.

General Pug Connor entered the room and took his seat at the end of the table. "The president's not a happy man. And neither am I." Everyone remained silent. "Where did he go, Carlos?"

"St. Louis, as best we can tell. We've tracked all eight limo drivers, interviewed them and showed them pictures. Two drivers ID'd Wolff, so one of them is mistaken. Or both of them are. One says he took his passenger to just outside Chicago. The other took his to Springfield, Illinois. They both transferred to another vehicle. It was the same story for all eight limos. Drive for six or eight hours, then change vehicles. But we've narrowed it down. The police found a body in the trunk of a Ford Taurus in East St. Louis, Missouri, yesterday morning. They caught two local kids trying to steal accessories off the car and found the body in the search. They identified his prints as belonging to a naturalized citizen, Devlin Hegarty."

"Hegarty?" Pug repeated.

"One and the same," Carlos replied. "SI's field man and the head of the pilot program for Domestic Tranquility. Two bullets to the head. I'd say Wolff was beginning to cover his tracks."

"Or starting his revenge on Harford and SI."

"That too," Carlos said. "No further trace. I'd speculate he took a flight from St. Louis. No leads so far. Maybe we should go have a talk with Harford."

Pug was quiet for a moment, then shook his head. "Don't want to alert him that we know anything. What are you hearing from your contacts among Harford's troops?"

"Harry?" Carlos said, turning toward one of the Trojan team members, a Delta operative on assignment to Trojan.

"I know a retired E-8 who works with SI, supervising the crew in Oklahoma and northern Texas. He knows Hegarty," Harry responded. "He said Hegarty's been out of the country for about a week. Rumor says he was in Holland."

"Any knowledge of what he was doing?" Pug asked.

"No, sir," Harry responded. "He hasn't seen him for about ten days."

"And if the police are right, he won't see him again, either," Carlos said. "I still think we could put the screws to Harford, General. We're going to have to call him out sooner or later."

"Right, but not now. I want to find Wolff first."

"But if you're right about Wolff believing Harford flipped him in East Timor, he might find Harford before we can talk with him. We won't get anything out of him then."

"Concentrate on finding Wolff. And one more thing. Have one of the team track down the ownership linkage for Strategic Initiatives. I want to know who the major share holders are. Especially any of our elected congressmen or politicians."

"Are you thinking—" Carlos started.

"I'm thinking that someone has a broader interest in Domestic Tranquility than meets the eye. I'm thinking that just in case Wolff *does* find Harford, we need to know who that someone is. Give our friend Senator Culpepper a call and you can meet with him to see what he knows," Pug said. "I'll check with Senator McKenzie. The rest of you pull out all the stops. Use every resource you've got. Find Wolff. Any questions?"

THIRTY-SIX

**CONQUISTADOR RESORT & CASINO
LAS VEGAS, NEVADA
AUGUST**

The second week in August, with the sun dropping behind the scrub-covered hills west of Las Vegas, a sleek Gulfstream 650 completed its flight, having originated in Los Cabos, Mexico. The private jet glided on final approach toward the Henderson Executive Airport, ten minutes south of the well-known strip. Besides the two pilots and one cabin attendant, each of whom were of Mexican origin, only one passenger was on board—a French citizen traveling under the name of Philippe Auclair. Immediately the aircraft shut down engines, a solid white limousine pulled alongside and the passenger disembarked, entering the vehicle. The flight crew proceeded to the operations building, where the pilot filed a flight plan for 9:00 A.M. the following morning, non-stop to Santiago, Chile.

Following three weeks in the luxurious accommodations of the five-star Pueblo Bonito Sunset Beach resort in Cabo San Lucas with its award-winning cuisine, Jean Wolff had erased most of the unpleasant memories of six months' incarceration in the Thomson Federal Correctional Facility. Newly refurbished with a European wardrobe, obtained during a four-day side trip to Paris, Wolff, AKA Philippe Auclair, emerged from his limousine with a far brighter outlook than when an orange jumpsuit had been his sole choice of attire.

Following a quick clearance through airport customs and a short drive to the north end of the strip, Wolff entered the massive, ornate lobby of the Conquistador casino, the newest addition to the opulence which made Las Vegas the most popular tourist and convention center in the world. He stood just inside the lobby for a moment, admiring the one-half scale model of El Castro, the Mayan temple at Chichén Itzá, rising just over fifty feet tall—five stories—the visual focal point from all points in the casino. The temple name instantly reminded him of an as-yet unfinished task: Carlos Castro. Wolff's lawyer had discovered the name of the person who had captured him, and his current assignment. But there would be time for Castro later, and his message tomorrow would make that clear.

Wolff turned and approached the VIP desk, where he used his Auclair ID and credit card and signed his registration form.

"What time is your last FedEx pickup?" Wolff asked the registration clerk.

The young man glanced at the clock behind the counter. "In about forty-five minutes, sir. May I be of assistance?"

Wolff reached into his briefcase and retrieved a slim FedEx prepaid overnight packet and handed it to the clerk. "Please see that this is made available for the courier."

"Certainly, sir. Will there be anything else?"

"No, thank you." Wolff turned back toward the casino and headed across the room, pausing again short of the bank of elevators to read the electronic display case which announced the conventions and gatherings for the week. He was not surprised to see a photograph of John Harford, Chief Executive of Strategic Initiatives, who was billed as the keynote speaker for the opening session of the International Association of Professional Security Consultant's annual conference. He allowed a small smile to cross his lips, then proceeded to the elevator, pressing the button for the thirty-second level.

After a shower, a change of clothes, and ten minutes of watching the news highlights, Wolff returned to the lobby and found a secluded corner table in the Yucatan Lounge. He ordered a drink and watched as the throngs of people made their way through the crowded casino. Over the next two hours, he watched an NFL football game on the large screen, ate a plate of boiled shrimp, and had a couple more drinks. At eleven P.M., a heavily bearded man in Dockers and a long-sleeved plaid shirt approached his table, making eye contact and then taking a seat opposite Wolff.

"I'm Thor Campbell," the man said. "We spoke on the phone last month."

Wolff just nodded, noticing that two other men in casual, but rural, attire took seats at another table across the lounge.

Wolff slid an envelope across the table. "Those are your instructions for tomorrow," he said. "Be in the parking lot before 9:00 A.M., but not earlier than 8:30. Don't arouse any suspicion by arriving too early. Just leave the vehicle and then station yourself at least five hundred yards away. You'll be safe at that distance. I'll handle the rest."

Campbell nodded. "Will you be there?"

"No need for you to know where I'll be, but I'll handle the rest. Just be sure to separate yourself from the vehicle. Where's the package now?"

"Right where you said it should be. In a garage in North Las Vegas with your French buddy. It's been there for five days. Me and my boys have been keeping an eye on it."

Wolff rose and handed Campbell another slip. "Your money has been deposited in this bank account, waiting for your instructions to transfer it after the event. This should fund your mountain boys for some time to come."

"And you?" Campbell asked again.

"I'll be in touch again in several weeks. There's more where that came from," he said, nodding toward the deposit slip.

HERNANDO CORTEZ CONFERENCE CENTER
CONQUISTADOR RESORT & CASINO
LAS VEGAS, NEVADA
AUGUST

At 8:45 A.M., Jean Wolff took a seat in the back of the assembly hall of the Hernando Cortez Conference Center, Room Three. There were about two hundred others present, mostly men, and about 250 seats in the auditorium. Attendees continued to drift in as Wolff sat quietly in his place. At 8:52, several people took their seats on the main dais, among them John Harford. Wolff took his cell phone from his pocket, keyed a short text message, and hit send. He watched as Harford took his seat, and then reached into his coat pocket to retrieve his iPod, glancing down to briefly read the message. Wolff glanced again at his original text:

Bright horizon is closer and sooner than you might imagine

Instantly, Harford was on his feet, whispered something to the man seated next to him, and departed the stage. Wolff also stood and exited the auditorium through the side door, careful to avoid contact with Harford. Wolff quickly strode to the main entrance to the casino and entered the back seat of a waiting limousine.

"Just wait," he told the driver.

Within three minutes, John Harford exited the hotel, his anxiety visible in his body language. He spoke to the concierge, who motioned for a taxi to pull forward. Harford entered the vehicle, which immediately departed.

"Henderson Executive Airport," Wolff told his driver.

HOOVER DAM
ARIZONA/NEVADA BORDER
AUGUST

Thor Campbell, commander of the Blackfoot Brigade, sat in the right front passenger seat of a dark blue Ford Explorer with one of his associates in the driver's seat and another in the rear. Campbell had parked a white Chevy Suburban in the visitor parking area on the Nevada side at 8:48, left the keys in the ignition as directed, and then joined his associates for the short trip across the dam and up the hill on the Arizona side to the main parking area. Traffic on Highway 93 across the new Hoover Dam bypass, a quarter mile south of the face of the dam and high above the canyon, continued unimpeded.

Campbell waited for the expected explosion that would demolish the parking lot and the visitors center on the Nevada side. From his location, he would have an excellent view without danger of being injured by debris.

EISENHOWER EXECUTIVE OFFICE BUILDING
OFFICE OF INFORMATION & PUBLIC RELATIONS
DEPARTMENT OF HOMELAND SECURITY
WASHINGTON, D.C.
AUGUST

At 12:05, EST, three hours ahead of Las Vegas, Carlos Castro strode briskly down the hall toward the office of General Pug Connor, ignoring the general's secretary and entering Connor's office without knocking. Connor glanced up, a surprised look on his face.

"General, I've just received a FedEx package you need to see."

"From who?"

"No name, General, and probably a false address. But as sure as I'm standing here, it came from Wolff."

Connor reached for the folder Carlos placed on his desk. "Summarize," he said.

"He's given us everything we need on Harford—dates, places, the Kansas City and San Antonio terrorist events, even the Internet contact methods with the roving shooters. Nothing admissible in court, but he's given Harford to us on a silver platter. He even names the Secretary of Defense, Acting Secretary of Homeland Security, and several Army generals who were part of the conspiracy to pass the Domestic Tranquility Act and select SI as the contractor. He doesn't say they all knew about the shooters, or SI's involvement, but they were paid under the table to support SI and passage of the bill. A dozen or more congressmen, also."

Connor stood and stepped around his desk, taking a seat in front and motioning for Carlos to be seated. "Not legally enforceable, you say?"

"No, sir. DOJ couldn't take this to court, and given the political involvement, I don't think the president would want to. But from an intelligence perspective, everything fits." He paused for a moment. "I'm afraid that's not all, General. He's indicated there will be another event today in. . ." Carlos glanced at his watch, ". . . twenty-four minutes."

"Did he say where?"

"No, sir, he just said 12.30 Washington time. That probably means it's in some other time zone."

"Did he give any indication of a nuclear device being in the country?"

"No, sir."

"Recommendations?"

"General, the FedEx package originated in Las Vegas. If we called Air Force security at Nellis—"

"He's long gone," Connor interrupted. "Or soon will be. Anything else?"

"One terse handwritten note. '*We shall meet again*'."

"Directed at you, no doubt. You made him look like an amateur in East Timor. He's not the kind to forget it."

"No, sir, he's not. And I won't make the same mistake twice."

"It wasn't a mistake to let him live, Carlos," Connor said. "We got information, and now we have even more."

"Are you going to present this to the president?" Carlos asked.

"I don't know. I need to consider it. If, as you say, several cabinet level officers and congressional people are involved, it goes far deeper than we imagined. We'll discuss it later. Twenty minutes, you say?"

"Twenty-two, General."

**HENDERSON EXECUTIVE AIRPORT
LAS VEGAS, NEVADA
AUGUST**

Jean Wolff watched as John Harford walked swiftly across the tarmac and boarded a Lear jet, which immediately taxied toward the runway. Wolff then departed his vehicle and boarded the Gulfstream 650 which was manned and ready for departure. As he took his seat and nodded to the pilot standing in the cabin doorway, he took out his cell phone again and keyed another text message.

Safe flight. Your horizon will not be as bright as it once was, but you will live . . . for now.

The Gulfstream spun up the engines and began to taxi toward the main runway. Wolff watched out the port side window as Harford's Lear lifted off, turned northeast, and began to climb. He turned his attention to his cell phone once again, keying in a series of numbers and placing the phone beside him on the aisle seat. Then he buckled in as the aircraft turned to the west and the engines spooled up for departure. They lifted off and turned due south, beginning to climb out through cloudless skies. Wolff watched out the port window as Henderson disappeared beneath the wing and, slightly to the southeast, Boulder City appeared on the horizon.

To his left, the large body of water known as Lake Mead appeared and narrowed toward the southern end, capped by the massive engineering structure known as Hoover Dam. Millions of people downstream, as far as Los Angeles and San Diego, with hundreds of communities along the way, depended on the water and electricity generated by this 1930's federal works project.

As the dam came closer into view, about twenty miles distant to the east, he could see the narrow ribbon of Highway 93 and the newly constructed Hoover Dam bypass bridge. He turned to his right and retrieved his cell phone from the seat next to him, glanced out the window once more, and pressed Send.

HOOVER DAM
ARIZONA/NEVADA BORDER
AUGUST

Thor Campbell glanced again at his watch, which read 9:28 A.M., and shifted in his seat, wishing that he had taken a moment to use the toilet before beginning his observation. For a moment, he considered walking several hundred yards to the small, public restroom facility located on the southern end of the parking area. He decided to wait another ten minutes before making the trip. It was the last decision of his life.

**EISENHOWER EXECUTIVE OFFICE BUILDING
OFFICE OF INFORMATION & PUBLIC RELATIONS
DEPARTMENT OF HOMELAND SECURITY
WASHINGTON, D.C.
AUGUST**

General Pug Connor, United States Marine Corps, and Carlos Castro, Sergeant Major, United States Marine Corps, Retired, sat in the general's office while Connor listened to the party on the other end of his telephone. He was silent, nodding occasionally, and then hung up the instrument.

"A two-kiloton nuclear explosion at Hoover Dam," he said to Carlos. "That's all they have so far."

"It's Wolff," Carlos replied. "That bastard Wolff. I should have slit his throat in Timor."

Connor nodded. "This will change the dynamics completely. If Harford is still alive, SI will gain complete control now, with unlimited powers for his domestic security operation, and Congress will be begging him to expand his force."

Carlos stood, pausing behind his chair. "Not if I kill him first, General."

Connor also stood, his jaw set and his voice soft. "I think we've come off the bench, Carlos. You and me, personally. And we're back in the game. This may have to be done off the books. Off *everyone's* books. There's one person I can contact for advice, but that will be the extent of outside knowledge."

"Lock and load, General. Semper Fi."

Sneak Preview
Blood and Treasure

One

**Air New Zealand flight 5361
Auckland — Christchurch
September, 2013**

Brigadier General Pádraig "Pug" Connor, United States Marine Corps, had been reading an article in *The Wall Street Journal* — "Dateline: New York, September 12: Angela Broadbent, Editorial Writer — **Blood or Treasure: The American Choice**" — on his Kindle e-book reader as Air New Zealand flight 5361 entered final approach to Christchurch, New Zealand. The ninety minute flight had followed the overnight twelve hour marathon from Los Angeles to Auckland.

'The cost in American blood has always trumped the cost in national treasure, at least in public statements made by politicians,' Broadbent had opined. In fact, she posited, the opposite is true.

Such was the case with the aftermath of the nuclear explosion that destroyed the Hoover Dam and hydroelectric facility and the attendant radiation contained in the water supply that was released upon collapse and continued to flow.

Thousands of people were killed in the hours and days following the explosion as the flood waters ravaged downstream communities, collapsing smaller tributary dams, and destroying buildings, bridges, infrastructure, towns, and people. Thousands more would yet die from radiation poisoning as the contents of Lake Mead and the Colorado River continued to flow through the polluted nuclear zone with no engineering solution in sight. Politicians beat their chests, promising to 'find those responsible' and bring them to justice. Privately, they counted the cost and cringed at the financial demand that would be made upon them by the very same corporate executives who had funded their elections. To top it all off, the insurance companies had refused to pay claims, citing 'war damage,' which was a policy exclusion clause, as the source of the catastrophe.

Together with Carlos Castro, Deputy Director of the Office of Information and Public Relations, Department of Homeland Security, where Connor served as Director, the two men were on their way to a private—and unofficial—meeting at the request of Clarene Prescott, former president of the United States and the person who had created Connor's task force. Buried within the organizational structure of DHS, General Connor had a very small staff of highly trained, tip-of-the-spear military officers and non-coms. Internally, the group was known as Trojan, and, at the direction of the president, they acted as deemed necessary, with or without legal sanction, against terrorists, abroad and within the borders of the United States. What Trojan did *not* do was information or public relations.

Angela Broadbent, a recognized conservative columnist, had written the WSJ article and had pulled no punches. Her indictment of corporate greed and political acquiescence to their demands shielded no one, least of all those in the forefront of the latest assault on the public treasury.

Federal, state, and local politicians made all the requisite statements, decried the loss of life, and promised retribution, but it was the captains of industry, power company executives, elected water district board members, and farming communities who were the most vocal about the unacceptable impact on their livelihood. They *must* be made whole, became the hue and cry.

Federal bailouts were the only possible solution, according to congressional representatives from across the width and breadth of southern California. Public sympathy for those who were devastated in the disaster prevented a national backlash against the proposed federally funded Southwestern Relief Act, sponsored by two dozen Arizona, California, and Nevada congressmen. Compassionate reaction was unanimous until OMB projected the price, and then some courageous—or foolish—spokesmen began to speak out against the largesse.

In the same way that tens of millions of dollars had been paid to the families of victims of the Twin Towers disaster, national approval being the order of the day, every person remotely affected by the terrorist action at the Hoover Dam should "be made whole and productive with the assistance of their neighbors," voiced Senator Marjorie Hamersley, Democrat from California.

In the case of the Twin Towers payouts twelve years earlier, who had spoken up for the thousands of everyday citizens who had put on the uniform to defend their country, losing their life in the process, Broadbent asked. A pittance of an insurance policy went to *their* beneficiaries. Why, then, were the survivors of people trapped in the Towers so richly rewarded? Why were they more deserving than those who had agreed to stand on the wall and had paid the price? And since terrorists had struck again, and people were terribly affected, were we going to repeat the process? Would there be a whole new class of millionaires created with nothing for the police, fire, and military families who were always the front line of defense? And who had made these choices? What were their motives? And who were the *true* beneficiaries? Broadbent asked.

Rumination on Broadbent's commentary was placed aside for the moment as General Connor leaned toward Carlos Castro, who had the window seat in their first class accommodations, courtesy of Prescott.

"Beautiful country, isn't it?" Pug asked as the eastern flank of New Zealand's Southern Alps twinkled in the bright blue sunlight of a cloudless day.

Carlos nodded. "I've been thinking the same thing, General. How can such tranquility exist in a world gone mad? Are they so damn far away from everything that peaceful life is the norm? Are these New Zealanders unaware of the turmoil that is encompassing the world?"

"You've got to view their history, Carlos. They're really quite a new country, as nations go. But they've had their share of world events. You've read about Gallipoli, right? I was there once about ten years ago and walked the battle sites. As a Marine infantryman, that's one of the last places on earth I'd like to attempt a frontal assault. Yet these Kiwis were there for eight months, trapped in worse conditions than those on the western front in France during World War I. They even captured the heights, as their inept British leadership demanded, but they were never reinforced and were eventually driven off. No," he said, looking out the window again, "don't let the bucolic paddocks and millions of placid sheep fool you. Kiwi's have earned their peaceful existence. You'll see their pride in every little village we drive through today on the way to our meeting. There are statues everywhere. 'Lest we Forget,' is their motto, along with the Australians. A very patriotic people, yet I have to admit, they've stepped away from the confrontational nature of today's world, choosing a rather isolated international posture."

Castro was quiet for several moments as the landing gear groaned and crunched its way to a locked position, then he spoke again. "What do you think President Prescott wants from us, General?"

Pug tightened his lap belt, leaned back against his seat and closed his eyes for a few moments. He'd thought about the same question for several days after Prescott's original invitation had arrived. "Blood," he answered, his eyes still closed.

Rakaia Gorge
Canterbury, New Zealand
September, 2013

Two hours later, in a rented four-wheel drive Holden Captiva SUV, Connor and Castro were in the shadow of Mount Hutt and the popular ski fields at the western edge of the Canterbury Plains, an hour from Christchurch. In September of 2010, the area had been devastated by a 7.1 early morning earthquake which destroyed hundreds of buildings and thousands of homes, yet not one life had been lost. Within hours, the local and national governments had restored power. In days, the water was back on to residential homes, and emergency food and welfare services had been made available to every community affected by the natural disaster. The magnitude of the quake had made international news and had demonstrated the capability of a nation of people who relied on themselves, pulled up their socks, and got on with life. And somehow they had done it without a plea to America.

As the road paralleled an ice-blue, glacial stream, Pug asked Carlos to look at the map once again, confirming the approaching turnoff. "We're supposed to meet Prescott at the Mount Hutt Ski Resort. That signpost should be coming up shortly. She's reserved a couple of rooms for us tonight and tomorrow. The meeting will be later tonight, at a private residence, or so she mentioned in her message," Connor said.

As stated, several smaller communities through which they traveled had a central plaza, each containing a military statue of someone in World War I or II uniform, some even from the Boer War era in the late nineteenth century. Quite often, the names of those who had served and died were engraved into the stone for eternity.

As they pulled into the parking facility at the ski resort, Carlos retrieved their bags, only one each, and they entered the foyer.

Clarene Prescott was already seated in the lobby and rose to greet them. Had she not initiated the approach, Pug would not have recognized her. She wore a wig of different length and hair color and had a scarf around her head, with sunglasses. She had aged since her ascendency to the presidency over a year ago upon the death of President Eastman. There was no Secret Service visible, although Pug knew that former presidents always traveled with a security detail.

As she approached them, she casually put her finger to her lips, which Pug took to be a "*no recognition or honors*," sign. Pug took the clue.

"Good afternoon, Clarene," he said, embarrassed at the lack of courtesy to his former boss.

"Pádraig, how nice to see you again," she replied, taking the younger man in an embrace. "And Mr. Castro. It's nice to finally meet you," she added, reaching to shake his hand. Carlos remained silent, not fully understanding the lack of protocol for a former president.

"Why don't you both check in, and we can go up to your room."

They approached the front counter, registered under their own names, without titles, and obtained their electronic pass keys. Clarene Prescott joined them and they took the stairs to the first floor.

"I've never gotten used to the 'first' floor bit from Europe and other countries where the first floor is the *ground* floor and the second floor is the *first* floor," Carlos said.

"Different strokes for different folks." Prescott chuckled in return.

Once inside Pug's room, he grew a bit more serious. "Madam President, I—"

She held up her hand. "That's not who I am here, Pug. I hope you can accept that requirement of our meeting. I'm Clarene Wainwright, which was my maiden name. You'll understand that a bit more this evening. But first I have a quick question for you. The answer will determine whether this is a short vacation to New Zealand, or if it will turn out to be a very important step in your life."

"Madam . . . Clarene, can you clarify?"

"Pug, how long have we worked together? On how many projects?"

Pug thought for a moment before responding. "I recall we met about eight, maybe nine years ago when you were Ambassador to the United Nations. We did some work together with the Russian ambassador, as I recall. And then the presidential task force in California for the secession issue."

"Do you trust me, Pug?" she said, looking sternly into his eyes. At five feet, ten inches, she was not much shorter than Connor.

"Yes, ma'am," he replied.

"*Completely?*" she added.

Pug hesitated momentarily. "Yes, ma'am."

"And since I don't know Mr. Castro, do you trust him completely?" she continued.

"Yes, ma'am."

"With your life?"

Pug looked at Carlos and smiled. "I wouldn't be here if I didn't, ma'am."

"Well then, here's your question. The meeting I mentioned will be held in two hours, about ten kilometers from here. A car will pick you up and return you to the hotel when we're finished. You can come or not. Your choice. If you come, it's an irrevocable decision. You'll be committed to our objectives. You'll be sworn to secrecy. I can only give you one answer for the myriad of questions that are running through your head, and here it is: I give you my solemn oath that what we are involved in is of world importance. It is not treasonous to the United States, nor is it solely in American interests. It is, however, worthy of your consideration, and you're the first person outside of our group whom I thought of as capable of directing the project. We are not speaking of a liberal or conservative ideal, and it's not political in the current meaning of that word, but we are addressing the question of good and evil in today's world. If you trust my judgment and are willing to come with that limited assurance, I would be very grateful to have you. There will be nine people present, including myself, plus each of you. Have I given you enough information to make your decision?"

Pug looked to Carlos briefly before he answered.

"General," Carlos said in answer to the unspoken question, "I'm confident that you'll make the right decision for both of us. I sense we're not here to play bridge."

Pug gave a soft laugh, and looked back at Clarene Prescott. "Will this change our lives completely, Madam President?"

Without hesitation, Prescott answered. "Yes, it will, and it will most likely require you to leave government service, but not immediately. That will be your decision. General Connor, as God is my witness, what we have asked you here to discuss will change the lives of many people in the world who need help."

"We'll be ready when the car arrives, Mrs. Wainwright."

Ninety minutes later, the vehicle was out front when Pug and Carlos stepped through the doorway. They entered the rear of the car and departed the hotel. In fifteen minutes, after several steep switchbacks climbing into the foothills of the Southern Alps, they arrived at a stately English Tudor-style mansion. As they exited the car, they could see east across the Canterbury Plains toward the horizon where the lights of Christchurch reflected off the evening clouds. They were ushered into the building by a older, quiet gentleman who led them to a large room filled with shelves of books and oil paintings on several walls, who then closed the massive double doors and departed. There were eight individuals seated around the room, seven men and one woman, plus Clarene Prescott, who was standing just inside the entrance, smiling. Pug immediately identified several of the attendees and tried not to let surprise reflect in his face.

"Welcome, General Connor and Mr. Castro. May I introduce our host, Trevor McAlister, a former prime minister of New Zealand," she said, gesturing toward a sixtyish man in a brown leather chair. Without exception, everyone in the room, other than Pug and Carlos, was well over fifty-five years of age.

"You may recognize some of the other people seated around the room. From left to right, this is Harold Usher, former British Chancellor of the Exchequer; Yoshita Takamura, a retired chief executive of Hanniban Electronics; Admiral Rostenkowski, former Chief of Naval Operations, Russian Navy; Lawanda Mitubi, former Secretary General of the United Nations; Christina Peterson, former Vice President of the Norwegian parliament; David Wiederman, formerly Director General of Israeli intelligence; and on our far right, Klaus von Klausen, former Chairman of the Board of Euroil Petroleum. As you can see, General, we come from varied nationalities and government, military, and corporate experience. We have some rather enlightening debates, I can tell you," Prescott concluded. Then she made a sweeping gesture with her arm toward the two visitors.

"Members of the Cloister, allow me to introduce a trusted and experienced friend of nearly a decade, General Pádraig Connor, and his close associate, whom I am informed is equally worthy of our trust, Mr. Carlos Castro. These two gentlemen currently head a small private task force under the direction of the president of the United States. General Connor is a serving Marine officer and Mr. Castro is a retired Command Sergeant Major of the United States Marine Corps. To our advantage, Mr. Castro is also a lawyer."

Prescott paused for a moment after the introductions. Pug and Carlos remained standing just inside the great room.

"General Connor, the big question is, what is the Cloister? Who are we, why have we invited you here, and for what purpose?"

Pug smiled and nodded his head. "That would be the first of several thousand questions, Madam President."

"Well then, let's get some of those questions out of the way. We are a council of former leaders of nations and corporations from around the world united in our understanding of the importance—and volatility—of our current world situation. In short, General, we agree that self-serving and often corrupt political solutions have gotten us where we are in the world today, and we need to change that. Large corporations, especially those who fund political campaigns, have often determined the policy of a government, working toward the advantage of that corporation, rather than toward the peace and harmony of those nations they serve.

"Some years ago, the people in this room, or some of our predecessors, recognized the need to overcome our geographical and philosophical differences. This Cloister," she said, again sweeping her arm around the room, "is the result. We call our council the Cloister because of the secluded nature of our work. None of us reports back to our respective governments. And our primary requirement is that we be unanimous in our decisions. Not a majority, but unanimity. Does that give you sufficient understanding, at least initially, as to who we are?"

Pug shook his head slowly. "No, Madam President, it doesn't. But it does remove some of my initial concern. I'm beginning to understand the concept, if not the purpose, of your multi-national association."

"Good," she replied. "Now that brings us to why have we invited you to meet with us. General, it's very likely that in six weeks time, with the November elections in the states, America will become two countries. That would prove disastrous to future prospects for the world, but we'll talk more about that tomorrow. As you might imagine, we have access to a great deal of information. More detailed information, in fact, than any single intelligence agency from any single country. As you well know from your current position, various intelligence agencies, even allied nations, only share what they determine is in their national interest. The big picture is not always available, and analysis is often wrong as a result. Maintenance of those in power is always the prime objective of any government. Information that might ease a world situation, but would not benefit an individual nation with access to that information, is often not shared.

"As to how we are able to operate, you'll be pleased to know that financial resources are not an issue. Transportation is always available from many different sources. And even special operations military support is available as required, although a bit more difficult to keep quiet, and some covert cooperation is required."

The entire time of the presentations and explanations, Carlos had stood a few feet behind Pug, remaining quiet. He took two paces forward to stand alongside Pug, but remained silent.

"So, with that background," Prescott continued, "why did we ask you here? I could put the answer in formal protocol terminology or politically acceptable language that we often use when ordering a distasteful task to be performed, but quite simply put, General Connor, and Mr. Castro, the Cloister has prepared a list of people we want to discuss with you. Mostly corporate and government leaders from around the world. And our list will undoubtedly grow over the next several years."

"And the purpose of this list?" Pug asked, all too certain of the answer.

Prescott looked around the room once again, gauging the mood of her compatriots, then she looked back at Pug and Carlos. "When I said unanimous, General Connor, I meant it. A 'yes' vote from you, and from Mr. Castro, is also required to achieve final approval of the names on this list. What we are going to ask of you is not that different from your responsibilities at Trojan. Simply stated, General Connor, there are eleven people on this list, both men and women from nearly as many countries. To use a term both you and I understand, the Cloister has classified this project as 'Troy.' We are asking you to create and direct a task force to kill them."

"*Madre Dios!*" Carlos exclaimed.

Acknowledgements

The Pug Connor series has required technical input from a variety of sources, but none more important than that received from my military colleagues and associates who provide the security for our nation and those of our allies. I am indebted to these people, some of whom are not individually listed below. They know who they are.

William A. Tolbert, Major, USAF (Ret.) a life-long friend with whom I have spent many hours discussing the concept of American governance, states' rights, and public turmoil.

Kate Ryan, Lieutenant Commander, Royal Australian Navy. Kate's contribution to scenes in upcoming volumes were indispensable, and her critique of RAN naval terminology is essential to the accuracy of the story. We share the same name, but there is no family connection..

Pete Bartos, Lieutenant Colonel, USAF, (Ret.) As a former "Eagle Driver," an F-15 pilot, and a veteran of Operation Noble Eagle, the domestic air cover operation designed after 9/11, Pete provided first-hand knowledge of the prospective air battle over American cities as we continue to prepare for the next assault.

Tristi Pinkston, a first-class author in her own right, who edited the manuscript and provided much needed variation and insight into the story. I express my sincere appreciation for her contribution.

Novels by Gordon Ryan

State of Rebellion — A Pug Connor Novel, Book One — California is on the brink of secession. Daniel Rawlings, a twelfth generation American whose ancestors fought in the Civil War and aided in the settlement of California, finds that his patriotic heritage sets him apart from those who seek California's independence. With a growing economy exceeding that of many third world nations, an independent Republic of California could become a major economic and political player on the world stage—incentive enough for unscrupulous and greedy men to foment a violent rebellion, aided by the Western Patriot Movement, a militia cadre for whom insurrection is a dream come true.

Torn between his allegiance to the Union and his desire to be true to his California roots, Rawlings must decide which faction he'll support—a decision that both his friends and enemies are more than willing to help him make. From the first sentence in *State of Rebellion*, this gripping political thriller grabs the reader by the throat and never lets go.

Uncivil Liberties — A Pug Connor Novel, Book Two — On inauguration day, 2013, President Clay Cumberland assumes office and is immediately advised that a hijacked commercial airliner is headed for Washington D.C. He only has two choices: allow the plane to choose its target and potentially kill thousands of people on the ground, or authorize the Air Force to shoot down a civilian airliner and kill 350 innocent people on board.

From page one, *Uncivil Liberties* take the reader on a thrilling ride that involves a domestic terrorism plot, including American terrorists and ends with a nuclear disaster in America. Congress panics, Americans are imprisoned in their own homes, afraid to visit the mall, sporting events, and even to drive the highways. *Uncivil Liberties* gives new meaning to the freedoms inherent in our Constitution, thereby creating an America our Founding Fathers would not recognize.

Blood and Treasure — A Pug Connor Novel, Book Three—(Spring 2011) Domestic terrorism, both imported and home grown, runs rampant in the streets of America and it has risen to nuclear proportions.

Congress has passed the Domestic Tranqility Act, greatly expanded the Patriot Act, and authorized unprecedented law enforcement powers including those granted to civilian contract security firms.

President Bill Snow is faced with a divided America, a rebellious Congress, and a frightened populace.

General Pug Connor faces his own demons, trying to determine what kind of man he is and how he will respond as the warrior in him competes with the man who yearns for stability, an understanding of the America that has disappeared before his eyes, and the love of a beautiful United States Senator. When he is introduced to the Cloister, a secret group of former international leaders, his vision of who he is becomes even more confused.

Pug's deputy director, Carlos Castro, a former Marine Sergeant Major, faces no such conflict. He fully understands his nature: he is a stone cold, instinctive killer, single handedly seeking to rid the world of evil, one terrorist at a time. However, determining who are the terrorists is not as easy as it seems.

A Question of Consequence — **Matthew Sterling** is a man on the way up. As Assistant City Manager in the Wasatch Range community of Snowy Ridge, Utah, and a Brigham Young University law school graduate, the 21st century looks promising. Returning east to New York, to settle the estate of his deceased grandmother and to direct the demolition of Riveroaks, her two-hundred-twenty-year-old Hyde Park home on the Hudson River, Matt discovers the historic journal of **Major Andrew McBride**, his sixth-great grandfather, plus a Revolutionary War manuscript that uncloaks a true patriot—and reveals the misguided citizens that pilloried McBride as a traitor.

When Matt returns to Utah, local government elections and their tumultuous aftermath shatter his image of democracy and he finds his future is in the hands of unscrupulous politicians and bureaucrats who value personal gain above honor. As the modern-day political drama unfolds, and the glare of negative publicity turns against him, Matt is astonished by the similarity to McBride's early American tale of deceit, dishonor, and public shame and the consequences that affected the rest of his life.

Amidst the whirling maelstrom, his life is further complicated by a growing attraction to a beautiful genetic biology PhD candidate from England, **Kasia Somerset**, who serves as the Assistant Director of the Molecular Genealogy Project at BYU.

When Kasia examines Major McBride's historic documents, the incredulous DNA revelation she discovers turns Matt Sterling's world upside down as it did his ancestor, and he is forced to come face-to-face with his true lineage—and a heritage of epic proportions.

Spirit of Union: Destiny — Fleeting an abusive father and a hopeless life in Ireland in 1895, nineteen-year-old Tom Callahan takes passage on a ship bound for America. On board the *Antioch*, he meets pretty Katrina Hansen, a young Norwegian woman traveling to Utah with her family. Their meeting results in a promise: Katrina will wait one year before accepting any other proposal of marriage; within that time, Tom will somehow find his way to Utah to try his hand at winning her heart.

It's not a likely match. The brash Irishman is a Catholic, a brawler, and a young man without prospects. Katrina is a refined young woman—one whose wealthy and domineering father heartily disapproves of the uneducated "Paddy" who has invaded their lives.

Destiny is a sprawling historical novel set at the end of the nineteenth century, during one of the most turbulent times in the history of America. It is filled with memorable historical and fictional characters and packed with romance, high adventure, and political intrigue. The story plays out in such far-flung places as New York City, the gold fields of Alaska, Old Mexico, and a vibrant and growing Salt Lake City.

In his first historical novel, master story-teller and best-selling author Gordon Ryan has spun an exciting tale of romance, tragedy and adventure—one that will satisfy your itch for a rollicking good read even while it leaves you wanting more.

Spirit of Union: Conflict — It's 1917, and America has entered World War I. Along with the rest of the nation, the Callahan's have enjoyed relative peace and prosperity. But now their son has joined with thousands of other young men in what President Woodrow Wilson is calling "the fight to make the world safe for democracy."

Other conflicts are more personal. Twenty

years into their marriage, Tom and Katrina Callahan have not yet resolved their religious differences. While Tom stubbornly clings to his Catholic roots, Katrina yearns for spiritual unity in a temple marriage. And when a tragedy befalls their family, it brings with it a stern test of the love that binds Tom and Katrina to each other and to their children.

Set against turbulent, turn-of-the-century events in both Utah and world history, and filled with vivid historical scenes as well as tender emotion, *Conflict*, takes the reader around the world and into the homes and hearts of a beleaguered family.

Best-selling author Gordon Ryan has skillfully captured the flavor of an earlier day, but he has also crafted a moving story about the forces that can unite or destroy a family regardless of the age in which they live.

Spirit of Union: Heritage — Tom and Katrina Callahan's three children have grown up and are making their way in a world that is propelling itself toward World War II. Tess has her heart set on the glamour of a Hollywood movie career; PJ is a successful sheep rancher in New Zealand; and Tommy is pursuing his career in the Marine Corps and learning not only about war but about the perils of romance.

In this, the final volume of *The Spirit of Union* trilogy, author Gordon Ryan follows Tom and Katrina Callahan into their middle and late years. Tom must finally decide whether to remain true to the promise made to his mother not to abandon the Catholic faith or to embrace his wife's Mormon religion. Living in a time when aviation is just becoming a viable industry, the stock market is booming (some say growing out of control), and Hitler's evil machinations are on the horizon, the Callahan's face challenges that threaten to rob them of all they hold dear.

Set in Hawaii, the Dominican Republic, South America, Great Britain, and the United States, *Heritage*, is a novel filled with scenes and characters that will linger in your mind long after you close the book.

Threads of Honor — The process that Air Force Major Bill Tolbert was required to go through in his attempt to obtain flight clearance for Troop 514's flag would have deterred a lesser man. But the responsibility he felt for those young men, now numbering fourteen scouts, and the image of their eager faces at each meeting kept him going. Their excitement over the possibility that their flag might actually go into space and return inspired him to persist. He enlisted the help of all his resources to get the flag included in the official flight kit. Finally, beaming with satisfaction, he stood one night before the troop and announced that their request had been approved. Troop 514's flag would be on the next shuttle mission, due to launch in eight weeks.

Upon the Isles of the Sea — *Isles* is a particularly LDS story, taken from the Book of Mormon and rendered as a fictional account. When Seth, a young Stripling Warrior comes home from the wars after nearly eight years of fighting, he barely has time to settle in before Helaman, his former commander, now a missionary, comes to the village and calls him on yet another assignment. But Lilliana is determined that Seth will not leave the village again—at least not without her.

Jared, Seth's best friend and also a former Stripling Warrior, is persuaded by General Moroni to remain in government service to infiltrate the devious "Secret Combinations." When Seth and Jared meet Hagoth—an "exceedingly curious man,"— in the City of Bountiful, their quest takes on a whole new dimension.

Upon The Isles of The Sea, an adventure tale from *The Nephite Chronicles*, is a story of courage, sacrifice, and honor.

Dangerous Legacy — In the light of reduced world military tension, the United States and New Zealand move to restructure the dormant ANZUS pact. But as they do so, they inadvertently encounter a nuclear plot initiated decades ago by Soviet premier, Nikita Khrushchev to undermine the U.S. In its new incarnation, if the plot is successful, tens of thousands of people will die, and the U.S. will lose the trust of all its allies.

Air Force Major Zachariah O'Brien assigned to the National Security Agency, finds himself face-to-face with an international puzzle for which he has neither all the pieces nor time in which to avert disaster. All he has, in a situation escalating into war, is his basic instincts and a determination to see this thing through, even when he finds it necessary to leave his secure intelligence billet and place himself in harm's way.

Dangerous Legacy takes the reader to New Zealand, Russia, Great Britain, Japan, Iraq, and the United States as diverse events reveal a panorama of intrigue, suspense, espionage, and nuclear warfare. From a peaceful attempt to mend the New Zealand and United States alliance to a second battle with Iraq, *Dangerous Legacy* sweeps like a tornado through the area of global politics. In the process, it shows how much good one dedicated person can accomplish in a world grappling with uncontrollable forces.

The Leashes of Dogwood Hollow — In a departure from his normal thrillers or historical fiction, Gordon Ryan has penned a raccous political satire which takes the reader on a romp through a fictional city hall run by dogs, both purebred, who are of course, in charge, and mixed breeds who do not share the same level of prestige. Not since George Orwell's *Animal Farm* has the government been so cruelly displayed, warts and all. **Adult reading with a cautionary warning to parents and younger adults.**

About the Author

Gordon Ryan is a writer with a varied history. He has lived and worked in six foreign nations and a dozen or more states, including Alaska. He was a Recon Marine in the aftermath of the Cuban Missile Crisis, served in the Air Force in Thailand during the Vietnam War. He also served as a member of the American Embassy staff in Dublin, Ireland, during the violent seventies. His first published novel, *Dangerous Legacy*, was released in 1994 and he has published nine more over the intervening years with the Pug Connor novels, *State of Rebellion and Uncivil Liberties* being his newest releases.

Needing to feed his family, he never gave up his day job as a city manager and chief executive of large homeowners' associations, but once he discovered the joys of fiction, writing has been the driving force.

Now writing full-time, Gordon and his wife, Colleen, spend their time between the American northwest and the beautiful South Pacific.